THE
ADDISON KENT
MYSTERIES

THE
ADDISON KENT
MYSTERIES

THE GAUNTLET OF ALCESTE

THE GOLDEN SCARAB

HOPKINS
MOORHOUSE

COACHWHIP PUBLICATIONS
Landisville, Pennsylvania

The Addison Kent Mysteries, by Hopkins Moorhouse
Pseud., Herbert Joseph Moorhouse (1882-1960)
Copyright © 2011 Coachwhip Publications
No claim made on public domain material.

The Gauntlet of Alceste published 1921
The Golden Scarab first published 1926 in *McLean's Magazine*

ISBN 1-61646-080-6
ISBN-13 978-1-61646-080-8

Cover Image: Scarab © Roman Malanchuk

CoachwhipBooks.com

Contents

The Gauntlet of Alceste

The Golden Scarab

THE GAUNTLET OF ALCESTE

1
UNEASINESS

The twinkle of amusement died out of Traynor's eyes as he took note of the dark circles beneath those of the beautiful, stylishly dressed girl who sat opposite him in the vine-clad arbor. Foolish indeed as it seemed to him, the fact that she was frightened was undeniable. There was a telltale nervousness in Rose's manner which was beyond her power to repress completely, and although she tried to smile it was not a very successful attempt. Had she been a neurotic young woman, her present state could have been discounted at once; but the daughter of Henry C. Radcliffe was far from neurotic. Although raised to peer over the edge of Luxury's lap at the busy world about her, she was as healthy as outdoor sports could make her and possessed an ample share of that independence and poise which is the birthright of North American womanhood.

The young man hesitated, therefore, to dismiss as utter nonsense the strange things she had just finished telling him, to belittle her apprehensions as structures without other foundation than her own imagination and therefore mere folly. His very visit for the week-end was in direct response to her frightened appeal for his advice. Yet what possible danger to her or her father could lurk about "Hillcrest," the luxurious Radcliffe home in Westchester, scarcely more than fifty minutes by motor from the corner of 42nd Street and Broadway, New York City?

"Listen, Rose. Somebody is trying to play a practical joke. There is no occasion to get excited about anything. You are within 'phone

call of the finest police force on the continent and as for the supernatural—" He smiled and waved a hand eloquent of skepticism at
the flowering shrubbery of the well-kept grounds, the sunny woodlands beyond which gleamed the blue waters of Long Island Sound.

"I know it must seem very silly of me," she interposed hastily,
"but—Tommy, I simply can't help it. It is because everything is so
vague, so mysterious and persistent and because my father has
been acting so unlike himself that I feel something is wrong. If I
only knew what! At least there is nothing intangible about those
messages you are holding in your hand. Who sent them? And why?"

The appeal in the expressive eyes stirred him to a deep elation.
It was to him Rose had turned in this trouble. Unconsciously his
shoulders straightened and he frowned fiercely at the three pieces
of ordinary notepaper which he still held in his hand as he allowed
his mind to race in review of the events which she had just confided to him.

They were perplexing enough. Of late Rose had become aware
of a subtle change in her father's manner. Also he had taken a sudden liking for books dealing with psychic phenomena and seemed
to be giving the subject his keenest attention. All his life Henry C.
Radcliffe had been a practical business man, a money maker, and
had earned a national reputation as an expert in precious stones,
rare jewelry and antiques. Upon his retirement from business his
chief interest in life had been his beautiful daughter, an only child
whom he literally worshipped. His only other hobby had been his
valuable collection of rare gems—until this new notion of reading
every book he could find bearing upon phantasms of the living,
phantasms of the dead, visions in the waking state and other phenomena upon which the psychic research societies were accumu-
lating data to establish the existence of a spirit world.

Then one night Rose had heard her father pacing his room restlessly and finally she had crept to his door and overheard him conversing with someone in considerable agitation. Upon opening the
door she had found him in a state of great nervousness—but alone
in the room. In an awed whisper he told her that he had been talking to the spirit of her mother, long since dead. Rose had never

known her mother, and upon the rare occasions that the subject had come up her father had evinced a strong dislike for it, dismissing it usually with the promise that they would go into it fully some day when she had grown up. In secret the girl had wondered greatly over this reticence. As for his present strange behavior, his firm belief that he had had a vision—Rose was greatly alarmed. Certainly she had never known her practical, hard-headed old dad to believe in ghosts and she would have laughed at the idea but for his evident agitation. On the following morning, however, he had so far recovered his normal state that he was inclined to regard the whole thing as due to overwrought nerves and told Rose curtly to keep silence and forget the incident altogether.

Then Rose herself began to receive mysterious messages which at least had the merit of being tangible. The first had come a few days later; she found it early one morning, pinned to the pin-cushion in her boudoir with a perfectly normal and intelligent pin. Also it was written on plain notepaper—typewritten in quite an up-to-date way— and read: "Go away from Hillcrest for a visit of three or four weeks to some friend and leave before the end of the month." It was signed in typewriting: "One Who Wishes You Well." When the startled girl had shown it to her father his face had paled and while he had passed it off as "a foolish prank of some sort" he had been unable to hide from his daughter the fact that the incident worried him.

Exactly one week afterward the second message reached her. It was thrust into Rose's hand as she came out of the Metropolitan one night with a party of friends in the city. The after-theatre crowd had been jostling about them while they waited for their car to pull up in response to their number, megaphoned by the uniformed starter, and she could see nobody who looked as if he were watching her. The note might have come from any one of a hundred persons in that crowd. Its message was an echo of the first: "Do not forget to leave home for your visit before the end of the month," and it was signed as before.

The third message arrived at the end of the following week— through the mail this time. It was more imperative: "Why do you not go away? Do so at once—O.W.W.Y.W."

By this time her father had become alarmed and talked of placing the matter in the hands of the police. He urged Rose to leave
home for a visit, as directed; but the idea of being dictated to in
this mysterious manner by some unknown was deeply resented by
the girl. She was now so worried over her father that she refused
to leave him. If anyone were trying to get her out of the way in
order to harm her father, she determined that they would fail.

"I think you're inclined to take the whole thing too seriously,
Rose," Traynor ventured at length. "In the first place, if your father
wants to study up on this psychic stuff, why shouldn't he? It is quite
the popular thing just now and everybody's doing it. As for that
vision of his—well, given a good imagination and a think-tank full
of other people's experiences along that line, it would only require
an extra large piece of cheese with one's pie to bring on an exceptionally vivid dream. In a semi-waking state one can doze through
one of those dreams very realistically and merge into wakefulness
with the dream still hanging around one's neck, so to speak.
Frankly, I think that this is the explanation."

"But what about those three messages?" objected Rose.

"That's harder to understand," admitted Traynor slowly. "I can't
see any object to be gained by the sender. If harm were intended
to Mr. Radcliffe how on earth could your presence at Hillcrest prevent it? Unless— Did you show these messages to anyone besides
your father?"

"Only to Mrs. Stanton, who sews for us. She is a well-bred
woman who has seen better days, and I have never looked upon
her as a servant, rather as a motherly companion and confidante.
She is refined and gentle at all times and very discreet. Knowing
the matter would go no farther, I did show her the messages. I was
greatly worried."

"What did she say about them?"

"She agreed with my father—that it was best for me to go. She
did not think any harm would befall; it might be just a clumsy joke
or a business appointment of some sort—somebody wanting to have
a long and secret interview with my father at Hillcrest when none
of the family were around. It was just as liable to be a blessing in

disguise as anything of a harmful nature. But I felt she was just trying to quiet my fears and I decided I wouldn't budge a step."

Traynor smiled at the uptilted, spunky little chin.

"Well, you didn't go and the end of the month came and nothing happened and here we are getting along into the new month—"

"You are forgetting the arrival of our two guests."

Traynor looked at her in silence. For the time being he had quite forgotten the presence of the two other guests at Hillcrest. He had been introduced to them shortly after his arrival—as he and Rose passed the tennis court where the strangers were in the middle of a lively exchange—and had promptly dismissed them from mind, his full attention being already centred upon the distractingly lovely young woman by his side.

"You mean that Mrs. Lomer Saint-Anton and her nephew with the spectacles? What a name! Is she French? Tell me about them, Rose."

And as she did so Mr. Tommy Traynor pursed his lips and listened with a quizzical expression on his tanned and youthful face. For it appeared that Mrs. Saint-Anton had been coming to Hillcrest so frequently of late that she had worn out her welcome. As an old-time acquaintance of Henry Radcliffe she seemed to think she could come and go as a guest whenever the fancy took her. At first Rose had regarded her merely as a recurring inconvenience—one of those "friends" who barnacle themselves to every social ship and to whom one is polite without enthusiasm. Her father had requested Rose to treat Mrs. Saint-Anton with every courtesy, yet it was evident that he devoutly wished she would pack her trunk for Jericho and stay there.

"The present visitation has annoyed him particularly. I think that's because it's the first time she has dared to bring anybody with her. Mr. Levering is a complete stranger to us and she has no right to presume that he would be a welcome guest, Dad has no use for him and it is astonishing the number of excuses he manages to find for disappearing for hours at a stretch and leaving the pair of them for me to endure. I—" She hesitated for an instant. "Frankly, I do not like Mr. Levering's manners."

"Why? Has he dared—?" Traynor sat up alertly.

Her smile of gentle reproof at hasty conclusions faded slowly and the look of apprehension that flitted across her face was not lost upon her companion.

"I want to be entirely fair and perhaps I should not say it," she said soberly, "but although daddy only laughed and told me not to be nonsensical when I asked him about it, I feel that for some reason he is powerless to send them away openly. The whole thing is so silly!—I don't know—Mr. Levering is almost too polite—and besides—" She stopped abruptly and the color came into her cheeks.

"Excuse me, Miss Radcliffe, but Mrs. Saint-Anton desired me to tell you that tea is served and she would be glad to have you join her."

Traynor turned to find the butler bowing deferentially. He frowned resentfully, for he strongly disliked pussy-footed servants who came and went without a little noise at least.

"Thank you, Thompson. Tell her we are coming at once."

"You were saying, Rose—?" Traynor prompted when the man had withdrawn. He noted that she was disturbed.

"Nothing much. I was merely going to add that Mrs. Saint-Anton and Mr. Levering arrived on the thirty-first, the date mentioned in those precious messages of mine. But come, Tommy, let's have a cup of tea and be human."

2
MR. TRAYNOR BECOMES MORE SERIOUS

Mr. Tommy Traynor was a brisk young specimen of mental and muscular activity, so completely absorbed in his work that his thoughts ran naturally in practical channels. He was what was known in business life as a "live wire," an exceptionally promising young man. Not that he lacked imagination; it was his wealth of imagination that enabled him to achieve success, and his fund of bright ideas that had graduated him logically from journalistic ranks into the advertising field. His present position as advertising manager of the famous Lamont establishment on Fifth Avenue—jewel experts and silversmiths—kept every commercial facet of his intelligence highly polished. But even in his newspaper reporter days he had harnessed his imagination to common sense and had had scant patience with certain types of emotional women with whom he had come in contact on the trail of the day's news.

It was as a newspaper reporter that he had first met Miss Rose Radcliffe under somewhat unusual circumstances—a fire at a charity bazaar; in fact, he had rescued her—and had fallen hopelessly in love with her. But even a fifty-dollar-a-week reporter may look at a beautiful heiress and admire her and, if he has enough nerve and ability and finds favor in her sight and is of excellent family and has cultivated a "poker face"—eventually he may look her father straight in the eye! Tommy had made wonderful progress; for with his rapidly rising income he was able to assume his proper social status and become "a desirable acquaintance." With youth calling to youth, the "friendly footing" followed quickly and in time

15

as the mutual attraction ripened they called each other by their first names. Some day he would muster up courage to leap the barrier of wealth that frowned between them and compel her father to listen to reason.

Just now his thoughts were fully occupied with what Rose had been telling him. He did not anticipate any great trouble in getting to the bottom of the mystery and setting her mind at ease; it probably would prove to be simple enough when he had uncovered the missing link. He studied the two guests across the wicker tea-table with lively interest and decided that neither of them was cause for alarm or could have any relation whatever to the messages which Rose had received. Their arrival on the last day of the month might very well be a mere coincidence.

Although far from an ordinary woman, Mrs. Saint-Anton was the typical grand dame of the smart set, full of the inconsequential chatter of her world and capable of carrying herself with dignity and charm. In spite of her grey hair—perhaps partly because of it—she was still of striking appearance with a cold stateliness that was impressive. Observing her even features, large dark eyes and finely preserved figure, Traynor could well imagine that in her time the lady had been, in the argot of the street, "some chicken." A hen of such antecedents might be forgiven charitably for a tendency to strut still! She was dressed in the height of fashion and Tommy could not help wondering if possibly Mrs. Saint-Anton was "setting her cap" for the wealthy widower who owned "Hillcrest." If that was her scheme the cap was certainly awry.

Or was it her nephew who was the fortune hunter, seeking a match with the daughter of the house? Tommy glared at him with unreasonable resentment. He was somewhat foppishly dressed and affected a blasé air and an inclination to patronize. He wore gold-rimmed glasses with thick lenses which contracted his eyes to abnormal smallness; these glasses were equipped with side lenses—blinders on a mule, thought Tommy disagreeably—so that Roger Levering's natural expression, if he had such a thing, was completely hidden. As he peered at Traynor the stare seemed to Tommy like nothing more intelligent than the vacuous gaze of a toad which stupidly watches for bugs. It only needed Levering's drawling accent to realize that in this gentleman lay infinite possibilities for boredom. His only redeeming features were his broad shoulders and the athletic suppleness of his carriage; he may have been something over forty and there was an easy grace in his movements that bespoke devotion to outdoor sports. His self-centred talk was interesting only when it veered to athletics.

Strangely enough, his present predilection appeared to be the game of chess about which he was keen to talk. He seemed greatly disappointed when he found that Traynor knew nothing about the game. Who in the mischief, thought Tommy, would want to play an indoor game like that in the golden summer time? No doubt the chump would argue that they could play it outdoors, don't you know—under the trees, as it were!

"Poor Roger has been *so* disappointed at finding nobody here who can play with him," Mrs. Saint-Anton murmured to Traynor in what was evidently an apology for her nephew. "He is simply chess crazy, Mr. Traynor; but I am hoping it will pass. Roger always overdoes his enthusiasms and it is fortunate that they do not last long. Just now he is getting reports from a chess instructor who is endeavoring to make a player out of him, and if I am not mistaken here comes another message for him now."

As she spoke a messenger in the regulation uniform wheeled up the driveway, looking hot and dusty. Levering had risen eagerly and presently waved the message in front of them, excusing himself in order that he might consult his chess board. Traynor caught a glimpse of a jumble of chess notations and as Levering disappeared, taking the messenger with him, Tommy decided that he could stay with the chess-board till dinner time for all he would be missed. Which is exactly what Levering did.

In trying to analyse his dislike for Roger Levering it did not take Traynor long to reach the conclusion that nine-tenths of it was due to his own prejudice and he was forced to smile at his momentary jealousy. If "poor Roger" was guilty of "intentions" he was certainly starting off on the wrong foot in antagonizing his host.

Immediately after dinner Henry Radcliffe carried Tommy off to the library for one of their customary talks over the cigars. He liked to talk to this young advertising manager of Lamont's, finding in him a listener who was intelligent enough to allow the elder man to do most of the talking and who had a keen appreciation of his host's favorite subject—rare gems. How many of Tommy Traynor's invitations to Hillcrest were due to his listening accomplishments it would have been hard to estimate. What Henry C. Radcliffe would have said had he known that the mendacious Tommy was trying deliberately "to make a hit with the old boy" at these interviews for the ulterior purpose of robbing him eventually of his most precious possession—! But Mr. Traynor took good care that her father did not know and Henry Radcliffe liked him immensely.

The tired lines which Tommy had noted in his host's face at the dinner table vanished in animation, once they were alone in the library, and as he chatted away there was no sign whatever of those inward forebodings which Rose had recounted a few hours before. But for the incident which followed there might have been no sign at all of the strain under which Henry Radcliffe was living.

Opening the library safe, he had taken out two large oblong cases of black velvet and handed them to Tommy with the pleased air of a small boy who proudly exhibits a new jackknife. One of the cases contained a diamond necklace of remarkable beauty; the other a wonderful collar of pearls. Traynor drew in his breath at the dazzling display. He knew something of precious stones and the evident value of these startled him. He was about to remark on the danger of keeping them at "Hillcrest" when Roger Levering walked into the room with a large book under his arm,

"Oh, really—I beg your pardon! I—did not know the library was occupied," he stammered and withdrew in haste after laying the volume on the nearest bookcase.

Traynor hardly noticed the interruption, it was so fleeting; but the scowl remained on Radcliffe's face. Then as Tommy was admiring the lustre of the perfect pearls, twelve rows deep, the butler entered.

"Did you ring, sir?" he asked, civilly enough.

Traynor hastily closed the case of pearls and slipped it out of sight beneath the newspapers on the library table. Henry Radcliffe's face was furious as he turned on the man and angrily told him to get out. Tommy picked up the second case containing the diamonds and closed it nervously.

"I'll take that, Traynor." He literally threw it into the safe and slammed the door with a clang, muttering something about a man being unable to call his house his own these days. "You will have to excuse me, my boy; but let us defer this display until another time. I am feeling out of sorts to-night. To-morrow we'll have a long talk where we will not be interrupted. I think I will retire early, if you don't mind."

Tommy's face was thoughtful as he walked slowly out and bent his steps towards the pergola in search of Rose. That Henry Radcliffe's nerves were taut, almost to the breaking point, he no longer doubted. Of course, it was provoking to be interrupted with those jewels of great value open to observation; but the only way to ensure secrecy would have been to lock the library doors. The library was a room that was usually open to all members of the household and Traynor could not help feeling sorry for Levering whose embarrassment under the reproof of his host's frown had been painfully apparent. It was likely the butler would be sufficiently thick-skinned after years of service, to stand anything; but for a host to treat a guest, unwelcome though he might be, with anything but courtesy—well, it was sufficiently foreign to Henry Radcliffe as Tommy knew him to illustrate the change which had come over him. His show of temper and sudden termination even of Tommy's company seemed out of proportion to the cause.

"'Out of sorts' is right," nodded Traynor. Then he caught sight of Rose's welcoming smile and promptly forgot everything else for the time being.

The evening passed very pleasantly, featured by a stroll about the grounds with the girl who had come to mean so much to him. Afterwards they all had quite an enjoyable game of billiards at which Levering was very proficient. They left him finally amusing himself with practice shots and presently the ladies excused themselves for the night.

"Mr. Traynor, please. You are wanted on the telephone, sir."

The butler showed him the location of the instrument in the hall and with some surprise Traynor listened to the voice on the wire. It sounded muffled and indistinct but he thought it must be Baker, Lamont's private secretary. The man rang off, however, as soon as he had delivered his message and left Tommy somewhat irritated that he had done so.

He was annoyed, too, at the message itself. Mr. Lamont was requesting him to return to the city by the first train in the morning for an hour's conference on a matter of immediate importance. He was sorry to intrude, but it was important. He would be free to return to Hillcrest in the afternoon, however.

Darn the luck! But business was business. Anyway, he could be back by six in the evening at latest, possibly much earlier; so it might be worse. He thought Lamont was going out of town for the week-end; but apparently his chief had changed his mind.

He retired to his rooms. A comfortable armchair, drawn up to the open window, appealed to him and he proceeded to fill his pipe. He did not feel sleepy yet and a quiet review of things before turning in was in order. He must decide just how best to act to arrive at some satisfactory explanation of those messages which were worrying Rose.

Traynor was more disturbed than he cared to have her know, and with the coming of night the situation had begun to appear more complex than he had at first imagined. Undoubtedly something was wrong at Hillcrest—with Henry Radcliffe. And a man of his experience and initiative did not lose grip on himself without cause. That fear of Rose's that some menace to her father might be creeping in upon them seemed less foolish, sitting here in the dark and gazing out into the moonlit night, than in afternoon's sunlight. Plenty of men found secrets of their past refusing to stay buried in oblivion—particularly when they had grown as wealthy as Henry C. Radcliffe. Traynor stirred with irritation at this line of speculation which threatened possibilities that were bounded only by the elasticity of his imagination. He must stick to the facts or he would get nowhere.

He got up and for a moment leaned out over the window-sill, breathing deeply of the cool flower-perfumed air. It was a night of piling cloud movement and the changing lights and shadows checkered the woodlands. His room was next to that of his host, on the side of the house where an elaborate fire-escape had been installed; the long platform of it ran beneath the window of the guest room which Traynor was occupying, and also beneath the adjoining windows, descending finally to within ten feet of the ground directly above the driveway.

One by one the lights disappeared from the upper chambers of the graystone mansion, but even after the last light in the servants' wing had gone out, Tommy Traynor still sat on in the darkness, smoking and thinking. At last he began to undress in the dark and had just climbed into bed when he paused at sound of a knock on Henry Radcliffe's door and soon the murmur of conversation reached him. The voices were indistinct at first and the persistent mumble prevented him dropping off. to sleep immediately as was his habit. Presently the sound grew louder and a snatch of excited conversation reached his ears.

"Well, out with it," came Radcliffe's irritated accents. "What do you want now?"

A woman's voice murmured on for a space, then rose in a passion.

"I tell you, you must do it. You must!"

Traynor heard the door close at last. Silence ensued. He wondered sleepily what Rose could be discussing with her father at that hour. Well, that at least was none of his business. No 'casion— make mystery out of—molehill. He'd soon clear everything up— to-morrow. To-morrow—

He fell asleep.

What it was awakened him Traynor could not say. What time it was he did not know. He started up in bed and looked around him dazedly. It took him a moment to get his bearings.

The moonlight was streaming in through the latticed window of his room. It fell to the rug in a patch of silver. As he stared blinkingly at that patch of light he noted a shadow stealing slowly across it. A cloud, of course—No! His gaze lifted quickly to the window. Perspiration came out on his forehead.

A hideous, grinning face was peering in at him—a face—a half of a face, white in the moonlight!

3
IN THE MIDDLE OF THE NIGHT

Traynor was no coward, but it took him a few moments to collect his wits. The face had been withdrawn instantly and Tommy sprang from the bed and threw wide the French window. Nobody was there. He went out onto the fire-escape in his pyjamas and even walked to the end of the runway and looked down. The moon had gone under an extra large cloud and the light was not of the best; but his eyes had become more or less accustomed to it. Not a motion was discernable as his swift gaze swept the shrubbery and lawns. Nobody was anywhere in sight and although he listened intently there was no sound except the whisper of the leaves in the faint night breeze.

"That's darned funny!" he grumbled to himself. Shivering, he crept back to his room and nestled in beneath the covers, his mind swimming. He was sure that he had not been mistaken; but he must have been. It was the only solution; he must have been half dreaming. He felt beneath his pillow for his watch; the hands pointed to 1.55.

Then he held his breath to listen. Somebody was tapping cautiously at Henry Radcliffe's door. Tommy could hear no response; no doubt the sleeper had not awakened. The silence within the house was so heavy that every sound was magnified. He distinctly heard a rustling of garments out in the hall and a moment later a similar sound seemed to come from within the room next to his own. A queer scratching followed. Then Traynor's heart stood still at a smothered cry of terror.

Springing from bed, he switched on the light and grabbed up his dressing-gown. He snapped off the light again and peered cautiously out into the upper hallway just in time to catch sight of a hurrying figure at the head of the staircase. The woman's hair hung about her shoulders in a billowy mass and as she disappeared quickly down the stairs Traynor followed without hesitation as far as the staircase. He hung back until she entered the library.

Instantly he was in motion, slipping noiselessly down the heavily padded stairs and hiding for a moment or two behind a curtain in the lower hall. But as she had closed the door after her and did not reappear at once, Traynor decided to risk discovery for a peek through the keyhole, a procedure which he felt justified in taking by virtue of the circumstances.

He saw the woman kneeling in front of the large safe, her hand on the handle as if she had just closed the door. Her back was toward him and it was not until she straightened up and turned that he got a look at her face. It was Rose Radcliffe!

She came out so quickly that Traynor barely had time to get behind the curtains alongside the door. A rustle of her silk kimona, a whiff of subtle perfume and she had brushed past him. She seemed in a great hurry and as she glanced over her shoulder apprehensively his heartbeats quickened in fear that she had seen him. But she hurried to the staircase and ran all the way up. He listened until he heard the door of her room close before he ventured to move.

Greatly bewildered, Tommy stole back to his own room on tiptoe. He crawled slowly into bed where he lay thinking for a long time in an effort to understand what he had just seen. What was Rose doing in the library at that time of night? Why this nocturnal secrecy? Above all, why was she clutching to her breast a large oblong jewel-case of black velvet? There was no mistaking it. He had seen it and recognized it at once as one of those her father had shown him after dinner with such pride.

He decided that as soon as he got back from town the following afternoon he would have a talk with Rose, tell her exactly what he had observed and ask her to be frank with him. It was the only way that he could hope to be of use to her in the troubles which seemed to be hedging her about.

He shut his eyes, but he was not to be permitted to sleep just yet. Even as he settled himself once more for slumber a new sound brought him again to elbow prop. The sound was distinct to his alert senses. Someone with the utmost stealth was creeping down the hall past his room!

Breathlessly Traynor listened. The blood throbbed in his ears. Then after a moment he slipped quietly out of bed for the third time, wrapped the ends of his pyjama legs about each ankle in turn and drew his socks over them; next his trousers and the dressing-gown and his rubber-soled tennis shoes. Then he carefully opened his bedroom door, determined this time to explore the house till he found out what was going on under that roof during the hours when its inmates were supposed to be wrapped in sleep.

The night light which had been burning dimly at the end of the hall had been turned out by somebody. The place was in darkness except for a lone shaft of moonlight that filtered through the small cut-glass panes at the top of the long stained-glass window of the stairway landing. The occasional whispering of the leaves outside as they held converse with the night zephyrs penetrated at intervals the dead silence that hung like a pall in that high, arched hallway. As he advanced slowly in the dark Traynor's feet made no sound. He paused. A door closed somewhere on the floor above him, and presently a breath of cold air reached his face like the passing touch of unseen fingers.

Then he saw it. In perplexity he stood still—perplexity that altered slowly to pure astonishment. At first it was but a pale blur, high in the darkness that enveloped the upper reaches of the stair that ascended to the floor above; but it grew in luminosity as he watched, and he became aware that the dim smudge in the dark was floating steadily towards him as if wafting down the stairway on unseen feet. There was no sound whatever except the pounding of his own blood in his own ears.

Clutching the carved supports of the bannister rail, Traynor crouched, straining his eyes in the dark, wondering what it was that he saw. It took form slowly as it approached—then the thing flitted across the landing where fell the refracted rays of the moon that filtered in through the cut-glass panes. The moon went under a cloud and he had only a glimpse; but in spite of himself he felt his spine prickling.

Although Mr. Thomas Traynor did not believe in ghostly manifestations, he could not prevent his mind flashing back to everything that Rose had told him about her father's strange conviction that he had been conversing with the spirit of a dead woman. And the figure of the apparition was that of a woman. But it had no face! It was dressed in gray habiliments that trailed and floated about it like figments of vapor. The torso was wound round and round with this substance. The trunk had no arms and in place of a head the diaphanous wrappings curled upward to a peak. The upper part of the figure seemed to exude a faint glowing light; the lower part— There was no lower part! The mystified onlooker knew that the wrappings reminded him of something which at first eluded his memory. Then he had it—a picture he had seen one time—of Lazarus coming forth from the tomb, still wrapped in cere cloths!

Scarcely believing the evidence of his senses, the fascinated young man stared after the vision as it floated onward and downward in the blackness. For a space his limbs seemed paralyzed and he could not move in his sheer amazement. Then his mind righted itself and he started forward. The figure now was on the floor below, moving swiftly and silently towards the rear hall. As fast as he could go without noise Traynor went down the stairs in pursuit.

The thing was not in sight when he gained the ground floor; but without hesitation he turned to the left and sped through an archway into the rear hall that led towards the kitchens. At the end of the passage he got just a glimpse of the Gray Woman vanishing through an open doorway and ran swiftly in that direction. A basement entry stood open and presently he found himself outside the house, running through the shrubbery.

He stopped short at a rustle of leaves near him. The next instant he was knocked flat on his face.

His assailant fought furiously. Although Traynor exerted every effort to dislodge him and tried every wrestling trick he knew, the man was too strong for him. Certainly there was nothing intangible about this fellow's muscles; for soon Tommy found himself thrown on his back and pinned helpless to the earth with the hot, angry breath of his antagonist blowing in his ear.

"Now, damn you, we'll have a look at you!" growled a voice.

There came a slight click and the glow of an electric torch fell full on Traynor's face, blinding him. The result was rather surprising, for at once the man released him and sprang back in evident astonishment.

"Traynor!" he muttered. "You! Wh-what's this mean?"

It was Roger Levering—a dumfounded Roger Levering with his pyjamas showing under his coat and in his stocking feet. As Traynor stared back at his dishevelled fellow guest he was no less amazed. But the meaning of it was too apparent to them both to waste time.

"Which way did it go? Quick, man!" cried Tommy in an excited whisper.

"Oh, my word! I don't know. I don't know. You—you saw it, too—that white thing? I—I thought you—"

With impatience Traynor brushed him aside and ran for the gate in the wall at the foot of the garden. As he expected, it was unbolted. Levering came panting behind him; but although they both explored the hedges and shrubbery, and after that the highway outside the grounds, the thing they were pursuing had vanished as if drawn into the night sky by some invisible power and lost among the clouds that marched there in silent majesty.

It was then Traynor realized that Roger Levering was shaking with chill—or fear—or both. The man had received a bad fright if his face was any barometer. It was like chalk and drops of moisture covered his forehead. Traynor eyed him, surprised that one of his muscular vigor should become such a coward of his imagination at the first hint of the supernatural.

"I say, do—do you think it was a spook?" asked Levering in an awed whisper. The hand with which he clutched the other's arm was quivering. "Do you believe in spirits—and all that sort of r-rot?"

Tommy, on the point of casting off the trembling grip with an impatient denial, paused.

"Sometimes," was what he said.

Levering's teeth chattered like castenets.

"I once—knew a—chap—"

"Speaking of spirits, Levering, how about a scoot of Scotch? You look as if you needed a drink. We'll catch cold if we stand here," he said practically. "Let's beat it for the dining-room."

The suggestion was approved instantly by Levering. When they had turned on the light he almost ran to the sideboard; but the decanter shook so badly that Tommy took it from him and poured out a stiff drink of whiskey. Levering swallowed it at a gulp and immediately held out the glass for a second one.

"What's that mark on your finger?" asked Traynor curiously. As he peered more closely he saw that it was a purple stain as from an indelible pencil—or ink.

"I was writing a letter in my room—not sleeping well, you know; so I got up to do it. Was right in the middle of it when I heard suspicious sounds and came out into the hall to investigate. Then I saw that bally ghost thing and popped back into my room, quite upset—knocked over the ink, you know—quite a turn, I assure you. But I got back courage to come out again and when I could see nothing of it I went on downstairs. Got as far as the lower hall when I heard a slight noise up above again and there the damned thing was again—coming right down after me. I ran ahead of it and when I saw it was making for outdoors I slipped out and lay for it. I heard you in the bushes and jumped right on you—for which accept my apologies, Traynor, like a good fellow."

"Some jumper!" grinned Tommy, rubbing his arm which was still aching. "It was you I heard, then, creeping past my door." In the explanation of his own movements he left out all mention of Rose Radcliffe, of course.

"Dash it, old boy, I'm going to get beneath the blankets," decided Levering abruptly. He was still looking pale and unwell. He took one more drink and promised to say nothing of what they had seen. There was no need to alarm the ladies unnecessarily, argued Tommy.

"Right-o. If I'd known the dashed house was haunted, I'd never have set foot in it," murmured Levering with a shudder. "The bally thing was whimpering and moaning when it went past me—whimpering and moaning, Traynor. It's God's truth!"

His starey little eyes behind their thick lenses turned upon Tommy with such solemnity that Traynor slapped him on the back with a word of encouragement as he switched off the light. Arm in arm, they went upstairs.

"There's nothing to get scared about, Levering. Go to bed and forget it. Good-night."

"Nothing to get scared about," echoed Levering in a husky whisper. "No, nothing to get scared about." And as he went on down the hall to his room he seemed to be repeating to himself this comforting phrase.

4
CONSTERNATION

Nobody, meeting Roger Levering in the breakfast-room that morning, could have found fault with his appearance or questioned the peace of his night's repose. Under the invigorating influence of a cold bath and a brisk walk before the dew was off the grass, all traces of his disturbing experience had vanished. He looked immaculate—even more so than usual—in his smart riding breeches and leather gaiters; with his snow-white stock at the neck and a clean shave, Levering was a very presentable gentleman and, but for the displeasing effect of the thick lenses of his glasses, might have been considered handsome.

The breakfast-room was bright with sunshine; the morning-glory vines at the windows nodded their funnels of color in welcome of it and approval of the songs the birds were singing. No thought of gray apparitions, whimpering and moaning in the dead of the night, could live in that setting and as he stood at an open window, chest inflated, there was a self-reliant poise in the well-dressed athletic figure that bespoke a much-travelled cosmopolitan who was entirely sure of himself.

Pausing in the doorway, Rose Radcliffe envied him his poise. She was conscious that her own appearance this morning was not as fresh as it might be; but she was not quite prepared for comment upon it from Mr. Levering.

"Good-morning, Miss Radcliffe," he greeted urbanely with an easy bow. "I hope that you rested well; but I am afraid the hope is not borne out by the facts, if you will pardon my saying so." He interrogated with his eyebrows and smiled. "But I guess you are not the only one; I happened to overhear my estimable aunt complaining to the maid of a bad night as I passed her door. And your father seems to be oversleeping." He held out his watch and she noted that breakfast was later than usual. "We were to go for a canter this morning and planned an early start. Pity to waste such a glorious day as this."

"I saw the valet knocking at my father's door as I came downstairs and I have no doubt he will join us soon," said the girl somewhat coldly. She turned to greet Mrs. Saint-Anton who swept into the room with vivacity.

"Dear me! I though I would be the last one in," she smiled.

"Oh, it is quite all right," assured Rose, noting with her woman's eye for such things that the rouge on her guest's cheeks had been applied with less delicacy than usual. "Neither daddy nor Mr. Traynor—"

"Miss Radcliffe! Your p-pardon, p-please—but I—"

They all gazed at the agitated servant who stood in the archway. It was Follis, her father's man, leaning weakly against the woodwork, white and shaken.

"Why, Follis!" Rose cried, starting forward in alarm. "Are you ill! What—? Speak out. What is the matter with you?"

But as she asked it she seemed to sense the answer and shrank from it involuntarily, the valet's horror reflected in her own eyes.

"Your father, Miss— lyin' on his bedroom floor when I opens the door—dead!"

Rose swayed unsteadily and Mrs. Saint-Anton stepped quickly towards her. Levering strode forward uncertainly, stopped and stared at the valet, his face the picture of shocked disbelief.

"Do you know what you are saying?" he almost shouted.

"It is true, sir. Mr. Radcliffe has been shot to death—murdered, sir—during the night!"

At this terrible news all three seemed paralyzed for the moment. Then with a bound Levering was out of the room, and going upstairs, three steps at a time, followed by the valet. Thompson, the butler, on his way to the library, turned to watch them, his bland expression of surprise giving way to sudden excitement. He, too, rushed up the stairs.

With a quick cry, Rose broke away from the older woman's restraining hand and made wildly for the staircase, Mrs. Saint-Anton close behind her. But Levering met them at the door of Henry Radcliffe's room, his arm extended to stop their entry.

"Ladies—please—it is no place for you—"

Rose pushed past him and gave a quick gasp at sight of her father's huddled form on the floor. She would have advanced farther into the room but for Levering who gently but firmly barred the way.

"Nothing must be touched, Miss Radcliffe," he warned imperatively, "until the police arrive. Thompson, 'phone for them at once."

"The police!" cried Mrs. Saint-Anton in consternation. She shaded her eyes with her hand. "Horrible! How horrible!" she murmured to herself.

A torrent of questions broke from Rose Radcliffe's lips. Her agitation was pitiful. She tried once more to get into the room. But Roger Levering was firm and signalled Mrs. Saint-Anton to take charge of the distracted girl who suddenly bowed her head on the supporting shoulder and suffered herself to be led slowly to her room where she threw herself, sobbing, upon the bed.

Slowly shaking his head, Levering locked the door and thrust the key into his pocket. The awed faces of the servants peered into the hallway from the rear quarters as he came thoughtfully downstairs. Then he turned upon Follis with a startled expression.

"Where is Mr. Traynor?" he demanded.

"I understand he left this morning, sir—on the early train."

"What? Left Hillcrest altogether?" His face showed surprise. Rapidly he questioned the man; but the valet could give him no information as to the purpose of the sudden departure or the young man's destination and, recalling the night's encounter, it was excusable that Levering's manner betrayed a hint of suspicion.

He was given no time to question further; for Thompson, who had rushed back down to the library, now came running out into the hall, his complacency completely shattered.

"There's been a robbery, too!" he called out, forgetting all formalities in his excitement. "The safe in there—wide open!—empty!"

Levering ran to the library door and looked in. It was as the butler had said. A few scattered papers alone were visible in addition to the little metal deposit-box which his aunt had handed to her host for safe-keeping; it did not appear to have been tampered with. It contained only her personal papers—deeds and so on.

Rising from his examination, Levering stood looking down in silence for a moment. He grunted "Hmph!" once or twice while a little mirthless smile played about his cynical lips. Then the lines grew grim in his face.

"Nothing is to be touched—nothing whatever, Thompson. You are sure you understand?"

"Very good, sir."

"You 'phoned the police station?"

"They are sending someone at once, sir."

"Is Mr. Traynor the only member of this household to be—missing—this morning, Thompson?"

"I believe so, sir."

"It is very awkward—very awkward indeed. That will do, Thompson."

5
THE POLICE TAKE CHARGE

Within two hours of the 'phone call Lieutenant Robert Fargey, of the detective bureau, was on the scene, accompanied by the coroner. It was the second jewel robbery of importance reported within the week and the instructions that had reached the precinct captain of detectives had been explicit. Lieutenant Fargey had been taken off desk duty in order to handle the case in person with every resource of the bureau and the Central Office at his back; for the murder of such a prominent citizen as Henry C. Radcliffe was a complication indeed.

Fargey was one of the keenest plainclothes men on the force. Of medium build physically, there was nothing very striking about his appearance unless it was the fastidious neatness with which he dressed. His manner was gruff, his movements energetic. There were those who did not like his ways, particularly his sarcasms of speech and his inordinate vanity; but as a detective he was undoubtedly a man of great ability. If he was a lover of publicity for what it could earn him by way of promotion, he never let it interfere with the thoroughness of his investigations. With the newspaper reporters, of course, he was perhaps the most popular man at the bureau; for he made it a point to tip them off on the news whenever possible and many a favorable mention in the columns of the New York press was due to this—and a certain largess in cigars.

The brisk assurance with which he took charge of the present case, once he reached "Hillcrest," showed that he knew his business. While Hays, his subordinate, at a nod, rang the doorbell he stood back and took a swift survey of the surroundings. As the butler opened the big door with its plate glass protected by grill work of intricate design, he stepped forward, brusquely introducing himself, and without waiting to be invited, walked right in.

"Where's Miss Radcliffe?"

The butler indicated the drawing-room and Fargey entered. He threw the briefest of glances at the elder woman and introduced himself at once to the younger.

"Sorry to worry you at a time like this, Miss Radcliffe, but it is my duty. Please have everybody who went to bed in this house last night brought here—including the servants."

Rose nodded to Thompson and the butler bowed and withdrew. The servants filed in presently—eight of them besides the butler—Rose's maid, the housemaid, and the valet, the cook and the scullery maid, the laundress, the gardener and the chauffeur. They stood awkwardly in line, self-conscious and ill at ease.

"Is Mrs. Stanton—? Oh, here she comes now," murmured Rose as the seamstress came slowly into the room.

Fargey eyed her sharply; but in that gentle face with its aureole of snow-white hair and its marks of refinement was a wistful sadness that commanded sympathy.

"There is nothing unusual in this, madam—just a necessary formality," explained Fargey as he noted her nervousness. "We will not detain you long." He turned to Detective-Sergeant Hayes. "Run over them, Sergeant, in the presence of Miss Radcliffe and give them to understand that they are not to move out of the house, use the telephone or write until given permission."

Rose had introduced him to the two guests while they were awaiting the arrival of the servants and Fargey now turned to Roger Levering.

"I will ask you, sir, to show us the room where it happened. I would like to ask some questions, Miss Radcliffe, after I come down." He bowed in acknowledgement of her acquiescence and followed Levering from the room.

"Who first discovered the body?" he demanded as they went upstairs.

"Follis, Mr. Radcliffe's valet."

"Anybody been in the room since?"

"Only in the doorway," replied Levering. "I thought it best to lock the place up until you arrived."

"Quite right," grunted Fargey, covertly eyeing the other more closely as he turned the key and threw open the door.

For a moment Fargey stood on the threshold, surveying the sitting-room with its fireplace and mantel. Across the room was a wide alcove at the back of which a huge cherrywood wardrobe was built in, extending almost to the ceiling. Through an archway was visible the bedroom beyond. Through the sitting-room window the iron railing of the fire-escape showed.

These details Lieutenant Fargey's busy eyes took in at a sweeping glance before coming to focus upon the body of Henry Radcliffe which lay in a huddled heap in front of the fireplace. The rich, brocaded lounging-robe and slippers, an open book inverted upon the small library table beside the reading lamp—these were eloquent of the fact that Henry Radcliffe had been sitting quietly in his room, reading. The bed had not been slept in.

Fargey stooped quickly and picked up a small S. & W. revolver that lay a few feet beyond the outstretched arm. He examined it for a moment, noting that it was fully charged, then dropped it into his pocket without comment. He knelt on one knee and studied the body more closely. In the fingers of the right hand was clutched a gold pencil of the sort that is worn by ladies upon a chain. Fargey reached over and secured it; a bit of chain dangled from the ring in the end of it.

"This looks important—assailant evidently a woman—been a struggle an' this got torn off, eh? All right, Doc." Be waved the coroner towards the body and rose to examine the room in detail. While he poked about the coroner proceeded to ascertain the cause of death.

A sharp ejaculation from Roger Levering drew the eyes of both men towards him. He had been standing in the background, an interested observer, but saying nothing. As they looked at him now they saw that his face was pale and that he was pointing excitedly towards the body which Dr. Charles had just turned over. The left arm which had been doubled underneath was now visible and it was to this that Levering's finger directed attention.

"What's that?" cried Fargey, striding briskly across the room.

"The shirt-cuff!" repeated Levering. "See, it's been torn off! The cuff's—gone!"

"Gone!" echoed the detective. He stared blankly, not at the torn sleeve but at Roger Levering. A muttered imprecation escaped him as he confirmed the fact that the left cuff of the white shirt was indeed missing—ripped completely off, leaving a frayed sleeve. The starched linen cuff was intact on the right sleeve which at first alone had been visible.

"Don't—don't you understand? Somebody's taken it!"

"How deucedly clever of you, Mr. Levering!" There was almost a sneer upon Fargey's face as he eyed the other suspiciously. "When a thing's missing, of course somebody took it. Now, who was it? And why did they take that cuff?"

"I'm sure I can't say," faltered Roger Levering. "The door's been locked."

"Since breakfast," snapped Fargey irritably, and the coroner looked at him in mild surprise. "What's the verdict, Doc?"

"Shot through the lung—dead over twelve hours, I would say. Here is the bullet—automatic, .25 caliber, fired at comparatively close range."

"Could he have lived long enough to write a message on his shirt-cuff?" The detective looked at him eagerly.

"I believe so—a few minutes possibly."

"That's what he did—and somebody interested in that message discovered it—removed it."

Fargey was on his feet now, making systematic search of the room, every corner of it. He went on into the bedroom and searched there without success.

"Did you find the shirt-cuff?" asked Levering, as the detective returned to the sitting-room.

"Didn't expect to," grunted Fargey. "Through, Doc?"

He locked the door after him and they all went downstairs. In the drawing-room Hayes had finished his questioning of the servants and his superior waved them back to their own quarters peremptorily. But he halted them at the door for a moment.

"Did anyone hear a shot fired during the night? Think now—all of you."

Nobody had heard any such sound. The detective considered this strange fact for a moment, then waved the servants out.

"You are sure, Miss Radcliffe, that I have seen everyone—?"

"There was one other guest who was recalled to the city early this morning—Mr. Thomas Traynor," replied Rose. "He left word for me that he had received a message from his employer unexpectedly that required his presence in the city this forenoon. He expects to return by six o'clock."

"Expectations are no good in a case as serious as this, Miss Radcliffe. Who is his employer, please?"

"Armaund Lamont—the Fifth Avenue jeweler."

"'Phone headquarters, Hayes, to look him up. If he did not see Lamont, have them locate him and report. I would like to know, Miss Radcliffe, who occupied the rooms adjoining those of your father last night."

"Mr. Traynor was in the room on the left side and Mrs. Saint-Anton on the right."

"May I see those rooms please?"

"You poor child!" murmured Mrs. Saint-Anton as soon as they were alone. "What a disagreeable man! Your American policemen—" She rolled her eyes upward and raised her hands in a gesture more expressive than words.

"He is only doing his duty," defended Rose, wondering somewhat at the feeling of resentment which possessed her. Mrs. Saint-Anton had been kindness itself in her ministrations of the trying hours just passed; yet the girl found herself wishing both these strangers in the house would go away and leave her alone. Her poor father had felt the same way. "From what I have seen I am inclined to believe that Lieutenant Fargey is a thoroughly reliable and efficient officer and will find out who killed my father. That is what he is here for and that is what we all want him to do, is it not?"

"Oh, my dear Rose, how can you ask it? By all means! Oh, it is terrible, terrible—and *so* inconvenient. Roger and I had planned to run down to Atlantic City on Tuesday; the Van Alstynes are expecting us. But I suppose this policeman—you might ask him, my dear, how soon we shall be allowed to leave. Of course—if you prefer me to remain with you—if I can be of any service—"

"There is nothing you can do, Mrs. Saint-Anton, and I really would prefer to be alone at this time—" Rose began frankly.

"Quite so. I understand. Yes, of course," murmured the elder woman, and while she tried to throw only sympathy into her tones there was a false note in it that did not escape the girl's sensitive ear.

"But I am afraid nobody will be allowed to leave here—until after the fullest investigation has been made by the police."

Neither of them said anything more upon the subject and before long Fargey returned, followed by Roger Levering.

"We are going into the library now, Miss Radcliffe. Will you please attend—you, too, madam."

Except for the open door of the safe the room was in perfect order. Fargey approached the safe, but made no attempt to touch it.

"Was your father in the habit of keeping valuable gems in—that?" he demanded incredulously.

"Oh, no—not usually," Rose replied. "His collection is in his safety vault—at the bank. But occasionally he brought some of the jewels home for short periods and when he did, that was where he kept them."

"Know what was in the safe last night? Any inventory of the contents or anything like that?"

Rose hesitated, then shook her head. Lieutenant Fargey frowned thoughtfully, his lips pursed in disapproval.

"Can you describe your father's actions last night, Miss Radcliffe?—what he did during the evening, I mean—who was with him last, and so on?"

"Immediately after dinner he came into the library to smoke a cigar with Mr. Traynor as usual—"

"As usual?" She colored under the detectives' shrewd look.

"Mr. Traynor is quite often our guest. Father liked to talk to him about—" She hesitated.

"Yes? About his collection of jewels?"

"Yes."

"So last night they were in this room, discussing precious stones—perhaps looking at some of them?"

"Excuse me, but I can verify that," Levering vouchsafed. "By accident, I came upon them in here, not knowing the room was being used for an interview. Afterwards Traynor and the rest of us played billiards, Mr. Radcliffe having complained of a headache and the desire to retire early for a good night's rest."

"You saw them—examining jewels?"

Levering hesitated.

"Remember, I was intruding. Yes, they were looking at some cases of gems. I was in the room but a moment. But surely you do not think—?"

"Never mind what I think!" snapped Fargey. "That will be all for the present. I am returning to town with the coroner, Miss Radcliffe, but I will be back some time in the afternoon. Meanwhile Sergeant Hayes will be in charge here and we will appreciate it if you will afford him every opportunity in his further investigations about the house and grounds. I must request that all of you remain on the premises. No communications of any sort can be allowed for the present except through Sergeant Hayes."

"Mrs. Saint-Anton was wondering whether she and Mr. Levering could leave—"

"Decidedly not!" cried Fargey, flashing both of the guests a quick look of anger. "I do not want to be forced to take harsh measures, Miss Radcliffe; but it must be understood that until permission is granted, nobody is to leave this house. Have I your word on that point—all of you?" He grunted as each one nodded in turn. "You will be required to give evidence at the inquest. After that— we'll know more than we do at present."

Dr. Charles, the coroner, was already waiting in the car under the porte-cochere and Fargey, climbing in, paused to give final instructions to his subordinate.

"Keep a sharp lookout, Sergeant. And comb house and grounds for a cuff torn from a white shirt. Not that I expect you to find it; but look anyway—an' look good."

His face relaxed as he sank back on the cushions. He seemed very tired.

"You did not get much sleep last night, old man," ventured the doctor. "Better ease up a bit. You are working too hard, Bob."

Lieutenant Fargey glanced at him sharply. Then he laughed.

"Ease up! That's a good one. Do you know, Doc, that this is the second big jewel robbery this week! And now it's murder as well and a man as prominent as Radcliffe—!" He broke off impatiently. "They've put it up to me an' I've kissed sleep a fond farewell for a while—till I run down the gang. It was four o'clock when I turned in last night."

6
MR. ADDISON KENT

In his comfortable suite of rooms in Minaki Annex, Mr. Addison Kent, the well-known author of popular detective stories, had just finished a late breakfast and the latest extra. It was nearly eleven o'clock; but the ordinary divisions of night and day meant little to Addison Kent when he was at work and daylight had been blue at his windows when he had put the last finishing touch to his new novel with a sigh of relief. Once in the grip of those mad fits of literary production that periodically swept him away upon the high seas of his imagination, Addison Kent preferred to divide the clock according to demands of circumstance, scattering the hours to suit his own convenience. Thus, breakfast at three in the afternoon or dinner at three in the morning were matters entirely ungoverned by the complexion of the sky.

To find suitable quarters and to make household arrangements that fitted his special needs had required a lengthy search. Minaki Court on its quiet street off Riverside Drive had been a discovery; the location of the Annex with a frontage of its own on the little boulevarded crescent at the rear had further aroused his interest; it was really the old house originally on the property, converted into five-room suites, two on each floor, and the minute he had stepped inside that top-floor suite he knew that his search was over. Then had come the biggest discovery of all—the elderly Mrs. Madden across the hall, retired housekeeper, author of delightful pies and cakes, dramatist of the oven, creator of the famous Madden salads and master of all the culinary arts. It had required some coaxing; but the good woman was naturally a motherly sort and there was no resisting this attractive young man. Not only had she agreed to look after his rooms for him, but as she became better acquainted with him and his work she found many other ways of making herself useful, answering the telephone when he was out and guarding him against aggravating interruptions.

But it was not of his fortunate accommodations which Kent was thinking as he lolled in a worn old Morris chair by the window this morning, puffing thoughtfully at his favorite briar pipe. Sunday was always a lazy day with him; but he would have been out in the sunshine somewhere except for the glaring headlines of the latest murder sensation that stared at him from the front page of the latest extra, just delivered from the little news-stand where he kept a monthly account for the service. In itself the murder of Henry C. Radcliffe at his Westchester home was sufficiently startling; but to Kent it carried special interest by reason of the fact that Mr. Thomas Traynor was his friend and confidante of long standing. The two had learned to know and admire each other in the old newspaper days when both were cub reporters; each regarded the other as his best friend. Kent was waiting for the 'phone call which he felt sure would reach him sooner or later.

As he lounged and smoked, carelessly at ease, he was good to look upon, this strapping, athletic, professional novelist. The fact that he kept himself always in physical trim was apparent in the healthy color of his skin and the clearness of his eyes. They were the eyes of a dreamer and an idealist in repose with little hint of the keen logical mind which enabled him to construct the fascinating plots over which the public clamored at the bookstores. Poet and romanticist by inclination, he dreamed of the literary masterpiece he would write sometime much as the fat comedian longs to play Hamlet; in his spare time it was one of his amusements to compose verse, a habit which Baxter, his publisher, never lost an opportunity to frown upon.

"Look here, Kent, cut out that slush!" he protested anxiously one day. "It's a sure sign of insanity, and if it ever spreads on you— Good night! You've hit a paystreak. You're outselling every book on the market with that last one of yours. It's real literature, boy, even if it is a detective yarn and I'm telling you—"

And so on. Baxter was never through telling him, it seemed, and the funny part of it was that Baxter's enthusiasms were founded upon the public's insatiable appetite for Kent's novels. To Kent himself it was an unfailing source of amusement; for he took neither the novels nor his publisher very seriously. His financial success had not turned his head in the least; money interested him mostly as a resource for self-improvement and the relief of others less fortunate than himself.

So he continued to fill his long-term contract with Baxter. Yet he enjoyed the mental exercise of plot building, too. It was a game of hare and hounds, a literary adventure that developed surprises as the trail lengthened. And because he was a thorough craftsman, Kent had become a keen student of crime and criminals. The bookcases in the room he had fitted up as his "fiction factory" were filled with valuable volumes, bearing upon all manner of researches; he had accumulated that library with an eye to rare books long out of print and not readily obtainable at the public libraries. It was a unique collection. So were the newspaper clippings, stored in his filing cabinets—perhaps the most complete collection in New York City, not even excluding the newspaper offices or police headquarters. The mind of Addison Kent was trained for his work with an efficiency that began in the Canadian university from which he had graduated and to which he had added as the years went by; odd bits of information upon an amazing range of subjects were stored there like clustering constellations in a kaleidoscope, forever grouping into new combinations as the need for their application arose.

It was this ready knowledge, coupled with his keen reasoning powers in analyzing human motives under given circumstances that at last had brought him into contact with the official police. He had been instrumental in assisting the police to unravel one or two baffling mysteries and the fact that he had been ready to step aside from the limelight without accepting credit for his work had established very friendly relations at headquarters. Kent had considered himself more than repaid by the experience itself, having found the work highly interesting.

The details of what had happened at Hillcrest, as reported in the early extras, were necessarily meagre and he had soon tossed them aside. He knew of Traynor's deep interest in Rose Radcliffe, of course; also that Tommy had gone to Westchester for the week-end. Under the circumstances, he was surprised that Traynor had not called him on the 'phone long before this and he fully expected to hear the buzz of the instrument at any moment.

He was not quite prepared, however, for a familiar signal knock on the hall door and the unceremonious entry of Tommy Traynor himself. Kent sprang from his chair and hurriedly closed the door behind his visitor, aware at first glance that Traynor brought strange news. He went back to his chair without speaking.

"You've seen the papers, Ad." Traynor jerked his head at the discarded extras. "You're wondering why I'm not at Hillcrest. I was called on the 'phone last night and told that Lamont wanted to see me first thing this morning for a business conference. I left Hillcrest on the first train down this morning and the first I knew of—what's happened—was when I bought that extra. My God! it's awful! And me away—just when Rose needed me most!" He clenched his fists and took a turn across the room and back to get control of his voice. "I'm going back to Westchester on the first train out. I want you to come along."

"Calm yourself, Tommy," advised Kent quietly. "There's no need for me to go; I'd only be in the way and you'll have all you can manage, handling the crowd of reporters and photographers—"

"No need for you to go?" echoed Traynor. He laughed mirth-lessly. "Listen, Ad. Lamont didn't want me in here this morning; he's out of town, I find, over the week-end. It was a fake message!"

"Recognize the voice on the 'phone?"

"The wire wasn't very clear—I thought it was Baker, Lamont's secretary; but Baker denies it absolutely."

Kent laughed softly.

"Do you know that you were followed here, Tommy? Come here. Without disturbing the curtains take a look across the boulevard yonder." He pointed with the stem of his pipe and Traynor gave an exclamation as he noticed a man pausing to light a cigar and covertly glancing up at the windows of Kent's apartment.

"But I thought—the paper says Bob Fargey's been detailed on the case— Why, Bob and I know each other like a book!"

"Bob takes no chances," chuckled Kent. "You were missing when he got there and Fargey'd shadow his own mother if she crossed a murder trail. Now, sit down and tell me everything you can."

Traynor did so with the thoroughness of the experienced reporter and without interruption Kent listened attentively. Once or twice he stirred with interest; but it was one of his characteristics to remain perfectly motionless with every muscle in repose for minutes at a stretch so that it was hard to tell how deeply he was impressed by what went on about him at the moment. As the recital reached its climax with the vanishing face at the window of Traynor's room, the strange behavior of Rose Radcliffe in the middle of the night, the still stranger encounter with the Gray Woman, and the frightened Levering, Addison Kent's eyes brightened and he smoked a little more rapidly at his pipe.

"Less than half an hour ago I was on my way to the Grand Central to find out when the next New York, New Haven and Hartford train pulled out, when I got my first glimpse of those headlines. I came straight here to get you. I want you to come along."

"Why?"

"Do you need to ask that, man? You're my friend and I request it for one thing. Rose is going to need our best help, poor girl. The wisdom of the police—even Friend Bob—in a difficult case isn't to be relied upon and you know it. And I miss my guess if this doesn't prove to be a corker. It's going to tax even your best wits, Ad."

Kent smoked in silence for a moment.

"I don't know that I'm altogether prepared to agree with you, Tommy—that it is too complicated for Fargey to handle alone, I mean," he said slowly.

"But there is something so infernally queer about what happened out there last night—" Traynor shuddered involuntarily and paced the room restlessly.

"On the face of it—yes. But that's just it, Tommy. It's these unusual features—outré, if you like—that may lead to quick solution. In simplicity lies—complication. There's a paradox for you!" He smiled. "You don't believe in ghosts, do you? I don't think Bob Fargey does either. He'll probably go after that spook and have the bracelets on it within forty-eight hours. He might resent my interference at this early stage."

"To the dickens with Fargey!" cried Traynor. "If Rose and I retain you to make an investigation outside the police enquiry altogether—that's our own business, isn't it?"

"But why not give Bob a chance at least?" objected Kent. "That's his business, Tommy. My business is writing detective tales, not actually attempting detective work. This super-detective thing is all right on paper, but when it comes down to brass tacks— Say, do you know what would happen to that famous story detective of mine, Professor Jefferson Crate, if he went up against the real thing? They'd lasso him and haul him away to an asylum!" Kent laughed whimsically.

"No, no, old man! I may get away with a lot of crazy nonsense in a piece of fiction that would only bring loud laughter if tried in practice. Suppose I do override the courtesies and tackle this case, how am I to make certain, for instance, that I have lots of footprints to work with? It doesn't snow in the summer time and there hasn't been a drop of rain for a week! My friend, Crate, would be utterly lost, you know, unless 'it had rained heavily the night before,' or 'snow had fallen and footprints were plainly visible.' And as for clues—"

"Oh, for heaven's sake, Kent, have a heart! This is no time for kidding. What about that Acheson case you worked on? Donovan admits that if it hadn't been for your assistance—"

"Don't forget that the Blarney Stone is somewhere in Ireland."

"Bob Fargey's going to need all the help you can give him. Mark my words. Anyway, isn't it enough that I want you to help us— Rose and me?"

There was a note in Traynor's voice that made Kent look at him quickly. Tommy's face was worried, drawn in its anxiety, and at once Kent's whole manner altered. He laid aside his pipe and stood with his hands on his friend's shoulders in sudden contrition.

"Forgive me, Tommy. As it happens, I've just got the new thriller ready for Baxter; so I'm free. I've already looked up the time-table and our train leaves at 2.20."

Traynor sank into a chair with a breath of relief and reached for a cigar.

"Now you're talking," he grunted.

7
THE OBLITERATED CLUE

The shock which Traynor had received that morning as he stood in the street, excitedly reading the terrible news of the tragedy at the very place he had left but a few hours before, had thrown him into such a state of mental turmoil that for a time he scarcely knew what he was doing. He had come nearly being run down by the street traffic several times as he rushed for the nearest telephone booth he could find. The cool, insolent voice of the operator, informing him that the line was out of order, had steadied him finally, and immediately he had thought of Addison Kent.

Kent, of course. Kent would know exactly the best thing to do—Kent, the quiet, unassuming, long-headed, clever son-of-a-gun! As he made straight for Minaki Annex Traynor had thanked his stars for a friend like this to turn to, and he had not been long in Kent's presence before his mental tension began to relax. His confidence in Addison Kent's unusual abilities was supreme and with Kent's assurance of his best endeavor, he felt that the Hillcrest mystery was as good as solved.

As they went more thoroughly over all the details as Traynor knew them Kent already had helped him to a saner view of the whole situation. In his confusion of thought and under the influence of Rose's fears and his subsequent nocturnal adventures, he had been imagining too much—creating mystery where no mystery was and so on. Was it so very strange that Miss Radcliffe had visited the library after the household was asleep? Had he forgotten that one of the two cases of jewels had been left out of the safe

49

beneath the magazines on the library table when Henry Radcliffe
had closed the door in irritation at being interrupted! In their
excitement both of them had overlooked the fact. Suppose Miss
Radcliffe, happening in to get a magazine, had discovered the jewel-
case, would it not be natural for her to take charge of it—take it to
her room, her father being asleep? Then, worried at the responsibility, suppose she went back to the library to see if she could open
the safe or find some other hiding-place for the gems until morning. Suppose she was not satisfied to leave them there after all and
decided to take them back to her room and keep them under her
pillow for the night. Wouldn't that explain what he had seen her
do? Was Traynor fool enough to think Rose Radcliffe was robbing
her own father?

And Tommy had smiled and tried again to raise Hillcrest on
the telephone. This time he got the connection and had talked a
few moments with Rose herself, assuring her that he and Kent were
even then getting ready to go to the depot. The tremble in that sweet
voice at the other end of the wire, the relief in it, made Traynor
realize more fully the strain under which she was bearing up
bravely. He chafed at the delay after that and insisted upon reaching the Grand Central half an hour before train time. Not until they
were rattling off through the canyoned vistas of endless hives of
rusty brick did his impatience begin to subside.

The sight of policemen, guarding the gateways of the Radcliffe
residence, brought full realization of the change that had taken
place since morning. The news of the murder already had attracted
to the spot the usual crowd of morbidly curious people and Traynor
counted at least five newspaper cameras and two motion-picture
machines; no doubt a dozen or more newspaper reporters were
roving around the great house—perhaps indoors, pestering Rose.

As if divining his thought, Kent reminded him that his first duty
was to assist Rose and relieve her of as much detail as possible.

"I'll look after Fargey, Tommy. There he is now, filling that
bunch of ink-slingers with wonderful copy."

A cigar tilted at a complacent angle and a patronizing smirk on
his face, Lieutenant Robert Fargey at last had consented to give an

interview to the reporters. It was something to which he was not unaccustomed; he was an adept at handing out a "story" without really saying anything very vital to the case of the moment. As Traynor and Kent approached he dismissed his audience with a wave of the hand and preceded the new arrivals into the house, not altogether pleased at the interruption and evidently surprised to see Addison Kent. However, he grinned at Tommy Traynor, whom he knew of old, and shook hands with a show of cordiality.

"Kent's an old friend of the family, Bob; so I brought him along to help you," explained Tommy.

"Very kind," murmured Fargey, eyeing Kent non-committally. "We are always glad of expert assistance."

"I see you're right in the thick of it, Lieutenant," laughed Kent pleasantly, ignoring the emphasis on the adjective. "Just about cleaned up, eh?"

"Just about. You may as well see things for yourself, though. Come upstairs and I'll show you."

"Go ahead, Lieutenant. I'll be with you in a moment," and following Traynor, he stepped aside to pay his respects to the wan-faced girl who stood awaiting them at the drawing-room arch.

"This is the room," said Fargey when the other rejoined him and he unlocked the door.

The body of Henry Radcliffe had been removed, but he gave Kent a rapid review of the case and pointed to a chalk outline on the floor.

"Can you remember the exact attitude? Do you mind posing for me?"

With a smile at the request, Fargey allowed his body to collapse into the position in which the murdered man had been found. Kent studied the situation very closely. Then, when Fargey had risen, he stood over the spot and stretched out his left arm. It came in contact with the mirror over the mantel and he stepped closer to examine the glass.

"Did Mr. Radcliffe have a diamond ring on his left hand?" he asked. Fargey nodded. "Look at this, then."

A short curved scratch was visible on the surface of the mirror. At a point where the scratch ended a piece of bric-a-brac on the mantel had been newly chipped. Fargey glanced at Kent enquiringly.

"It looks as if there had been some sort of a struggle. The dead man's hand, possibly held in the grip of another, has swooped downward in a wide curve, the diamond in his ring scratching the glass."

"Might be an old scratch," suggested the lieutenant.

"Possibly. If you don't mind, though, we'll have one of your Bertillon experts look over these ornaments."

Standing once more within the chalked outline, Kent surveyed the room slowly. His eye focused suddenly upon something at the edge of the fireplace and, stooping quickly, he held out a tiny bit of yellow cardboard. It was scarcely half an inch long and about an eighth of an inch wide, torn at one end and burnt black at the other—

"A match," nodded Fargey, "evidently used to light a fire in the fireplace. It's often done, you know." His amusement was apparent.

"No doubt," smiled Kent. "I dare say Henry Radcliffe was in the habit of carrying these little packets of cardboard matches even in the pockets of his dressing-gown, advertising Somebody's Cigars; but the matches in that smoker's set on the table—"

His voice trailed away as he pocketed the fragment and walked into the alcove to examine the huge cherrywood wardrobe, built in solidly at the back. He opened the doors of it and peered in among the hangers that displayed a neat array of suits. Then dropping to hands and knees, he began a systematic search of the carpet within the alcove.

"We're progressing a little at any rate," he said with quiet satisfaction as he came out, and the surprised lieutenant saw that he held another of the yellow cardboard matches in his fingers.

"No doubt you have your own ideas of what happened in this room—," Kent began.

"Oh, never mind me!" retorted Fargey. "Go ahead. You're doing fine!" He grinned; but it was without mirth. He was beginning to wonder if he had really examined the room. Not that those yellow matches mattered in the least—

"Twenty-five caliber automatic, I believe you said, Fargey?" pursued Kent, amiably ignoring the other's manner. "Did anybody hear the shot fired?"

"Not a soul in the house."

Kent pondered this fact for a moment, then strode swiftly towards the window of the sitting-room. He threw open the French lattice, glanced at the direction of the fire-escape, then drawing in his head, began a careful inspection of the velour hangings. As he parted fold after fold he presently gave a grunt of satisfaction.

"Here we are, Lieutenant. Look."

Fargey's face was a study as he came slowly across the room to examine the curtain which Kent was holding out to him. He gazed at the small hole, stained brown all around, but said nothing. He nodded with the air of one who already had discovered the hole.

"The shot was fired from the fire-escape, of course."

"Of course."

"By a short man perhaps, although we can't rely on this bullet-hole as an indication of height. He might have been on one knee—"

"What's the matter with making it a tall woman?—might have stood at the railing at that!"

Kent shook his head and chuckled.

"Or it might have been somebody of medium height like you and me," growled Fargey. "Can you decide which of us did the deed?"

"Let's take a look out here," said Kent, climbing out onto the fire-escape as he spoke.

His gaze swiftly covered the surroundings. The view of the grounds and the wooded reaches beyond was magnificent; but Addison Kent was not admiring scenery. The lure of the chase was taking possession of him and his immediate concern was the fire-escape and more particularly the metal landing directly in front of the window. He waved Fargey back and got down on hands and knees to examine every inch of it closely, slowly working his way towards the point where the steps descended.

His next move was somewhat surprising. He scuffed the metal floor with his boot, examined the sole, then the spot where he had rubbed it. Abruptly he reached for the police officer's ankle, lifted his foot and glanced at the sole. Both of them were wearing fine boots with sewn soles and he shook his head as he looked up.

"No, neither of us did the deed," he said with utmost gravity. "Unless, Lieutenant, you've changed your boots."

Fargey stared at him blankly. Then he laughed and placed a hand over his heart in mock distress.

"Don't scare a fellow out of his boots like that, Kent!"

"The man who committed this murder was wearing heavy boots, thick soles, worn down so that the nails were prominent. He paid a visit to this fire-escape since the shooting—perhaps during the night; perhaps to-day some time."

"Wha—what's that?" gasped Fargey. "Surely you're not serious?"

"There's the proof of it," and he pointed to a spot near the railing where the paint had been scuffed completely off a segment of the grating. The whole fire-escape had been painted recently; the scratches of the boot-nails were quite distinct.

"But, good heavens, Kent—!" protested Fargey skeptically.

"I confess that I have the advantage of you, Lieutenant. You see, Traynor has given me quite a lot of information. During the night Tommy was awakened by some sound and saw somebody looking into his room. He lost a few valuable moments, trying to collect his senses, so that when he opened the window and looked he could neither see nor hear anyone. The light was poor; the moon was behind a large cloud—"

Fargey, who had been listening in a sort of trance, came to life suddenly.

"I know," he interrupted. "You mean an athletic person could climb over the railing and hang by his or her hands from the grating?"

"Exactly. You note that this platform extends beneath both windows—Traynor's and Radcliffe's—and the mark is about half way between. It's the only way to account for the disappearance."

"But you say this person has been back here since the shoot-ing?"

"I think so. I can only guess at the time, of course."

"But the risk of discovery—"

"Was not greater at the time than it would be now if the mur-derer had not returned." He pointed to the scuffed grating and to two or three similar spots on the railing where the paint had been thoroughly scratched away. "A perfectly good clue has been com-pletely obliterated there, Lieutenant."

Fargey rubbed his chin reflectively and nodded.

"Finger-prints," he muttered. "By George, Kent, that's good work—even if it doesn't get us anywhere." The sarcasm was en-tirely missing from his tone now and he looked up with a new re-spect. "Let's get inside before some of those snooping reporters catch sight of us." He hesitated. "What d'you say if we work this thing together, old man?"

"That's what I'm here for—to give what help I can."

"Come on inside and I'll show you everything I've picked up and tell you everything I've learned since I came here."

Addison Kent smiled quietly to himself as he followed through the window. He had not hoped for such quick capitulation.

8
"The Lady is Lying"

Lieutenant Fargey passed over his cigar case with friendly insistence, then felt in his pocket and handed Kent the small, fully-loaded S. & W. revolver which he had found in the room.

"It was like that when I picked it up," he explained. "And this here gold pencil with indelible lead was clutched in the right hand like it was grabbed from its chain in the struggle. A woman did this murder, Kent. That's a lady's pencil. There was a woman in here with Radcliffe last night—"

"Maybe. But she did not do the shooting—"

"Why not?" objected Fargey. "She had an argument with Radcliffe. They struggled. She broke away to escape by the window, turned and fired through the curtain."

"It was a man's face Traynor saw looking in on him in the moonlight."

"Moonlight is deceptive, and Traynor was only half awake," argued Fargey eagerly. "And I know lots of women could do that stunt of hanging beneath the fire-escape out of sight—dead easy."

"The boots—"

"There's coarse boots for women as well as men."

"Then, those yellow cardboard advertising matches—"

The lieutenant made a gesture of impatience.

"I don't put any stock in them. One of the servants might have dropped 'em—chambermaid with a wastebasket in her arm—anything you like. I've got a hunch it's a skirt we've got to look for, Kent."

"Do you believe in ghosts, Lieutenant?" asked Kent abruptly.

Fargey's hand hovered over the ash-tray as he looked up quickly. He knocked the ashes off his cigar with a smart tap of the finger.

"I dunno," he grinned. "Do you? There's a lot o' people in Ireland believe in banshees— You're referrin' to this here spook last night Traynor an' this man Levering say they saw—"

"You've heard about it, then?"

"Levering told me the yarn this morning—seemed to take it seriously enough, too." Fargey smoked thoughtfully. "Traynor told you about this Roger Levering?—guest in the house—queer-looking fish, but seems decent enough. We'll look him up after a bit. What do you make of the ghost business?"

"Somebody masquerading, of course."

"I think so, too—a woman, don't forget. It was a woman they saw. We've got a pretty unusual case here, Kent; we'll get to the bottom of it when we find who tore off the shirt-cuff that was missing from the left sleeve of Radcliffe's shirt."

This was news to Addison Kent and he leaned forward intently.

"Tell me all you know about that."

"We don't know much—except that the cuff's gone. We've ransacked the place inside and out, of course, without finding it. I asked myself why anybody would want to tear off one of the sleeve-ends like that and there seems to be only one answer. The doc says Radcliffe might've lived a few minutes after he was shot and it's my guess he wrote a message of some kind on his cuff—perhaps with that gold pencil that was in his hand."

"And someone interested returned to the room and removed the message?"

Fargey nodded. There was a glint of satisfaction in his eyes as he looked importantly at the other's thoughtful face.

"I'm willin' to bet dollars to doughnuts that message identifies the murderer."

"At any rate it is very important," agreed Kent. "Too bad. Another good clue very likely destroyed by this time."

"Damn the luck!" Lieutenant Fargey savagely bit the end off his cigar and spat it out in disgust. "But we'll get her if it takes a year!" he vowed. His jaw was set and there was a menace in his eyes that boded ill for the object of his wrath. He saw Kent studying the expression with interest and he gave a short laugh and gestured with his pudgy hand. "I take this thing pretty serious, Kent; I admit it. It's the second robbery of the kind within the week and feelin's beginnin' to run high at headquarters. I—I've got to make good on it, y'understand. I've got to make a good showing—" He broke off and gazed at the floor in abstraction for a moment. "It ain't that there's a bunch o' fellows at the Central Office waitin' for my job," he said slowly, "I don't want you to think that for a minute. But my work's what I live for and it gets my nanny when things ain't goin' right."

"All the more credit to you, Lieutenant." Kent smiled reassuringly; the jealousies which he surmised lay back of Fargey's words were easy enough to understand. "Obliterated finger-prints or missing shirt-cuffs are not going to stop us. What else have you got?"

"I searched his clothes without finding anything. This is the thing that did the trick." He handed over the bullet which the coroner had extracted and Kent turned it over in his fingers.

"No sign of the ejected shell anywhere?" Fargey shook his head. "How about the servants?"

"There's ten of 'em altogether, counting the seamstress who sleeps out and the butler who bosses the bunch. They don't seem to know very much—all been with the family for some time, except Thompson, the butler; he's on'y been here about a month. The bureau is looking him up."

"Who else was in the house last night?"

"Besides Miss Radcliffe and her father, there were three guests—Traynor, Mr. Levering and his aunt, Mrs. Saint-Anton. Everybody's accounted for."

"And not one of them heard the shot fired?"

"So they say."

"Twenty-five caliber, automatic—it would not make a very loud noise if it were—"

He rose and went over to examine the heavy velour window drape once more, presently reaching down and lifting up the bottom of the curtain which was of double thickness where the end had been turned up in a wide hem. As Kent held it out for inspection, the lieutenant of detectives saw several minute creases and counted no less than three more bullet-holes.

"Been wrapped around the gun, eh?"

"Evidently," nodded Kent. "That would muffle it effectively. Besides, it was not fired indoors. Got identification of this revolver yet?" He handed back both it and the bullet as he spoke.

"Miss Radcliffe says it's one her father always kept handy in his room. Looks like he was expecting trouble of some kind, eh?—knew the woman who visited him last night was dangerous."

"You think he was expecting this visit?"

"Don't know for sure; but the bed hadn't been slept in. Doc. fixes the shooting somewheres around two o'clock in the morning."

Kent was eyeing the detective keenly now. He got up and stepped to the window. For a moment he leaned out, studying the descent of the fire-escape, then slowly drew in his head.

"Entrance to the room may be had—?"

"Two ways and two ways only," replied Fargey, "—the hall door and the fire-escape."

"The last section of the steps is hauled up high on the wall by weights just heavy enough to hold it there," stated Kent half to himself. "A person to reach the fire-escape without using this hoisted section would require a ladder probably; if they used the fire-escape steps—the chances are the pulleys would squeal loud enough to wake a pretty heavy sleeper. The section has not been disturbed from its position for some time—"

"Exactly," nodded Lieutenant Fargey eagerly.

"So that whoever came into this room last night came through the hall door in the regular way—that's what you want me to say, Lieutenant?"

"The hall door—yes."

"Then the conclusion is that the midnight visitor—"

"Wait!" Fargey held up his hand for silence, stepped softly across to the door and suddenly yanked it open. Satisfied that nobody was eavesdropping, he came back eagerly.

"The woman who came here last night to see Radcliffe," he said in lowered tones, "was already in the house."

"A member of the household?" Kent's tone was indicative of disbelief.

"She slept here last night."

"It isn't a good plan to go upon any preconceived theory, Lieutenant," warned Kent with a doubtful shake of the head. "Once it is exploded, your investigation is all at sea."

"I'm not just guessing," objected Fargey. "Everybody—the women folks, that is—was in bed before one o'clock last night—except two. Miss Radcliffe went down to the library during the night—"

"What time?"

"About two o'clock, she thinks it was. She found a case of pearls under some magazines in the library; she wasn't sleeping very well and that's what she went down for—to get a magazine. She doesn't know how the jewels got left out of the safe; but there they were and she took 'em to her room, not wanting to disturb her father."

"And the other woman—?"

"Owns that gold pencil that was clutched in the dead man's hand. Mr. Levering recognized it at once as one belonging to his aunt."

"Mrs. Saint-Anton?"

There was a gleam of triumph in Fargey's eyes as he nodded his head.

"You've said it. She admits it's hers but says she lost it shortly after she arrived here. She also denies that she was outside her bedroom last night."

"You have reason for thinking otherwise?"

"The maid that was attending her says the lady told her this morning she'd had a miserable night. Besides, how did that pencil come to be where we found it?"

"Mr. Radcliffe might have found it, intending to return it to its owner and have forgotten to do so—"

Lieutenant Fargey interrupted impatiently.

"Here's the rest of the chain that belongs to the pencil," he said, drawing it from a pocket of his vest. "Hayes picked it up outside."

"Outside the house?" asked Kent in surprise.

"Just underneath the fire-escape!" Fargey slipped his thumbs in the armholes of his vest and leaned back in his chair with the air of a man who has proved his case. "And if that ain't enough, Mr. Levering'll tell you that he found the pencil and chain unbusted yesterday morning—out in the grounds somewheres—and gave it back to his aunt half an hour afterwards."

"Does she deny that?"

"No. She's too clever to deny that part of it. She says she left it on the dresser in her room and didn't miss it till this morning."

Addison Kent smiled a little.

"And suppose what she says is the truth, Lieutenant?"

"Excuse me, Kent, but I ain't been in this business with my eyes shut. I *know* when people are telling me the truth. The lady is lying— lying to beat the band!"

A knock on the door startled them.

9
Concerning a Belief in Spirits

"Well, what do you want?" demanded Fargey as he stood with his shoulder against the half open doorway and glared at the butler with no great friendliness.

"Sorry, sir, if I am intruding. Mr. Traynor asked me to find you and say that he would be glad if you and the other gentleman could join him in the library, sir. He is waiting there now, sir. That is all, sir."

"We'll be down in a minute or two."

"Very good, sir."

As Thompson bowed and made a dignified retreat, the lieutenant of detectives stood watching him, chewing on his cigar. When he closed the door and came back to his chair the frown still lingered between his bushy eyebrows.

"Some o' these here servants get my goat for fair," he growled as he resumed his seat. "That bucko's too polite to be a real guy. Say, it must be fierce to be livin' with flunkeys like that always hangin' around you. He took my soup away from me when they served me a late lunch to-day, and I rather liked the stuff, too—had a hard time cleanin' anything off my plate. If I was one of these High Muckymucks—"

"Oh, heaven forfend, Fargey!" laughed Kent. "I'll bet that guy's been in Yurrup, and was born quiet in some dock's kitchen while his mother was washin' the dishes or something. He acts like his whole family'd been purrin' around palaces over there for a couple o' hundred years. Over in Yurrup—"

"Ever been in Europe?"

"Who? Me! Not Robert Fargey! Couldn't get me over there on a bet. This country's good enough for me. You can't go nowheres these days that you ain't seen it already in the movies or on picture-postcards anyways. Well, what do you say if we go down and see what Tommy Traynor wants?"

"You go on down and I'll join you in a minute. I want to take one more look around the room, if you don't mind."

"Oh, all right. Go as far as you like," and with a wave of his hand Lieutenant Fargey sauntered out.

As soon as the door had closed Addison Kent slipped across to the window without noise and crawled through. He ran down the fire-escape as far as he could, then dropped easily to the driveway. Here he began a careful scrutiny of the hard packed chipped gravel. He glanced up to locate the windows and, gauging the direction, continued the search on the farther edge of the driveway. Almost immediately he found what he was looking for, half hidden by the edge of the turf. The crunch of a heavy step sent him behind a large lilac bush and he chuckled as he saw the lieutenant of detectives approach and begin to duplicate his own actions.

"'Great minds run in the same groove,'" he quoted as he revealed himself. "No use wasting time there, Lieutenant," and he held out the article he had just picked up, laughing at the chagrin on the other's face.

"You found the shell?"

"As you see. Does the bullet fit?"

Fargey fumbled in his pocket and tried it. It fitted perfectly.

"So much for that," he grunted. Then he eyed Addison Kent coldly. "Tryin' to put one over on me already?"

But Kent only laughed and slapped him on the shoulder and assured him that nothing of the sort had been intended.

"You can rely upon me collaborating fully, Fargey. Without absolute frankness between us, we cannot hope to work together successfully."

"I've heard Donovan praising you up often enough to know better, Kent; so forget it," growled Fargey, apparently half ashamed of his insinuation. "I'm used to working alone and I get my eats by being suspicious—of everybody. For all I know, you may be the guy that committed this murder. Get me?"

"I thought you said it was a woman!"

"So it was! Come on, Traynor's waiting."

They found Tommy pacing slowly up and down the library, his hands behind his back and his mien one of deep thought. He had just come from his interview with Rose Radcliffe and it had been rather a trying ordeal in some respects. Although she was putting on a brave front in public and going about her duties with her usual efficiency, she had given way to her grief when talking to Traynor and he had been strangely stirred. It was as if she looked upon him as the only one who could be leaned upon absolutely—as if with her father gone he alone was nearest and dearest enough to be turned to without restraint in her great trouble. And as Traynor had tried to comfort her as best he might he had accepted the trust and made a silent vow that he would not rest until Henry Radcliffe's murderer had been brought to justice. It was no time to talk of love, but the light of understanding was in their eyes. To remove the shadow of mystery from this beautiful girl's life, to bring again the smiles to her lips and the brightness of happiness to her eyes— surely this were a privilege which transcended all else in life! And his face had grown very tender as these thoughts possessed him.

There was nothing of tenderness in the expression with which he greeted the two men when they entered the library, however. His eyes were alert, his face somewhat hard, the face of a young man who had justly earned his reputation in business circles as being "a live wire." Tommy Traynor was "on the job."

"I think we'd better hold a council of war, Bob. Should we call in Levering or not? I'm leaving that for you to say."

"By all means. Why not? I want Kent to meet him and he seems anxious enough to help."

Traynor's finger went out to an electric bell button at the edge of the huge library table.

"See if you can locate Mr. Levering and ask him to come here at once, Thompson."

While they waited Lieutenant Fargey and Kent examined the safe which still stood with doors yawning wide. Nothing had been touched, upon Fargey's strict instructions. Traynor recited briefly the facts of his short interview with Henry Radcliffe on the evening preceding.

"I've questioned Rose pretty closely, Ad., but her actions last night are easily explained. It was as you surmised. She knocked on her father's door about two o'clock but got no answer. That was just after she found the pearls under the papers there. She came back down to the library, rather than wake him up, hoping to find the combination, then decided to keep the jewel-case in her own room until morning. That's all there is about it. She said she had reported the facts to you, Bob."

Fargey nodded.

"What I can't understand is why a man with lots of money like Radcliffe kept an old model like that— Why, I know a dozen yeggs could get into that thing in two minutes—and keep their soup in their pockets at that."

"Mr. Radcliffe wasn't in the habit of using that safe for valuables, Bob," volunteered Traynor. "Anyway, the combination was stolen— At least, it can't be found. Hello, Levering. Come in."

Kent turned, but there was nothing in his manner to indicate the interest with which he took in every detail of the newcomer's appearance. He acknowledged Traynor's introduction with casual friendliness. Roger Levering, however, was more effusive.

"It was only a few moments ago, Mr. Kent, that I learned from Traynor we were honored by the presence of a real live author in the house. I am indeed delighted to meet you, sir. Is it permissable for me to tell you that I read that last book of yours with tremendous interest?"

"Permissable—if you are utterly reckless of your reputation for literary taste," smiled Kent rather wearily. He was so used to this sort of thing!

"I've read every book you ever wrote—and enjoyed them all, Mr. Kent; I am partial to detective stories and I am not literary snob enough to be ashamed of it," declared Levering, looking around at the others with a challenge. "But pardon me, Traynor. You sent for me?"

Tommy explained and at once Levering's manner became serious; there was no doubting the sincerity of his appreciation that he had been invited to the conference. He was anxious—even eager to help in every possible way and placed himself entirely at their command. He seemed to recognize at once that Traynor had assumed a rightful place as Miss Radcliffe's representative in the household.

As briefly as possible Traynor stated the situation. The police were in absolute charge of Hillcrest until after the coroner's inquest and as much longer as Lieutenant Fargey should see fit. Every member of the household had been subpoenaed to give evidence and it was hoped that the formal enquiry would clear away much of the mystery that seemed to hang about the tragic event that had taken place last night. Meanwhile, it was Miss Radcliffe's wish that every possible assistance be given the police in arriving at the facts.

She had been worrying about the collar of pearls that she had found in the library; the safe was no longer—safe. Traynor had thought it best to ask Mr. Armaund Lamont to run out to Hillcrest to advise Miss Radcliffe in regard to her father's collection of precious stones with which he was more or less familiar; also he could take charge of the pearls for her and it was just possible he might be able to throw some light upon the mysterious telephone message which Traynor had received, calling him into town unnecessarily. Mr. Lamont had promised to come at once.

"Will you be sleeping here to-night, Bob?"

"That's hardly necessary with you three fellows in the house," replied Lieutenant Fargey. "Some of my men will be about and I'm within easy reach if needed."

"I thought you might like to take a whack at the ghost," grinned Traynor.

"The ghost's out o' business. She won't worry you no more," assured Fargey. "She knows she's liable to get a bullet through her bread-basket if she pokes her nose around here again—"

"She had no nose, Bob, and ghosts are unaffected by bullets."

"Bunk, Traynor! You don't believe in the thing, do you?" demanded the lieutenant. "Mr. Levering here—"

"We both saw it—," began Tommy, regarding him with amusement.

"And even if she was the genuine article—the ghost is through here. 'Cause why? Her work's done."

"You mean the ghost—killed Henry Radcliffe?"

"We'll see—what we'll see," said Fargey grimly.

"I would be glad to hear Mr. Levering's explanation of the strangest feature of the case," suggested Addison Kent who had been studying Roger Levering's expression which had altered subtly at mention of the apparition that had frightened him so the night before. "I believe you can corroborate Traynor's yarn about the thing, Mr. Levering?"

Levering's starey little eyes behind their thick glasses turned directly upon his questioner. There was a faint indication of moisture on his forehead and he wiped it away with his handkerchief rather impatiently.

"It is one of the strangest experiences I ever had," he murmured solemnly.

"Tell us exactly what you saw or think you saw."

"There can be no question that both Mr. Traynor and myself saw the phenomenon. We are agreed on its appearance in every detail," and Roger Levering proceeded to relate his version of the encounter; it coincided perfectly with what Traynor had already described to Kent.

"You are not satisfied altogether that it was a masquerade?" suggested the latter.

"I would not like to say that," Levering replied after a moment's hesitation. "It probably—" Again he hesitated.

"You believe in spirit manifestations?" persisted Kent.

"Frankly, gentlemen, I do." He glanced at each of them in turn with something of challenge in the look as if he feared they might laugh at the admission. But none of them was even smiling. "I have given some study to psychic phenomena and I may tell you at once that I have every reason to believe the evidence in favor of visualization. In fact, I myself have had several experiences of the kind."

"The subject interests me greatly," said Kent soberly. "You mean you have personally experienced phantasms, Mr. Levering? Of living or dead persons?"

"Both," admitted Levering. "It is because of this that I hesitate to reach any hasty conclusion about last night. The evidence, Mr. Kent, is overwhelmingly in favor of the existence of a definite spirit world. If you have gone into the published documents of the psychical research societies—?" He paused for an answer.

"I have."

"Then you must admit that even discounting all cases where elements of doubt creep in, there still remains enough direct evidence—"

"I can quite understand your hesitation, Mr. Levering," nodded Kent. "It is a pretty deep subject and some of the keenest scientific minds all over the world have accepted the belief. Personally, I have never been able to get beyond reach of the subconscious mind. Our mental machinery is so complex and delicate that it plays us strange tricks at times—particularly in the matter of vision. Hallucinations and illusions—"

Levering interrupted with a gesture of protest.

"We must make due allowances for hallucinations, of course, Mr. Kent. But even so, if you will examine the 'International Census of Waking Hallucinations in the Sane' you will find narratives which will convince you—"

"That the narrators who claim to have been in the waking state when they saw their vision generally admit in the course of their accounts that they were feeling drowsy at the time or were not sure whether they were awake or asleep."

"Not all of them," said Levering earnestly. "Sane people with their eyes wide open—"

"See a straight stick appear bent when thrust into a pool of clear water," interrupted Kent. "And when a burning stick is swung in a circle they see a ring of fire when no such ring of fire exists."

"That is due to a persistence of impression upon the retina," retorted Levering.

"Or take an advertising poster," interjected Traynor. "What about a portrait or a pointing finger that seems to follow you wherever you move?"

"That's because the picture is a flat projection; the front of the portrait's eye and the pointing finger are presented to you from whatever angle you look. For the same reason the flat drawing of— a cube, say—may delude with the impression of solidity."

"What makes it look like the train you're on is standin' still while the freight-cars you're passing are doin' the travelling in the opposite direction?" This contribution came from Lieutenant Fargey with gusto; he was enjoying the baiting.

"Yes, or the whole landscape moving?" added Traynor.

"Or the moon plowing through the clouds," smiled Levering. "Optical delusions, all of them, quite beside the point."

"Seen by sane people with their eyes wide open," reminded Kent, laughing. "You can't get away from it, Levering. If we look through a prism we see objects doubled. If we press an eyeball we get divergence of the axes of vision. The sun appears to move around the earth when it does nothing of the sort; telegraph wires alongside the moving train seem to rise and sink rhythmically when they don't. The rising moon appears to alter its size as it climbs higher in the sky. People five or six feet tall seem to be pigmies when we look down on them from a high building. Does a railroad track really converge to a one-rail affair at the vanishing point?"

"Illusions of sight—mere fallacies of perception," protested Levering.

"So much for the reliability of the human eye. We can go on similarly with tricks of the brain, if you wish. What happens upon removing a tight bandage from your finger? It feels as if it were still bound up, doesn't it? The tingling sensation of the pressure remains. The conjuror presses the coin into your palm before removing it in order that you may think it is still there after he has closed your fingers. Fallacies like these are of universal experience. By the time we add to the list auditory hallucinations and loss of the sense of smell and taste, one is forced to the conclusion that not only is seeing not believing but about the only sense that can be relied upon is a sense of shame for man's precocity."

Levering shook his head, unconvinced.

"Do you believe in telepathy?" he asked quietly. "You admit, then, that there is a sixth sense, strange premonitions. You have only to examine the records of apparitions that have appeared to relatives prior to death or prior to some crisis—"

"It is difficult to obtain satisfactory evidence—of the coincidental character of the vision with the event," objected Kent.

"This sort of thing is of too frequent occurrence to be merely fortuitous," asserted Levering with conviction.

"Do you think the presence of this ghost woman last night had any such relation to the death of Mr. Radcliffe?" asked Traynor, suddenly thoughtful.

"That's the point. It may have a telepathic bearing. In my humble opinion it is quite possible; but then, I believe in the necessary premises—that there is such a thing as spirit life and that visual manifestations do take place."

"Have you ever talked to Mr. Radcliffe about this sort of thing, Mr. Levering?"

"No. The subject never came up between us."

"Do you know that of late he had taken up the study of psychic phenomena—and shared your belief in these things?"

"No, I was not aware of that," replied Levering with sudden interest.

Traynor turned to the lieutenant of detectives.

"There is a phase of this mystery, Bob, with which you are not yet familiar. Miss Radcliffe wished to confer with me before making any statement. There is no desire, though, to withhold any fact that can possibly have a bearing upon the situation."

He then told them all that he had learned in regard to the three warnings which Henry Radcliffe's daughter had received and the vision which the murdered man claimed to have had. During the recital Addison Kent covertly watched the other two auditors to whom these facts were new. Their astonishment and interest was manifest. Fargey was leaning forward, his mouth half open and his cigar neglected. Roger Levering plainly was deeply impressed by this unexpected support of the argument he had just been making.

"I take back what I said a moment ago," he declared at last, turning to Kent. "I do not think that what Traynor and I saw last night was anybody, masquerading as a ghost."

"You think it was a genuine psychic presence?"

"I believe so."

Fargey wet his lips. He swore softly.

Then he looked up with a start. Unnoticed by anyone, the butler was standing in the room, a tray with glasses in his hands.

10
Roger Levering Locks the Door

"Miss Radcliffe's compliments, sir," he murmured to Traynor as he deposited the tray with its liquid refreshments upon the table.

"You may close the door after you when you go out, Thompson, and kindly see that we are not disturbed."

"Yes, sir," bowed the butler and forthwith he retired softly with a somewhat abashed air.

"How much did that guy hear? That's what I want to know," scowled the lieutenant in a low voice full of resentment. "He's got to take the pads off his feet or I'll lock him up where he can't listen quite so handy."

Levering cleared his throat.

"It will be very awkward for Miss Radcliffe if this psychic phase of the case frightens the servants into leaving without notice," he ventured. "If I may make a suggestion, Mr. Fargey, it would be well if the whole matter were eliminated entirely for the time being— until some tangible evidence is forthcoming of its significance. It only complicates things unnecessarily and I agree with you that the apparition is very unlikely to make any further appearance, whether we admit its genuineness or not."

Traynor added his endorsement of the suggestion as he passed around the refreshments. Fargey looked enquiringly at Addison Kent who nodded slowly, his eyes fixed on Levering.

"It may help rather than hinder your investigations, Lieutenant," he said. "I think Mr. Levering is right."

72

"I think I'll take a mooch around," Fargey decided suddenly and emptied his glass. "See you later."

A few minutes afterwards Tommy Traynor also excused himself and Kent reached for a fresh cigar, first passing the humidor to Roger Levering who seemed to welcome the opportunity for a confidential chat.

"I've noticed you looking at me rather intently once or twice, Mr. Kent," he began, "and as I am sure that we have not met before—you don't mind me mentioning such a trivial matter? People frequently look at me that way and I have traced it to my rather uncommon glasses. Do they make me look like a freak, or what?"

There was no resentment in the tone and he smiled at his own question.

"Oh, I wouldn't like to say that!" protested Kent, somewhat taken aback for the moment at the man's perspicacity in voicing the very thought that was passing through the author's head.

"I am troubled with hypermetropia, to give it its full name."

"It sounds impressive. You are far-sighted."

"Very far-sighted, Mr. Kent."

For a moment it almost seemed to the novelist that he sensed some vague threat underlying the repetition, a double meaning. Or was it merely that the expressionless stare behind the distorting lenses conveyed an undue solemnity to the words? He laughed softly, recalling his own advice to Fargey about the importance of not jumping to theoretical conclusions upon mere suspicion.

"To be short-sighted would be a much greater handicap, I should think," he said easily as he proceeded to light his cigar.

"I suppose so," sighed Levering. "I have had to wear these confounded things constantly and there are times when I abominate them. It annoys me to see ladies—" He stopped abruptly as if saying too much.

"Do you never leave them off, then—the spectacles?"

"I dare not do so because I am lost without them. However, one is helpless in these matters at birth and should be philosophical about it." He smiled in dismissal of a disagreeable topic. "Forgive me, Kent, for talking trivialities when there is so much that could be discussed with greater profit. You are not busy for a while, are you? Suppose you come up to my room where we are sure of absolute privacy. There is something of grave importance about which I would like your advice as a friend."

"Certainly," said Kent, rising at once. "I have nothing to do but finish this cigar. If I can be of any service—"

Murmuring his thanks, Roger Levering led the way upstairs to the rooms he was occupying. It was a suite arrangement, like the other guest chambers on the first floor, consisting of sitting-room with open fireplace, bedroom and beyond that a private bathroom. As they entered Kent noted that Levering's rooms were at the end of the passage, two doors distant from the room where last night's tragedy had been enacted.

"Who occupies the rooms next to you?" he asked.

"My aunt, Mrs. Saint-Anton. You will not meet her until dinner to-night as she is lying down with a bad headache. Then come the quarters which poor Radcliffe occupied, and next past that is where Traynor is. Take that easy chair, Kent. Throw off your coat and make yourself at home."

Levering set the example by tossing his own coat aside and, nothing loath, Kent did the same. Collars and ties followed and in spite of Kent's protest Levering rang for the butler and requested him to mix long cool drinks "a la Johnathan Collins." Kent could not resist a smile; he was unable to decide, however, whether Levering was indulging in the facetious or whether he really was unfamiliar with the Christian names of our great inventors.

One of the first things that caught Kent's roving eye was a small bottle of purple ink that stood on the open lid of the writing-desk, where it had been spilled on some of the notepaper and envelopes scattered there. Levering, returning from boosting the window higher, noticed the direction of the glance and apologized for the untidy appearance of the desk.

"The routine of the servants has been somewhat upset by the general excitement, I guess," he said as he walked over and closed the desk. "I upset the ink last night when I was writing some letters; I wasn't sleepy and got out of bed to do some correspondence

I'd forgotten when I heard—or thought I heard—someone out in the hall. I went to the door and looked out and that was when I first caught sight of the lady ghost. It gave me quite a start and I shut the door quickly and dropped into the chair at the desk. I was trying to put the cork in the bottle and upset the thing. Scarcely a man's prerogative, eh—fumbling corks?" He laughed. "By George! Kent, I was all in a tremble for a minute, it was so unexpected, don't you know? I got over it after a bit and went out to investigate. I've nearly rubbed the skin off my fingers with pumice and lemon, getting the indelible ink-stain off," and he laughed again as he held out his hand for inspection.

"Say, you play chess, of course?" he asked suddenly.

"Why no, it's a game I have never learned," replied Kent as he followed Levering's glance towards the chessboard that stood on the mantel beside its box of pieces and pawns. "I guess it's a good enough game all right; but it has always seemed to me too complicated to take time to learn it."

"It's the greatest game in the world!" cried Levering enthusiastically. Then a shade of disappointment crossed his face. "Pshaw! I was sure you knew how to play it. In that last novel of yours— Surely you are spoofing, Kent?—Why, those chess moves you describe in that chapter near the end are almost professional in their ingenuity—where you have your hero playing a game of chess with the criminal, you remember?"

"Oh, yes," laughed Kent, "but you don't realize, Levering, that a writer has to go to experts in many different directions at times to get correct data. I got all that from a friend of mine who is a fiend at the game; I am indebted to him entirely for that passage."

"I am very much disappointed," declared Levering, and he showed it. "I have been taking lessons with one of the New York experts in the game and have been trying to find someone to practice with ever since I came here. You ought to take it up; I'm sure you'd like it and become very proficient in it. Later on I'll give you your first lesson or two, if you like. But that is not what I brought you up here to talk about— Ah, this looks good," he finished as the butler entered with two tall glasses, tinkling with ice.

Levering took the tray from him and dismissed him. He waited a moment, then went to the door and turned the key in the lock.

"I have a few questions to ask first, Mr. Kent, and if I seem to presume upon such short acquaintance, I hope you will allow my anxiety to excuse my apparent impertinence. The questions are pertinent rather than impertinent."

Kent nodded politely, but for a few moments Roger Levering stirred and sipped his drink in thoughtful silence.

"Just what is your status in this police enquiry?" he began at length. "Are you a professional detective as well as a professional writer of detective stories?"

"Not at all, Levering. I am a writer by profession, as you know. I am here merely to help in any way I can—like yourself, I presume—because I am a friend of Miss Radcliffe and Mr. Traynor."

"Are they engaged? But no, I should not have asked that; it doesn't matter. You are not officially connected with the police, then?"

"No."

"But you have done work for them, I understand. Haven't you?"

"Who told you that?"

"Fargey. However, that doesn't matter either, as long as you are not working officially with them on this case."

"Just what do you mean?" asked Kent in surprise.

"Presently, presently; but please let me go on in my own way, Mr. Kent. I must be sure that I understand your position thoroughly before I can speak—I— Frankly, old chap, I am worried about—" He hesitated again and Addison Kent's eyes never left his face.

"About what?" he prompted with just the right shade of polite sympathy in his tone.

"Something—which is too personal not to be—very disturbing. Please let me come at it in my own way. I am surprised to learn that you are not in charge of this case instead of the official police. Frankly, I am not overwhelmingly impressed with the perspicacity of this man, Fargey; I am in complete agreement with your Professor Crate—in your novels, you know—in believing that the official police are a pack of stupid asses—"

"I must correct you there," interrupted Kent with a smile. "As a reader of detective stories you are making the mistake of confusing fiction with reality. It is the customary privilege of the story detective to make jibes at the official police in order that his own wonderful genius may show up in sharper contrast. But there are many such liberties taken in a piece of fiction. There is a vast difference between the work of the Master Detective of the story pages and the detective in real life; the former finds the tiny clues and makes his amazing deductions and solves his problem because the author has planned carefully to have him do so, but the detective in real life has to rely upon honesty, obedience and leg work, well mixed with common sense, and then trust largely to good luck. Lieutenant Fargey no doubt has his limitations; he is only a human being with no guarantee of infallibility. But he has the reputation of being a hard worker and a man who is thoroughly posted in his work."

Roger Levering had listened to this speech with great interest and a growing astonishment.

"But I thought— You yourself as the creator of such clever tales, Mr. Kent—surely you would be able to bring to actual detective work a superior power of deduction and induction— Do I understand you to infer that in a real mystery such as this that seems to surround the killing of poor Radcliffe, you—at least you would not make stupid blunders—"

"I might—some very stupid ones perhaps."

"You amaze me."

"My 'Professor Crate' character does not make half the fun of the official police that the official police make of him, I am afraid," laughed Kent. "He is really impossible, my dear Levering. Ask Bob Fargey. Ask Fargey what he thinks of 'Sherlock Holmes,' Gaboriau's 'Lecoq' or Poe's 'Dupin'; he's probably read a lot of the detective tales available. Of course, I am not arguing that the fiction detective with the abnormal gifts has not his legitimate place—in stories; he is a standard type which the public accepts, even expects. But you make a mistake if you attempt to place him outside the printed page and confuse him with your real detective from the Central Office."

"I understand what you mean," nodded Levering. "Then you yourself as the creator of one of those characters with abnormal powers as a detective are yourself unable to apply those powers on a real case?"

"I leave it to your own common sense to answer that. If you told me that John Smith had just been robbed of a million dollars, I am very doubtful if I could walk around the nearest corner and arrest the first man I met just because he had a mole on his right cheek and had a bit of clay adhering to his left heel. No matter how many moles the robber had or whether the money had been dug out of a clay-bank, I could never land the culprit that way."

"How would Fargey go about it, then!" smiled Levering.

"He'd probably go first to the Rogue's Gallery and the whole machinery of the police system all over the country would be set in motion to run down every crook whose record made him a 'prospect' for a job of the kind in hand. He would have to trust to chance to a large extent. He certainly wouldn't start out, carefully disguised in a bunch of whiskers, to trail every man he met with a mole on his right cheek and mud on his boots!"

"Fargey is a man of reputation, you say?"

"Yes. I believe he is a first-class detective. But you understand, of course, that even a Central Office man who stands high may make mistakes—plenty of them. It is a business which must be learned like other businesses, by experience, and I would not say that the average detective was mentally any keener than—the average chauffeur, let us say. You have no more right to expect any greater brain power in an ordinary detective in real life than you would expect from a fireman or a plumber or a clerk in an office."

Roger Levering heaved a breath of relief.

"I am glad to hear you say that, Mr. Kent, yet—I don't know, after all, that it— Listen. I am going to tell you something in confidence which by no means must you repeat to a soul. I do not know whether you can help me or not; but you are the only man in this house whom I care to consult on what you will recognize at once is a delicate situation—for me."

"Your confidence will be respected, Mr. Levering."

"Thanks. Then—" He drew a big breath like a man taking a plunge into deep water. "I must tell you that Fargey has discovered a clue to the—what happened last night—that is likely to result in grave consequences. He has told you perhaps about the missing shirt-cuff—?"

"Yes."

"And the gold pencil that was clutched in Radcliffe's hand?"

"Yes."

"And the broken chain that belonged to it— Has he told you where it was found?"

"Yes."

"The pencil belongs to my aunt, Mr. Kent."

"So I believe."

"She lost it but I happened to find it yesterday morning and returned it to her. She says she left it on the dresser in her bedroom and that she missed it again for the first time this morning. She says she wasn't outside her own room last night." He got to his feet and paced about in sudden agitation.

Kent watched him intently, waiting quietly for him to recover his equanimity and not a little interested in what might follow.

"Yes?" he prompted at length.

"Fargey seems to attach great importance to this gold pencil and the fact that the chain was found beneath the fire-escape. He has not told me much, of course, but I strongly suspect that he does not believe the truth of what Mrs. Saint-Anton has told him."

"That is his privilege, of course," nodded Kent. "But it does not follow that he is at all justified. What possible object could your aunt have in trying to deceive him?"

"That's the very point!" muttered Levering as he again took a turn across the room and back. Kent noted that his hands were clenched.

"You mean—she had an object?"

"Yes." He stopped directly in front of Addison Kent.

"My aunt—I am afraid—for her," he said in a hollow voice.

He clutched the novelist's arm and Kent could feel the tremble of his fingers.

"I am afraid that she was not in her room every minute of last night," he whispered hoarsely. "I am afraid that she—that Fargey may be—right!" He sank into the chair and buried his face in his hands.

Kent stared at him in silence, tense and alert.

11
AN EYE IN THE DARK

He leaned over and touched Roger Levering's shoulder.

"Come, come, Levering, this thing's getting on your nerves, man. Your fears are not logical at all—unless you have some knowledge which you are withholding. Perhaps if you tell me all you can about your aunt and her relation to Henry Radcliffe I may be able to set your mind at ease."

There was not much to be said in this connection apparently. Mrs. Saint-Anton had not confided in her nephew in regard to Henry Radcliffe, except to say that he was an old-time acquaintance whom she had met first in France. Levering went on to explain that until recently he and his aunt had been comparative strangers as she had travelled a great deal on the Continent while he had grown up in somewhat hap-hazard fashion as a lazy sort of dog who took life rather easy. His father had been a barrister in Dublin, he said, and had spoiled him by giving him a good education and plenty of spending money. His roving spirit and association with certain scions of the British aristocracy at Oxford had led him into several hunting trips in Africa and South America and it was not until the unexpected death of his father that he learned he was practically penniless. A letter had reached him from his father's sister, whom he had seen but seldom, inviting him to join her on the Riviera. The visit had proved preliminary to Mrs. Saint-Anton's proposal that he accompany her on a trip to America, as a sort of escort, and he had accepted it at once. His aunt wished to visit several friends and some of these had met them when the liner

from Cherbourg had docked in New York harbor. Since then they
had visited the principal watering places, his aunt's chief concern
apparently being to have an enjoyable time. She was alone in the
world and as her husband had left her with a large annual income
she was in a position to go and come as she might choose.

"Has your aunt said nothing which would throw any light upon
your visit to Hillcrest?" asked Kent, not without surprise.

"Very little. Beyond the fact that she spoke of Mr. Radcliffe as
an old friend, I know nothing. She told me how wealthy he was
and how beautiful his daughter—" He stopped in some confusion.

"I see," nodded Kent. "And you were to make yourself agreeable and—who could tell what might happen, eh?"

Roger Levering shifted restlessly in his chair.

"I would rather not discuss that, if you please," he protested.
"I am not altogether dull, Kent. I have sensed that I was not very
welcome here and have been anxious to get away. I have felt that
my aunt's presumption was altogether unwarranted. I trust that
you will credit me with that."

"If you know nothing of your aunt's past relations with Mr.
Radcliffe, what makes you jump so readily to your conclusions?"
demanded Kent bluntly. "Without some reason they are utterly
foolish. Did you see her outside her room during the night?"

"No."

"Then why do you think she may not be telling the truth? Was
there any apparent ill feeling between her and Mr. Radcliffe?"

Levering hesitated and wet his lips.

"There have been times when I—thought perhaps there was,"
he admitted uncomfortably. "I have seen Mr. Radcliffe looking at
her somewhat strangely, I thought, and once or twice I happened
upon them when there appeared to be a decided coolness between
them. I thought at first it might have to do with my aunt's match-
making tendencies; but now I am not sure but it may have been
deeper than that."

"Even that suspicion does not justify your present fears, Mr.
Levering," said Kent with a note of severity in his voice. "You are

evidently upset by what's happened and are giving your imagination too free a rein."

"I hope you are right, old chap. You understand that all this is in strict confidence. This Fargey seems so sure of himself that it has made me realize my position very keenly. I feel a lot better for having had this talk with you. I want to get this situation cleared up as quickly as possible. I am going to have a frank talk with my aunt; it will probably mean a bit of a row, you know, for she has a temper of her own. I want to help, though, in every way I can."

"Of course," murmured Kent as he stood up and reached for his coat.

He stepped past Levering's chair and in the act of thrusting his arm through the sleeve one of his fingers swept across the other's face and knocked his glasses upward into his hair where for a brief instant they hung in jeopardy before their startled owner could grab for them, adjusting them once more behind his ears.

"Oh, I say!" cried Roger Levering, springing to his feet. His face flushed angrily.

"Great Scott! Are they broken?" gasped Kent in dismay. "How infernally careless of me! I beg your pardon, old man. It was an accident. If they had been broken I could never forgive myself." He heaved a breath of relief, his manner one of abject apology and concern.

"They're all right. Ac—accidents will happen, old chap," murmured Levering, dismissing the incident with a hasty wave of one hand. "See you at dinner, Kent." He expressed his gratitude once more for the interview as he unlocked the door and smiled pleasantly as he bowed his visitor out.

On his way to his own room Kent, leaning over the bannister, saw Detective-Sergeant Hayes in the hall below and whistled softly to attract his attention. In answer to his beckoning finger, Hayes came quietly upstairs and followed into the suite of rooms to which Kent had been assigned.

"You are to be in charge here to-night, Sergeant, I believe."

"Yes, sir," he saluted. "Loot'nant Fargey has just given me the word."

"The grounds will be picketted, of course?"

"That is the intention, Mr. Kent. I have 'phoned headquarters for a squad of patrolmen to report for night duty and I have several plainclothes men besides."

"Good. I believe it may be of importance to keep a sharp lookout to-night. No special liberties are being allowed anyone, I suppose?"

"The orders are strict, sir. Nobody is allowed to leave."

"Not even me?" smiled Kent.

"Oh, yes,—you, of course, sir," grinned the sergeant. "And Mr. Traynor. The orders refer to the servants."

"And Mrs. Saint-Anton?"

"Queen high, Mr. Kent," and Sergeant Hayes drooped an eyelid. It was evident that he shared the confidence of his chief to a high degree.

"In drawing to the queen, Sergeant, be careful not to discard the jack."

Detective-Sergeant Hayes was bright. His response to this cryptic warning was another slow wink to signify appreciation of the fact that nephews and aunts were close relations.

"About this missing shirt-cuff, Hayes—," Kent continued, "just how thoroughly have you searched?"

"High and low, sir. We've been through every room in the house, garages and stables, tool-house, and every part of the grounds. Everything has been turned inside out."

"Much to everyone's annoyance no doubt. The lady guest was annoyed very likely. Was she, Hayes?"

"Very much, Mr. Kent. But we can't help that."

"No, of course not. All right, Sergeant. If anything interesting crops up, you might let me know. I'll be up late most likely; but don't hesitate to wake me if you happen to need me after I've turned in."

For a few moments after Detective-Sergeant Hayes had taken his departure Addison Kent stood at the window of his room, his hands in his pockets, lost in thought. Once or twice he shook his head slowly and at last he smiled faintly as if in skepticism of his own speculations.

"Well, 'we'll see—what we'll see.' That's one wise remark that can be accepted anyway and by the time—"

For a moment he stared vacantly at the object which his hand had idly withdrawn from his pocket; then his thoughts focused upon it—the master key which Traynor had obtained for him from Miss Radcliffe at his request. It was her own private key and it would admit him practically to any room in the house. He smiled at the responsibility its possession entailed and tossing it on top of the cheffonier, proceeded leisurely to dress for dinner.

In the bathroom, drying his hands upon a towel, his thoughts turned to the convenience of all the appointments in this house of luxury. Although it was such a large place, the clever architect had designed a use for every corner of space; thus, the bathrooms of the various guest suites were let into the wall at one end of the large clothes closets—

Kent dropped the towel abruptly and came out into the sitting-room to study the layout more closely. Yes, it was the same as the suite Levering occupied; there would be uniformity of design in all the guest chambers likely. Then, why was there no clothes-closet in the rooms which Henry Radcliffe had occupied? None of the other suites had a huge wardrobe or any alcove—

He went to the window and gazed out again, this time with seeing eyes, noting that the wing where the servants were quartered was of much more recent construction than the rest of the house; the masonry was new, the whole wing un weathered. There was a certain impression of newness about these guest rooms, too,—as if extensive alterations had been made in the house proper at the time the new servant's wing had been added.

Kent began to whistle a little soundless tune to himself as he slipped on his coat and reached for Miss Radcliffe's key. He glanced at his watch. Nobody was in sight in the hallway and he moved quietly along to the door of the late Mr. Radcliffe's apartment and let himself in. It was the same as the suite he had just left except for the lack of a clothes-closet in the bedroom and the addition of the alcove off the sitting-room.

Kent studied the partitioning of the room with particular care. The alcove was wide but not deep; the big cherrywood wardrobe that was built in at the back across the full width required most of the space. He opened all the doors and stood back, chin in hand, then turned on his heel and went into the cuter hall for a glance at the relative distances between the various doors that opened upon the passage from the neighboring rooms. Satisfied, he returned to the alcove, carefully locking the door that gave entrance to the suite, and took from his pocket a small flat flashlight.

With this thrust inside the wardrobe he patiently explored the woodwork, running his hand over every inch of it, feeling every edge with which his fingers came in contact. He dusted his knees at last with an ejaculation of disappointment; yet he was sure he was right. The measurements at the back of the thing were abnormal, even allowing for a bulky solidity; besides, when he tapped gently He stepped inside, shoving away the hangers on their sliding rod, and found that he could stand upright; he could even move sideways behind the clothes—

There was a slight click beneath his advancing foot. The little disk of light revealed the centre panel sliding noiselessly into a hidden recess, cunningly provided for it; through the aperture the thin ray from his tiny torch penetrated the dark. He turned it to the floor and without hesitation stepped through the back of the wardrobe, finding himself in a small compartment where the air hung heavy like that of a catacomb. There appeared to be no opening of any kind in the four walls but presently the tiny investigating ray of light revealed the beginning of a staircase not ten feet in front of him.

With elation Kent sent the thin beam of light dancing upward. His calculations had been correct. This was evidently a section of what had been a back stairway for the use of the servants. The passage had been swallowed completely in the alterations after the new wing had been built—all but this portion which, for some reason of his own, Henry Radcliffe had chosen to leave as a secret exit from his own quarters.

A dozen questions crowded on the heels of the discovery. Where did it lead to? How many people in that house of tragedy knew of this secret stair? Had the murderer used it to gain entrance and exit to the dead man's rooms? Had the ghost—?

He released his finger from the button of the flashlight and as he stood there in utter blackness Kent listened with bated breath. Some sixth sense seemed to warn him that he was not alone, even while his reason told him that it was folly to think otherwise.

Suddenly his muscles tautened and every nerve thrilled in spite of himself. A long sigh reached his ears, which were straining for sound. It was followed by a low, piteous moan that ended in a half-choked sob. There was no mistake about it; for the sobbing was repeated. Even after it ceased, which it did in a few moments, Kent stood motionless in his tracks, seeking the direction of the sounds; but in those cramped quarters there was little room for direction and the sound seemed to come from all sides at once.

Suddenly he started and his hand went quickly to his hip where he carried his police automatic. From the top of the stair something was looking down at him—like a cyclops whose single eye stared balefully downward in the dark. The sobbing had not been renewed; not a sound reached him as he stood there.

He pressed the button of the light, holding it well away from him and throwing the thin beam upward. There was nothing standing or creeping upon the stair from top to bottom—not a thing. Yet when he extinguished the ray, the eye still regarded him with silent menace.

Kent laughed at himself. The sounds, of course, must come from the rooms adjoining this passage on one side or the other. The passage was flanked by the room he had just quitted, Henry Radcliffe's bedroom, on the left; on the right—Mrs. Saint-Anton, to be sure. It was Mrs. Saint-Anton, then, who was indulging in emotion in the secrecy of her own room.

He noted as he advanced that the treads of the stair were padded to allow of silent negotiation. Very carefully he ascended, directing his ray of light at the spot where he had imagined—

Kent smiled again as he reached it and ran his fingers over it tentatively. With the light out they glowed, faintly luminous.

"A daub of luminous paint, forsooth!" he mused with interest.

It was on the wainscotting, directly at the head of the steps. He fumbled about for several minutes before he located the right point of pressure and had the satisfaction of seeing a panel open. He held back as the daylight came through and stuck his head out very cautiously before venturing to advance.

He found himself now in what seemed to be a trunk room and general storeroom. Trunks, suitcases and various other articles were arranged neatly against the walls; near the door on the far side was a badly-scarred steamer-trunk, covered with hotel labels. He tip-toed across the little room to the door and found it locked; but it yielded to his key and he slowly opened it. It gave on the third-floor hallway. A few yards away the main staircase descended.

Kent's watch told him it was time to be moving and after relocking the door he retraced his steps. As he thrust a foot through the opening in the wall his eye noted something upon which he pounced with a mutter of satisfaction. He closed the panel quickly and descended the secret stairway, his mind busy. He lost no time in regaining his own room, leaving everything behind him as he found it. He was sure that he had succeeded in avoiding observation and his eyes were alight as he dressed hastily.

"Somebody claims that heaven is a Picadilly sort of place—spiritual cigars, top hats and all the rest of it!" He grinned at his reflection in the glass as he applied his military brushes. "I wonder if Levering believes that the lady ghosts go in for cigarettes or what?"

He felt in his pocket and with whimsical amusement, eyed the little object he had picked up.

"The Hillcrest servants must be a very careless lot," he nodded.

It was another of those flat, yellow, cardboard matches.

12

A Man Who Calls Himself "Alceste"

Up in the rooms occupied by Mr. Thomas Traynor two after-dinner cigars glowed in the semidarkness. It was the first opportunity of a quiet smoke together that the two friends had had since they had reached Hillcrest that afternoon and both Kent and Traynor were enjoying the relaxation. Long association with one another had established that mutual understanding which enables old friends to discard the burden of making conversation for the mere sake of appearing sociable; there is a silence more eloquent of true companionship than the liveliest repartee.

Dinner had not been a cheerful function and everybody at the table had been glad when it was over. Miss Radcliffe had done her utmost to banish the spectre of Tragedy; but in spite of her bravery, the strain under which she was laboring was apparent to her sympathetic guests. The purpose of their presence as guests obtruded in spite of the carefully directed trend of the conversation and a certain restraint seemed to have settled down upon the whole household with the arrival of the police on the scene. Roger Levering maintained a politely melancholy mood; Traynor and Kent had been more or less pre-occupied; even Lieutenant Fargey had sensed the general depression and devoted himself almost exclusively to the food set before him; the servants came and went with silent efficiency. Mr. Armaund Lamont alone exhibited any degree of vivacity and at last he had reached the limit of his ability as a monologuist. Mrs. Saint-Anton had elected to remain in her own room and did not put in an appearance.

If Addison Kent had been disappointed at not meeting the visitor in whom his interest was aroused, he gave no hint of it. He had managed to have a few moments alone with his hostess, and during their confidential chat discovered that she knew nothing of the hidden stair. The alterations had been made and the new wing built while she was away for the summer in the Adirondacks. Their butler had given notice a short time before and Mrs. Stanton had acted as stewardess for several months, taking full charge of what servants had been left on the premises. Why did he ask?

Kent professed mere architectural interest in the house. There was nothing to be gained in adding to Miss Radcliffe's perplexities and he had decided to keep secret for the time being what he had discovered. He excused himself, therefore, and sought out the seamstress who had been ordered by Lieutenant Fargey to remain at Hillcrest for the night, instead of returning to the cottage where she usually slept.

Without revealing his purpose in questioning her, Kent soon came to the conclusion that Mrs. Stanton could throw no light upon the situation. It was apparent that she worshipped the very ground the charming mistress of Hillcrest trod upon, and to one of her years the shock of events had been severe. Kent felt sorry for her without quite knowing why unless it was the wistful appeal of her faded face and saddened eyes; as Miss Radcliffe had told Traynor, the seamstress at Hillcrest was a woman of education and refinement above her present station and one always feels a certain pity for those whose education has but served to sharpen the arrowheads of misfortune.

Mrs. Stanton was able to tell him, however, that the late master of Hillcrest had given personal supervision to the alterations in the house. This seemed to point to the probability that he had planned the secret exit from his room deliberately, though what his object was in so doing was a matter for wide speculation. It may have been only a whim. A pretty expensive one, thought Kent soberly; for there seemed little reason to doubt that the secret stair had played some part in last night's tragedy. Whoever had gained

entrance to Henry Radcliffe's rooms through the hidden passage
had done so during the night and had carried no light to announce
approach, but had relied upon the little cardboard matches for an
occasional flare to light the way.

Mr. Armaund Lamont, the Fifth Avenue jewel merchant, had
taken a run over to Long Island for the weekend, but caught the
first train back to the city when the news of what had happened at
Hillcrest reached him. He had called up Traynor on the 'phone to
learn if there was anything he could do and to express his deep
sympathy for Rose in her distressing bereavement. In response to
Tommy's suggestion that he come out to Westchester, he had ordered his chauffeur to bring around the limousine at once and had
lost no time in making the call.

For an hour or more he had discussed the situation with Traynor and Miss Radcliffe, giving his best advice in regard to her
father's valuable collection of gems. Rose had been grateful for the
information he was able to impart; as a friend of her father's he
was very familiar with the Radcliffe collection and her father's
wishes in regard to it. He had consented at once to take charge of
the collar of pearls and remove it to a place of safety. Traynor had
left him after dinner, arranging with Lieutenant Fargey for one of
the detectives to accompany him in the car back to town as a bodyguard.

"You ought to have seen Lamont's face when I told him about
that fake appointment in town this morning," mused Traynor
aloud. "At first he thought I was kidding him, then he went right
up in the air and swears he'll fire everybody in the office from Baker
down if they've dared to put up such a joke on me."

Kent continued to stare out the window at the moonlit vista of
shrubbery, lawn and flowerbeds, but offered no comment.

"If it was intended as a practical joke it was very much out of
place in view of what's happened since," Traynor went on. "If it
wasn't a joke, what possible object could anyone have—?"

"You are wasting energy, Tommy, on what can be but a paragraph, a sentence, a phrase in the book of mystery which we seek
to read."

"A whole book of it! I knew you'd agree with me. What chapter are you at—? But you haven't had time to more than look at the binding," laughed Traynor, toying with the metaphor.

"The leaves are still uncut—most of them," admitted Kent. "But it looks interesting. The story will start to-morrow morning with the inquest at ten o'clock—and I have every expectation that that part of it at least will prove very hackneyed."

"You do not expect any new evidence?"

"Possibly. But I doubt it. However, it will serve to assemble the situation on a working basis."

"What are the police doing?"

"Standing pat—and searching everywhere for that missing shirt-cuff."

"Is it so very important?"

"Undoubtedly. But it was removed most likely for the purpose of destroying it. If it were incriminating it would hardly be left about for the police to find. Tell me, Tommy— You are quite certain that it was a man's face which looked in at your window from the fire-escape?"

"I'm positive it was," Traynor replied without hesitation.

"And you are equally positive that the thing you saw on the staircase was a woman?"

"It had a woman's figure—yes."

"And came down from the third floor, I believe you said?"

"Yes. It was swathed in draperies and glowed in the dark— It's darned queer, that. If somebody were playing ghost how would they get that weird glow? I happen to know that the druggists handle phosphorous mighty carefully; it would burn the skin off."

"There is a luminous paint on the market that does not contain phosphorous in any form, yet would achieve the effect. Undoubtedly that was what was used."

"You don't share Levering's belief in spirits, then?"

"I am not at all sure that he does believe in genuine phantasms."

"The devil you say!" exclaimed Traynor. "You mean—?"

"I am more interested in the genuineness of the fright the apparition gave him. No doubt about that, I suppose?"

"No. He was scared half out of his boots."

"Keep to the facts, Tommy," smiled Kent. "He was in his stocking-feet, remember."

"You have formed some theory, old man. What is it?"

"Theorizing is the most useless thing we can do, Tommy," protested Kent. "It is too early for that sort of thing—until all the facts are in front of us. You were right, however, in predicting that this case is going to require our best efforts. There is something more in it than murder incidental to theft—"

Kent had turned towards Traynor as he talked, but the speech remained unfinished as Traynor clutched his arm in sudden excitement.

"Look!" he gasped. "The window!—the face!"

Kent jerked about in his chair just in time to get a passing glimpse of a face at the lattice. It was not much more than a flash of pallor in the moonlight before it vanished.

With an inarticulate sound in his throat Traynor leaped across the room with Kent at his heels. As they reached the window pell-mell they recoiled involuntarily at sight of two shadowy bulks on the fire-escape, crowding out the light. Came the gruff, dictatorial voice of Lieutenant Robert Fargey.

"Hey, you fellows! Mr. Lamont and I are comin' in. Go ahead, sir."

"Why, come right in, gentlemen. We were sitting here in the dark, finishing our cigars— Just a minute till I switch on the light." As he crossed the room, Kent seized Traynor by the arm with a warning squeeze. "Control yourself, man!" he whispered tensely.

Mr. Armaund Lamont's snappy dark eyes danced from one to the other and his even teeth gleamed whitely beneath his black moustache in an ingratiating smile.

"We are intruding, gentlemen—yes?"

"Not at all, Mr. Lamont," Traynor assured his employer. "You'll find this chair more comfortable. But you startled us, coming in through the window; we didn't hear you on the fire-escape."

The Frenchman chuckled as he settled his stout, well-groomed body into the chair and proffered his monogramed cigar-case. Lieutenant Fargey had just been showing him around, he said. He had examined the safe in the library and had seen the room where the shooting took place. No less strange than sad, that! While inspecting the fire-escape they had heard voices and the Lieutenant had seemed anxious to join them.

"Mr. Lamont here has been telling me some mighty interesting things I didn't know about jewelry, Kent. Thought perhaps you might like to hear some of it," Fargey explained.

His face still retained a trace of the animation with which he had listened to the conversation of the expert upon the subject that had been a life study. It was a good opportunity for Fargey to post himself and he had been taking advantage of it.

The diamond ring on the little finger of Armaund Lamont's plump, white hand flashed with his gesture of deprecation. For the next five minutes they listened in absorption while he concluded his dissertation upon the excavations of the British Museum in the ancient graves near Salamis in Cyprus and discussed the gems found in Etruscan and Roman ornaments. Both Kent and Traynor were qualified to ask intelligent questions on these matters and to comment upon the development of the goldsmith's art and soon Lamont's eyes were alight with the enthusiasm of a connoisseur.

The conversation became studded with diadems and necklaces of strange words quite beyond the depth of an ordinary lieutenant of detectives. Fargey was not sure whether lapis lazuli was a serviette which the ancient princesses spread upon their bare knees between dances, while they sipped their wine in the cabarets of Dahshur, or whether it was one of the seven veils which they discarded when they did a "shimmy" dance before the king! For all he knew vitreous paste might be the favorite dentifrice of the mummies! A pair of sirens, repoussé, telling each other the latest fibulae they'd picked up in the streets of Cameiros or a fourth-century horse with wings on it, having a feed of oats in a godforsaken temple at Tunis—it was all Greek to Fargey! But he floundered along in the rear of the conversation all the way from the sarcophagus of Queen Aah-hotp (who admired herself about 1400 B.C., in spite of her name!) down to the exhibits of René Lalique in the Salon of 1895 and the activities of A. Lamont, New York, United States. On the way the discussion drifted over to Enkomi, wherever that was, and had a pleasant time going through the cemetery there, afterwards travelling to various interesting points in Egypt, Chaldea, and the Far East; the archaic temple of Artemis at Ephesus was visited and at last the talk arrived in Europe and took in the jewelry factories in Paris, Vienna, London and Birmingham, reaching home at last somewhat tired out but happy!

"Home," for Fargey in this connection, meant the subject of artificial gems, faking of famous jewelry, sensational robberies by notorious jewel thieves and so forth. It was a remark of Kent's that turned the conversation at last into these channels and Lieutenant Fargey awoke all at once to the suspicion that Addison Kent had been directing the jewelry expert in such a way as to lead up to this very climax, but so subtly as to hide the intention.

"Tell them about that chap who has been cutting loose lately across the pond, Chief," suggested Traynor. "You know who I mean."

Mr. Armaund Lamont either did not hear or chose to ignore the remark. He continued to address himself to Kent, in further explanation of cleavages in crystallized gem-stones and flaws in the cut stones. Then he hurried on to speak of the color upon which the beauty and value of many gems depended mainly. Some stones were exceptions, of course—the diamond, for instance; the less color it exhibited, the more "water clear" it was, the higher the value. It was this which made the diamond necklace which had been stolen from the Radcliffe safe so very valuable. Why Henry Radcliffe had risked the two finest pieces in his collection just to have them where he could look at them when he pleased— But then, when one has so much money and worships beauty with the understanding eye, one does not think of risks. Assuredly not.

Pardon? But yes, the collar of pearls was of great value also. Such size and uniformity! Such "skin"! Such "orient"! No finer pearls had come from the Persian Gulf, off the islands of Bahrein. The Frenchman's eyes gleamed as he spoke of their lustre and freedom from flaws. He had offered much money to Henry Radcliffe for this precious possession; but *pouf!* what was money one did not need compared to ownership of such pearls!

"If that cracksman could hear you, Chief, those pearls would be as good as gone," laughed Tommy Traynor.

Lamont frowned at his advertising manager and gestured impatiently.

"By any chance, are you referring to a man who calls himself 'Alceste'?" Kent's question was intended for Traynor; but it was Armaund Lamont at whom he looked as he spoke.

"Ah! You have heard, my friend. And how did you know?"

"Oh, there's an old acquaintance of mine over in London—a Scotland Yard superintendent," smiled Kent. "He keeps me posted more or less on what's going on."

"Scotland Yard, yes. They would know," murmured Lamont as if talking to himself. "My hat is no longer on my head when you speak of Scotland Yard, Mr. Kent, is it not? What they do not know they find out. A dangerous thief, this Alceste. We have been— warned."

"By Scotland Yard?" enquired Kent with interest.

"In Paris the police quite well know him also." He shook his head. "All over Europe, I guess, they know that rascal. But do they ever catch him? *Mon dieu*, no! He is here—there—nowhere! Jewels, rarest of gems, always the precious stones that he takes and nothing else! He knows the fine ones—always the very finest he takes. The police run after him like hens after food. But he is always— gone! He has wings! He sinks under water! He buries himself in the earth! He is *le diable!*"

"A highly entertaining individual," commented Kent, gazing with some amusement at the excited Frenchman.

"It was he, this Alceste, who walked into the Hermitage Palace in St. Petersburg and removed the famous Princess ruby from one of the early ivories—in broad daylight, with the noses of the guards right over it! You heard of that, perhaps, Mr. Kent? Later he came back and restored it to its place on the breast of the ivory goddess and— *Voila!* he was gone! There was so fine a fuss! For why? It was not the Princess ruby at all—just a doublet with a slab of real gem-stone on top to cover the paste beneath! Truly, a dangerous thief, my friend!"

"The gentleman is a humorist," smiled Kent. "Alceste! What a name to travel under! the name of the hero in Moliere's *Misanthrope*—an enemy of social hypocrisies! But sooner or later he will be captured like all the rest of them—"

"Pardon, Mr. Kent," interrupted Armaund Lamont with a negative shake of his large head, "the police will never catch this Alceste. He is *le diable!* He strikes, he disappears, he is dead, he is forgotten; then when least expected— *Voici!* he is alive, he takes what he wants and is gone again!"

"Well all I gotta say is he better not go tryin' to pull any o' that stuff over here," declared Fargey boastfully. "We'd put a crimp in him inside forty-eight hours if he showed his nose in this burg!" He laughed as he scratched a match to relight his cigar.

Armaund Lamont regarded the lieutenant of detectives in silence. He shook his head doubtfully at last and smiled a little uncertainly.

"My friend," he whispered in a slow, impressive way, one fat white finger upraised, "this Alceste—he is already here!"

13
"Guard Well Your Tongue"

A sudden silence had possession of the group. The jeweler had spoken with the conviction of one who asserts a fact, not as one who expresses an opinion merely. The match in Fargey's fingers burned on unheeded until at last he threw it down with irritation.

"Go on. Spring it. I'll be the goat. What's the joke, Mr. Lamont?" he urged.

"One does not joke upon a so serious matter, Mr. Fargey," was the sober reply.

"You are sure, Chief?" asked Tommy Traynor in disbelief. "What's happened to make you think that?"

Addison Kent alone seemed to have accepted the startling statement without question. He nodded his head in thoughtful approval.

"You see certain indications of this particular crook's handiwork, then, in the jewel thefts of the past week, Mr. Lamont. May I ask just what these are?"

"Organization—deliberate preparation, Mr. Kent,—a certain finish in the execution of the actual robberies and complete obliteration of all clues. Come, my Lieutenant, you will admit that the police are—how do you say it?—up in the atmosphere! I have talked with your Commissioner about it. We have had a delegation to him from our Association and the insurance people are not easy minded—nervous over what may happen, surmounting what already has happened."

"And what is it that may happen, Mr. Lamont?" asked Kent quietly.

"Anything! Everything!" cried Armaund Lamont in sudden agitation. "I tell you, this man Alceste—he is the very *diable* himself! He will come and take as he pleases—in spite of all the precautions in our vaults! Burglar-alarm systems are nothing to him; he knows every surprise! He could rob the government mint itself if he wanted money; but it is the rare gems—always the rarest of the gems he comes to take. Wait and see!"

"But you are not sure that Alceste is even contemplating a trip to America—," Traynor began.

"He is here. I know it because I feel it in my marrows, Tommy. Last Wednesday he got the Van Tuyl lavalliere in Chicago. We have secret reports. Last night it was the Radcliffe diamonds. To-morrow he may be in Philadelphia. To-morrow— Ah, *mon dieu!* we can not tell what next!"

"Yon think—he was here?—at Hillcrest?" gasped Traynor in amazement.

Lieutenant Robert Fargey's eyes were glittering with a subdued excitement. He saw great headlines in the newspapers all over North America—London, Paris, Vienna—all over the world and his head felt hot; his fingers twitched. What a catch! What a catch!

"From what you say, this 'Alceste' is spectacular," came the even tones of Addison Kent. "I would judge, Mr. Lamont, that he would be bold enough to come right here among us, if necessary,—in this very room, say—and tell us how very impossible it was for the police or anyone else to capture a master thief by the name of 'Alceste'!"

The laugh which greeted this bit of foolishness relieved the tension. Kent joined in heartily; so did Armaund Lamont. Afterward he stole a glance at the novelist once or twice as if he searched for innuendo without discovering anything to justify the suspicion. These writers—one could never be sure when they were laughing!

"He'd make a good character for your next novel, Ad," said Traynor.

"That's where he would seem to belong—in a story book," smiled Kent. "If the police can't lay hands on him it is time to call in a gumshoe expert with a large magnifying-glass and a false moustache!"

"The police will never catch Alceste," repeated Lamont. "They have the men, the system; they are fine—our police, yes. It is that they lack the imagination, is it not?"

"Well," growled Fargey, tossing his cigar-end out the window and getting to his feet, "sittin' here, workin' imagination overtime ain't going to get us anywheres. I'm going home to hit the hay. Whenever you're ready, Mr. Lamont, Detective McVey will ride in with you. I'm leaving Sergeant Hayes in charge, Tommy. Goodnight, Mr. Kent. If the ghost shows up, give her my compliments." He grinned as he waved a hand from the doorway.

"If you see Alceste hanging around anywhere, Bob," called Traynor, "you'll arrest him, of course?"

"Does a duck swim?"

"Not on dry land."

But Lieutenant Fargey closed the door and was gone.

"I think if you will excuse me, gentlemen," said Armaund Lamont presently, glancing at his watch, "I will be going also. It is not well to be too late when one carries—responsibilities."

After the jeweler had bowed himself out, Traynor closed the door and locked it. He stepped across to the window and closed it also. Then he looked at Addison Kent who was lighting his pipe, eyes crinkling with amusement.

"I believe you are getting nervous, Tommy." Traynor said nothing but threw himself into the chair Lamont had vacated and frowned at the floor. "You did not see who it was that looked in at the window. You can not even tell me that there was any resemblance to the face last night. You were merely startled for a moment at seeing a face looking in when you were not expecting anything of the kind—a face in the moonlight. Am I right?"

"Yes. It—must have been that—just that I was startled. Any other idea of it would be too—utterly ridiculous."

"Exactly. Secretly you have been entertaining the hypothesis that the face at your window last night was the face of the murderer—because the shot was fired from outside Mr. Radcliffe's room. But can you give me any good reason why it could not have come from some distance outside the room—say a couple of hundred yards? Some automatic pistols are sighted up to a thousand yards. For all you know to the contrary, the murderer may have climbed a tree nearby and fired from there. The fact that nobody heard the shot would even seem to favor this idea, wouldn't it?"

"I hadn't thought of that," nodded Traynor. "Then you believe—?"

"I did not say so," interrupted Kent. "I am merely presenting two possibilities to ease your mind—either that the whole thing was part of a nightmare and there was no face looking in at your window at all—"

"I won't admit that."

"At any rate, there can be no resemblance— You surely don't suspect Bob Fargey of having anything to do with the killing?"

"You are kidding me, Ad."

"As for your worthy boss—come to think of it, though, what do you know about his early life in France?—before he came over to the United States?"

"Great Scott! you are not trying to make me believe anything against Lamont, are you?" cried Traynor with a touch of resentment in his tone. "He's white clean through, a prince—!"

"Then quit worrying over foolishness and go to bed, Tommy." Kent laughed and stood up, yawning behind his hand.

"The chief certainly has a very great respect for this wonderful cracksman he was telling about, hasn't he? I suppose, though, he was exaggerating—"

"Not as much as you might think. Lamont, of course, is influenced by his own apprehensions and he is ready to believe that there is no limit to Alceste's powers. Nevertheless, Alceste really is perhaps the smoothest crook loose at the present time. The fact that Scotland Yard has failed at every turn, as well as the best detectives in Europe, proves that he is a very accomplished gentleman."

"Do you put any stock in the chief's idea that he is operating over here—had a hand in this affair last night?"

"I think it is quite within the possibilities." Kent's face had grown thoughtful. "I was about to remark that I had come to some such conclusion when we were interrupted. The solution to this mystery lies much deeper than surface indications, Tommy. Beyond doubt the thing was planned carefully in advance. The occurrence of these other jewel thefts indicates that a regular campaign is being followed as there are certain similarities that point to them all as the work of the same directing mind. All of them exhibit systematic cunning of conception, carried through without a hitch and without leaving a single clue behind. The only thing that seems to be established in each case is that the gems have vanished."

Traynor moved over to the door, opened it and glanced out into the hall. He relocked it and came close to Kent.

"Is it possible that the man is in this house—now?" he asked in an excited whisper. "Anything is possible—even that."

"Well? Let me have your reasons for thinking so, Tommy. You won't get a wink of sleep without cleaning your mind of disturbing suspicions. Whom do you suspect?"

"There is one man here who is a stranger—"

"I thought so. You have had a dislike for Levering from the first. Neither he nor his aunt have been welcome guests here because both Miss Radcliffe and her father have sensed the fact that they are fortune hunters. But you are overlooking the possibility that Levering himself is not to blame for this visit; he was brought here by his match-making aunt. He is well educated and extremely sensitive; he admitted to me this afternoon that he had been very angry at his aunt for coming here at all. Be fair, Tommy."

"I am trying to be fair," protested Traynor, "but what are the facts? He comes here, a total stranger, from Europe, on a visit; he shows his interest in the jewels in the library safe by nosing in on Mr. Radcliffe and me—"

"So did the butler."

"Then in the middle of the night I find him roaming about—"

"So were you—and others."

"He tries to make out that the ghost thing was real—"

"Mr. Radcliffe believed in it. Lots of educated people are sincere in such beliefs."

"But he doesn't look right or act right, Kent."

"His glasses make him look queer, distorting his expression. He has a bad case of long-sightedness, a common enough affliction, Tommy, and he abominates those glasses himself. As for his acting ill at ease, would you feel very comfortable if you were in his shoes?"

"What do you mean?"

"He comes to America as travelling escort for an aunt who has hitherto been a stranger to him. He has been highly educated with plenty of spending money until his father died and left him stranded—accustomed to go off on hunting expeditions with prospective dukes and baronets. He lives off his aunt's bounty; she drags him around to marry him off to some wealthy American girl. He is sensitive of being disliked and is anxious to get away from Hillcrest where he feels he is not welcome. Then this tragedy happens and he finds, himself subject to the inquisitiveness of the police, discovering that Fargey is suspicious of his aunt. The possibilities of newspaper publicity loom large; he even begins to wonder whether his aunt's relations with Radcliffe in the past have anything to do with the situation. The thought is very disturbing and he is greatly worried. He picks out your humble servant as the only one with whom he can discuss the situation—"

"And proceeds to fill said humble servant full of misinformation," grumbled Traynor.

"You are prejudiced, Tommy."

"All right. What about the new butler, then?"

"Fargey does not like him—"

"Neither do I. He's too sneaky to suit me."

"Yet what has he done? Nothing—except go about his duties with the *savoir faire* of the well-trained English servant. He has been taught to efface himself, to move silently and surely about his work."

"It's at least a positive fact that you are in a negative mood tonight. Then who is there left that could be this man Alceste under cover?"

"You won't allow me to suggest that in spite of his established position as an American gem expert, Mr. Armaund Lamont—"

"Oh for heaven's sake, be sensible!" cried Traynor in disgust.

"If it were a detective novel I were writing—what would be the matter with having Mrs. Saint-Anton the clever Alceste masquerading as a woman, then?"

"Impossible!" breathed Traynor. He stared at his smiling friend.

"Yet there are very clever female impersonators who could perform the feat and surely such an exceptionally clever artist as this gentleman cracksman—"

"Aw, get out of here, Kent! I'm going to bed," laughed Tommy. "You're the limit! By process of elimination we'll be arriving at the conclusion that there has been no robbery and no murder—"

"That is why it is foolish to lose sleep over it," chuckled Kent. "Do you think Alceste would be fool enough to camp on top of a bombshell? One of the best things he does is to put distance between him and the scene of his operations. Also he is too much of an artist to spoil his pretty thefts with anything so unaesthetic as murder. His past record is clean in that respect at least. Well, I'm going now. Good-night, Tommy."

Addison Kent did not retire to his room immediately. A glance at his watch assured him that it was not so very late and he had a fancy to get outdoors away from the lights of the great house and in some quiet corner of the grounds classify the impressions which had been crowded into the last twelve hours. From the pergola he noted that Armaund Lamont's limousine was drawn up at the porte cochére and the chauffeur was lolling in his seat, smoking a cigarette and reading a newspaper while he waited for his two passengers to put in an appearance. A patrolman stepped from behind the shrubbery and stopped Kent as he wandered off across the lawns in the direction of the summer-house, apologizing and withdrawing as he recognized him in the flash of his electric torch.

The moon was almost smothered in the murk which was spreading across the sky and Kent had to proceed cautiously until his eyes grew more accustomed to the half gloom that prevailed. He had selected the vine-clad arbor as the most isolated spot where he could give his thoughts rein without fear of intrusion; but as he approached he paused in surprise at finding it already occupied.

The voices which reached him in a confused murmur were those of a man and a woman and Kent half turned to retreat, having no inclination to spy upon a lovers' tryst; but at sound of a subdued sob he halted uncertainly and after a moment of listening, he stole closer under shelter of a hedge. This was no mere maid's foolishness; the carefully lowered voices were tense with an excitement which was with difficulty suppressed and the colloquy was being held in French. It was a language which was very familiar to Kent and curiosity took him still nearer to the arbor to listen with both ears as he recognized the accents of the man's voice. It was Mr. Armaund Lamont beyond a doubt!

Who was the woman? Why was it necessary for them to meet in this clandestine manner? Lamont must have come straight to this prearranged meeting from Traynor's room. Kent felt justified in eavesdropping when circumstances were so palpably not above suspicion. The interview had been a hurried one evidently and it was being hurriedly concluded as if the risk of discovery was a vital matter to both.

"I must go. I cannot tell you more—not here, Armaund. It is too dangerous," whispered the woman anxiously. "The black shadow of the château is creeping far beyond the old bridge. Ah, *mon dieu!* Am I never to escape it? It is more than I can bear, more than I can bear!"

"Nothing can harm you, my Yvonne, now that you have me to shield you," came the soothing voice of the man. "You must be brave a little longer, my dear girl. Ah, it is such a joy to have found you again, Yvonne! You will let me help you—"

"Ssh! What was that? Did you hear nothing? Oh, Armaund, I am so afraid, afraid!"

"It is but the leaves in the breeze, Yvonne. I will let no harm befall you. I am strong; I am rich; I have influence. To-morrow, then, you will come to me and tell me all your troubles? And see, they will be gone like little clouds before the rising sun. It is indeed so, dearest one."

"Ah, you are so good, dear friend!"

"That is nothing. Guard well your tongue and all will come out aright. We will be happy at last—happy together at last, my Yvonne."

They were coming out now. Kent pressed deeper into the leafage. The two dark forms separated hastily and melted into the shadows in opposite directions. Kent hurried after the woman and soon caught sight of her; She was making a detour which would bring her to the house by way of the garden. If he cut straight across the lawns to the pergola he could intercept her at the basement entry for which she was heading. He must discover her identity.

So intent was Addison Kent upon this that he failed to see a third figure which slunk away in the bushes on the farther side of the arbor—slunk with the greatest of caution, like a shadow of the night, along the hedgerows to the rear of the estate. The man vaulted the stone wall and disappeared at top speed along the highway to the woodland path which struck through the park over the ridge to the shore drive.

14
SURPRISES

Meanwhile Kent lost no time in taking up a position in the back hallway, behind a door. Through the crack he had a good view of the short flight of steps up which anyone must pass who used the basement entry. The hall light was switched on and unless he had made a bad guess—

A light footfall apprized him that he had not. The basement door was open and he heard the scrape of boots on the cement floor. She threw back the cape of a light cloak as she came up the steps and paused for an instant to pat her hair, heaving a sigh of relief as her eye swept the empty hallway.

When he got a clear look at her features Kent had difficulty in preventing his surprise from revealing his presence. It was Mrs. Stanton, the seamstress.

The novelist certainly had not expected this and he debated the advisability of stepping from his concealment and questioning this gentle woman who enjoyed the confidence of Miss Radcliffe, had been with the family for a long time and so evidently held her mistress in affectionate regard. As he hesitated the faint sound of stealthy footsteps just beyond the basement doorway decided him; he drew back out of sight and allowed the seamstress to continue down the hall. The sound of the inner door closing behind her came to him distinctly.

It was followed at once by a quick light patter of feet. Addison Kent's eyes glinted with interest as he peered through the crack of the door. He recognized the young woman as the housemaid who had been assigned to attend Mrs. Saint-Anton during her stay at Hillcrest. Traynor had pointed her out that afternoon as she passed in the hall; her name was Lucille Beliveau.

She came up the steps on tip-toe, craning her neck for a cautious survey of the hallway and casting nervous glances over her shoulder. She fairly jumped when Kent stepped out from behind the door, her eyes widening in surprise and a little ejaculation of dismay escaping her. His smile, however, reassured her somewhat as did also his bantering greeting.

"Where do you come from, my pretty maid?" he paraphrased.

"I come from the milking, sir, she said," retorted the girl pertly. Her black eyes flashed at him in coquetry; for he was good to look upon and the girl evidently was a born flirt.

"The cows, no doubt, were in the pasture 'far beyond the old bridge.' Were they? But 'nothing can harm you, my Yvonne, now that you have me to shield you.'"

She shrank away from him, staring at him in utter amazement. If she was not completely dumbfounded by these strange words she was a wonderful actress.

"My name is Lucille, sir,—Lucille Beliveau," she faltered in a voice and manner from which all pertness had vanished.

"Why, yes, to be sure," smiled Addison Kent. "How stupid of me! You are in attendance upon Mrs. Saint-Anton, are you not? She sent you out on a message, perhaps?"

"No, sir. She is ill in her room. She said she'd ring if she wanted anything. She wanted to be left alone."

"Look here, Lucille, you have nothing to lose by being frank with me. I am not the kind that tells everything I know. It is important that you tell me exactly where you have been. And why do you come in as if you were afraid of being seen?"

"Miss Radcliffe sent Catharine to look for me. I did not want her to know I had been outside the house."

"Catharine?"

"Mrs. Stanton."

"Oh, so her name is Catharine, eh? You knew the police have requested everyone to remain indoors to-night, I suppose?"

"Yes. But I have a gentleman friend on the Force; he is on duty here to-night."

"I see. And you went out at his request?"

"No." She studied him a moment. "I will tell you, if you promise not to get either of us into trouble, sir. He had not had his supper and—I took him out some sandwiches and a piece of pie."

Kent laughed and she smiled up at him a little doubtfully.

"All right. We'll let it go at that, Lucille. It is a terrible thing for a policeman to be hungry and I am sure it was very thoughtful of you. I believe I would welcome you with open arms myself under those circumstances." She flashed him the smile of a piquant little minx. "What time did you leave Mrs. Saint-Anton last night?" he asked unexpectedly.

"About eleven o'clock, I think it was, when she dismissed me for the night, sir."

"And you did not see her until this morning, eh? Was she taken ill in the night?"

"Oh, no. She is all right—except for a bad headache."

"But she was up part of the night, wasn't she?"

"She said she had not slept very well, sir. That is all I know about it."

It was evident that the girl was growing restive under this volley of questions, and Kent allowed her to go without further inquisitiveness. He had heard Lamont's big car depart some moments before, so there was nothing to be gained in that direction. Accordingly he retired to his own rooms, threw off his coat and made himself comfortable for his deferred mental review of the whole situation.

There were several angles to the mystery surrounding Henry Radcliffe's death which puzzled Addison Kent not a little. Not the least of these was the latest development. Lucille Beliveau was an exceptionally bright girl. Was it she who had met Lamont in the arbor and talked so strangely? An *affaire d' amour* between a pretty maid and a confirmed old bachelor was by no means beyond the possibilities. Or was she acting in some way as a go-between for

Mrs. Saint-Anton? Perhaps Mrs. Saint-Anton herself had been in the arbor while Lucille remained on guard—

For over an hour he sat there, lost in deep thought and a blue haze of tobacco smoke. A sharp tap on the door aroused him at last and in answer to his invitation, Detective-Sergeant Hayes entered.

"Oh, it's you, Sergeant. Come and sit down. Have a cigar."

"Thanks, Mr. Kent. You said to report to you at any hour, sir, and I bring some bad news."

"That so?"

"I've just been talking to Mac on the 'phone, Mr. Kent, and he's rattled complete. Has reason to be, too. McVey went into town in Mr. Lamont's car on purpose to see that he got home safe, as you know. Well, they reached Lamont's house O.K. and went inside— into the library. It was not till then that they found they'd been robbed."

"What?"

"That collar of pearls has been stolen slick as a whistle, Mr. Kent."

"Are you sure? What does McVey say?"

"He says they didn't touch the parcel till they got into the library. Mr. Lamont carried it on his knees all the way in. The jewel-case was in a cardboard box and the whole thing was wrapped in brown paper and tied with a string. McVey swears nobody touched it after they left. Yet when Lamont comes to open the velvet case to take a look before sticking them in his safe, the pearls were gone. The case was empty. Lamont is wild about it, Mac's feelin' kind o' sick himself."

"What have you done? Did you 'phone Fargey?"

"Yes. He was swearin' mad. But he's on his way to Lamont's by now an' will look after that end of it. Ought I to report this to Miss Radcliffe immediately, sir? She's asleep, I'm told."

"It will only upset her unnecessarily. The morning will do, Sergeant. Were you on hand when they left here—Lamont and McVey?"

"Yes, sir."

"When was the parcel handed to Mr. Lamont—just before he left?"

"No, sir. Miss Radcliffe got it from her room personally and gave it to him after dinner some time. He turns it over to McVey an' Mac spent the whole evenin' nursin' it like it was his lunch-box. He's flabbergasted, Mac is. And I'll be blessed if I know what to make of it myself."

"Well, I wouldn't try to make too much of it, Sergeant. I think it would be best not to talk of it at all or some of the newspaper men may get hold of it and we don't want that. It may turn out that Miss Radcliffe forgot to put the pearls into the case when she did up the parcel."

He bade the other good-night and began to get ready for bed. He knew that this was no instance of neglect upon the part of his hostess, and he laughed a little as he reached for the dangling chain of the reading-lamp.

"The clever beggar!"

Addison Kent's prediction that the coroner's inquest would be productive of little, if any, new evidence of importance was fulfilled the following morning. It was a tiresome session which disappointed the curious spectators who had fed upon the newspaper reports of the murder and robbery at Hillcrest and fully expected some thing unusual to happen. One after another the servants took the witness stand and told in tedious detail their routine on the Saturday night; none of them had anything to report which could throw the least light on the crime; all of them had been in their beds at a respectable hour and had slept through the night without alarm. Mrs. Stanton was the only member of the household who "slept out" and when she testified to having left for home at her customary hour, Coroner Charles ordered her to stand down, unable to conceal his irritation; he did not relish wasting questions upon useless witnesses.

Interest centred upon Miss Rose Radcliffe, because of her relationship to the murdered man and because of her great beauty rather than upon her evidence. It was apparent that she was under a heavy strain; but she bravely answered the questions put to her and earned the sympathy of the court.

Mrs. Saint-Anton also gave her evidence in a straightforward manner, adhering consistently to the story she had told already to the police. She had not been out of her room after retiring for the night, she said. The whole affair had distressed her so greatly that she had been confined to her room most of the time since with one of her terrible headaches. She looked ill and had recourse to her smelling-salts in the witness-box. As she retired with a rustling of silk and an air of profound relief Lieutenant Fargey caught Addison Kent watching him and smiled contentedly.

There was something puzzling about Fargey's whole manner this morning; at least, Kent fancied so. The lieutenant of detectives might have been excused for being in no very amiable mood; for the police investigation appeared to be making no progress at all and the theft of the pearls the night before was nothing short of a taunt to the detectives. It certainly would not improve the feeling at headquarters. Yet Lieutenant Fargey was full of smiles, or, at least, the scowls were absent, even when the jury filed in with the usual verdict of murder in the first degree by "person or persons unknown." It was as if he viewed the paucity of evidence, the lack of eye-witnesses, the opaqueness of the mystery with the unconcern of a man who already held the key in his hand.

Kent did not return to Hillcrest with the others after the court proceedings were concluded. He went to his own apartment in Minaki Annex to look over his mail. While he was in the middle of it the telephone rang at his elbow and he took down the receiver. There was a business-like briskness in the salutation which came over the wire.

"Fargey talking, Kent. Where's Traynor?"

"Gone back to Westchester with Miss Radcliffe and the rest."

"Well, I'm going out there myself now and I thought perhaps you might like to come along in my car."

"Thanks, Lieutenant; but I'm just going over my mail—"

"Bring it along with you. I think you'll want to come."

"Why? What's doing?"

Fargey's throaty laugh was expressive of triumph.

"Tell you that when I see you. Pick you up in about twenty-five minutes."

"All right—if it's important."

"Important enough, I guess. We've found the shirt-cuff!"

15
THE SECRET OF THE STEAMER TRUNK

"Well, gentlemen, things have come to a showdown." Fargey took in the circle of faces with evident satisfaction. He had assembled them in the trunk room on the third floor at Hillcrest— Kent, Traynor, Roger Levering, Detective-Sergeant Hayes and Smith, a chirographic expert from the bureau whom he had brought along in the police auto. As Fargey's gaze came to rest upon Levering his eyes narrowed and his mouth set grimly.

"What I have to say concerns you specially, sir. I am giving you the chance to say what you think before action is taken. I am going to lay my cards down, face up, and if any of you gentlemen think I am not playing fair I'd like you to say so frank an' open. Personally I see only one thing left for me to do and as the representative of the Law, that's what I'm here to do. Murder ain't what you might call a pretty thing an' when the Law has to deal with it there ain't any reason for being polite an' all that. I ain't here to preach a sermon but to do the best I can to bring the party who killed Henry Radcliffe to justice. Who that party happens to be, man or woman, rich or poor, don't matter; it's all the same to the Law."

Fargey paused, as if to note the effect of this preamble, and was gratified to observe the gravity on every face. Roger Levering seemed to sense the crisis which he faced and it was apparent that he held himself in repression with difficulty. He offered no comment.

"You are all familiar with what happened here between Saturday at midnight and Sunday morning. Henry Radcliffe was found

114

shot to death in his room and the safe in the library was robbed. I ain't prepared to say whether the robbery had anything to do with the murder. The first question to answer is: Who killed Henry Radcliffe? In the course of our investigations we have discovered certain evidence which points conclusively to the guilty party and I have to inform you that we are about to arrest the woman who has been a guest in this house for the past week. I refer to Mrs. Saint-Anton."

"No, no! Surely—!" cried Levering. He stepped across to Fargey and clutched his arm. "Man, man—there must be some terrible mistake! You do not mean what you say?"

Fargey eyed him coldly as he loosened his fingers.

"Calm yourself, sir. I am not in the habit of making statements without good reason," he said sharply. "Allow me to proceed. We found clutched in Radcliffe's hand this gold pencil; as you see, it was worn on a chain. The rest of the chain was picked up beneath the fire-escape a little to one side of the window of the sitting-room where the body was found." He passed it to Addison Kent, together with the pencil, and asked him to compare the broken links. "Mrs. Saint-Anton admits that the pencil belongs to her, but says it disappeared from her dresser oh Saturday and she did not see it again until Sunday morning; she also swore on her oath, at the inquest this morning, that she had not been outside of her room after retiring on Saturday evening about eleven o'clock.

"We might accept these statements as true but for other and more damning evidence of her guilt. That she was in Henry Radcliffe's room is proved by the fact that her finger-prints were left upon certain ornaments on the mantel which had got knocked over in the struggle which took place and which she put back in order; we had no difficulty in obtaining her prints and our Bertillon department has identified them beyond question."

"They might have been left on the ornaments at some other time," objected Kent.

"Very true, Mr. Kent. We'll let that stand for what it's worth and pass on, if you don't mind."

"But, hold on, Bob!" protested Traynor. "You say there was a struggle. Between Mr. Radcliffe and Mrs. Saint-Anton? But how could she have killed him? The shot was fired—"

"From the fire-escape!" cried Levering, eagerly.

"And by a man!" supplemented Traynor. "It was a man's face that looked in at my window. I'll swear to that." Levering looked at him gratefully.

"Patience, patience!" cautioned Fargey. A faint smile flickered at the corners of his mouth, which hardened again almost immediately into its stern lines. "I'm coming to all that presently. Here is the bullet which the coroner extracted. Here is the ejected shell which Mr. Kent found on the driveway. Note that it fits, please, and that it belongs to an automatic of foreign manufacture—or at least, we will prove that soon. Here is the gun that was found near the body; it has not been discharged. Miss Radcliffe identifies it as one her father kept in his room. It doesn't matter.

"Very good. We come now to one clue which is unusual—the fact that one of the starched cuffs had been torn from Radcliffe's shirt. The gold pencil in his hand suggested to me at once that he might have written something on that cuff which was incriminating and for that reason was removed by the murderer. I started hunting for it without much hope of finding either it or the weapon which was used."

He paused and looked at Roger Levering with a flash of triumph. Fargey seemed to be taking a certain cruel pleasure in creating anxiety.

"Go on!" urged Traynor nervously.

"Please!" murmured Levering.

"Now, here's what happened as I make it out," resumed Fargey, turning to Kent. "I don't pretend to say what was between this woman and Henry Radcliffe; but they weren't on good terms. She goes into Radcliffe's room for an interview which ends in an argument. Radcliffe gets mad clean through and grabs the little gun out of the drawer or wherever he kept it—to scare her, perhaps. She takes it serious and grabs him by the wrists and there's a tussle for possession o' the gun. His hand swoops down and the diamond ring on his finger scratches the looking-glass and knocks over some bric-a-brac on the mantel. She knocks the gun out of his fingers and jumps across the room for the window—"

"Why not the door?" interrupted Kent, eyes twinkling.

"Because it was likely locked and there wasn't time—"

"But it was not found locked in the morning by the valet."

"Then because she didn't want to be seen in the hall," said Fargey testily. "As I was saying, she makes for the window to get away by the fire-escape and as she climbs out she sees Radcliffe reaching for the little revolver on the floor. She draws the automatic, wraps the heavy window drape around it to deaden the report—and lets him have it."

"You are making out a clear case of self-defence, then?" and Kent smiled a little at the blank expression of Lieutenant Fargey's face. Plainly the question disconcerted him for a moment.

"No, I'm not," he asserted emphatically. "That is, I— Say, I'm tellin' you the woman quarrelled with Radcliffe, ain't I? An' that he was expectin' trouble with her and kept the gun in his room, loaded for protection—from what? From this woman. He was afraid of her, see. Was she wearin' an automatic for a bangle or a brooch? I'm askin' you!" said Fargey with a sarcasm which converted his face into ugly lines of resentment; he found it difficult enough to convey things in their right order without all these interruptions.

"Where was I?—Oh, yes. Well, as soon as she shoots him she gets afraid the sound of the shot might have wakened somebody, especially Traynor in the room alongside; so she sneaks along an' takes a peek through his window. He says it's a man's face he saw. What I say is that nobody just wakened out of a heavy sleep can be sure of what they think they see for a minute or two. Traynor was sitting up in bed, wakened by the shot but not recognizing the sound. She just had time to climb over the rail of the fire-escape and hang out of sight from the bars of the grating beneath when out comes Traynor. The moon has just gone under a cloud and he fails to see anyone in the dim light—"

"Could your aunt have done a stunt like that, Levering?" asked Traynor doubtfully. "Isn't she too elderly?"

"I—I don't know—but what she could," stammered Roger Lever-ing reluctantly. "It seems to explain why you didn't see anybody when you looked. My aunt is quite athletic. She can beat me at tennis," he admitted. "She could do it all right, but it seems rather impossible, Lieutenant. The whole thing—"

"Anyways, that's what she did," reaffirmed Fargey. "She waited till Traynor went inside his room again, then dropped quietly to the ground—"

"Not in high-heeled shoes, surely?"

"Who said she had on high heels, Kent?" demanded Fargey tru-culently. "Besides, it was only a four-foot drop at that. But she was wearin' her tennis shoes."

"How do you know that?"

"I found the marks of 'em on the driveway, right underneath—the criss-cross marks of the heels, that is. An' if that ain't enough, I got a look at those tennis shoes in her room, and found gravel imbedded in the rubber—sunk right in."

He looked at each of them in turn, challenging further objec-tions. Somewhat mollified by the gravity on every face, he pro-ceeded less aggressively:

"It was when she dropped those few feet to the ground that the rest of the chain around her neck fell off, unnoticed. Radcliffe had made a snatch at her and busted it. She didn't miss it till she got back into the house through the servant's entrance in the base-ment; she had got a passkey that would open that door. Finding nobody anywhere in sight in the upper hall, she goes back into Radcliffe's room—"

"Again? That would take a lot of nerve, Bob."

"Nerve is this lady's middle name, Tommy," retorted Fargey.

"Were the lights still on in the room? You forgot to say, Lieu-tenant," Kent suggested mildly.

"No, they were out—or Traynor would have noticed them when he went out onto the fire-escape. That was the first thing she did after knocking the gun out of Radcliffe's hand—jumped for the light switch—"

"Which would bring her right alongside the door into the hall," nodded Kent. "Strange she did not just slip out instead of going clean across the room to the window where she would offer a good target against the moonlit sky for Radcliffe's gun. She was afraid he was going to shoot her, you said, didn't you?"

"Are— Say, are you deliberately tryin' to mix me up, Kent?" Fargey glared at him angrily.

"Not at all, Lieutenant. You have been so clear and logical that it is easy to follow you. I am merely wondering how she saw Radcliffe reaching for the gun on the floor when the lights were out and she was blocking the light from the window—"

"She *heard* him, rather than saw him."

"Please go on, Lieutenant," came Levering's anxious voice. "The lights are an unimportant detail, are they not? The little reading-lamp in the bedroom would still be lit and would throw enough light—"

"Exactly," snapped Fargey. "She came in to look for the gold pencil, but forgot all about it when she saw the writing on the cuff. She tore it off, greatly excited, stuffed it inside her dress, went in and put out the light beside the bed—and went back to her own room."

"What about the scratches on the fire-escape, Lieutenant?"

"She scratched out those finger-prints some time after daylight—with a pen-knife. It was done with a small knife, Kent—not with the nails in a boot-sole, as you thought."

"You will have great difficulty in finding a jury who would convict upon such evidence," said Roger Levering calmly. He mopped his forehead with his handkerchief.

"Would, eh?" grunted Fargey. "Guess you're right. I admit it. But— Say, who does that steamer trunk belong to?" He pointed across the room to where it stood against the wall near the door, its variegated labels eloquent of travel abroad.

"It belongs to my aunt," replied Levering promptly.

"Does, eh? Show them what you found this morning, Sergeant."

Detective-Sergeant Hayes stepped over to the trunk, undid the buckles, threw open the lid and stepped back. They crowded close, craning their necks with intense interest. The trunk was full of various odds and ends of clothing and travel accessories which had been rummaged about by the probing hands of the police.

"I tried to leave it the way I found it, as near as I could remember," volunteered Hayes. "If you lift that steamer rug, Mr. Kent—"

Kent did so. The missing shirt-cuff was staring up at them! He picked it up gingerly by the edges and held it where all could read the purplish writing which was scrawled across it in an erratic line. As if with one accord all eyes focused upon Roger Levering who turned from them in evident misery, walked across to the window and buried his head on his arm. Here was proof indeed!

The message on the cuff read: "Woman known as Mrs. St. Anton shot me." And it was signed, "Henry C. Radcliffe."

Tommy Traynor's startled gaze turned to Addison Kent. The novelist's eyes had narrowed; his jaw muscles were knotted, his hands clenched, but he stood motionless without other sign of what was passing through his mind at that moment.

"Here, Smith!" Fargey's voice sounded metallic as it struck across the ominous silence. "Here's a cancelled check of Radcliffe's. Compare those signatures. You'll have to allow for the conditions he was writin' under, of course."

The handwriting expert examined the cuff under a microscope for a few minutes, scrutinizing both it and the signature on the check very closely.

"I would not take oath that they are the same," he said, slowly shaking his head, and Kent glanced at him keenly. "But—allowing for the texture of the linen—and the fact that the man was dying and that the room was almost in darkness—neither would I swear that both signatures could not have been written by the same hand. Fact is, they are so similar I am inclined to believe that the signature on the cuff is genuine."

"Down in this corner of the trunk," said Detective-Sergeant Hayes, sinking to one knee and delving as he spoke, "I found this also."

He held up a small, neat, pearl-handled automatic hammerless pistol. Kent reached for it and examined it with interest. It was an exceptionally compact and well-made little weapon that lay flat on his palm. It was small enough to be carried in a lady's muff—a wicked looking little gun that undoubtedly could do deadly work at short range. He recognized it at once as a pocket model .25 caliber Browning, of Belgian manufacture—Fabrique Nationale D'Armes de Guerre at Liege. The magazine held six shots; it contained only five now.

Fargey drew their attention to the fact that the shell picked up on the driveway fitted the gun perfectly and that one shot had been fired from the magazine. "Can you identify this weapon, Mr. Levering?" he asked.

Roger Levering turned towards them and nodded dully.

"It's hers," he admitted in a low voice. Traynor moved over to his side and silently pressed his arm in encouragement.

"Thanks, old chap," murmured Levering huskily. He seemed to get a better grip on himself and cleared his throat. "Gentlemen, this thing is—a bit of a shock, you know. But there is no use in denying that Lieutenant Fargey appears to have ample justification for the worst suspicions against my—Mrs. Saint-Anton. With your permission, sir, I would like to summon her—"

"Just what I was going to do," interrupted Fargey. "Sergeant, will you bring the lady here immediately and Miss Radcliffe as well. It ain't going to be pleasant, Tommy; but I am only doing my duty."

Detective-Sergeant Hayes walked briskly to the door, threw it open—and almost collided with the butler!

"Miss Radcliffe's compliments, Mr. Traynor—"

"Hey, you, Thompson!" called Fargey brusquely. "We ain't handing out bouquets o' sweet lavender to-day. You beat it downstairs and tell Miss Radcliffe— Go along with him, Sergeant." He waved them out peremptorily and closed the door. He replaced the shirt-cuff and the automatic in the steamer trunk and dropped the lid, then drew Addison Kent to one side.

"Well, what about theories now, Kent?" and he grinned provokingly. "I said I had a hunch about this thing from the first, didn't I?"

Kent shrugged his shoulders and held out his hands in a gesture of helplessness.

"There is, of course, a point where theory may merge with fact."

Fargey fancied with satisfaction that the author's smile was a trifle sheepish.

"Think I've got the goods on her, eh?"

"The facts must speak for themselves, Lieutenant. In the face of this situation any opinion I might express would be entirely presumptions. You overwhelm me with evidence."

Fargey chuckled. There was a gleam in his eye as he lowered his voice to a pitch that could not be overheard.

"This is only a starter. We got this guy, Alceste, to deal with yet an' I want to warn you to lay low on that. The robbery an' the murder are two separate things. I'm workin' quiet an' I'll let you in on it when the fruit's ripe. Get me. If we pull it off right, it'll be the biggest thing you an' me—"

He broke off abruptly and turned away to talk to Levering. Traynor started towards Kent but stepped quickly across to the door as footsteps sounded on the stairs. The tension which everyone felt tightened at sight of the two ladies on the threshold.

As they came slowly into the room and noted the group that stood awaiting them with sober faces the expression of both was one of bewilderment. Lieutenant Fargey, however, wasted no time in explaining to the mistress of the house his reason for summoning them. The cloud of trouble which had hung over her for the past two days had left its mark upon the girl; she looked pale and worn and shrank instinctively closer to Tommy Traynor who stood beside her. He pressed her hand reassuringly.

"Our work here is just about over, Miss Radcliffe," Fargey was saying. "We have made some important discoveries this morning and I have a few questions to ask." He turned abruptly to Mrs. Saint-Anton and pointed to the steamer trunk. "That baggage belongs to you, I believe, madam?"

"Ye-es?"

He strode over and threw back the lid.

"And this also?" He held out the automatic for identification.

"Why—yes, that is mine, I think. I had one like it in that trunk. But what do you mean, sir, going into my things—?"

"That will do, madam!" commanded Fargey sharply. "It's me's askin' the questions. Why did you commit perjury in the witness box this morning? Will you answer that?"

"Perjury!" gasped Mrs. Saint-Anton, falling back a step.

"That's what I said." Fargey pointed his finger straight in her face. "You swore on your oath that you were not outside of your room on Saturday night after eleven o'clock. We have evidence to prove that you were in Henry Radcliffe's room after midnight!"

Her face went white. Her eyes widened in sudden fear as they swept the circle. Fascinated, she watched Lieutenant Fargey lifting from the trunk an oblong of white. She shrank back as he advanced upon her, holding it for her to see.

"Read it! Read it!" commanded Fargey sternly. He passed it to Traynor and laid his hand on the woman's shoulder. "Madam, you are under arrest—for the murder of Henry Radcliffe!"

"It's a lie!" she said weakly. "I did not kill him! I swear it!"

"The oath of a perjurer!"

"I did not, I tell you! Oh, *mon dieu*, you must believe me! You must! I was in the room—but as God is my judge—"

"It is my duty to warn you, madam, that whatever you say may be used against you."

"I tell you, it's a lie! I have never seen that thing before. How did it get in my trunk? I did not kill him!"

She turned frantically towards Rose Radcliffe who had bowed her head with a shudder at the accusation. She looked around in mute appeal, seemingly dazed by the crisis that had come upon her so suddenly. Her face was ghastly with its red spots of rouge pathetically apparent. Gone was all that poise, that superior air which had characterized her bearing, and she looked suddenly old.

Her frightened eyes at last encountered those of Roger Levering.

"Tell them, Roger—you at least do not believe—this terrible, impossible thing."

But even as she spoke she saw that he did believe it. His face was pale and set in grim lines that repelled her. He said nothing—merely turned his back upon her.

And at that a look of positive terror grew in the woman's eyes. Kent saw it and stepped closer to her. It was the look of a cornered animal. Weakly she sank down upon a trunk and covered her face as she emitted a tragic little moan.

Detective-Sergeant Hayes at a nod from his superior laid a hand upon her shoulder. Like one in a dream she permitted herself to be guided from the room.

16
A Packet of Cardboard Matches

The arrest of Mrs. Saint-Anton for the murder of Henry C. Radcliffe in his Westchester mansion was a front-page feature for the newspapers. The more sensational of them devoted considerable space to it and illustrated their "stories" by photos of all the actors in the drama, the shirt-cuff, the weapon that did the deed, the steamer trunk—marked X to show where the articles were found—, the house and grounds and so on. In the case of the *Mercury*, Tommy Traynor's former paper, an intelligent editor had dug into the files and reviewed the old story of the charity bazaar fire in which one Traynor, star reporter for the *Mercury*, had rescued the beautiful heiress, Miss Rose Radcliffe, etc., etc. This—illustrated by photos of Tommy and Rose, set in two artistic hearts, done in crayon and interlinked by a romantic newspaper artist—was so delicately handled that even Tommy with his appreciation of news values was forced to forgive it.

Less excusable by far were some of the veiled hints in regard to the possible relations between the late Henry C. Radcliffe and "the mystery woman," as she was called. A few of the reporters had found ready to hand in the "morgues" of their respective papers a fine sheaf of interesting clippings in regard to the wealthy gem expert's past activities; they had not hesitated to use imagination in drawing inferences from his goings and comings—all carefully worded, of course, with due regard to the libel law. Mr. Radcliffe had made several trips to France and the lady had a French name; ergo this and ergo that. Who was she? Why had she gone into his room after midnight? Was it a case of blackmail, jealous revenge or what? And so on to the yellow limit of daring!

And through it all stalked the heroic figure of Lieutenant Robert Fargey. The astuteness of the police, Lieutenant Fargey in charge, was played up from every angle. From the first the police suspected the very things that had happened and they had worked quietly and well, etc., etc. The speed with which they had followed the clues to an arrest was exceptional and reflected great credit, etc., etc.

Nor was Mr. Addison Kent overlooked. The presence of the famous novelist in the house as a friend of the family had been duly noted. Himself a writer of great detective stories which enjoyed phenomenal sale, he was qualified to appreciate the good work of the police. He had been prepared to assist them in their investigations but had found that Lieutenant Fargey had the case so well in hand that his own great powers of deduction were not required. Seen at his apartment in Minaki Court, he paid a graceful compliment to Lieutenant Fargey and admitted that the evidence appeared to leave nothing for him to say.

Kent smiled as he read and clipped the newspaper accounts. Fargey's vanity for once ought to be gratified by the flattering publicity he was receiving. Poor Bob! it was his very bread and meat. In handing out the details to the reporters he had made no mention of the "ghost," Kent noted; Fargey had told the author that he was sure that Mrs. Saint-Anton was responsible for the strange figure on the stair—if Traynor and Levering really had seen the thing. But that he was perplexed in regard to it was apparent in the fact that he was carefully concealing mention of it at all and had cautioned both Traynor and Levering to do likewise.

The business career of Henry Radcliffe, his rapid rise, his archaeological discoveries, the prominent part he had taken in the modern "arts and crafts" movement in the United States—all this was duly recorded and space given to the wonderful collection of Cypriot art objects which he had helped to assemble for the Metropolitan Museum of Art. His private collection of antiques and gems was not forgotten while the great value of the diamond necklace and the collar of pearls that had been stolen from Hillcrest came in for attention.

But of the many items of interest which Kent carefully clipped out and classified for his files he smoked longest over those which touched upon the late Henry Radcliffe's activities abroad. One of these in particular seemed to catch and hold his eye; yet it was only a paragraph which read:

> Fate seems to have a trick of singling out certain human beings and crossing their lives with lines of tragedy. It was while the late Mr. Radcliffe was on one of his excursions in France that his marriage to a young French woman took place. But after a honeymoon spent with his friends, Professor William Winterby and wife, on their French estate, Mr. Radcliffe returned to America without his bride whom he was forced to leave behind in Switzerland, too ill to travel. Some time later he crossed the Atlantic and brought back his infant daughter, Mrs. Radcliffe still remaining in her native land. When at last his wife did make the journey to her new home she was killed in a railway wreck. Identification was made by a gold locket which he had given her on their wedding day. By a strange freak of the disaster she had been decapitated and the head was never found. Later his daughter nearly lost her life in a fire in New York. Now Henry Radcliffe himself lies slain by the bullet of an assassin.

Kent glanced at his watch and gave a low whistle at the fleetness of time. Hastily placing the clipping inside a leather wallet which he took from his pocket, he reached for his hat and gloves. His taxi was waiting and he had left himself little time to catch his train.

The newspapers he had been clipping were three days old. The funeral of Henry Radcliffe had served to keep public interest alive; but with the victim buried, the guilty person in custody—no question of that, of course!—and the trial a long way off yet, the Hillcrest case had slumped from columns to paragraphs in the current editions, much to Addison Kent's satisfaction.

It also was to his satisfaction that Miss Rose Radcliffe had acceded to the urgings of her friend, Miss Marjorie Struthers, to get away from Hillcrest with its depressing associations. She had gone to the Struthers summer home on Long Island that very morning for a visit of uncertain duration, leaving it to Tommy Traynor to assist the family solicitor in his adjustments. Roger Levering was gone—only the police knew where—and the servants were no doubt settling down to a quiet vacation after all the excitement.

It was Thompson who opened the door for him in response to his ring and it was the butler whom Kent had come to see. They went at once into the library and Thompson closed the library doors and locked them. There was a look of calm satisfaction on his mild countenance as he faced the visitor across the library table and reaching carefully into his pocket, he drew forth a long manilla envelope.

"I am glad to report that I have met with some success, Mr. Kent. I believe these are what you asked me to find, if possible."

As he spoke he emptied the contents of the envelope upon the table a little heap of paper fragments. Kent bent over them with close scrutiny as he poked and spread the scraps with his forefinger, assembling and reassembling them without a word for five minutes.

"Where did you find them?"

"In the furnace room where the sweepings go. I had to sort over a lot of rubbish in the dustbin, Mr. Kent,—personally; I could trust nobody else to do it thoroughly enough."

"Quite right. And you have made a clean job of a dirty one. I congratulate you, Thompson. This is what I wanted," said Kent as he carefully scraped the fragments off the table edge into the envelope, sealed it and placed it in his pocket. "I hope you found the other assignment more to your liking."

"She is a bit of a flirt, Mr. Kent, and I had no great trouble," smiled Thompson, unconsciously pulling down his waistcoat and straightening his tie.

"And is Lucille really keeping company with a policeman?"

"With Patrolman Carney, of the 8th precinct—yes. They are to be married in the fall, I believe, and she is wearing his ring."

"Officer Carney is to be congratulated," smiled Kent. "His gain, though, will be Miss Radcliffe's loss, no doubt. Miss Radcliffe got away this morning all right?"

"Yes. Follis looked after the trunks; but he had to send them by express through to Struthersholm because a telegram came from Miss Struthers this morning, asking Miss Radcliffe to take the Wading River branch line at Hicksville and get off at Woodland Cove. They plan to meet her there with the car and motor back."

Kent nodded and asked to see Mrs. Stanton. He was surprised to learn that she was ill and had sent one of the Stokes children up to the big house to ask Miss Radcliffe to excuse her for a few days.

"Where is this Stokes place at which she rooms? How do I get there?" and Thompson directed him to the path which cut across the wooded ridge of the park and down to the shore drive. "You will be anxious to get into action, Thompson. I want you to take the first train to Woodland Cove, just to make sure that everything is all right in that direction. You might call me on the 'phone from there. After that I leave you to your own devices."

"Very good, Mr. Kent."

The waters of Long Island Sound glittered in the afternoon sunlight in pleasing vista. The never-ending coastwise traffic that plied in and out of New York Harbor provided a constant movement of New England freighters and coal barges and small craft of all descriptions, making in through Hell Gate to the East River. But as Addison Kent took his way along the wooded path through the park his eyes were mostly on the ground and his thoughts busy with other things than his surroundings.

He had no great difficulty in locating the park attendant's little bungalow. Mrs. Stokes herself was enjoying a quiet half hour in the ham mock with a novel and Kent was amused to note that it was his own latest thriller in which her nose was buried. When he handed her his card the good woman stared at him in amazement. 6he was an omnivorous reader of popular fiction and she was not one of those careless ones who never look at the name of the author. To have the author of the very book she was reading walk in upon her like this startled her and her face flushed with excitement at an experience which provided such excellent material for subsequent conversation among her friends. He had no trouble at all in getting her to talk; for Mrs. Stokes was not only stout and good-natured but also sociably inclined to flexibility of the tongue with those she liked and it was apparent that Kent impressed her very favorably, as well he might.

Mrs. Stanton was not there. She had not returned home after the inquest; but had dropped a postcard into the mail to say she was not very well and had accepted an invitation to spend a few days with a friend in the city. She had asked them to send one of the children to notify Miss Radcliffe. No, she had not said where she was going. Yes, it was somewhat unusual, because Mrs. Stanton seldom went out and was not one who made friends readily although she was a dear little lady.

If Kent had wondered why Mrs. Stanton chose to room with the Stokes family when she might have had comfortable quarters at Hillcrest, he found a reasonable answer as Mrs. Stokes proceeded to dilate upon the pleasant way in which her household got along with one another. The children were off at play somewhere; she had three and every one of them loved Mrs. Stanton. Mrs. Stokes and her husband had considered themselves very fortunate in having a former governess of such ladylike and superior qualities take an interest in their children. The way Mrs. Stanton had helped Jenny with her school work was wonderful; the child was at the head of her class.

"I don't think she's had a very happy life, poor lady," said Mrs. Stokes thoughtfully. "The way she hugs those kids sometimes—!" She sighed. "She enjoys it here with us just like one of the family. We'd miss her awful if she went away."

"She seems to think quite a lot of her mistress—Miss Radcliffe. I suppose the murder has been a great shock to her!"

It had—a terrible shock. It was enough to shock anybody. When the detective had called at their cottage the other night Mrs. Stokes herself had felt positively—

"When was that?" asked Kent quickly. "A detective, you say?"

"Oh, he'd only been sent over to tell us that the police were keepin' everybody at the house to be ready for the inquest next mornin'—the Sunday night, it was—an' for us not to wait up for Mrs. Stanton."

"You are sure it was a detective who called?"

"That's what he said an' he flipped back his coat to show his shield. Mrs. Stanton asked him to fetch back her japanned box out of her bureau."

"Japanned box?"

"Yes. It was a little black box with a key to it; she locked up her trinkets in it. It had gold decorations on it—long-legged birds an' all that. I heard her say once it come from Japan."

"Do you know what was in it?"

"Well, I ain't sure. It was her private things an' I ain't one to nose in on what ain't none o' my business, Mr. Kent. Maybe she wanted a clean handkerchief or somethin' or a bit o' jewelry to wear at the inquest."

"Could you describe the man who called?" persisted Kent.

"Why—no, not very well," replied Mrs. Stokes, a little surprised at his inquisitiveness. "It was after dark an' he was on'y here a minute. He wasn't tall nor what you'd call short—just medium, sort of. Leastways, I think he was. I didn't pay much attention—just give him the box. Why, Mr. Kent, did I do wrong?"

Kent reassured her as he stood up and prepared to take his leave. No doubt Lieutenant Fargey had sent over one of his men and it was all right.

"Well, I must be going, Mrs. Stokes. I will see Mrs. Stanton later on, perhaps." He took out his cigarette-case, then felt for a match without success. "May I have these?" He stepped across the verandah to where a blackened pipe rested in a tin tray on the windowsill and picked up the packet of cardboard matches that lay alongside.

"Certainly. Take them with you," smiled Mrs. Stokes. "Bill's got lots more. He brought home a whole handful of those packets a while back; they always come in handy."

Kent thanked her and raised his hat. There was nothing in his manner to indicate the discovery he had made—that the cardboard matches advertised the same cigar as those he had picked up already in Henry Radcliffe's room and again on the secret stair at Hillcrest.

17
THE SHADOW OF THE CHÂTEAU

It was about six o'clock when Addison Kent got back to his own apartment. Mrs. Madden had been in and the sight of the table, spread with a snowy cloth and set for one, reminded him that he was hungry. He grinned like a boy at the scribbled note which his housekeeper had propped against the water pitcher to the effect that he would find a salad and a fresh-baked cake in the ice-box and a casserole of chicken pie keeping hot in the electric oven. He whistled a cheerful tune as he got into clean linen after a freshening shower-bath and bustled about the kitchenette.

Once the inner man was satisfied and his pipe going well, Kent retired eagerly to his desk and started what promised to be an interesting night's work. He tore open the envelope Thompson had given him, got out a sheet of cardboard and a jar of office paste, and began the slow, arduous task of fitting together the tiny torn fragments of what once had been—or was supposed to have been— a lesson in chess-playing. It was the very chess notation which had been delivered on the Saturday afternoon preceding the murder and robbery at Hillcrest to Mr. Roger Levering in the presence of Tommy Traynor and the others.

What there was in a mere notation of chess moves to interest a man who had confessed to Levering that he knew nothing about the game might have been a reasonable matter for wonder. The pains which Addison Kent was taking to reconstruct the sheet of paper were out of all keeping with the desire of a novice to learn the game. And when at last he screwed the top on the paste-pot and held the cardboard at arm's length, his head critically on one side, his grunt of satisfaction was too emphatic to be casual. The luck held good; the only part of the sheet missing was a corner of blank paper.

He got down his chessboard now, arranged the white and black pieces and pawns in their proper positions and with the eye of a chess expert studied the notation sheet. A move or two on the board and he laughed outright. He jumped to his feet and went over to the bookcases. Here he glanced through a few volumes, finally brought one of them back to the desk and began to put strange marks upon a sheet of notepaper.

Presently he sat back and stared at what he had written with a strange and growing excitement. He went again to the bookcases and looked through some books. Then he consulted the card index to his file of newspaper clippings, glanced at his watch and hurried out. Half an hour later he was pouring over an assortment of volumes in the reference room at the public library and remained there until closing time. Shortly afterwards he was swinging aboard a Fifth Avenue bus at Forty-Second street and climbed to the roof where he sat with his hat on his knees, completely absorbed in thought.

It was a favorite ride of his, this, through the illuminated canyons of the downtown streets on top of a bus and then away to the quieter spaciousness of great brownstone residences. But to-night he was not out for an airing merely; he was heading for the home of Mr. Armaund Lamont on upper Fifth Avenue. It was the second time that day that he had occupied a seat on top of a Fifth Avenue bus; for after his morning call at Lamont's place of business he had taken the bus line and from his point of vantage had uncovered by sheer good luck the lie that had been told him by Lamont's private secretary. For how could Mr. Armaund Lamont be out of the city for a ten days' absence on special business when Kent had just seen the gentleman pass swiftly and luxuriously by in his limousine? Kent had an excellent pair of eyes and he knew that he had not been mistaken. He had decided then and there that he would call upon Lamont this evening without fail; the matter he wished to discuss could wait that long, but no longer.

Confident that he had only to hand in his card to be admitted, he stood at last in front of the imposing glass doors of the jeweler's residence and pushed on the electric bell with the ferule of his cane. For a lone bachelor Armaund Lamont lived in somewhat pretentious quarters which were almost exotic in the richness and artistic harmony of the furnishings. He had his own peculiar tastes in this direction and on occasional visits to the wealthy Frenchman's home with Traynor, Kent had found much to arouse aesthetic appreciation.

He smiled now as he saw the inner door open and the familiar dark-skinned features of the Algerian servant peer out at him. This confidential man of Lamont's was a great silent slave of a fellow whose importation was justified a hundred times a day by the almost uncanny manner in which he seemed to anticipate his master's every wish. He had served Armaund Lamont for many years and lent a touch of the bizarre to the establishment both in dress and manner. The man recognized him with a grin which bared two rows of perfect white teeth and proceeded to inform him simply and plainly that his master was not at home.

"Hold on, 'Rastus'! Don't be in a hurry," said Kent pleasantly as he thrust his foot forward to prevent the door closing in his face. "Truth is one of the great virtues which you will do well to cultivate. In other words, why lie to me? I want to see Mr. Lamont very specially, as it happens; so take in this card at once."

The Algerian eyed him placidly and shook his head. Mr. Lamont was not at home.

"You mean he doesn't want to be disturbed by visitors. I'm sorry, but I must insist."

Again the man shook his head and tried to close the door. This time Kent shoved it open and stepped inside the vestibule.

"Now, look here, I'm not in any mood for fooling about this. Lamont is here and I know it." The flicker of uncertainty in the Algerian's eyes confirmed the guess. Kent turned his card over and wrote on the back of it. "Now take that in to him; he will be very angry with you if you don't. It's for his own good."

The man bowed his head silently and disappeared, leaving Kent to twiddle his thumbs with what patience he could command. The servant was back again in a moment, his dark face wreathed in smiles that he had done the right thing in submitting the card. With a low bow he held open the door and proceeded to usher the visitor down the wide hall. Beyond the great staircase was a closed door upon which he knocked discreetly before throwing it open.

Kent paused on the threshold and for a long moment the two men looked at one another in silent appraisal. Armaund Lamont had risen from the huge padded leather chair in which he had been sunk and he stood now in front of it on the far side of the room, nervously fingering the caller's card. He was a very different Lamont from the confident, advice-giving gentleman who had offered assistance to Henry Radcliffe's daughter a few days ago. A certain air of self-reliance which he had then possessed seemed to have vanished with the neatness of his dress. As he stood there in dressing-gown and slippers, collarless, unshaved, his thick black hair unbrushed and moustache uncurled he looked positively untidy. It needed only his bloodshot eyes and the decanter of cognac on the tray beside the chair to complete the impression of a man who had lost his nerve. His eyes shifted uneasily from Kent's. He waved his guest to a chair and was turning to the tray when the novelist stopped him with a gesture of refusal.

"I am not making a social call, Mr. Lamont, or I should not have been so insistent that you see me," said Kent as he seated himself. "I called at your office this morning and your secretary informed me that you had gone out of town for ten days. Your man at the door likewise insisted that you were not at home." Lamont held out his hands, palms upwards, and sank back into the big armchair. "You admit me only when I write upon my card: 'The black shadow of the château is creeping far beyond the old bridge.' It is about that we will talk, if you please."

"I do not understand you, Mr. Kent. It is because I do not understand that I admit you on my privacy, is it not?—to ask why you write these so strange words. It may be that you have gone—how do you say it in the slang?—like a nut? See, I am worried to know."

"The nut is hard enough to crack without you trying to make it more difficult for me, Mr. Lamont. Why this foolish pretense?"

"My dear Mr. Kent, please! I do not understand."

"Yes, you do!" contradicted Addison Kent sharply. "I have come here to ask you some questions and I want honest answers. Where is Mrs. Stanton?"

A startled look came into the Frenchman's eyes and Kent watched the fingers of his right hand close about the card which they still held till it was crushed in the tight clenched fist.

"Mrs. Stanton?" he echoed vacuously.

"Exactly—Mrs. Stanton, the lady who sews for Miss Radcliffe. Where is she? You know."

"But no, Mr. Kent—that is not so. How should I know where Miss Radcliffe's sewing lady is? Is she not at her place?"

"She is not at Hillcrest, nor at the Stokes home where she has a room," replied Kent. "I have just come from there. She mailed them a postcard to say she was ill and was remaining in the city with a friend for a few days' rest. She has not been seen since the inquest. She had an appointment to meet you—promised to tell you something important that would interest you—"

He paused as Armaund Lamont leaped to his feet in sudden agitation. During this speech the jeweler's fat face had paled. His bloodshot eyes were full of apprehension as he stared. The flaccid pouches beneath them were dark from sleeplessness. He paced up the room and back, gesturing, muttering to himself.

"It has come! It has come! *Mon dieu!*" he whispered hoarsely.

"What has come?" demanded Kent.

"We had business to transact—yes. After the inquest—yes. But she had her good health when she left my office, Mr. Kent, and she was going straight out to Westchester. She has no friends in the city to go on a visit—"

"Are you sure? The postcard was genuine. You think she may have written it—under compulsion?"

Lamont nodded miserably. There was nothing simulated in the apprehension which lurked in his restless eyes.

"It is the château! the accursed château!" he mumbled. He stared at Addison Kent with hollow, frightened eyes. His voice sank to a whisper. "It means—death!"

"The Château du Vieux Pont? Be more explicit, Mr. Lamont."

But with, a muttered imprecation Armaund Lamont fell back a step in astonishment.

"You know?" he gasped. "What do you know? Answer quickly. For God's sake, Mr. Kent—how much are you aware?"

"Enough to make it advisable for you to be frank with me, Lamont," said Kent firmly. "Now, first of all, what is this woman to you?"

"You must cease asking the questions—I cannot answer," protested the Frenchman, but the expression which crossed his face answered for him. "She is good—all that is good and pure and true. Ah, she is—!" He broke off abruptly and almost ran to lay an excited hand upon his visitor's shoulder. "We must do something! We must find her—so quickly as possible! You hear? Before it is too late, we must find her!"

"Then sit down and answer my questions," urged Kent. "You have nothing to lose and everything to gain by it. I am here to help you."

"Ah, if only that could be, my friend!" cried Armaund Lamont with a gesture of despair. He dropped disconsolately into the armchair again. "Alas! I can say—nothing."

"You will not tell me what you know?—even when it may mean the safety of the woman you love? Oh, I am not blind, Mr. Lamont."

"I can not— Ah, Mr. Kent, I believe you want to help but that you cannot do! You can never undo what is done, is it not? I would speak if I could do so; but that I dare not do."

"Why?"

"It is not—for a secret that belongs to me. But one whisper from me to you and it would be—the end!"

"Utter nonsense, Lamont! You refuse to talk, then?"

"Can you not see that it must be so?" cried Lamont miserably.

"Then perhaps you will listen while I say something," said Kent, his jaw set. "I tell you nothing new very likely, but it may serve to freshen your memory. The Château du Vieux Pont is one of those old relics of the feudal days which still stand in the Ile de France. When it was built in the fourteenth century by Henri d'Albrêt it was surrounded by the forest. Years ago it was abandoned and the owners of the surrounding lands have taken so little interest in their property that the whole section of the country thereabouts has retrograded into a wilderness that is almost primitive. You can see the Château du Vieux Pont from the road that runs between the village of Sainte-Genevieve and Monthery. There is an old inn of the coaching days still standing and offering hospitality to passing wagoners; but it is, on the whole, not a part of the country where one would wish to linger if sociably inclined. I can imagine even that its twisted beeches and oaks, centuries old, might strike terror to the hearts of the timid when the clouds were scudding past the moon and that in the season of mud, cold rains, rotting leaves and overcast skies it might provide a fitting theatre—for strange things, Mr. Lamont."

Kent's eyes were alight with eagerness as they fastened upon every changing expression of the pallid face before him. Lamont, his lips slightly parted, was breathing quickly with suppressed excitement. A little shudder passed through him; but he said not a word—merely stared with red-lidded eyes that burned with insomnia.

"That part of the country, as I say, has few inhabitants," continued Kent. "There are some small houses beside the road going to Corbeil and a village of charcoal burners on the highroad to Epinay; but the Château of the Old Bridge stands in a lonesome stretch of wooded country. There is one other old château not far away which was going to ruin also until an eccentric English savant and his wife took it over as a place of retirement and came there to live. I refer to the Château des Hêtres and to Professor William Winterby, F.R.S."

"Ah!" breathed Armaund Lamont. His black eyes glittered in the white of his big face.

"It was to visit Professor Winterby and his wife that Henry Radcliffe went some twenty years ago—shortly after his marriage. In fact, he was on his honeymoon. He and his bride were very happy together. It was a fine place to go for a honeymoon—the Château des Hêtres; for lovers provide their own companionship and it is all-sufficient."

Kent paused.

"Shall I go on, Lamont? Will you talk now about what happened at the Château du Vieux Pont?" He leaned forward and spoke in a low, tense voice. "Will you tell me why Henry Radcliffe came back to America—without his bride? Perhaps you will tell me why the shadow of that château is so black—why it has crept so far that after all these years it reaches even to New York—to Hillcrest—and strikes terror to the heart of one whom you say is all that is good and pure and true! Why do you cringe from honest questions? What have you to hide? Answer me, Armaund Lamont! What have you to hide?"

The Frenchman leaped to his feet, his eyes blazing.

"I refuse to answer!" he cried with spirit. "Who are you to come here—in my home—and torment me so? It is that I should have you thrown out! You do not ask these so many strange things by any right. I answer you not! *Sacré!* you make me all mad! Go! Go! Leave me with myself!"

"My right to ask these questions is the right of justice. I will not cease to ask them until justice is done, Armaund Lamont!" warned Kent. "I am here as the friend of Miss Radcliffe and of the late Henry Radcliffe, her father. I am here because I am on the trail of Alceste and will not rest until I run him down—"

"*Mille tonneurs!* No, no!"

"—for then I will learn who is the *man* who shot Henry Radcliffe to death!"

18
THE SOUNDLESS BULLET

"Hush! Hush! Not a word of that, Mr. Kent! You must keep silence immediately!" cried Lamont, hastening towards him, finger to his lips in warning. "*Mon dieu!* you must not say such things!" His frightened glance travelled about the room as if he half expected to see an enemy springing upon them from nowhere.

"Why not?" demanded Addison Kent, reaching for a cigarette and lighting it with an amusement which he made no attempt to hide.

"It is too much dangerous! That is why." The jeweler mopped the perspiration from his forehead with a plump hand that trembled. He was not feigning fear. He was really afraid—terribly afraid.

"Come, Mr. Lamont, you must not allow yourself to imagine so freely," said Kent more seriously. "There is nobody here except you and me—and that man of yours. Is there?"

"But no—of course not! But one is never sure— You must get away from here as soon as immediately."

"That is pretty soon," Kent admitted easily; but he made no move to go. "Why such haste? What are you afraid of?"

"Ah, you ask more questions. Everything I fear. Everybody I shun. I am in very great danger. Everyone who comes here is in danger. I cannot explain, but it is so and you must leave here without being seen, Mr. Kent. My word is given you that it is wisest."

"I do not scare very easily, Lamont—"

"If you were to be heard talking such fool things as you have said here to me you would not have time to scare, my friend. You would be too dead all over!"

Kent looked at him in wonder; for it was evident that Lamont really believed what he said. Then the novelist laughed quietly.

"Is it as bad as that?"

"Worse, I do assure you, sir."

"What I have been saying I can repeat at will. And it is not foolish talk, Lamont. I mean every word of it."

"But yes, it is foolish," insisted the other. "You do not know what you say. The police are right and she is a bad woman they have captured. She deserves to die!"

"So you know Mrs. Saint-Anton also, eh?" asked Kent with quickened interest. "Tell me about her."

Armaund Lamont paid no attention to the question, however. He was anxious only to be rid of his visitor as quickly as possible and he stepped to the door and clapped his hands smartly.

"Ho, my Mokra! Tell Pierre he will make ready the limousine at once with the blinds drawn down and wait in the garage. His passenger soon will enter by the garage. *Vite! Vite! Il se fait tard!*"

"Blinds drawn, eh?" mused Kent, his eyes narrowed as he drew on his cigarette. "Danger with all the trimmings!"

"Ah, Mr. Kent, you do not know how I am so anxious. I cannot explain. New York is big and many strange things happen every day. It is better to take care. How do you say it in the slang?—my goat is stolen?"

"So is that wonderful collar of pearls," Kent chuckled.

"*Sacré!*" cried Armaund Lamont. "Truly. It is very strange, that."

"This Alceste is a clever devil, Mr. Lamont. Have you any idea how the thing was done?"

"I do not know. There they are—*Pouf!*— Here they are not! It is done in a twinkle, is it not? Perhaps if I give him back the question, Mr. Kent himself will tell me how to do it?" His black eyes looked intently through half closed, reddened lids.

"Did you open the parcel Miss Radcliffe gave you? before you left Hillcrest, I mean?"

"I did not."

"You handed it to the detective who was to accompany you—when?"

"Miss Radcliffe brought me the parcel in the brown paper when dinner was over a little while. I gave it to Mr. McVey then."

"And it was not out of his hands until you were riding into town with it. You yourself carried it on your knees. The loss was not discovered until you were in this house, about to put the pearls into your vault here. Is that correct?"

"Quite correct, Mr. Kent."

"Then the theft was done in one of two places and at one of two times. Either the pearls were removed from the parcel while it was in Miss Radcliffe's room, wrapped up ready for you, or they disappeared after you got home!"

"Im—possible!" gasped Lamont. Then his face flushed with a quick anger that left it very white as he strode across the room in great excitement. "You dare to say—even that, sir!" he panted.

"Even what?" Kent smiled and blew a cloud of smoke into the face that scowled down on him.

"That I—Armaund Lamont—stole them?"

"Sit down, Lamont! I did not say so," cried Kent sharply.

"You will go, please—now. I wish to be with myself. It grows late and the car is waiting."

Kent stood up. He deposited the butt of the cigarette in the ash-tray and appraised the other for a moment in silence. Then without a word he accepted his hat, cane and gloves and followed the nervous master of the house to a rear door through which they could reach the garage unobserved.

"Pierre will take you where you want to go—anywhere but to your own apartment. He will not go there in fear that someone follows. It is well that you do my wishes in this matter."

"Mr. Lamont," said Kent as he paused with one foot on the running-board of the limousine, "I am sorry you have not seen fit to be frank with me. Think it over. I will call again. If I can be of any assistance in helping you to find the lady—"

"I will do the finding myself."

"But you will at least report—"

"Nothing. I bid you good-night," and he bowed coldly and turned away abruptly.

Addison Kent's eyes puckered with tolerant amusement as he took up the speaking-tube and gave directions to the chauffeur. He turned on the little electric light in the roof of the luxuriously upholstered car, glanced at his watch, put the light out again and relaxed on the cushions. The hour was near midnight.

That the novelist credited most of Mr. Armaund Lamont's excitability to a volatile temperament and did not take very seriously the fears which the Frenchman had expressed was apparent a few moments later. The car had no sooner glided smoothly into the street and got out of sight of the Lamont residence than Kent raised all the blinds and opened the windows. The gratifying breeze created by swift motion blew coolly against his face. He did not mind humoring a victim of "nerves," but not to the point of discomfort.

With an idea that he might step into Delmonico's or Sherry's or perhaps look in at the Players' he had asked the chauffeur to run him down the avenue as far as 44th Street. At 60th Street, in sight of St. Gaudens's bronze statue of Sherman and his horse on its polished granite pedestal, he suddenly changed his mind.

"I've decided to go home, Pierre," he said through the speaking-tube. "Cut through the park to Riverside Drive and take your time. There's no rush on such a fine night. You may drop me at 82nd and I'll walk the rest of the way."

The night was fresh with the sweet breath of flowers and growing vegetation in the vicinity of Central Park. At that hour particularly the place offered restful solitude. The peaceful sylvan setting was conducive to meditation and Addison Kent was soon deep in thought as they rolled along at a leisurely pace. The broad winding driveways, which at certain times presented a constant procession of fashionable equippages, motor cars of all descriptions and equestrians, were practically deserted. Only one powerful touring car, turning in through the southeast entrance, overtook the big brass-trimmed limousine, slowly edged its way past, then went cutting off ahead in a burst of impatient speed till it vanished around the next turn.

Lamont's chauffeur grinned spitefully after the irritated driver. Some people were never satisfied with anything less than the whole road apparently. He continued to smile as he recalled the altercation he had had over the rights of the road—last Sunday when he had been out with Marie. Pierre thought quite frequently of Marie when he was not too busy and as he dawdled through the park he allowed his mind to roam far away along paths of Romance. He was many blocks up Riverside Drive before he came to a full realization of his surroundings just in time to stop the car at 82nd Street according to instructions.

"We are here, monsieur," he called, swinging briskly down from his seat out in front.

He took hold of the handle of the monogramed door, but did not open it immediately. In the light from the electric standard nearby he saw something which drove every vestige of color from his cheeks. He stared downward with alarmed eyes. Beneath the closed door was seeping slowly a thin dark streak of liquid which widened upon the corrugated rubber tread of the running-board.

He gave a sudden cry of horror, pulled the door open—and recoiled, aghast. His passenger lay sprawled upon the cushions, head and shoulders fallen inertly forward over the edge. Upon the delicately patterned taffeta shirt was an ugly crimson stain where a bullet-hole showed plainly.

Shot! Why? How? When! There had been no sound of a shot!

In sudden panic the chauffeur slammed the limousine door, leaped to his seat and went tearing madly off into the leafy, night-hushed vista.

19
MENACE UNBELIEVABLE

When Addison Kent came to his senses he gazed with mild wonder at a little white-starched cap above a pleasant ruddy face.

"Where am I?" he asked in a weak voice.

"You are in the James B. Yates Memorial Hospital," replied the smiling nurse. She reached out and pushed an electric button which summoned the house-surgeon on duty. "You were brought by Mr. Lamont's chauffeur," she went on as if divining the questions he would ask. "It is now half after three in the morning. You are not to talk—just rest. The wound is nothing to be alarmed about—if you remain quiet."

She turned as the house-surgeon came softly through the doorway of the private room to which the midnight patient had been allotted. For a moment they whispered together, then the young doctor came quietly to the bedside and smiled cheerfully as he placed his cool soft fingers upon the wrist that lay outside the coverlet and felt the pulse. He looked very smart and clean in his white coat and white starched dickie that fitted snugly at the throat.

"You are feeling better. You will feel better still after a good sleep." Neither in tone or manner was any hint of the curiosity which the case must have aroused in him.

Kent winced with the pain in his upper arm, which was swathed in neat bandages. There was a bandage about his head also; his head ached and throbbed and he felt somewhat dizzy and weak. He relaxed impotently.

"I have been—shot?"

"Evidently. The bullet struck you on the head—a glancing contact fortunately—and passed through the upper arm. It just missed the humerus; but has torn the muscles of the *brachialus anticus* and biceps rather badly in its downward course."

"Downward! From a tree!" muttered the patient.

"It was the blow on the head which caused coma, Mr. Kent."

"How long does this—lay me up, Doctor—?"

"Brown. Oh, not long—four or five days, maybe."

"Four or five days!" echoed Kent in a dismayed whisper. He rolled his head on the pillow, frowning irritation. "Great Scott! Why, doc, I have to be out of here to-morrow—to-day, I mean—without fail!" he protested.

"Very well, then," soothed the house-surgeon. "Have a good sleep now and we'll see about it in the morning."

"I want to see Thomas Traynor—"

"Yes, in the morning. Everything will be arranged in the morning, Mr. Kent. No more talking, please," warned Doctor Brown, "or you won't be out of here for a week. Try not to think. Try to rest. Nurse Andrews will fix you up."

Although the hospital was not a large one and its accommodations were limited, the appointments were excellent. Kent had been in rare good luck that private quarters were available and that he had been recognized both by his card-case and from sundry excellent half-tone photo-engravings which had appeared recently in the magazines. The regular hospital staff was too small and too busy to be in constant attendance upon private patients—even a famous author like Mr. Addison Kent. His case, however, was not critical enough to require the calling in of a special nurse and the result was that the following morning he was left alone in his room for lengthy intervals.

He had had the "good sleep" which Dr. Brown had prescribed and he was feeling very much better. His wounds were easier and he felt so much stronger that be had been able to argue with spirit when the Superintendent informed him bluntly that he could not leave the hospital for at least three days. Kent finally had demanded

the presence of his friend, Traynor, as soon as he could be notified.

It was while he was waiting in no very gracious mood for
Tommy's arrival that the day nurse came in and informed him that
a gentleman had called to enquire after him and wished to see him
somewhat urgently—a Lieutenant Fargey, of the police.

"Send him right up! Good!" cried Kent. "And Nurse—you might
just see that we are not disturbed for a little while, eh?" He smiled
and nodded. Presently he heard an approaching footstep and
turned his head eagerly towards the door.

But it was not Lieutenant Robert Fargey who entered. The man
was a total stranger. Kent smiled at him.

"The right church but the wrong pew?" he suggested. "Who are
you looking for?"

"I do not go to church; but my business takes me to the cemetery occasionally and I know an open grave when I see it," replied
the stranger solemnly.

"Undertaker, eh? Well, friend, you'll have to look elsewhere.
You'll find the nurse outside there some place," and he turned away
in dismissal.

"I have taken the precaution to notify the nurse that we wish to
be left alone, Mr. Kent."

Addison Kent half sat up in his bed and stared intently. The
words alone were sufficiently disconcerting, but the tone of them—
! Yet—

"You wish to see me?—to talk to me? May I ask whom I have
the honor of addressing?"

"You may ask what you like. It does not follow that your curiosity will be satisfied."

"See here, sir! I am expecting a visitor—Lieutenant Fargey, of
the Police Department—who may be in here any minute. He's on
his way upstairs now—"

The sardonic smile with which this was received stopped him.
The man had a black Van Dyke beard and his mouth was partly
hidden by his moustache beneath which his teeth gleamed whitely.

"I am surprised that the clever Mr. Kent is not more astute," he sneered. "For the purposes of the occasion I am 'Lieutenant Fargey.'" A moment of silence followed. The author's keen eyes narrowed in concentrated study of the intruder. Something oddly familiar in the figure eluded his memory— Then as his gaze lifted once more to the face a sudden thrill of apprehension stirred him. It was the eyes—peculiar, light blue eyes—buttony, cruel, the whites as hard and dead as eyes of glass!

The visitor approached the bed slowly, hands in the pockets of his coat, a grim smile on his compressed lips as he watched the flicker of a dawning recognition on the face of the wounded man.

"You are surprised to see me, no doubt? I am always surprising people."

"Say, look here, what the devil do you want? And who told you I was here?" He sank back on the pillow, his blanched face tense, eyes alert, husbanding his strength.

"It is my business to know things—certain things, Mr. Addison Kent," came the low, unctuous voice. He nodded at the bandages. "You shook dice with Death last night when you called on Friend Lamont! You are meddling too freely for your own good!"

Kent shrank involuntarily from the look of intense hatred that accompanied the words; it played lambently in those evil eyes.

"You get right out of here."

"You annoy me exceedingly!" Quick-spoken words, vibrant with passion! "So—!"

Kent's fascinated gaze was bent upon the hands in the pockets. At the first movement he seized the pillow—almost automatically as he caught the glint of polished nickel and saw the hypodermic needle.

"Help!" he yelled at the top of his voice.

As they talked he had been edging imperceptibly to the far side of the bed and working the sheets loose with his feet. Now as his cry rang through the ward he cast the pillow in the malignant face and slid like a flash from beneath the covers just as the lunging arm struck, burying the needle harmlessly in the empty bed.

The instant his feet hit the floor Kent dashed past for the door and out into the corridor. Wild-eyed, he pointed back into the room.

"The man in there—who called to see me—is an imposter! I want him arrested! Quick! Arrest him! He has just tried to kill me!"

Pell mell, they rushed through the doorway. Then they stopped and stared at each other foolishly. The room was empty! The nurses exchanged meaning glances.

Kent knew they did not believe him—that to them it meant merely that he had fallen asleep and had a wild dream or else that he was delirious. He pointed to the open window and the fire-escape and sank exhausted on the bed. The reaction swept in upon him; he trembled from head to foot and for a moment nearly fainted.

He was still looking white and miserable when Traynor arrived. The news of Kent's whereabouts had been a shock to his friend who had remained at the apartment in Minaki Annex until a late hour the evening before, impatiently awaiting the novelist's return. He had sought him there again first thing in the morning without success, adding this new anxiety to the anxiety he was harboring already in regard to Rose Radcliffe.

That anxiety had been born as he listened to the perplexed voice of Miss Marjory Struthers who had called him on the telephone from Long Island to say that Rose had not arrived there, although her trunks had come. The Struthers car had met every train and she could not understand it. On calling up Hillcrest she had learned from the valet that his mistress had left that morning for Woodland Cove on the north shore as instructed in a telegram which purported to come from Marjory Struthers herself. Miss Struthers had despatched no such message!

"I don't like the looks of it, Ad," Traynor concluded with worry lines in his forehead. "Where could she have gone? I haven't reported this to Fargey yet; but I certainly am going to have that wire traced—"

"That is already being done, old man," Kent interrupted. "I was out at Hillcrest yesterday and I sent Thompson on a scouting trip to Woodland Cove—just to make sure everything was all right."

"Then you were anticipating—something?"

"Not until I heard of the wire, after Miss Radcliffe had reached the end of her train journey. I thought it rather strange that Miss Struthers should wire when she could talk on the 'phone to much better advantage; she usually calls up, long-distance, so Thompson informed me. I tried to raise her, but she was out."

"What do you think has happened?"

"Miss Radcliffe has likely been met by a touring car at Woodland Cove; but it did not belong to Struthersholme."

"Then who—? Good heavens!" cried Traynor in alarm. "You mean—she has been abducted?"

"I think it very likely. Now, don't get excited. I don't think she is in danger of physical harm."

"But you—" He pointed to the bandages. "You might have been killed!"

"They look upon me as dangerous," smiled Kent. "It is all the proof I need that I am getting too close to them for their peace of mind. They will work fast from now on; but we must work faster— Oh, hang the luck!" cried Kent in exasperation. "To think that I have to be laid up like an old woman with rheumatism just when— Tommy, I've got to get out of here! I want you to get busy with an ambulance—taxi—anything! 'Phone Mrs. Madden that I'm coming over right away. Get your own things moved over to the Annex; you're all the nurse I need and we'll lick them yet! I've been to the Commissioner—"

"Of Police?"

"Yes, yes. I will explain everything, once I'm home. Every resource of the police is back of us. I must talk to Fargey. I want you to go to Lamont's house—"

"I was there this morning to see what had become of you."

"You saw Lamont?"

"No. That's something I had to tell you. I found Mokra all worked up into a fine state of woollies because his master had gone out with a stranger in the middle of the night and had not returned."

The concern in Addison Kent's face deepened at the news. He scowled in silence, thinking; two flush spots burned in his cheeks.

"The showdown is coming even faster than I expected." He looked intently into his friend's eager face and spoke with an impressive earnestness that construed the seriousness of the situation. "Tommy, this is no Sunday School picnic you're heading into. It looks as if an organized gang is working, though I can't be sure of that yet. But one thing is certain—the men with whom we have to deal will stop at nothing. They are nervy and have the cunning of the devil himself. I must warn you that in mixing up with it you are taking the same risks as I am—"

"You know better than to waste time on that!" protested Traynor sternly.

"Very well. Last night I was shot from a tree in Central Park with a rifle that carried a Maxim silencer. This morning one of them actually visited me here and tried to finish the job with a hypodermic injection of quick-acting poison—"

"No!" gasped Traynor in disbelief. "Not right here?"

"The venom of a hamadryad, the deadliest snake of the East," nodded Kent. "Men bold enough to take such risks are dangerous and we'll have to be careful of every move we make."

"Was it anyone you knew?" asked Traynor in some awe.

"Yes, a man whom I had suspected already of being mixed up in this thing somewhere—a man whom you, too, have been inclined to doubt. It was our erstwhile friend, Roger Levering."

20
ADDISON KENT LETS FALL HIS MANTLE

A few hours later Addison Kent was in his own apartment, lying back with a sigh of contentment in his own bed. The very sight of the familiar things about him did him good and the success with which his removal from the hospital had been accomplished seemed to belie the dire predictions of the Superintendent. That excited official had washed his hands openly of the whole affair, refusing to accept any responsibility for the consequences.

In Kent's mind, however, nothing that could happen to himself balanced the vital necessity of an immediate talk with Traynor in order that Tommy might act intelligently in the crisis with which they were faced. Something of the seriousness of the situation the novelist managed to convey to his own physician who had been called in; nevertheless, Dr. Harvey shook his head disapprovingly at Mrs. Madden as he took his leave after giving her instructions.

As soon as Traynor had settled himself alongside the bed to listen, Kent began with the letter he had received some time ago from his friend, Superintendent Brownlee, of Scotland Yard, in regard to Alceste who was supposed to be heading for the United States after several bold thefts on the Continent. He had vanished completely about six months ago after a daring robbery in Norfolk. Scotland Yard had reason to believe he had left the country and reports from Paris were likewise negative. The police of Europe had co-operated to run him down but had failed in their efforts because they had so little information that could be relied upon regarding him; of his "works" they knew much, but of the man

153

himself they knew almost nothing at all. The cunning with which
he planned every little detail, the skill and boldness with which he
executed every manoeuvre, his elusiveness, the wide knowledge
which he seemed to possess these all pointed to the master mind
of a well educated criminal, probably of diseased mentality—a paranoiac,—the most dangerous sort of criminal whom the police have
to combat.

Superintendent Brownlee's letter to Addison Kent was entirely
outside the official warnings which had been sent through the regular police channels. In the past Kent had been of some assistance
to the Superintendent on two or three occasions in connection with
certain delicate matters that had been handled *ex-officio* and
Superintendent Brownlee was not one to overlook a trump card in
a game with an expert like this Alceste. Accordingly he had sought
privately the co-operation of Addison Kent and Kent in turn had
had a very private interview with the Commissioner. Following this
interview, steps had been taken to set a special watch upon certain famous gems throughout the country; for, if Alceste really were
on this side of the Atlantic, there was no knowing where he would
strike,—which particular bonanza had lured him.

All this, of course, was long before the events at Hillcrest.
Things had been going along quietly without the least indication
of anything unusual in justification of all the precautions that had
been taken. Then a rumor got into the papers that part of the crown
jewels of a certain bankrupt kingdom in Europe were being thrown
on the market and private word at last had reached Addison Kent
that Henry C. Radcliffe had acquired, secretly, the two most valuable items offered,—the diamond necklace and the queen's collar
of pearls.

In his pleasure over his latest purchase Henry Radcliffe had
not been able to resist the temptation of keeping the jewels beside
him for a while; he had argued, no doubt, that as nobody knew he
had them, the risk he took for a week or two was not great. That he
was indeed mistaken the tragic sequel had proven.

"There is no doubt in my mind that Alceste committed the robbery," said Kent, his brows wrinkled in a thoughtful frown. "I am

at a loss to account for the murder, though, Tommy. I am inclined
to agree with Bob Fargey that the two are separate and distinct
from one another—that is, that the robbery was planned with no
thought of murder and that if the same hand did both, the latter
was entirely fortuitous. Yet the robbery occurred in the library
downstairs, the shooting in the bedroom, and if Alceste climbed
the fire-escape to shoot into Henry Radcliffe's room, that certainly
would indicate premeditation on his part. It is not the sort of thing
his record would lead one to expect of him; therefore, I do not think
Alceste is guilty in this connection. The fact that he invariably plays
a lone hand in his depredations is another point in his favor.

"Against this argument must be pointed out the unlikelihood
of a big robbery and a murder occurring in the same house on the
same night by the hands of different individuals not connected in
any way and without each other's knowledge and co-operation. We
are therefore forced to the conclusion that for once Alceste has
broken his rule and used an accomplice,—perhaps as a lookout—
and that this accomplice did the shooting. We are at once faced
with two alternatives—either that the man who shot Radcliffe did
so because he was afraid of discovery during the robbery or that
he was actuated by some motive of his own, entirely unconnected
with the theft of the crown jewels. This uncovers a pretty wide canvas.

"We come now to a consideration of the specific. Let me reca-
pitulate for a moment. The coroner sets the hour between one and
two o'clock in the morning, nearer two. It was at two o'clock or
thereabouts that Rose Radcliffe tapped on her father's door. The
hands of your watch pointed to 1.55 when you pulled it from beneath your pillow after finding nobody in sight on the fire-escape.
You had just seen the face of a man in the moonlight, glancing in
at your window, after you had been awakened by the shot; for undoubtedly it was that which did awaken you. So that the shooting
took place within ten minutes of two. You heard Miss Radcliffe's
light knock on her father's door, heard the rustle of garments out
in the hall and likewise inside the room, followed by a smothered
cry which took you to the door just in time to see Miss Radcliffe

descending the stairs. You naturally thought it was she you had heard. You followed her down to the library and while you were there the third person inside the room had plenty of time to escape, for Miss Radcliffe found her father's door locked at that time and did not enter the room, proving that someone unknown was responsible for the little cry of terror which led you to spring from bed to investigate. Many things may have happened while you were downstairs.

"Well, then, the shooting had just taken place; yet neither Miss Radcliffe nor you noted anything amiss in the library. It is evident, therefore, that the robbery occurred later in the night and that would seem to contradict our first idea altogether and establish it as a fact that the murder and the theft of the jewels were indeed two separate events, happening in the one night in the same house. You note how we are travelling in a circle and getting nowhere when we try to reach a solution of the shooting with Alceste as the hypothesis.

"One thing, however, seems pretty clear that the shot came from the fire-escape. The carefully obliterated finger-prints on the freshly painted iron grating and rail, together with the holes in the heavy velour window drape, point definitely in that direction. The persons in the room, therefore, did not kill Mr. Radcliffe. So—"

"Persons?" interrupted Traynor, who had been listening with the closest attention.

"Yes—at least two, possibly three, different people visited that room during the night—after the shooting had taken place and each for different reasons. One of them was with Henry Radcliffe when he met his death—was having a secret interview with him which ended in a disagreement. Another entered to write the message on the shirt-cuff—"

"To—to what?"

"Write the message on the shirt-cuff," Kent repeated calmly. "The third person removed the cuff. It is possible that two entries were made by one person, but I have reason for believing that a third individual was on the scene."

"You mean—you suspect a frame-up? Against Mrs. Saint-Anton? Good heavens!" cried Traynor in amazement. "What makes you think that? You do not believe her guilty?"

"No. She was one of the three—in the excitement of her arrest she admitted being in the room, you may remember—but I do not believe she is guilty of the present charge against her. However, she has been concealing something undoubtedly and her arrest is a step in the right direction. I fancy it was she who was present when the shot was fired from outside the window and while it does not necessarily follow that she saw and recognized the man, it is possible that she may be able to throw considerable light upon the matter. She will prove to be an important factor in convicting the murderer, if he is brought to trial; for she is the only eye-witness of the crime."

"Yet Bob Fargey has worked up a strong case against her," ventured Traynor. "He has suspected this woman from the first—"

"And not without reason, Tommy. I admit that her actions have been very suspicious and I believe she may be involved. But the laws of New York look askance at mere circumstantial evidence and I have an idea that Fargey was playing for more direct evidence when he arrested this woman. In spite of his abnormal appreciation of his own abilities, Bob really is shrewder than you might think."

"I don't know, Ad; I've been at murder trials where the circumstantial evidence led straight to a conviction and a confession. While it's true that circumstances can combine in very strange ways sometimes to put a person in a false position, I don't know that this happens any oftener than the accused suffers from the direct testimony of a lying witness."

"You are voicing the belief of Jack Murray—you remember him in connection with those murder cases we both reported in Middlesex? Not only was he the greatest detective the Ontario Government ever had, but I go so far as to say that few have ever surpassed him in a practical way anywhere." Traynor nodded approval. "I had a long talk with him once about circumstantial evidence and he believed in it. He told me that he had sometimes been lucky enough to detect the liar, then the lie, and learned the whole truth simply by listening to the lie and thereby judging the truth. Few people are good liars because they don't know where to stop; they make their lies too probable. That is what has happened in the present case.

"What a minute now. You remember what the chore-boy on a certain farm once did in order to find a horse that had strayed away. After the neighborhood had been thoroughly searched without success and everybody had given it up as a bad job, 'Fat' strolled off by himself on Sunday afternoon and came back with the missing animal. When everybody wanted to know how he found the stray—for he was something of a lout and they were surprised—he said with a grin, 'Why, I just thought if I was a horse, where would I go. An' I went there, and he had!'

"So, Tommy, just imagine you are Mrs. Saint-Anton, have killed a man and have discovered that tell-tale shirt-cuff and ripped it off. What's the first thing you are going to do? Destroy it just as completely and ns fast as you know how! Isn't it? Are you going to smuggle it upstairs into your steamer trunk beside your automatic pistol and keep the both of them as treasured souvenirs to hand down to your grandchildren?"

"Hardly," laughed Traynor.

"Well, then, was her surprise that it was found in her trunk genuine or not? She cried out that she had never seen the thing before and demanded to know how it had got into her trunk. It got there because it was put there! Why was it put there if not to cast suspicion upon her? Who would do it if not the criminal himself or an accomplice?"

"What makes you think he both wrote the message and tore it off?" asked Traynor excitedly. "He could have returned to the room and discovered it. The message may be genuine and if that's the case, your argument—"

"The message is a forgery," insisted Kent. "Fargey's handwriting expert is not prepared to swear that the signature is not a clever forgery. But your own common sense should tell you that the thing has been overdone. Does a man whose life is ebbing away so rapidly that he cannot call for help or crawl to the door write a precisely worded message with a perfect signature to substantiate it or does he scrawl a fragmentary sentence with weakening fingers that make it trail out to wavering and meaningless marks?"

"But why should he tear it off instead of leaving it there for the police to find?"

"I did not say that the murderer tore it off," was the surprising reply. "He was content to leave it there for the police."

"Then, who did?"

"The third person who visited the room."

"But, hold on, Ad," objected Traynor in perplexity, "that would mean that this third person hid it in the trunk and you said the criminal himself did that."

"So he did— Wait, now! You are overlooking a lot of things that have made it very difficult to arrive at the truth of what happened. Since I saw you last I have made some fresh discoveries." Kent winced with pain as he shifted to a more comfortable position. "I have told you about the secret stairway that gave access to the room through the wardrobe panel; the luck was with me when I found that. The daub of luminous paint at the head of that stair could mean only one thing that our friend, the lady ghost, had passed that way. She is the third person who knows more of what actually occurred that night than she has seen fit to admit."

"Who? Who?"

"Give me time, Tommy. It was she who gave that muffled cry which took you out of your bed. She was inside the room then— had just discovered the body. It was she who tore off the shirt-cuff and fled—by way of the secret passage that admitted her to the trunk room on the third floor."

"And slipped the cuff into the steamer trunk?"

"No, I don't think she did. She remained in the trunk room for a little while, no doubt in great agitation and planning what was best to do. She decided at last to venture boldly downstairs in her ghostly disguise and trust to that to enable her to escape from the house unmolested. Meanwhile you had followed Miss Radcliffe to the library and were back in your own room; you came out a second time and saw the 'ghost' descending. She escaped through the garden gate while you and Levering were having your little tussle."

"Who was it?" demanded Traynor impatiently.

"The message on the cuff will help you to guess," smiled Kent, enjoying his friend's excitement. "It read, you will remember, 'Woman known as Mrs. St. Anton shot me.' Is it necessary for me to remind you that the period after the abbreviation was very faint and that the capital 'A.' was wobbly? If you read it all together as one word—"

"Mrs. Stanton!" Traynor leaned forward in his excitement. "Great Scott! the seamstress! I never thought of her!"

"It is quite clear why she removed the cuff, of course. She thought the name written there was 'Stanton'. Her actions are puzzling in the extreme. To begin with, why was she masquerading in the house as an outlandish ghost at an hour when she was supposed to be in her bed at the Stokes place away down in the park? How was it that she alone knew of the hidden passage into Henry Radcliffe's room and why was she going there? Once there, discovering the body on the floor, why did she not raise an instant alarm? Is it possible that she saw the deed committed and is shielding the murderer? Above all, if she is innocent of complicity, why did she not go to the police with the shirt-cuff? Why was she afraid that the message would incriminate her? To say the least, she has acted most foolishly."

"I should say so!" nodded Traynor. "Mrs. Stanton— Well, I'll be—! It looks bad, doesn't it? If she didn't put the shirt-cuff in that trunk, she must know who did—be in league with him, in fact; for she must have given him the thing."

"She did not give it to him. It was stolen from her on Sunday night. She took it home with her and hid it in a little Japanese box in which she kept certain personal belongings under lock and key. While she remained at Hillcrest that evening, according to police orders, a man who passed himself off as a detective, called at the Stokes bungalow, pretending to have been sent over from Hillcrest by Mrs. Stanton to inform Mrs. Stokes of her intention to remain at Hillcrest all night—and requesting that Mrs. Stokes give the Japanese box out of the bureau drawer to the bearer of the message. This man showed Mrs. Stokes his police badge; but he was no detective. He was the man who placed the shirt-cuff in the steamer trunk, beyond a doubt, proving that the interference with his plan to incriminate Mrs. Saint-Anton had been entirely unforeseen and that he was determined to carry it out at all hazards."

"How did he know who had removed the cuff?"

"He did not know—until Sunday night. I imagine he must have spent some anxious moments, wondering what had become of it. It was in the presence of a third person, unknown, on the scene that his greatest danger lay; for that reason—"

"By George!" cried Traynor, smacking fist into palm. "I have it! Levering! That was why he was so scared that night when he saw the supposed apparition. He knew it was no apparition. He only pretended to believe it was and posed as a spiritualist while all the time he was trying to find out—"

"And washing the stain of the indelible lead from the gold pencil off his fingers," supplemented Kent, "and upsetting the purple ink in the writing desk up in his room as an alibi, eh? I admit that your guess is not without seeming foundation, Tommy. As I said before, Roger Levering is mixed up in this somewhere and, judging by his attempt on my life perhaps both attempts it looks as if he was in this devil's brew up to his neck."

"Old man, you've done well with this thing," said Tommy with admiration. "How'n the mischief did you find it all out? Can you tell me how Levering—if he's the man—found out Mrs. Stanton had the cuff?"

"No, not yet. But it was Sunday night some time that he recovered it. The fact that the police had overlooked the steamer trunk in their first search and made their big find so promptly on Monday morning struck me as strange. When I questioned Hayes about it he said he had entrusted the search of the upper floor to McVey who was called off to other duties before he had quite finished the job and had given the steamer trunk very brief attention. A chance remark of Levering's before he left for the inquest—about how grateful his aunt was that her steamer trunk had been spared a clumsy mauling of its contents—had 'put a flea in his ear.'"

"Hm-hm—m! That fits in nicely," Traynor commented. "But how did you find out that Mrs. Stanton was the 'ghost'?"

"I called on Mrs. Stokes yesterday afternoon while I was out that way and had an interesting chat. I also picked up a packet of cardboard matches and learned that Mr. Bill Stokes had come home one night with a pocketful of them; each match carried the same advertisement on its flat shank and was otherwise identical with those I had found in Radcliffe's room and again on the stair of the secret passage where the daub of luminous paint had been left. It established the missing link; for there seems little reason to doubt that Mrs. Stanton put one of these packets that were lying about the Stokes place in her pocket and used the cardboard matches to find her way in the dark. If any other proof is needed that our deductions are not at fault, we find it in the fact that immediately following the inquest and preceding the arrest of Mrs. Saint-Anton for the crime, the lady vanishes."

"Vanishes!"

"She is the only one who can give evidence in favor of the accused. Tommy, Mrs. Stanton has disappeared in a manner that indicates—compulsion."

Traynor stared at him in bewilderment and passed his hand through his hair in a gesture of helplessness.

"What are we up against?" he asked in a low voice. "What is it, Ad? What does it mean?"

"It means that the man—or gang—trying to fasten this crime by false evidence upon the woman now in custody will remove every obstacle that crosses their diabolical path as completely as they have removed Mrs. Stanton and as cunningly. They made Mrs. Stanton drop a postcard to Mrs. Stokes, advising her of a visit to friends and asking her to request Miss Radcliffe to excuse Mrs. Stanton for a few days; that was the last heard of her. She had an interview with Lamont, following the inquest, and started for home immediately afterwards. Lamont tells me she has no friends in the city to visit—"

"Lamont? How does he know?" asked Traynor in surprise.

"Your worthy boss, Tommy, knows much that he refuses to reveal. I tried my best to make him talk; but he closes up like a clam. He was very much afraid that someone would see me leaving his place last night; he seemed to expect what actually happened. Now, he has disappeared and you may well ask what is the meaning of it all. That is what we have to find out. What powerful influence is at work to make everyone who knows the truth shut their lips tight together and refuse to divulge the secret while they turn pale with fright? What horror lies beneath this murder of a respectable citizen like Henry Radcliffe? That is what we must find out."

Traynor got to his feet.

"The first thing we've got to do is to find Rose!" he cried as he paced the narrow confines of the room like a caged animal. His face was anxious and he clenched his fists. "By heaven! Kent," he said through clenched teeth, "if they've dared to lay a finger on her or harm a hair of her head—!"

"Easy, old man. I'm doing my best. I don't think she is in any danger; in her case it's probably ransom they're after—that is, if it is the same gang that is responsible for the other disappearances— Ouch! confound this arm!— You've got to pick up the trail and you mustn't head into it blindfolded."

"Right now I'm as blind as a bat! In heaven's name, Ad, if you know anything, tell me! What have I got to do? Let me get busy on it!"

"It is the château!—an old feudal relic in France—which is throwing its black shadow down through the years to lie like a blot beneath this crime. What dire thing has happened there to end in the death of the master of Hillcrest I do not know. But Mrs. Stanton knows. Lamont knows. Roger Levering knows. Mrs. Saint-Anton knows. And we're going to find out in spite of bullets and hypodermic needles!"

Addison Kent's eyes were glittering with excitement. Pink spots burned in each cheek.

"Hand me the card you'll find inside the middle drawer of the desk, Tommy—the one with bits of paper pasted together upon it."

21
HIDDEN TRAILS

"Why was Henry Radcliffe killed? That is the first question which comes to the surface in connection with this case," resumed Addison Kent when he held in his hand the card for which he had asked. "The motive which leads a man to commit murder is usually more or less primitive, but it may be wrapped in mystery—as in the present instance. It is one of the first things the police look for as it quite frequently has a direct bearing upon the search for clues.

"You've heard it said, Tommy, that murder is committed for money, revenge or love; but these three subdivide into greed, ambition, inheritance, safety, jealousy, hate and so forth to the limit of the emotions. In casting about for a motive that would apply to the present crime we find absolutely nothing in Henry Radcliffe's maturer years to point the way. His life has been most exemplary— that merely of a useful citizen who has attained prominence both in financial circles and in the broader field of service to his fellows, respected by all and greatly admired by those who knew him best. We are therefore forced to fall back upon the belief that he became a victim of some 'enemy of wealth'—a 'crank'—or we must turn back many pages of the calendar to his earlier days to look for the enemy who has done this deed. Even in this direction I found nothing to give a definite clue.

"There was one event of Radcliffe's life, however, which attracts more than passing attention if only because he chose to be reticent about it—even to his own daughter. I refer to his marriage,

164

Tommy. When you told me what Miss Radcliffe had said—about her father avoiding the topic every time she asked questions about her mother—I agreed with her opinion that it was somewhat strange, even when making due allowance for the fact that Henry Radcliffe's life had been darkened by the tragedy of his wife's death in the railroad wreck, as announced in the papers at the time— In the inside pocket of my coat there, old man—hand me the wallet, will you?

"I am indebted to the *Mercury* for this particular 'squib,'" he said as he took out a clipping. "It is a fair example of the gossipy sort of filler with which the newspapers rounded out their recent reports of the arrest. Let me read it," and Traynor listened carefully to the account of the "lines of tragedy" with which Fate and the imaginative reporter had crossed the life of Henry Radcliffe. "There's no telling how much reliance can be placed in the accuracy of sensational 'copy,' as you know very well; but in this particular case the writer went to the 'morgue' for his 'dope' and the paragraph sums up briefly what appeared in the newspapers at the time of Mrs. Radcliffe's death. It sent me to the files and I read up everything I could find.

"I will ask you to note that the honeymoon of Henry Radcliffe was spent in France on the estate of Professor William Winterby; on looking him up I found that he was a Fellow of the Royal Society and a very learned man in a scientific way, being greatly interested in archegony and also in archeology, particularly the relics of the Ugro-Finnic—"

"Hold on, I'm just human, Ad! Come again. What's this 'archegony'?"

"The doctrine of the origin of life." Kent smiled faintly. "Winterby and Radcliffe had made some research trips together and were close friends. Professor Winterby was something of a recluse and it was this tendency which no doubt led him to purchase an old château in France and retire there to live, accompanied by his wife; he remained on this estate until his death a few years ago. Apparently, then that part of the newspaper accounts can be taken as true—that Henry Radcliffe and his bride spent their honeymoon, or a part of it, with the Winterbys.

"But I am getting ahead of my clock. Before I looked up Professor Winterby I had established the fact that Armaund Lamont and Mrs. Stanton had something in common—that so far as he was concerned, in fact, the attachment was deeper than mere friendship."

"What! You mean Lamont is in love with her? Aw, come off, Ad!" laughed Traynor skeptically.

"It is true, nevertheless," said Kent seriously. "When he left us on Sunday night he went straight to a secret tryst with the lady—in the summerhouse at Hillcrest. I happened to stumble on them there when I went out, looking for a quiet spot to think things over; I could not help hearing part of what was said. One remark of the woman's was so strange that I could not get it out of my head and it kept recurring because it seemed to me that it might carry some significance. She said: 'the black shadow of the château is creeping far beyond the old bridge,' and she spoke of this shadow as a thing from which she had been trying to escape. She was very much afraid. Lamont kept assuring her that she was in no danger if she guarded her tongue. Apparently she had been confiding in him to some extent and I happened along at the end of the interview. She said it was too dangerous to tell him all in that place and she agreed to see him at his office the following day.

"What it was she had on her mind you can now guess; no doubt she told him that she had something in the Japanese box at the Stokes place and she was turning to him as the only friend she could trust to guide her. We are safe in concluding that it was the shirt-cuff about which she wished to consult him; for the thought in her mind was, remember, that someone was trying to make out that she was guilty of Radcliffe's death— Get me a drink of water, Tommy."

Kent lay back on the pillows for a few moments before he continued. Traynor watched him anxiously.

"I come now to another piece of luck," Kent resumed, holding out the cardboard. Traynor took it and studied the chess notation, pasted there, frowning without understanding. "I remembered that you said Levering had received some chess instructions on the Saturday afternoon and with no other reason than curiosity I asked Thompson to see if he could find the thing among the waste paper; I had no great hopes that he would, but—there it is.

"You will recall how enthusiastic Levering pretended to be over the game of chess and how he tried to get each of us to play a game. I had no hankering for it at such a time and led him to believe I knew nothing of chess. One glance at that mixture there and I knew that Levering had been trying to discover whether it was safe for him to continue using his chess cipher."

"Did you say 'cipher'?"

"Yes. It's a message, Tommy, and an important one to us. It gave me no trouble at all. In fact, it is so simple to anyone at all familiar with chess that it was evidently never intended to be put to any greater test than a passing glance."

Simple! Scanning the thing, Traynor laughed a little and shook his head.

"He has used the text-book form of notation which places the moves of the white men above the line and the black below. It is hardly necessary to explain that a set of chessmen consists of sixteen 'white' and sixteen 'black' and that eight on each side are called 'pieces' and the remaining eight 'pawns'. The pieces consist of the 'King,' 'Queen,' two 'Bishops,' two 'Knights' and two 'Books'. The checkered board on which they are played divides into 'rows' horizontally and 'files' longitudinally, the rows designated by numbers and the files named after the piece which stands at the end of it when the game starts. It is thus possible to indicate any square on the board by setting down the initials of the piece to show the file and following these initials with the number of the row. A dash means 'moves to'; so, if we wished to indicate that the King's Knight was to be moved to the third square of the King's Bishop's file we would write it: KKt-KB[3].

"While the casual appearance of Levering's message is that of a genuine chess notation and it is set down in imitation of actual play, it would deceive only those who did not understand chess. I saw at once that it was a code message. Notice that last of all comes:

RICE GAMBIT

1. $\dfrac{\text{Q-R3}}{\text{Kt-B7}}$ 2. $\dfrac{\text{Kt-KB3}}{\text{P-KKt4}}$ 3. $\dfrac{\text{P-KR4}}{\text{P-Kt5}}$ 4. $\dfrac{\text{Kt-K5}}{\text{Kt-KB3}}$

5. $\dfrac{\text{P x Kt}}{\text{P-B6}}$ 6. $\dfrac{\text{R x B(ch)}}{\text{B-K3}}$ 7. $\dfrac{\text{Kt-Kt sq}}{\text{Kt-R6}}$ 8. $\dfrac{\text{P-K4}}{\text{P-K4}}$

9. $\dfrac{\text{B-Kt5}}{\text{Q-Kt7(ch)}}$ Black has advantage

---

1. $\dfrac{\text{K-Q3}}{\text{K-Q2}}$ 2. $\dfrac{\text{R-K sq}}{\text{Q-K2}}$ 3. $\dfrac{\text{Kt-Q2}}{\text{Q x P}}$ 4. $\dfrac{\text{Kt-Kt sq}}{\text{Kt-R6}}$

5. $\dfrac{\text{R-K sq}}{\text{Q-K2}}$ 6. $\dfrac{\text{P x Kt}}{\text{P-B6}}$ 7. $\dfrac{\text{P-Q4}}{\text{Kt-Kt5}}$ 8. $\dfrac{\text{P-K4}}{\text{P-K4}}$

9. $\dfrac{\text{Kt-Q2}}{\text{Q x P}}$ 10. $\dfrac{\text{B-Kt5}}{\text{Q-Kt7 (ch)}}$ 11. $\dfrac{\text{Q-R3}}{\text{Kt-B7}}$ 12. $\dfrac{\text{Kt-Kt sq}}{\text{Kt-R6}}$

13. $\dfrac{\text{Kt-K5}}{\text{Kt-KB3}}$ 14. $\dfrac{\text{Kt-B3}}{\text{Q-R3}}$ 15. $\dfrac{\text{Q-R3}}{\text{Kt-B7}}$ 16. $\dfrac{\text{K-Q2}}{\text{P-B8-Kt(ch)}}$

17. $\dfrac{\text{P-KR4}}{\text{P-Kt5}}$ 18. $\dfrac{\text{P-K4}}{\text{P-K4}}$ 19. $\dfrac{\text{Q-R4(ch)}}{\text{P-B3}}$ 20. $\dfrac{\text{P x P}}{\text{B-Q3}}$

21. $\dfrac{\text{Kt-Kt sq}}{\text{Kt-R6}}$ 22. $\dfrac{\text{P x Kt}}{\text{P-B6}}$ 23. $\dfrac{\text{Castles}}{\text{B x Kt}}$ 24. $\dfrac{\text{P-K4}}{\text{P-K4}}$

25. $\dfrac{\text{B-Kt3}}{\text{Q-Kt7(ch)}}$ 26. $\dfrac{\text{Q-R3}}{\text{Kt-B7}}$ 27. $\dfrac{\text{P-KR4}}{\text{P-Kt5}}$ 28. $\dfrac{\text{K-Q2}}{\text{P-B8-Kt(ch)}}$

29. $\dfrac{\text{R x B(ch)}}{\text{B-K3}}$ Black has better game

---

1. $\dfrac{\text{P x B(ch)}}{\text{K-B2}}$ 2. $\dfrac{\text{R x B(ch)}}{\text{B-K3}}$ 3. $\dfrac{\text{Kt-K5}}{\text{Kt-KB3}}$ 4. $\dfrac{\text{Kt-KB3}}{\text{P-KKt4}}$

5. $\dfrac{\text{B-Kt5}}{\text{Q-Kt7(ch)}}$ 6. $\dfrac{\text{Kt-B3}}{\text{Q-R3}}$ 7. $\dfrac{\text{2Kt}}{\text{Resigns}}$

---

1. $\dfrac{\text{K-Q3}}{\text{K-Q2}}$ 2. $\dfrac{\text{R-K sq}}{\text{Q-K2}}$ 3. $\dfrac{\text{Kt-Q2}}{\text{Q x P}}$ 4. $\dfrac{\text{P-KB4}}{\text{P x P}}$

5. $\dfrac{\text{K-Q3}}{\text{K-Q2}}$ 6. $\dfrac{\text{B-Kt5}}{\text{Q-Kt7(ch)}}$ 7. $\dfrac{\text{Q-R4(ch)}}{\text{P-B3}}$ 8. $\dfrac{\text{K-Q3}}{\text{K-Q2}}$

9. $\dfrac{\text{P-K4}}{\text{P-K4}}$ 10. $\dfrac{\text{R-K sq}}{\text{Q-K2}}$ 11. $\dfrac{\text{B-Kt5}}{\text{Q-Kt7(ch)}}$ 12. $\dfrac{\text{Castles}}{\text{B x Kt}}$

13. $\dfrac{\text{P-Q4}}{\text{Kt--Kt5}}$ 14. $\dfrac{\text{Kt-Kt sq}}{\text{Kt-R6}}$ 15. $\dfrac{\text{P-K4}}{\text{P-K4}}$ 16. $\dfrac{\text{P x Kt}}{\text{P-B6}}$

17. $\dfrac{\text{Kt-Kt sq}}{\text{Kt-R6}}$ 18. $\dfrac{\text{P-K4}}{\text{P-K4}}$ 19. $\dfrac{\text{Q-R4(ch)}}{\text{P-B3}}$ 20. $\dfrac{\text{P x P}}{\text{B-Q3}}$

21. $\dfrac{\text{P-KR4}}{\text{P-Kt5}}$ 22. $\dfrac{\text{11-EB}}{\text{6-97}}$ White mates in three moves

$\frac{11\text{-EB}}{6\text{-}97}$ which is different from the rest of it. I remembered you telling me that you had looked at the book which Levering left in the
library at the time he interrupted you and Mr. Radcliffe and that it
was Volume 6 of the 11th edition of the Encyclopaedia Britannica;
I had only to turn to page 97 to find what I wanted under 'Rice
Gambit.'

"'Gambit' is a chess term to denote a certain kind of opening
play and in the encyclopaedia's article on chess were given particulars of a game between Professor Isaac L. Rice, of New York,
and Major Hanham. The key to the cipher was staring me in the
face; for all that the sender of the message had done was to use the
first twenty-six moves in the Rice Gambit notation in the encyclopaedia to denote the twenty-six letters of the alphabet. The nu-
merals and the words written out— 'Black has advantage,' etc. were
inserted to make it look like a chess notation to the uninitiated.
The message resolved at once. You will see here how it worked out."

Traynor took the sheet of paper on which Kent had written
down the result as follows:

1-o 2-c 3-d 4-e 5-s 6-p 7-r 8-a 9-t

1-w 2-i 3-1 4-r 5-i 6-s 7-k 8-a 9-1 10-t 11-o 12-r 13-e 14-m 15-o 16-
v 17-d 18-a 19-n 20-g 21-r 22-s 23-h 24-a 25-t 26-o 27-d 28-v 29p

1-x 2-p 3-e 4-c 5-t 6-m 2Kt

1-w 2-i 3-1 4-b 5-w 6-a 7-t 8-n 9-w 10-i 11-t 12-h 13-k 14-r 15-a 16-
s 17-r 18-a 19-n 20-g 21-d

ocdesprat   oc desprat

wilriskaltoreinovdangrshatodvp   wil risk al to remov dangr
                                 shato dvp

xpectm2Kt   xpect m 2Kt

wilbwatnwithkrasrangd   wil b watn with kr as rangd

O. C. desperate. Will risk all to remove danger of château d.v.p.
Expect him to-night. Will be waiting with car as arranged.

"As a concealed message you see how crude it was," said Kent.
"The use of the initials of the Knight with the figure 2 before it to
represent 'tonight' is childlike in its simplicity. The only thing that
puzzled me was the 'dvp' following the word 'château'. I was tremendously interested and it occurred to me that the letters might
stand for the name of some château in France. I had just been reading up about Professor Winterby and remembered that the estate
he had purchased was the Château des Hêtres. I went to the library
and finally, found a description of this old castle of the beeches,
discovering that close to it was another old relic of feudal times—
the Château du Vieux Pont, which translates into the Château of
The Old Bridge. The connection was established; for the strange
remark of Mrs. Stanton to Lamont in the summerhouse on Sunday
night was: 'the black shadow of the château is creeping far beyond
the old bridge' and it was to visit Winterby in the neighborhood of
the Château du Vieux Pont that Henry Radcliffe and his bride—"
    "Good heavens!" breathed Traynor, staring, his lips parted.
    "—went on their honeymoon. We are safe in taking it for granted
that 'd.v.p.' stands for 'du Vieux Pont' and that 'O.C.' are the initials of the man who killed Henry Radcliffe!
    "No, don't interrupt. Let me finish. The questions you would
ask I have asked myself a dozen times and some of them remain
unanswered. Who is 'O.C.'? Why was he desperate—so desperate
that he was prepared to risk everything in order to remove the danger that threatened from this Château du Vieux Pont? What danger? Danger to whom? What was Henry Radcliffe's connection with
this danger? Was it he himself who was the menace? If so, what
had happened to make him so? Apparently it was only in his death
that safety for 'O.C.' lay. Where did Levering come in? Who sent
him the message? Why was Mrs. Stanton likewise in danger from

the château and what has so terrified Armaund Lamont that he has not slept for several nights? Why have they both been spirited away and where are they now? And finally, where is Miss Radcliffe?

"The message proves Levering's complicity beyond a doubt and makes three that we know of who were concerned in the crime— 'O.C.,' Levering and the third person who wrote the cipher message. It was a great mistake of the police to let Levering go; no doubt Fargey had him shadowed and thought he could lay hands on him at the hotel where Levering registered, but he underestimated his man. I am free to admit that the beggar's resourcefulness and daring are greater than I had thought possible and my own lack of caution has almost cost me my life."

"You are sure it was Levering who attacked you? How do you know that?" asked Traynor.

"By his eyes. It is the one thing to look for in penetrating disguise because it is the one thing that cannot be changed. That is why Roger Levering wore those glasses and took care that he was never without them—because his eyes were uncommon, a very light blue, small and of a particular coldness. They were the cruelest, most dispassionately calculating eyes I ever looked into—eyes almost inhumanly soulless. I got a good look at them up in his room when I—accidentally—knocked off his glasses. I recognized those light blue eyes in the man who visited me at the hospital; there was no mistaking them. The man was Roger Levering.

"Having established Levering's status as that of a criminal by intent at least, the question arises as to where his so-called aunt stands in relation to the Hillcrest murder. That she is involved in it seems altogether probable. What was there between her and Henry Radcliffe? What were they quarrelling about at 2 o'clock in the morning in his room? If she was a member of the gang, why was Levering—for it must have been he—so anxious to fasten the crime upon her that he took the risk of faking evidence against her? What had she done to arouse his displeasure—or failed to do? This is something which we cannot hope to answer at present.

"Similarly, we cannot yet find an answer to the identity of 'O.C.' or the motive which actuated him. Neither do we know what it was

that happened at the Château du Vieux Pont to place Henry Radcliffe's life in danger from these men. Also we are unable to say
whether one of the three is Alceste or whether the theft of the jewels is a thing apart. However, the fact that the pearls which were
missed when the safe was robbed first were gathered in so promptly
the following night seems to point to the presence of the thief
in the house still; I am inclined to think it is not improbable that
Levering is the very gentleman we are after."

"Alceste himself?"

"Yes. He seems to have all the qualifications. At best we can
only guess at these things. The fact that the man who wrote the
message was to be waiting with a car as arranged may indicate provision of a 'get-away' for 'O.C.' or for the transfer of the 'bundle' to
a safe place.

"There remain to be accounted for the strange actions of Mrs.
Stanton and Armaund Lamont. I have given very close thought to
their connection with events and can reach a solution of it upon
one hypothesis only. It is so strange as to be startling; but it would
account for Mrs. Stanton's fear that the evidence of the shirt-cuff
might be believed against her by the authorities; also for Lamont's
refusal to reveal what he knows; and again, for the authorship of
those typewritten messages received by Miss Radcliffe from some
unknown well-wisher. If you look at that newspaper clipping again
you will note that the body from the train wreck identified as that
of Mrs. Radcliffe was—decapitated."

Traynor gave an ejaculation.

"You don't mean—?"

"Tommy, I believe that Henry Radcliffe's wife is still alive! Fur-
thermore, I believe that Mrs. Stanton is the lady herself—Rose
Radcliffe's mother!"

Speechless, Traynor stared at Addison Kent. In the silence of
the moment the telephone in the adjoining room trilled loud and
insistent summons.

22
CAPTURE

Much can happen in a short space of time. Much did happen in the three days that followed Addison Kent's removal from the hospital to his own apartment. Thompson's voice on the telephone had been dominated by urgency; but Tommy Traynor had needed no importunity of the butler's nor the excited commands of the novelist to send him speeding to Thompson's assistance when he was likewise flying to the rescue of Rose Radcliffe. Thompson had verified the fact that the young and beautiful heiress had been met at Woodland Cove by a powerful touring-car and whisked away into the labyrinth of automobile roads that veined the interior of Suffolk County, Long Island. With all the cunning of a born sleuth Thompson had secured an excellent description of the car and its occupants and had managed to trace it. Traynor joined him in the hunt; then on the fourth morning, just as they found the trail nearing an end, they had encountered not the missing girl alone but also Armaund Lamont and Mrs. Stanton, making for the nearest railroad point in a hired auto.

A strange story it was the missing trio had to tell—of an isolated place to which each had been taken separately, of bandages tied about their heads in order that they might not be able to take notice of landmarks as they approached, of comfortable quarters and good food and courteous treatment but nonetheless vigilant guard. Judging by its equipment, the place was some sort of private sanitarium. There each had found the other two; no effort had been made to keep them apart, once they were on the premises, but they had been denied any outside communication whatever. Then, quite unexpectedly, on the fourth morning they were ordered out into the same car in which they had arrived and with the side curtains buttoned tight and eyes once more bandaged they had been driven for several miles and abruptly set down in the middle of the road and left to their own resources after promises had been extracted from each that they would go straight home as fast as they could get there.

But much had happened in those few days—much! Mrs. Stanton had been approached as she left the office of Armaund Lamont by one who showed her the official shield of a plainclothes man; he stated that he had been sent from Headquarters to request her presence there immediately and he had hailed a taxi. But they had not gone to police headquarters; they had gone to the waterfront where they boarded a tug. She was told that no harm would befall her if she did exactly as she was instructed; she had no means of knowing where they went for she was kept in the tiny cabin out of sight and personally guarded by her captor. They landed somewhere on the north shore of Long Island and transferred to the automobile. At the end of the journey she had been forced to write the postcard to Mrs. Stokes.

Rose had been met at the station by a man in the livery of the Struthers' chauffeur who said he had instructions to take her to Miss Struthers who was waiting at a summer hotel some miles away, having been taken suddenly ill. Her suspicions had not been aroused until they turned off the main road and had gone for some distance; then the driver had coolly informed her of the facts and put it up to her common sense to decide whether she would go peaceably and without harm or whether he would use force. He told her that he was taking her to the lady who had written her the messages signed "One Who Wishes You Well" and no harm was intended. He had ended by informing her, to her utter amazement, that the writer of the messages was her mother who was alive and well. Scarcely knowing what to believe, but having no choice in the matter anyway, she had decided to make the best of it. When the bandage with which she had been blindfolded upon nearing their destination had been removed she found herself in a large, airy room alone—with Mrs. Stanton. In the astonishment of that meeting, their joy at seeing each other kindled anew the strange bond of affection which many times they had sensed in one another. The hour that followed was an hour of confession and wonder—wonder, growing to belief, to pity, to tender emotion—an hour of infinite happiness.

Then had come the revelation of a purpose behind their forced "visit." In an interview alone with Mrs. Stanton—or Mrs. Radcliffe, as she may be called—the suave, immaculate "Doctor" who seemed to be in charge of the establishment informed her that he expected Mr. Armaund Lamont to join their little "house party" shortly. In order that Mr. Lamont might accept the invitation in the right spirit he deemed it advisable for Mrs. Stanton to write a little letter which he would dictate. She had demurred at first until he calmly warned her that refusal to do as he said would endanger not herself alone but her daughter as well. At his dictation, therefore, she had penned an urgent note to Armaund Lamont, advising him that she was with Rose and that both of them were in danger. The letter implored him, if he still loved her and had any regard for his own safety, to do exactly as the bearer of the note directed and on no account to attempt communication with the police. If he placed himself completely in the hands of the bearer of the message, everything would come to a happy conclusion and not all the money in the world nor all the precious stones in the world could be as important as life and hope.

That had been the gist of it. In great apprehension she had signed it and heard the car depart. What did it mean? She was not long left in doubt; for the car returned just before daybreak, bringing the jeweler in a state of collapse—and the choicest gems from his vaults in a leather travelling bag! His captor had taken fiendish delight in playing upon his fears and had recounted horrible tales of murder as they rode the wooded highways in the dark, finishing the torture with the shocking news of Addison Kent's death; with evident gusto his informant had described in detail the terrible throes which mark the end of those who die by the particular snake-poison with which in some mysterious manner Kent had been inoculated.

"They may take the jewels and escape, yes," whispered Lamont in breathless relation of his adventures to the two women, "but so terrible a thing as that they cannot—how is it in the slang?—cannot gallop off with it!"

Addison Kent, however, was very much alive when Tommy Traynor telephoned his great news that everybody was returning, safe and sound. The author's superb physique and three days of solid rest had worked recuperative wonders. He was out of bed, perforce with one sleeve empty; but the bandaged arm did not prevent him getting about. As arranged with Traynor over the 'phone, he motored out to Hillcrest in company with J. K. Yelland, of Fraser & Yelland, the young lawyer upon whom had devolved the formality of defending Mrs. Saint-Anton. Since her arrest his client had sunk into a despondency from which it had been impossible to arouse her; she seemed to have given up all hope, refused to talk and wished only to be left alone. Something in Kent's manner as they discussed the case en route, however, awakened the lawyer's flagging interest and when he learned that Mrs. Radcliffe was alive and had an important statement to make his surprise and eagerness left nothing to be desired.

It was a cheerful group who awaited them in the library at Hillcrest. None of the three principals were experiencing any ill effects from their adventure and the revelation of Mrs. Stanton's identity was too wonderful for depression; its effect upon Rose was like the sudden burst of sunshine through a rift in sombre clouds and the others shared her joy. Even the loss of a fortune in precious gems, stolen in such a simple and audacious manner, could not dampen the spirits of Mr. Armaund Lamont who was once more his confident, well-groomed self with a jaunty rosebud in his coat lapel. *Pouf!* What were a few gems compared to the jewel of happiness at the end of a season of sorrow and anxiety? Less than nothing! Besides, those thieves had not escaped yet with their loot; for Thompson had asked permission to remain behind to follow up his clues and the police were hot on the trail. *Parbleu!* Assuredly.

As a preliminary to more intelligent action, Mrs. Radcliffe was eager to tell her story to Addison Kent and the lawyer. It was a trying ordeal for her, but she faced it bravely. And as that terrible tale of the black night which had ruined her life unfolded behind locked doors, the listening group fell silent. In her simple language as the scenes of that drama followed one by one like pictures upon a screen, the late afternoon shadows lengthened across the sward and crept like ghosts into the room; the dark oak panellings of the great library seemed to fade out while those who listened were transported on the wings of imagination to other surroundings in another year.

In the Convent of St. Ursula in the City of Montreal in the great Canadian province, Quebec, had grown to beautiful young womanhood little Yvonne Prefontaine. She had known no other home; for she was an orphan, left to the guardianship of an aged parish priest who planned for her a life of consecration. But although reared behind the sheltering convent walls, there was that within her which yearned for the freedom of worldliness with the irrepressible spirits of youth. There were times when the call of the musical bells in the old stone belfry found no response in her heart and when the sylvan quiet and the feeding of doves and all the peaceful routine of her life palled upon her to an extent little dreamed by the good Sisters in whose care she dwelt.

She had just celebrated her eighteenth birthday when what promised to be the great event of her life occurred. Past the Convent of St. Ursula one day Fate trended the footsteps of the young, impetuous and handsome Harry Radcliffe, in Montreal on a business trip. The early harvest apples were ripening in the gnarly old orchard; it was against orders for Yvonne to climb, but that was what she had done and it was while perched on the convent wall, munching an apple from a limb that hung across it, that young Radcliffe caught sight of her roguish eyes and piquant beauty. Being nothing if not bold, he had essayed acquaintance and the two had sat there for some time, laughing and chatting about nothing at, all. So elated by this charming adventure was Yvonne that she promised to meet him there again the following day at the same hour.

It was but the first of many such meetings. For nearly two weeks Harry Radcliffe wooed her with all the fervor of complete captivation. To the young and impressionable girl his stories of his travels were like the pages of a wonderful book of adventure. He was about to leave on a trip to France and he urged her to marry him quietly and accompany him abroad. Swept off her feet by his ardor and by the glittering temptation of a trip across the ocean, the petite Yvonne agreed at last to go to him over the convent wall.

The appointed night arrived at last and without incident she stole from her room and down through the moon-mottled orchard. He was waiting, as promised, and they were married an hour later in the home of a Protestant clergyman. Their boat sailed that same night and not a trace of Yvonne Prefontaine was left behind except the tear-stained inadequate little note which she had addressed to the Mother Superior, saying she was going away of her own accord and leaving instructions as to the disposition of her pets—a kitten, a tame crow and a young rabbit.

It was a deliriously happy time, the three weeks that followed. His young bride's sweet face and charming grace had completely turned Henry Radcliffe's head. To the convent-bred girl everything she saw, every casual shipboard acquaintance, attracted her notice; in her unsophistication all people were kind and good. Her naiveté and great beauty in turn awakened interest in those around her and it was not long before she learned that her headstrong and quick-tempered young husband was abnormally jealous by nature. He took to lecturing upon the wickedness of men and the devious ways of the world with such zeal that she rather resented the close watch he kept upon her at all times and once or twice she teased him with harmless flirtations just to see the masterly manner in which he asserted his prerogative and sent her admirers flying and took her to task; for she had grown to love him dearly and she liked to tease him for the joy of "making it all up" afterwards.

Once away from the restricted limits of shipboard, however, she dropped these tactics and settled down to enjoy to the fullest the wonderful honeymoon jaunts which he planned. They visited many beautiful spots in that beautiful old country of France and they wound up at last with a visit to Radcliffe's old friend, Professor William Winterby, who with his wife and a few old servants lived in the ancient Château des Hêtres in the midst of wildwood solitude. The Winterbys were very much surprised to learn of the marriage and, Yvonne fancied, were inclined at first to look at her askance; when they were alone Mrs. Winterby asked her many questions about her parents which she was unable to answer. But they were hospitable enough and it was a happy visit.

A happy visit! Without warning came that night of terror, blotting all the light from her life as black thunderclouds blot out the sun—as the ruthless lightning rives the innocent tree in its path.

Yvonne had been warned by her husband to keep away from the other old château which was in the neighborhood. He gave no reason for this mandate except that she might get lost if she wandered off the Winterby estate. He did not tell her that the Château du Vieux Pont had been leased by the Countess Marinelli, a woman who was notorious in every capital of Europe and noted for many things of doubtful savor. She only knew that many guests had come flocking down from Paris for a house party at the neighboring château and that there was much laughter and gayety; but she had no intention of seeking to join them in their frivolities.

As she wandered alone in the woodland park behind the Château des Hêtres, picking flowers one morning, she was quite startled, therefore, to come suddenly face to face with a smiling young man of handsome carriage and fascinating manners. He gazed at the beautiful vision of her in bold delight. She did not know that the "gentlemen" in the train of the Countess Marinelli were roués, underworld characters and political spies; but her intuition warned her not to linger in conversation with this stranger, who only laughed when she hastened away.

That night the week of roystering at the Château du Vieux Pont was to be capped by a grand *bal au masque*. In the afternoon Henry Radcliffe had taken the dog-cart and gone away on a leisurely message of some sort for Professor Winterby that took him far along the high road to Epinay. As he had not returned by dusk, but was expected momentarily, Yvonne ventured to stroll a little way down the road in order to ride back with him. It was a little lark of her own conception—to surprise him like this—and she said nothing of her intention to Mrs. Winterby or the *concierge* at the gate.

She did not go far—only around the turn in the road at the end of the estate. She was on the point of retracing her steps when to her surprise she saw hurrying towards her the tall, handsome young gentleman whom she had encountered accidentally in the wood that very morning. She half turned to run, but he held up his hand in an urgent gesture; she saw then that he was panting for breath as if he had been running and he seemed to be too excited to speak as he stood for a moment, mopping his forehead with a silk kerchief.

Then hurriedly he informed her that there had been an accident—yes, her husband!—and he had volunteered to run on and give the alarm at the Château des Hêtres. He told her that Mr. Radcliffe had been pretty badly hurt in a runaway and was calling for her; they had carried him into the inn at the crossroads. Without giving her time to think, he hurried her along the road in the direction of the inn and she, forgetting everything in the wild anxiety of the moment, went with him. Ah, if only she had insisted upon running back to the château gate to notify the *concierge* before going to her husband's aid!

Nearly opposite the neighboring château two men suddenly appeared from a path that came out of the woods to the road. All three set upon her so unexpectedly that she had no time to cry out before a heavy cloak was thrown over her head. Her screams thus muffled, she was carried off she knew not where; for in her mad struggles and hysteria she fainted.

When at last she came to her senses she found herself alone in a bare-walled room of the Château du Vieux Pont—a tower room with no window or opening of any kind—in a deserted wing of the massive feudal castle.

She ran to the heavy oaken door and found it locked. She pounded upon it with little futile fists until they were bruised. She called for help at the topmost pitch of her voice. But her cries were utterly swallowed by the great thickness of the stone walls.

23
LA NUIT NOIRE

The hours crept by. She would have been in the dark but for a lone taper in a niche of the wall. She knew she would be missed and a search for her started, but recalled with dismay that none had seen her leave the Château des Hêtres and there was no way of tracing her. She pictured her husband's return; he would be frantic with alarm and would insist upon arousing the entire household to an all-night search. He would come here to the Château du Vieux Pont and they would tell him that they had not seen her. The hopelessness of her position grew more and more manifest.

Calling for help until she was exhausted, Yvonne huddled down at last in a sobbing, forlorn little heap. Then from some hidden source within her was born a certain desperate courage and cunning. She would fight! She would use a woman's weapons and perhaps the way would open. As time dragged and none came near her the hope that she would escape brought her strange calm. She knelt in prayer for guidance.

It was almost midnight when a key grated in the lock and her captor entered with a queer ancient-looking lantern in which a candle burned. It evidently went with his costume; his pink mask was shoved up on his forehead and he grinned cheerfully as he set the lantern on the floor and turned to relock the door.

Like a flash she darted across the room and snatched the key from his grasp. He put his back against the door, ogling her, assuring her with exaggerated politeness that he appreciated her spirit. It added zest to beauty, did it not?

Still smirking at her, he advanced until she had retreated to the farther wall. Then as she tried to dodge past him for the door he caught her by the wrist with strong fingers and drew her toward him slowly and irresistibly by sheer strength until he pulled her other arm within reach. He twisted her arms until she cried out and the key fell from her nerveless fingers. He picked it up, locked the door and put the key in his pocket, still smilingly unruffled.

She knew then that it was useless to match her strength against his and she suddenly began to laugh. She made a gesture of helplessness and scolded him for twisting her arms. He apologized most humbly and welcomed her change of attitude eagerly. She pleaded with him to let her go but he shook his head. He had been drinking, but not enough to lose his cunning. She tried wheedling him into unlocking the door without success. Then she learned that the big masked ball was in full swing down below and that the crowd were having a high old time in the banqueting hall.

"Oh," she cried, clapping her hands, "take me down and show me, won't you please? I have never seen a big party like that and I think you are very selfish if you keep me out of all the fun. Besides, I have had nothing to eat and I am very hungry, and—and nothing to drink," she added in desperation.

Anything were better than her present situation. There was at least a chance of escape there; here there was none.

"Will you dance for the ladies and gentlemen if I take you down there?" he asked at last.

She promised that she would. She saw that he hesitated, saw him waver, and she urged along the idea eagerly. It seemed to appeal to him; for he suddenly slapped his leg and chuckled as he glanced down at his costume, improvised to go with the ancient lantern and pass for that of an old-time linksboy.

"But you have no costume and you cannot dance properly, dressed like that. Dancing girls don't need clothes," he laughed gleefully.

She tried to avoid him, but he grabbed at her gown and ripped it from her shoulders. She cried out in anger and slapped his flushed face, even bit and scratched as he began to disrobe her, laughing boisterously at the joke of it. Frantically she told him that she would not dance at all if he did not let her dance as she wished. If what she had read were true, most dancers did their own disrobing—as they danced—did they not?

It was an inspired argument. He desisted at once. With a chuckle he felt for the key and unlocked the door. Together they descended the winding stair, he gripping her arm painfully to make sure of his prize. Together they passed through echoing corridors, musty with age and decay, until at last they came within sight of the great central stone staircase and within sound of revelry from the banquetting hall.

She shrank back, struggling madly to escape, but he forced her over the flagstones, through a small anteroom and the whole roystering midnight carousal burst upon her horrified gaze. She had pleaded with him for a mask to wear and he laughingly had ripped the flounce from her petticoat and poked two holes through it for her eyes and bound it around her head. On the stroke of midnight all masks would have to come off; it was the rule of the night, he said.

Above the din of their noisy welcome from that inebriated company she heard as from a distance her captor's loud voice, announcing that Mademoiselle Wildcat, caught alive in the forest, would dance for them—and take off the rest of her clothes herself! Drunken shouts and laughter greeted this unexpected novelty on the program. The Countess was celebrated for her delightful surprises, *n'est-ce pas? Vive la Comptess!*

A space was quickly cleared in the centre of the long table and, frightened and trembling, the mortified little girl from the Convent of St. Ursula was forced forward and lifted upon it. Her terrified glances had not been idle for a moment; but in none of the faces which she scanned could she find a single look of sympathy to which she could appeal. Through the holes in the array of masks looked only eyes which were evil or which were dulled by wine.

So she danced to please them, to gain time, while in agony of soul she tried to figure out some way of escape from her awful predicament. She danced on, planning, locating the doors and windows, weighing her chances of success by a sudden leap from the table for liberty and honor. Someone had twined a vine from the table decorations about her. So she danced, in what clothes were left to her, her white shoulders gleaming in the light from hundreds of candles, her bare knees flashing.

Suddenly she paused in dismay as a gong sounded the midnight hour. With one accord hands went to the masks. Panic-stricken, she stood, she alone remaining covered. A howl of protest arose. The nearest cavalier leaped to the table beside her and tore away her impromptu mask; he fell back with a gasp at the beauty of her.

Just then came a great commotion at the door and bursting in upon that ribald scene like one demented Yvonne saw—Henry Radcliffe, followed by the staid Professor William Winterby. For one long moment husband and wife stared at each other in disbelief. Then with a great cry of joy and relief Yvonne leapt off the table and ran towards him, sobbing hysterically.

But with an oath he flung her from him to the floor. His face was black with passion. He hid his eyes on his arm, turned on his heel, fled out into the night with an exclamation of horror.

"Harry! Harry!"

There was but a moment to act in the confusion of the interruption and she seized it, running from the room at top speed to overtake Henry Radcliffe. But he had dashed out of the château with the dumfounded Winterby after him and even as she ran down the corridor she heard the massive outer door slam with ironbound finality.

She could not open it! The sound of pursuit was close at hand. She darted for the huge stone staircase that descended into the hallway and had just time to creep out of sight; trembling and heartsick, into at dark corner beneath it. Here she cowered while running feet passed her on all sides. Laughter and shouts arose in the melee of the pursuit about the grounds.

Slowly the company straggled back to the feasting. Long after comparative silence had fallen upon the passageway little Yvonne

Prefontaine still crouched in her retreat, afraid to venture forth. Then, just as she was about to pluck up courage to try for the outer door again or seek some other exit, she heard angry voices approaching and above them the protesting accents of a woman.

"Gentlemen, please! If it is that you must fight, why not with your fists—like the canaille, *n'est-ce pas?* Or with your fencing foils—like vagabond players? Truly, it is but pretence, my brave gentlemen, *n'est-ce pas?* Surely you do not intend to fight over me as fought the cavaliers over their ladies—perhaps in these very halls! *Voila!* the swords! *Mon dieu!* they mean it!" gasped the woman; but there was a note of exultation in the tone that belied the hollow words she had spoken.

The frightened little girl from the far-off Province of Quebec shrank in fresh terror at the low tense passion in the masculine voices, their muttered satisfaction, the rush of the men's feet as they ran to snatch from the wall the glittering rapiers crossed there—rapiers to which the woman so artfully had directed their attention. Ancient arms hung upon those walls—broadswords and battleaxes of bye-gone days, steel armour, helmets and bucklers, rusty with age and neglect; but there was no rust upon the two rapiers, the blades of which glittered wickedly in the candlelight of the candelabrum which the woman held high above her head. It was as if they had been placed there for this very occasion.

Curiosity got the better of Yvonne. She peered out upon the strange scene from her hiding-place with bated breath. One of the gentlemen was dressed in an early sixteenth-century costume with flaring-topped leather boots and large spurs, a wide hat with a red plume and a great wig of black curls which fell to his shoulders to match the swaggering false moustache upon his lip, just below his black mask. The other was in a red brocaded coat, knickerbockers and white silk stockings of the seventeenth mid-century fashion with powdered periwig tied behind with a ribbon.

It was like a play to see them cross rapiers. There was a vicious-ness in the hiss of the steel blades, however, and a grim earnest-ness in the thrust and parry that bespoke deadly determination;

those sharp, shining blades in the hands of these practised swords-
men—for each apparently was familiar with the weapon—held infinite possibilities of tragedy.

The Countess Marinelli—for it was she—stood on the stone
steps of the descending stair, one white bejewelled hand gripping
the stone balustrade, the other holding high the candlestick from
which came uncertain, flickering light that cast gaunt, elongated
shadows on the walls.

The younger of the two men, he of the powdered periwig, was
fighting with wonderful aggression. He pressed his opponent without permitting a breathing space. Even the inexperienced Yvonne
saw that the cavalier was tiring. He retreated slowly to the bottom
step of the stairway, beating off the flashing menace of the other's
blade with remarkable skill but giving ground steadily.

The end came swiftly. Yvonne saw the Countess Marinelli with
catlike tread step noiselessly down behind the man who was so
hard pressed. At a critical moment in the lightning play of the rapiers the frightened watcher saw the woman give a sudden push
against the broad back. Thrown off his balance, the cavalier fell
forward just as the thrusting blade of his adversary came on the
lunge. The sharp point of it came through the man's back. He
toppled in a heap.

"*Mon dieu!* What have you done? Ah, *mon dieu!*" moaned the
Countess.

In the fall of the body the wig of black curls had come away,
revealing the gray hair beneath. The younger man, completely sobered by what had happened, bent down and removed the mask
that hid the features of the dead man. With a strange choking cry
he leaped back, the whites of his eyes showing in the surprise and
agitation of that moment of recognition. He threw the rapier from
him in abhorrence; it clattered and slid on the flat paving-stones.
He leaned weakly against the staircase, his head buried for a moment in an agony of remorse.

Then he straightened abruptly. His face looked terrible in the
candlelight as he stepped towards the Countess Marinelli who
watched him, fascinated by his pointing finger.

"What have *you* done, you evil one?" he cried hoarsely. "Why did you not tell me it was my father with whom I was quarrelling—my own father?" His face grew dark with rage and at that she smiled at him, calculating him with cold assurance.

"And what does Monsieur O'Carrol intend to do now?" she demanded. "The Law does not recognize affairs of honor like this, monsieur. The Law to-day calls it murder. Two gentlemen quarrel over a lady's favor; they insult one another and fight; one dies and the Law calls it murder and seeks a life for a life. What are you going to do, I ask you? Perhaps the matter may be hushed up—if the young Monsieur Dermod O'Carrol will do as I say. Yes? Monsieur knows how to be discreet, does he not?"

But the young man recoiled from the woman as from a loathsome thing and with an inarticulate cry—fled—fled to the sound of the Countess Marinelli's low, mocking laugh in the empty corridor behind him.

So badly frightened by what she had witnessed that she felt faint, little Yvonne Prefontaine at length was able to venture out from her hiding-place and make her way down a side passage at the end of which she found a small door. To her immense relief it opened on a courtyard with a great gate through which she sped like a shadow—out, out and away into the perfumed air of God's peaceful summer night.

From that towering bulk of the Château du Vieux Pont she ran as from a place accursed.

24
A BLANK WALL

Straight for the Château des Hêtres she flew and it was only at the very gates of the Winterby estate that she realized her appearance. She could not go in to them that way. She must first awaken the wife of the *aged* concierge and get the good woman to lend her a cloak. With this about her she hurried on, pressed hastily past the servant who opened the door and came upon the group by the fire-place; for the events of the night had upset the routine of the household completely and they were not yet abed.

At sight of her standing there in the doorway Henry Radcliffe sprang from his chair, a black frown upon his face, pallid and worn with the mental suffering through which he was passing. He pointed imperiously to the staircase and told her in a voice which was cold and even and determined to go to her room and pack her belongings; in the morning she would be driven to the train.

He refused to listen to her pleadings at first; but at last she fell on her knees before him and with tears rolling down her cheeks she swore that she could explain everything if he would only listen. So he laughed skeptically—ah, such a laugh!—and listened. Panic grew upon her as she realized how unsatisfactory that story sounded in the bald telling and that the faces of her audience remained unmoved. They did not believe her!

Her husband told her so bluntly at last. All his jealous nature had arisen to a cold fury that crowded out his reason; his better instincts and his judgment were alike smothered in rage and bitter humiliation. She had been seen by one of the servants, talking to a stranger from that nest of iniquity—the Château da Vieux Pont—talking to him that very morning! She could not make him believe that the whole thing had not been arranged in order that she might have her gay fling—not if she knelt there for a hundred years! If what she said were true, why had she not at once notified the *concierge* of the alleged accident? She was but a little way from the gate, according to her story; yet she went off with this "total stranger" of hers as if she had known him all her life! Bah! He was through with her and never wanted to see her again. She could take the return ticket to where she came from. In the morning she must leave that roof whose hospitality she had insulted.

Heart-brokenly she turned to the Winterbys; but they stood like ice before her entreaties. To people who were snobs at heart and had secretly resented Radcliffe's choice, the evidence of her guilt appeared too damning. "Blood will tell," they had whispered not half an hour ago. "Blood will tell," Henry Radcliffe echoed from the depths to which his injured pride had sunk.

Then to little Yvonne Prefontaine who had never known her parents came a dignity of her own. She ceased her abasement before them and gazed at them with pity. Her voice did not falter as she bade her husband goodbye; something seemed to have snapped within her. She refused to accept the boat passage back to Quebec. The early morning train carried her to Paris.

She had a vague idea of seeking work to earn her passage-money home, knowing that it would take months. She was a little stranger in a strange land and but for the fact that the good God had raised a friend in her extremity there was no telling what might have become of her. Attracted by the pathos and beauty of her face as she stood hesitating in the railway depot, a young man approached and after much hesitation ventured to ask if there was any service he could perform for her. With his help she found her way to a temporary refuge in a respectable boarding-house and finally secured employment in a millinery shop.

The young man who had thus befriended her was named Armaund Lamont, connected at that time with a Paris jewelry establishment. The acquaintance between them ripened and when he had learned part of her story he took her home one day to visit his aged mother. To her sympathetic ears the heartbroken young woman confided her whole story.

When the time approached that her baby was to be born Mrs. Lamont found shelter for her with the Gray Nuns and from there she obtained employment as a governess. She heard nothing from Henry Radcliffe until the little baby girl was two years old; he had not acknowledged her letter, advising of the little one's birth, but one day a notary called upon her and advised her that her husband desired the child to be with him. Knowing that it meant education and greater advantages than she could hope to provide, Yvonne let the child go. The unfortunate woman found it hard to give up her baby; but she steeled herself to start life anew and try to forget.

She accepted a position as governess in an English family and several years passed by. In time she returned to Quebec and found a similar position there. Once a year she made a secret pilgrimage to New York to get sight of her little girl, unknown to Henry Radcliffe whose heart had remained adamant towards the woman who had ruined his faith in women. On her part Yvonne made no effort to force herself upon him; for she was quite able by this time to take care of herself. Her one concern was his treatment of Rose and in this direction there was no fault to find; for Henry Radcliffe lavished love and care upon his daughter if ever a man did.

It happened that upon one of her secret pilgrimages she was in a railroad disaster and although uninjured, she lost all her personal travelling possessions in the wreck of the car, including the gold locket which her husband had given her at the time of their wedding. To her astonishment she found her name listed among the victims of the train wreck, the locket and her handbag being found beside the decapitated body of a young woman. Instead of trying to correct the mistake, she allowed the news to reach Henry Radcliffe and let things take their course, believing that it was better for him to think of her as dead if he could not forgive and believe in her innocence.

The years of suffering had wrought a great change in the once beautiful Yvonne, so much so that in time she could come and go more freely; for none who had known her as a girl-bride would now recognize her in this white-haired woman with the sallow face. She took up permanent residence in New York at last and watched her little girl growing to budding womanhood. Her hunger to be near Rose overpowered all fear of discovery finally and she became the seamstress of the family, assuming the name of Catharine Stanton and going to live near Hillcrest with the Stokes family.

When Mrs. Saint-Anton first put in an appearance at Hillcrest Yvonne recognized her instantly as the notorious Countess Marinelli, much changed by the years but still recognizable to one upon whose memory those haughty features had been so indelibly imprinted that night when she had stood on the stone staircase, unmasked, in the Château du Vieux Pont. It seemed like a strange trick of Fate that this wicked woman should once more cross her path. Yvonne made it her business to find out why "Mrs. Saint-Anton" was at Hillcrest and was not long in discovering that the woman was blackmailing Henry Radcliffe by threatening to reveal to Rose the disgrace which the girl's mother had brought upon the Radcliffe name at the Château du Vieux Pont.

How this woman had learned that Henry Radcliffe had kept these facts from his daughter sedulously and that it was the one weak spot in which to attack him Yvonne could not fathom. It was true that it was a positive obsession with him to guard against Rose learning this secret; some day he would be forced to tell her—when she came of age—but he dreaded that day's arrival as if he were afraid of his daughter's condemnation. The latter years had softened Henry Radcliffe not a little; there were times when he no doubt wondered if he had been too hasty—if his forlorn little bride perhaps had been innocent, as she had claimed. That doubt was the cross which was with him always and there were moments of poignant remorse that were very bitter. He sought penance by worshipping Rose and gratifying her every whim.

Yvonne, although she avoided the master of the house as much as possible, was not ignorant of these things. Her intuition told her of the change that was taking place in Henry Radcliffe's attitude. She occupied her thoughts with plans for sending this blackmailer about her business. The scene she had witnessed that night in the drafty corridor of the old château recurred to her. She had recounted all the details to the Lamonts at the time and Armaund had gone to the police with the story. However, the party at the Château du Vieux Pont had broken up immediately following the masked dance; the place was untenanted and the Countess Marinelli had disappeared none knew where. Her aliases were many in the capitals of Europe. Certainly she had left France on some dark mission of her own; so that she had never been brought to book for this particular misdeed.

It seemed to Yvonne that here was a weapon with which her husband could silence this woman definitely and for all time; but how to convey the information to Henry Radcliffe was the problem. The fact that recently he had started serious study of spiritism gave her the fantastic idea. She knew that he was reading many volumes upon psychic phenomena and Yvonne hit upon the extravagant plan of appearing to her husband in the guise of her own spirit and holding converse with him. She knew that the books he had been reading had more than half convinced him it was possible for visions of persons deceased to appear to the living at times of crisis and she decided to risk such an interview.

She planned to appear in his room by way of the secret passage, the existence of which he was likely to have forgotten as it had never been used. A mistake of the architect in planning the alterations or of the workmen in carrying out instructions had been responsible for the surplus space during Henry Radcliffe's absence; upon his return he had ordered the workmen to proceed and bury the section of the old staircase in the new walls, the conversion of it into a secret exit from his own room being a later whim. Only Henry Radcliffe and the workmen were supposed to know of it at all; Yvonne had discovered it by accident during the summer she acted as temporary stewardess at Hillcrest. It therefore enabled her to appear and vanish with the necessary mystery when she undertook to materialize as a spirit and by keeping well within the alcove, where the light was uncertain, she managed the deception successfully.

She appeared to her husband in this guise on one occasion only—the night Rose had so nearly surprised them in their séance. Yvonne told him that "Mrs. Saint-Anton" was really the woman known as the Countess Marinelli. She told him that she, his wife, knew the difficulty he was in and that for Rose's sake he must get rid of Mrs. Saint-Anton. To this end he was to ask her about the sword combat at the Château du Vieux Pont on the night of the *bal au masque* and the manner in which the elder O'Carrol had been sent to his death; he was to threaten the woman with exposure if she did not stay away from Hillcrest and leave them alone. He had promised that he would carry out these instructions and she had left him hurriedly; for her own emotions at his pleadings for forgiveness threatened to overcome her and reveal the hoax that she was perpetrating.

Mrs. Saint-Anton had been coming there whenever she happened to run short of money and Henry Radcliffe was expecting her next visit about the end of the month. To prepare the way for the showdown, Yvonne was anxious to get Rose out of the way; if necessary, she intended to reveal her own identity, explain to her husband the fact that her announced death was a mistake and as the eyewitness in the case, denounce the Countess Marinelli to her face.

She therefore wrote the three mysterious notes to her daughter, not realizing how foolish it was until afterward when they failed of their purpose; she had thought that her husband would see that Rose did go visiting and she regretted not having warned him to do so instead of merely succeeding in arousing the girl's curiosity and alarm. It had been a silly, inadequate performance in keeping with that other foolish notion of playing at ghost. It would have been much better if she had revealed to her husband her true identity in the first place; but it is not always easy to be wise in a difficult situation even when one has wide experience at command.

She saw that Henry Radcliffe was very anxious and worried. Here again, frankness with Rose would have been best; for one's fears so often were groundless and it was time Rose should know the truth. In his nervous uncertainty her husband was praying

nightly for the spirit of his wife to advise him once more. His belief in the vision he had had was firm and there would be little
difficulty in convincing him if she tried it a second time. Mrs. Saint-
Anton and Roger Levering, however, were on hand now and with
them on the premises the risks were tripled. Nevertheless, she decided to take the chance and advise her husband to lay all the facts
before Rose and let the girl order the intruders out of the house.

But it was too late. The night Yvonne chose was the night of
the tragedy and she narrowly escaped capture in her masquerade.
It had been a simple matter for her to acquire a duplicate key to
the servants' entry and, knowing the habits of the establishment
so thoroughly, to time her approach correctly. She had made herself a diaphanous costume which with the assistance of luminous
paint enabled her to obtain the effect of a ghostly, indeterminate
shape in the dark; she assumed these habiliments in the sewing-
room on the third floor. After her horrible discovery of Henry
Radcliffe's body she had recoiled with a cry of horror and started
to retreat from the room by way of the wardrobe panel, but as she
was about to release the hidden spring the shock of the grewsome
find suddenly reacted in a wave of weakness that almost made her
swoon. She was forced to wait a few moments before she could
proceed.

It was then that she heard someone enter the room from the
door that led out into the hall and she shrank within the wardrobe
and held her breath in great fear. Whoever it was evidently knew
what he was about, for he lost no time in approaching the body on
the floor. Yvonne heard a slight click and peered cautiously forth
through the crack of the wardrobe door to see a man's hand, busy
writing upon a cuff of the murdered man's shirt with a gold pencil—just a pair of hands, illuminated in the rays from an electric
flashlight which lay upon the floor alongside. As methodically and
swiftly as he had come the intruder departed; the whole thing took
only a moment and Yvonne wondered for an instant whether she
was the victim of false perception.

There was nothing intangible about the message on that cuff,
however. The only light she had with her was a packet of cardboard

matches. When she struck one of these flares and read the writing her heart sank at what appeared to her to be an accusation directed against herself. Why was this false evidence being deliberately manufactured against her? Thinking the name was "Stanton," she stooped quickly, ripped off the cuff and fled as she heard someone stirring in the next room. Up the hidden stair to the trunk room, thence to the sewing-room she went, half crazed.

She hardly knew what she was doing. Her one idea was to get out of that house as quickly as possible; but for a while she felt too weak and upset to move. What if she were seen escaping? She decided to keep on her masquerade till she was safe outside in the shrubbery. At last she summoned her courage and descended the staircase. She sensed that she was being followed and fear speeded her feet once she was out in the grounds. Sounds of a struggle in the shrubbery behind her sent her flying for the garden gate, divesting herself of the flowing draperies as she ran. Once on the highway, she sped for the woodland path by which she was accustomed to take a short-cut through the park. She was confident that nobody could have recognized her; but to make certain that she was not followed she hid beside the path, watching and listening for half an hour. As nobody came that way she went home at last with relief and let herself quietly into her own room.

Her state of mental uncertainty was terrible. It was not until she calmed down that she began to wonder if the accusation on the cuff was directed at Mrs. Saint-Anton. Someone knew that the woman had killed Henry Radcliffe and had taken this means of directing the police? Mrs. Saint-Anton had shot to silence Henry Radcliffe when he revealed his knowledge of the O'Carrol affair at the Château du Vieux Pont! That was the motive, then, and the grief of Yvonne that this should be the result of her advice to her husband was bitter. She was sorry now that she had removed the cuff.

But she could not take it back. She dare not reveal her presence on the scene. It would come out that she was Mrs. Radcliffe and all manner of false impressions would result. She did not know what was best to do and in all New York was only one in whom she could place implicit trust and to whom she could turn in her extremity. That one was Armaund Lamont and he even did not know that she was alive. She had avoided him all these years because after time had softened the acuteness of her misery in France he had never ceased to urge her to secure a divorce and marry him. He had wooed her with such persistence that she had left France altogether. Marriage, she felt, was a failure in her case and she would not wed where she could not give heart as well as hand.

It had been a bitter disappointment for Armaund Lamont, who loved her sincerely. This friend and benefactor had remained a bachelor as a result of it. He had gone to America and had risen in the world. That she had only to reveal herself to him to command his utmost help, Yvonne knew.

His arrival at Hillcrest on Sunday gave her the opportunity which she could not resist and she had met him in the arbor that night. Someone must have spied upon them there and overheard her confess her identity and tell Armaund of the shirt-cuff which she had concealed in her Japanese jewel-box at the Stokes bungalow; for that night it was stolen. Her abduction occurred the very next day after she had reported the matter to Armaund Lamont.

What the meaning of the terrible things that had happened could be, Yvonne did not know. She learned of Mrs. Saint-Anton's arrest only when Rose told her. Even if the woman were guilty of the crime with which she was charged, Yvonne felt it her duty to relate all these facts; for undoubtedly the evidence of the shirt-cuff was forged. She was anxious to assist the police in every way and was prepared to give her testimony in court.

The twilight had deepened in the Hillcrest library until the final sentences of the narrative were spoken in semi-darkness. The silent figures of Mrs. Radcliffe's audience surrounded her dimly. For a long time after the gentle voice ceased a silence reigned in the room a silence broken at last by long breaths, eloquent of tension.

Tommy Traynor rose and pressed the button that flooded the library with light. Mrs. Radcliffe lay back in the club chair she occupied, resting, her eyes closed; it had not teen easy for her to lay bare these intimate details of her life and the recital had stirred anew the wellsprings of her suffering. From beneath her closed lids the tears coursed down her cheeks. Her daughter stood beside the chair, one arm along the back of it, the other stroking the white hair while she regarded this newfound mother of hers with eyes which shone mistily. Armaund Lamont had blown his nose violently and stepped to the window, gazing out as if he really could see the landscape.

Addison Kent got up quietly and went across to where J. K. Yelland was sitting. He held out his hand.

"My congratulations, Yelland," he said in a low voice. "While it is true that Mrs. Radcliffe's testimony will provide the prosecution with a perfectly strong motive, it will likewise destroy the strongest evidence against your client—completely. Taken in conjunction with certain discoveries which I have made, it should result in prompt acquittal beyond a doubt."

Before the smiling lawyer could make reply, there came a light knock on the door and the voice of Follis, announcing that Mr. Yelland was wanted urgently upon the telephone by Mr. Fraser, his partner. He excused himself and went out into the hall.

"May I ask you, Mrs. Radcliffe," said Kent gently, "if you recognized in Roger Levering anyone you had ever known?"

"He was a complete stranger to me, Mr. Kent," she replied.

"Did you recognize anything familiar in the appearance of the men who were responsible for your enforced visit on Long Island?"

"No. They were total strangers also."

"This man O'Carrol who killed his father in the duel at the Château, then— Did you ever hear anything more of him what became of him, where he went and so on?"

Traynor leaned forward in his chair as Kent asked this question, his expression suddenly eager. O'Carrol—O'C! He waited breathlessly for the answer.

"No," was the reply. She shook her head. "That is something which I have often wondered. I have never heard of him from that day to this."

"But you are quite sure the name was O'Carrol?"

"Oh, I am quite sure of that, Mr. Kent. I have an excellent memory for names and the whole thing was so impressed upon me at the time—"

She paused with a start. Everyone in the room turned suddenly towards the door as the agitated voice of J. K. Yelland at the telephone rose loud in ejaculation.

"*WHAT?* Oh, Fraser, surely— My God!"

They all watched him as he entered the room slowly, his face blank with astonishment.

"What's wrong, Yelland?"

The lawyer eyed them in silence for a moment. All animation seemed to have gone from him.

"Our evidence has arrived too late," he said heavily. "My partner 'phones me that the Commissioner of Police has just informed him that Mrs. Saint-Anton—has committed suicide—"

They all gasped.

"—and has left behind a signed confession that she killed Henry Radcliffe!"

Traynor threw a swift glance of bewilderment at Addison Kent. The novelist got slowly to his feet and stood with a hand on the back of his chair to steady himself. His face had gone white.

25

SCOTLAND YARD SITS IN

Intimately as Tommy Traynor had known his old newspaper friend, he had never seen Addison Kent in such a mood as possessed him in the hour that followed. In spite of confirmation of the startling news from Police Headquarters—confirmation obtained over the telephone from the Commissioner himself—it was plain that the novelist was not only greatly disturbed by the sudden turn events had taken but puzzled as well.

Yet to Traynor, in the light of Mrs. Radcliffe's disclosures, the thing was understandable enough. The fact that "Mrs. Saint-Anton" was in reality this Countess Marinelli, a notorious adventuress, seemed to point to her suicide as a logical ending to such a life as she had led; a woman of her antecedents, finding herself in a position where her identity would become known and her past exposed, would be bold enough to choose such an end in preference to the legal punishment from which there could be no escape. Heaven alone knew what crimes she had committed, what secrets she preserved when she swallowed the small capsule of poison which she had concealed for this last desperate act! It was what might be expected from an intrigante who had dallied with European polities.

Her confession of the present crime certainly put a period to the murder case in Traynor's mind, as it would in the minds of the police and of the public. Confessions of murder were not in the nature of a popular pastime. Her guilt had been known to Levering who for some reason dare not accuse the woman openly yet was so anxious to have her brought to book that he directed suspicion towards her by means of the shirt-cuff, making the accusation appear to come from Henry Radcliffe himself. If Levering were Alceste, as Kent suspected, the woman probably was his accomplice and sought the secret interview as an excuse for ensuring Radcliffe's presence in his room while the safe was being rifled down in the library. Discovering that he knew of the O'Carrol affair at the château, she had been seized by panic and had shot down the master of the house as she fled by way of the fire-escape. This sort of complication no doubt angered Alceste greatly and he determined to get rid of the woman who had been guilty of such a *faux pas* and work alone in the future.

Rather proud of this reasoning, Traynor was of a mind to discuss the situation with Kent, but found no opportunity of doing so in the rapid developments which followed. Kent was in no mood to talk; the news seemed to galvanize him to action and he behaved like a man who suddenly realizes that there is no time to be lost. As he talked to Headquarters his queries were almost staccatto with nervous energy. His chief concern now seemed to be the arrest of the thieves who had robbed Armaund Lamont by the bold ruse of abducting the woman who was dearer to him than life itself. The name of Thompson was mentioned several times during the conversation and Traynor gathered that the butler had been heard from and that the police were about to close in on their quarry.

No sooner had Addison Kent hung up the receiver than he was eager to leave Hillcrest. He took Traynor to one side.

"I don't want to drag you away, Tommy, but you made me promise to tell you—"

"Something doing?"

"We are going over to Long Island to-night. It may prove an interesting trip."

That was all he would vouchsafe. The presence of Yelland in the car may have been responsible for the silence which Addison Kent maintained nearly all the way in. He gradually dropped out of the conversation and for the last half of the journey sat so wrapped in thought that he seemed oblivious of his surroundings.

Occasionally he muttered to himself in his abstraction and once Traynor, who sat next to him, caught the words.

"Devilish! Devilish!" was the almost inaudible murmur.

They dropped the lawyer finally near his own apartment and Kent at once directed the chauffeur to drive as fast as he could to Minaki Annex.

"Thompson is waiting there," he explained.

"Thompson? He seems to be mixing in pretty freely for a servant," commented Traynor. "I thought Fargey had the butler rather under suspicion."

"Hmph! Fargey!" grunted Kent. "He knows by now that that is at least one mistake he has made. Inspector Arthur Thompson, of Scotland Yard, is scarcely to be mentioned in the same breath with a man of Lieutenant Fargey's caliber on a difficult case."

"Inspector Ar—!" Traynor's surprise held him silent for a moment. "Good night! And he's been on the case from the first?"

"Yes. He has been on the trail of Alceste ever since the robbery in Norfolk—six months ago. It was he who looked me up and handed me Superintendent Brownlee's letter. I took him to the Commissioner and we have all been working quietly ever since."

"And even Bob Fargey didn't know—"

"Does Washington tell the policeman on the corner everything that goes on in the Secret Service?" countered Kent. "I dare not let even you into the secret before, Tommy. This Alceste is the most resourceful, slippery— Here we are! Out you go! We're due at Headquarters in twenty minutes or so and Thompson has a lot to say first."

Inspector Arthur Thompson, quiet, unassuming, smiled his deprecation as Tommy Traynor approached him in mock fear and shook hands. There was nothing of the butler in his manner now and Tommy marvelled at the perfect naturalness with which he had played the part in the Hillcrest household. There was a dignity and reserve about him, a confident carriage that bespoke self-reliance and initiative. As Tommy listened to the report which Inspector Thompson had to present it did not need the glint in Kent's eyes to tell him that the discoveries made by the man from

Scotland Yard were very important. There was no longer the need for preserving the incognito which he had maintained up to that very morning when Traynor and the others had parted from him to return to Hillcrest; during the succeeding hours Thompson's suspicions had been confirmed.

He had acted at once. The strange story which had been related by Lamont and the two ladies had given him a clue to the situation by reason of the special study which he had devoted to the history of Alceste's activities in Europe. The police records in regard to Alceste's personality were scant enough; by wearing rubber gloves he avoided leaving finger-prints behind him and the fact that his eyes were blue and that he was likely to prove of Irish ancestry practically sum-totalled the available information as to Alceste himself. He had never been captured and the few who had seen him on occasion could not recall his personal appearance with any accuracy; if these casual, untrained observers were to be believed, the man was tall and likewise short, dark and likewise fair, young and likewise old, but none who had stood looking into those eyes forgot them. They were blue.

It was Addison Kent's description of Levering's eyes that had made Inspector Thompson wonder if his man had been living right under his nose at Hillcrest for days. Traynor had told him what had happened at the hospital and it might well be that Roger Levering was Alceste himself. The thought was somewhat disconcerting and it had sent Thompson on the trail of his new clue with all the determination that was in him.

That clue lay in the fact that the place to which the three had been abducted was some kind of private sanitarium which had everything to establish it as such—except patients! This was a favorite scheme of a certain clever doctor, known to Scotland Yard and "wanted" for sundry nefarious dealings—a Dr. Shane Mac-Murrough. As a surgeon this man's prospects had appeared brilliant; for he had stirred things up during his college days and had carried off many honors. What had happened in his life to send him off on a tangent to criminal practices could only be surmised; the fact remained that he had figured in a scandalous affair in which his so-called "sanitarium" turned out to be nothing more nor less than a private gaol for the detention of wealthy "patients" whose relatives wished to get rid of them under the plea that they were insane. A "wild Irishman," this MacMurrough, who had entangled himself in the political imbroglio also; the police believed that he knew more than a little about certain dark pages which had been written in that connection by the particular "Brotherhood" of which he was a member.

The two outstanding facts which interested Inspector Thompson were—first, that Dr. Shane MacMurrough was suspected of having assisted Alceste on occasion, although it was impossible to prove it by direct evidence; second, that MacMurrough had dropped out of sight at the same time that Alceste disappeared. If Alceste were in the United States, why not Dr. Shane MacMurrough also? If the redoubtable Doctor had assisted Alceste before, might he not be doing so now? If the theft of Lamont's gems pointed to Alceste, the "sanitarium" to which they had been taken indicated Dr. MacMurrough. The description of the man who had visited Addison Kent in the hospital tallied with the description of the driver of the touring car who had so boldly compelled Lamont to open his own vaults and accompany him; Kent recognized the peculiar blue eyes as those of Roger Levering and the eyes of Alceste were blue; Roger Levering, therefore, was Alceste, had robbed the safe in Hillcrest, had purloined the collar of pearls out of the package which Miss Radcliffe had left in her room for a short time on Sunday evening, had subsequently visited Lamont after attempting Kent's life in Central Park, and had gone back to finish the job at the James B. Yates Memorial Hospital, having trailed Lamont's limousine and learned that Kent was still alive. The description of the man in charge of the "sanitarium" where the abducted trio had been taken was not out of harmony with the known description of Dr. Shane MacMurrough. This "sanitarium," then, was the retreat upon which the police must focus attention.

Thompson had telephoned his tip to Headquarters and the Commissioner had got in touch with the District Attorney's office and set the machinery in motion for fullest co-operation between

State and city police. Several discreet plainclothes men had combed
the neighborhood and as a result of this quiet investigation the
"sanitarium" had been located and unobtrusively had been under
surveillance all day. The orders were that no arrivals at the place
were to be accosted; but if anyone tried to leave the premises they
were to be arrested at once. Lieutenant Fargey had been sent over
to take charge with a Strong Arm Squad and a detail of motor-
cycles. The place was to be raided at ten o'clock.

"Fargey, you say, Inspector? Were you talking to him at all?"

"Yes, Mr. Kent. He was very eager to take a hand in the capture—"

"Trying to steal your thunder, eh? Drunk with the wine of success over the Saint-Anton confession, he must climb aboard this
other bandwagon! Well, that's like him!"

Traynor glanced quickly at Addison Kent into whose tone had
crept an irritation that was unusual with him. Was it possible that
Kent was jealous of Bob Fargey's triumph?

"I would not say that exactly," smiled Thompson. "I rather fancied he would resent it when he discovered my identity, you know,—
feel a bit upset over it. But by Jove, he was quite friendly with me
and congratulated me! Quite friendly. Turns out he's been suspicious of this man Levering—"

"From the first, I suppose," drawled Kent with amusement.

"Just so. He'd just gone to the Commissioner to tell him he
thought Levering was this Alceste—was in the office, I believe, when
I telephoned. He requested to be allowed to take charge of the raid
to-night. I rather fancy, you know, Fargey wants to redeem himself for letting the bounder slip through his fingers the way he did.
Silly asses, all of us! What?"

"Yes—if we linger here much longer," agreed Kent, rising.
"Fargey will get more satisfaction out of his raid if he has us as
spectators and if we don't move, we'll be late for the performance.
Here, Tommy, help me on with this coat—careful of that arm,
dammit!"

"I say, old chap, you'd better go armed, you know," warned
Thompson and he nodded approval as Addison Kent tapped his

hip and passed an automatic to Traynor. "It's a meeting of the Irish and there's liable to be a bit of a fracas. It takes an Irishman to catch an Irishman—what?" and he chuckled at his own paraphrase.

He stepped out into the hall as he spoke and failed to see the startled look that suddenly came into the novelist's eyes. It did not escape Tommy Traynor, however, and he followed down the stairs to the waiting automobile with an uneasy feeling that beneath the surface of impending events flowed an undercurrent of danger which he could not fathom.

They stopped at the big gray-stone building in Center Street only long enough to learn that reserves under Kent's friend, Donovan, were just leaving in response to a call from Fargey. They were just in time to go along.

26
THE EYES OF ALCESTE

In silent majesty the full moon, a mellow ball of light, lifted slowly above the heavily-wooded ridge to the east; across its golden face the lacey fingers of the tree-tops slipped as if reluctant to release it to the star-sown sky. A bird stirred and twittered sleepily in the nearby leafage and the warm summer night was under-toned by the chant of crickets in the wayside grass. In the neighboring village a hound bayed and was answered by the sharp bark of a dog on a distant farmstead. Down in the river bottom an owl whooed, tremulous, uncanny.

Lieutenant Robert Fargey parted the bushes and pointed.

"Over to the left there a ways—you can see one o' the gables an' a chimney sticking up against the sky," he directed in a low voice.

Kent, Traynor and Thompson peered forth with interest. The time for action was at hand. From the rise on which they stood the quiet countryside stretched in the moonlight. There was nothing of alarm in that peaceful scene; the far-off staccatto of a motor-cycle was innocent enough. Yet each of the four men knew that every road converging on the point where they stood, disappearing like white ribbons into the woodlands, was under vigilant patrol—that concealed in the undergrowth a close-drawn cordon of police surrounded the comfortable old house that stood back from the road, almost hidden behind its sheltering elms.

Fargey's preparations left nothing to be desired. He had met the reserves some miles down the road and turned them over to Detective-Sergeant Hayes for disposition in their proper places.

He had made good use of his rural constables as outlying pickets. Great care had been taken to keep everything under cover in order not to arouse the suspicions of their quarry. The touring car had returned to the place early that morning and was still in the yard; no attempt had been made by anyone in the house to depart during the day.

"We've got 'em an' got 'em right!" exulted Fargey as he finished explaining the situation.

The elation in his voice was not that merely of official approval and satisfaction; it was that of a man keyed to a high pitch of subdued excitement—a man who concentrates every fibre of his being upon achieving—publicity? Surely it was deeper than that, thought Addison Kent, as he studied the lieutenant stealthily. It was revenge Bob Fargey was seeking to-night—revenge upon Roger Levering for bamboozling him, for coolly slipping through his fingers, for making him appear ridiculous? Possibly. Fargey's vanity would be unable to stand ridicule or censure at Headquarters; he was much too jealous-minded himself for that.

"Time's up," said Fargey, extinguishing his flashlight again as soon as he had glanced at his watch. "Follow me carefully, gentlemen, please. Watch your step. This is a surprise party."

In single file they made their way slowly down the hill to the road and advanced towards the gate. A light was burning in the lower hall; but outside of this the house was in darkness. Hayes and Donovan joined the group as they went lightly across the lawn to the verandah, hands in coat pockets, automatics gripped for instant use. There was no telling what the next few minutes might beget and as Tommy Traynor brought up the rear, a position to which he had been peremptorily relegated by Fargey, he experienced a genuine thrill of excitement.

Inspector Thompson pointed silently to the brass plate alongside the door— "Dr. H. B. Shane." Lieutenant Fargey pulled the knob of the door-bell and they could hear the tinkling of the bell within quite distinctly; but there was no sound of an approaching footstep in answer to the summons. As Fargey gave the bell an impatient tug, Kent quietly tried the door. It was locked.

"Locked, eh?" muttered Fargey. He scowled for a moment, thinking. To break down the door by force would rob them of the advantage of surprise for which he had hoped.

He took a key-ring from his pocket and was about to insert a skeleton key in the lock when Kent seized his arm and cautioned silence with a look. It was then that they heard stealthy footsteps inside, approaching the door. The sound of bolts being quietly slipped followed, the door opened slowly and a man stepped out, finger to lips, closing the door behind him.

A murmur of surprise passed among them as they saw that it was Donovan who had slipped away unnoticed and had gone around the house.

"I found a window open at the rear, Loot'nant," he explained simply.

With a grunt of approval his superior pushed the door open and they all tip-toed into the hall. Hayes closed the door carefully and they stood where they were, hastily surveying their surroundings in the dull light that came from the hanging lamp in its frosted globe. To the immediate right and left two doors opened off the hall; each stood wide open. Directly in front of them a wide staircase ascended at the right; the hall extended past it to a third door which was shut. An old-fashioned hall rack and a hall bench of golden quartered oak were the only articles of furniture in sight; the rugs on the floor were costly.

The silence was oppressive; their own breathing was audible. Did it mean an uninhabited house or was it portentous of enemies who concealed their presence but to make their attack more effective?

Lieutenant Fargey motioned with his police automatic and they followed him into the room on the right—evidently used as a consulting-room. Nobody was in sight there. They crossed to the left-hand room and went through it without discovering any sign of life or place of concealment; it was fitted up as a bed-sitting-room and Traynor recognized it as the room Rose had described to him in detail, the room where she had met her mother.

Very cautiously, ready for any emergency, they crept along the hall now to the closed door. Lieutenant Fargey quietly turned the knob and found the door unlocked. The faint but unmistakable, sweetly pungent odor of chloroform greeted their nostrils and they saw that the place had been used as a sort of surgery and library combined.

Addison Kent pushed forward, his eyes moving swiftly and no detail escaping him. He picked up and examined several pinches of cottonwool that lay on the plate-glass surface of a small table near the window; there was a tinge of blood upon them and, as nearly as he could tell, it was fresh. He went over to the case of surgical instruments and gazed at them intently. As Tommy Traynor watched him, some instinct told him that all this was of importance or at least that Addison Kent considered it so. But it was apparent that Fargey's mind was focused only upon the importance of keeping a sharp lookout against the possibility of a shot in the back. He waved Kent away impatiently.

A door at the right, opened by Hayes, disclosed a downward flight of steps. Fargey motioned him back and himself ran down noiselessly. He shot the bolt in another door at the bottom and stepped back with a muttered imprecation at the shadowy figure of a man who promptly thrust the muzzle of a pistol into his face. Fargey laughed a little at his own nervousness. It was one of his own men who had closed in on all exits, as instructed.

Wiping his forehead on his coat-sleeve, the lieutenant of detectives rejoined the group at the head of the steps and curtly explained.

"They must be upstairs," he whispered. "Be ready, everybody. We're goin' up now."

At the foot of the stairs they paused to listen and Lieutenant Fargey sent the beam of his flashlight dancing upward. They climbed slowly, one step at a time, hugging the wall, eyes unwaveringly on the landing at the top.

They reached it at last without a sound to indicate what lay beyond in the darkness of the upper hall. A short flight of stairs continued around the turn. Fargey thrust his electric torch through the uprights of the banister above his head, snapped on the switch and ducked back; but as no pistol fire was drawn by this manoeuvre, he advanced stealthily. The upper hall was likewise empty.

Several doors were visible, all open but one. The carpet was thick and they made almost no sound at all as they crept from room to room, investigating. Every bedroom was empty; so also one which was fitted up as a den. The smell of cigarette smoke still hung here in the air.

Alert, every nerve at tension, automatics ready, they joined Donovan who had gone on guard outside the closed door. What lay beyond that door? By process of elimination it was the only room which could reward their search. Kent pointed silently to the hasp and padlock which fastened it on the outside and Fargey motioned Hayes forward to pry off the hasp.

To their straining ears then came a sound from within the room—the first sound of any presence in that house except their own. They looked at each other in the bright rays of the flashlights, surprise on every face. Had their men been so sure of themselves that they had gone to bed with unconcern? The sound was recognizable at once—the heave of a body on a spring mattress!

Again Fargey motioned to Hayes. Kent might stop to wonder why the room should be padlocked on the outside; but just now Fargey thought only of getting inside that room as quickly as possible. He leaned forward in his eagerness, body bent, breathing rapidly in his excitement.

Hayes stepped back and saluted. Slowly the knob turned under his superior's hand and the door gave an inch. Satisfied then that it was not bolted on the inside, Fargey jerked his head in command and kicked the door wide on its hinges.

Together they all sprang into the room, the electric torches flooding the place with blinding light in every direction.

"Hands up!" shouted Fargey hoarsely, levelling his weapon.

Traynor thought he was prepared for anything. He fully expected gun-play; but there was none. Surprise held them all motionless for a moment.

The room was small and almost bare of furniture—a bed and a chair. The floors were uncarpeted. One small window alone was visible, high in the wall, iron-barred. On the bed lay a figure beneath the bedclothes, face to the wall. The back of a head, covered with unkempt black hair, protruded from the bedspread at one end—a head with a white bandage encircling it.

"Hands up! Quick, you!" commanded Fargey again, covering the form on the bed.

Then very slowly, as if the effort were painful, the form turned beneath the bedclothes, facing them. The man made no move to show his hands. His eyes were blindfolded by the bandage. A chill ran down Tommy Traynor's spine as he saw that white face turn to them,

"I say, watch out for the beggar, Lieutenant," warned Thompson. "He's going to shoot!"

"Want me to plug you as you lay?" cried Fargey at the limit of nervous restraint.

Addison Kent pushed aside the lieutenant's gun, stepped calmly to the bed, took hold of the bedclothes and flung them back.

"We know you, Levering!" Fargey's voice came gratingly. "No use tryin' to cover up your eyes! No use—!" He broke off in astonishment.

No man with a fast-spitting automatic in either hand lay on that bed. The man there was as helpless as a baby. He was strapped and buckled in a strait-jacket the contrivance used to control demented or delirious patients!

After that first mutter of astonishment which passed their lips, dead silence fell in the room as they stared at the creature on the bed. Thompson was the first to break it.

"My word, Mr. Kent!" he murmured in a shocked voice. "Now there is no room for doubt that MacMurrough was running this place. This is his work. The bounder has kept a genuine lunatic in the house to carry out the scheme!—to deceive anybody who got too inquisitive! By Jove!"

Addison Kent said not a word. Keenly he studied the man in the straitjacket, then bent over and gently removed the bandage.

The immediate result was startling. The man rapidly grew as violent as the strait-jacket would permit. He tossed about, rolled to the edge of the bed, swung his feet to the floor and, before anyone could interfere, butted his strapped-up body against Kent so forcibly that the novelist fell back into Traynor's arms.

He charged at Fargey who promptly knocked him back on the bed with a cruel uppercut to the chin.

"Would, would you?" he snarled. He sprang forward, but with a cry of protest, Kent interfered.

"Can't you see the poor devil's helpless!" cried Kent, his eyes blazing with anger. "Look at him!"

The man's ravings and curses had dwindled to a meaningless mumble. He was crying now. The tears rolled down his white cheeks. Gently Kent replaced the bandage across the bloodshot eyes, talking soothingly as to a hurt child. Almost at once the man quieted.

"Can you tell us who you are?" suggested Kent in matter-of-fact tones. "Try to think. We are friends. We want to help you. Who are you?"

"Friends!" muttered the fellow. "Friends? FRIENDS!" he shouted. He threw back his head, opened his mouth and gave vent to a loud peal of laughter that sent a shiver through Tommy Traynor. It was terrible, that laughter—wild! "I have no friends! They all died!"

"Who are you?" repeated Addison Kent quietly.

"Who am I? Well, who am I? I'm nobody. That's who I am—Mr. Nobody from Nowhere! NO! WAIT! I'm—I'm Mr.—Mr.—" The raucous voice dwindled off into a gibber of mouthed nonsense—the gibbering intonations of insanity.

Kent looked helplessly around at them.

"Poor unfortunate beggar!" muttered Thompson.

"Unfortunate nothing!" cried Lieutenant Robert Fargey scornfully. "That don't fool me for a minute, see! If Levering's really gone crazy, it's the on'y thing'll save him from goin' up the river; but I miss my guess—"

Inspector Thompson's look of quiet disdain made him pause.

"You believe this man to be Roger Levering!"

"Surest thing you know! I ain't taking no chances—"

"Did you note the color of his eyes?"

"Well!" glared Fargey resentfully.

"The eyes of this man are dark brown. Those of Levering are light blue; Kent can verify that. So are the eyes of Alceste; I can verify that. This man is quite apparently one of Dr. Shane MacMurrough's insane victims. God knows who he may prove to be!"

He turned to Addison Kent for approval of his statements. Fargey knew that he spoke the truth but he leaned forward and peered long and earnestly as the novelist once more carefully removed the bandage. There was no mistake about the color of the bloodshot eyes; they were a chestnut brown. Kent restored the bandage and stood back, nodding thoughtfully.

"Your best plan is to leave one of your men to stay with the poor devil," suggested Inspector Thompson, "until you can arrange for his removal. I think a doctor ought to see him first."

Lieutenant Fargey, almost beside himself with disappointment over this culmination of his expectations, gritted his teeth in a passion. He was obsessed by the conviction that he was being duped in some manner and he refused the evidence of his own eyes. Roughly he caught Thompson by the arm and pulled him out of the way.

"The hell you say!" he exploded. "That's our man, I tell you! And by— I'll take no chances—!"

Before they realized what he was doing he had sprung forward and was in the act of thrusting the muzzle of his automatic against the bandaged temple of the man on the bed when Kent leaped. The novelist was just in time to knock the gun aside as it went off, the bullet spatting harmlessly through the ceiling.

"Fargey!" Kent stared at him, dumfounded. "In God's name, man, have you gone crazy yourself? Control yourself!" he said sharply.

"I's just bluffin'," panted Fargey. "I wasn't goin' to plug him, you fool!" he protested. "You come near makin' me do it!"

Again the wild peal of laughter broke from the man in the strait-jacket. They stared at each other in awe as it dwindled away once more into the meaningless mumble.

Then across the brooding quiet of the night came a new sound that drove every thought but one from their minds—a fusillade of pistol shots. The firing came from the direction of the river, several hundred yards from the house. The open window at the rear through which Donovan had climbed! The men they were after had escaped from the house before the police entered it!

Shouting to Donovan to remain behind in the room until a man could be sent to relieve him and instructing him to follow then as fast as he could, Fargey flew out the door, dashed downstairs and out of the house, followed by the others.

They raced across the lawn in the direction of the firing as hard as they could go—across the road—over a fence into a meadow—over another fence into the bush and down a long slope to the very bank of the river. Along the highways behind, specks of light were speeding through the dark and the staccatto of motor-cycles seemed like echoes of the cracking pistol-shots that mapped the location of the running fight.

The firing ceased all at once and a loud halloo was sent out from a point over to the left. A police whistle sounded with piercing distinctness and the signal was taken up by the squad at the house and went relaying in every direction into the distance. Escape from that network of pursuers was next to impossible.

"You hear that?" Fargey had stopped them with upraised hand to listen and he turned jubilantly as he spoke. "We've got 'em! That signal means we've got our birds. Come on!"

The party hurried along the riverbank and presently came within sight of a group, gathered about the base of a huge elm tree. A plainclothes man, bathed in the light from the electric torches, stepped forth as they came up and saluted Fargey. It was McVey.

"There was on'y one of 'em, sir. He broke cover ten minutes ago an' showed fight. He wouldn't be taken alive."

"Good work, good work, boys!" approved the lieutenant as he strode towards the tree. The men fell back.

For a long moment they gazed down upon the still form that lay there—a man of middle age with iron-gray hair, brushed back in a pompadour from a low, wide forehead. Inspector Thompson identified him at once.

"It is Dr. Shane MacMurrough," he said.

Addison Kent stood close to Lieutenant Fargey, silently watching him. The officer's heavy jaw was set, his hands clenched. The expression of his eyes was hard, triumphant.

"Two!" he muttered.

As if in answer, Inspector Thompson spoke again.

"There is only one of them here. Alceste did not return to the house. I hardly expected we would find him here. The bally eel is too slippery for that. Alceste has got clean away again, by Jove! What?"

Kent said nothing. His eyes were still fixed reflectively upon Lieutenant Fargey—in doubt as to whether congratulations or condolences upon the result of the night's work were in order, thought Tommy Traynor.

27
BOLD PLAY

Up and down, up and down the room Addison Kent continued his restless pacing, a fixed furrow between his eyes, so deep in concentrated thought that he was oblivious of his surroundings. It was nearly two o'clock in the morning, but the excitements of the night left neither of the two friends inclined for sleep. They had returned to Kent's rooms half an hour before and the abstraction which the author had exhibited during the journey back to town had become profound as soon as they were alone at Minaki Annex. He seemed nervous and worried and Tommy Traynor watched him anxiously from the depths of a Morris chair.

"If I'd known this thing was going to bother you as much as this, Ad, I'd never have got you into it," he protested. "For heaven's sake, sit down somewhere! You make me nervous. Do you know that you haven't said two words in the past fifteen minutes? Be a little more sociable. What's wrong, anyway?"

Kent paused in front of him and looked at him strangely.

"Wrong?" he repeated. The hand of his uninjured arm clenched unconsciously. "It's all wrong—everything—terribly wrong!" He resumed his pacing.

"Nonsense! The shooting of MacMurrough on top of the suicide has been too much for the state of your nerves with that arm in a sling—"

Kent stopped in front of him again and Traynor looked up with some surprise at the tensity of the other's expression.

216

"Tommy," he asked slowly, "what would you say if I told you that in spite of everything that has transpired—in spite of the woman's suicide—in spite of her signed confession— I still believe she did not kill Henry Radcliffe?"

"I'd say you were crazy," responded Traynor promptly.

"And supposing I told you that I was beginning to wonder if Bob Fargey was not right after all—out there to-night—the man on the bed—"

"What! Was Alceste, you mean?"

"Yes."

"I'd say you were getting crazier every minute!" Traynor smiled skeptically. "What on earth next! I saw his eyes and they were as brown—as a horse-chestnut!"

The novelist's solemn expression remained unchanged.

"There's something infernally queer about it, now that I think it over," he said slowly. "I saw something which perhaps escaped your notice—when I was removing the bandage. The man's scalp in one spot was black—like the hair—as if it had been hurriedly—dyed!"

"Dyed! But that doesn't mean anything. The eyes were brown, I tell you. You saw that yourself. You can't get around that fact."

"No. They were brown. But I am wondering— I have been trying to recall where I— Tommy, did you ever hear of an operation whereby the iris of the eye could be—tattooed?"

"Tattooed?" Traynor sat up in his chair with a jerk. "The color changed?"

"From light to dark—yes. I should not have said 'the iris'; it is performed upon the cornea in front of the iris—in cases where through injury or otherwise a blemish has occurred in the natural pigment of the iris."

"Gre—at Scott!"

"But it is a very painful operation and only a small portion of the area can be tattooed at a time; the complete job would take weeks. That is what I am wondering about. It is only a little over four days ago that Levering visited me at the hospital and his eyes then were blue—light blue."

"Could that man have been the fellow mentioned in the message Levering received?" asked Traynor thoughtfully. "You know—'O.C.'?"

"I have considered that possibility." Kent shook his head. "MacMurrough must have written that message, Tommy. There is every reason for believing that the letters 'O.C.' stand for O'Carrol, the man who figured in the duel at the château. But I have a reason for thinking that O'Carrol is elsewhere than in that room we left a little while ago with a policeman on guard. No, if the man is not what he appeared to be—an insane victim of MacMurrough's—he is Alceste himself."

"Yet the color of the eyes could not be changed in four days, you say?"

"That's what puzzles me. I seem to have a faint recollection of having read something somewhere about a new discovery or an operation of the kind that was performed in much shorter order—in fact, the whole operation completed at one time. It was quite a while ago— By George! I believe I ran across the item while I was clipping Old Country newspapers for the file. Look up 'Surgery,' Tommy—in the file beside you—under 'Eye'—Let me have the folder."

Eagerly Kent took it over to the desk and began rapidly to go through the budget of clippings which the folder contained. In a moment he held out a tiny clipping, his face alight with satisfaction—just a few lines of type from a medical journal, briefly describing the discovery of Dr. Shane MacMurrough.

"MacMurrough's own special process!" cried Traynor with growing excitement. "That accounts for the chloroform smell and the— Gee Whiz! Alceste himself! For sheer nerve—!"

Addison Kent was already at the telephone.

"Police Headquarters!" he instructed in a low, tense voice.

"Pay-station calling," responded the languid voice of the telephone operator unexpectedly.

"Hey! Get off the line! What?—Who? Donovan? Well, for the love of— You what?—What's happened?"

A strange expression flitted across Kent's face as he listened to the detective. Traynor leaned forward.

"What is it, Ad?"

But for a moment after he had slowly hung up the receiver, Kent sat silent, still clutching the instrument. He turned with a quizzical look.

"Always twenty minutes late, Tommy! I've got the cow's tail beaten a mile when it comes to being behind! Donovan slipped out to a pay-station just now to tip me off to the fact that the man in the straitjacket has got away."

"Got a— What's that?" His incredulity was apparent.

"He escaped a couple of hours ago—in the uniform of the policeman who had been sent to the room to stand guard over him. Officer McCann went up to confer with his fellow guard and found him lying on the bed, in the straitjacket and gagged! Alceste had slipped out of the thing somehow—that was provided for, you may be sure—and the first thing 'Flatey' knew the muzzle of an automatic was staring him in the face. Alceste walked calmly downstairs in uniform—outdoors—helped himself to a motor-cycle in the yard and was miles away before any suspicions were aroused. By the Lord Harry! but we've got to give him credit, Tommy. He's smooth! He's nervey!"

He got to his feet and resumed his restless pacing, deep in thought once more.

"Alceste!" he muttered. "The man was Alceste! Eyes bloodshot, face white with the pain he'd been through and was still suffering! Caught in a tight corner, surrounded by police,—knew his eyes would give him away—bluffs it out right there under our noses— and gets away with it! And—gets—a-way—with it! Oh, the nerve of it!—And Fargey with his pistol right at his head! Yet he deserved a fighting chance and I'm glad I—"

His voice trailed away. New lines of worry grew in his face until it looked almost haggard. Traynor watched him breathlessly; for he saw that there was something else which Kent had not yet divulged. He waited patiently. The novelist's voice was edged with suppressed excitement as he stopped midway of the room and turned slowly on his heel.

"O'Carrol is the murderer," he said with solemn finality. "We must find him. No matter what the consequences, it is our duty. Tommy, I am being slowly forced to a conclusion which I have hesitated to entertain. Every time it has faced me, I have set it aside as a foolish idea. But the proof keeps crowding it in on me. It has haunted me for days and I have refused to entertain it as being altogether preposterous—imbecile! I have been afraid to put this fear into words! Tommy, I want you to prepare yourself to receive the shock of your life. It is—awful!—awful!"

Scarcely knowing what to expect, Traynor watched him and waited. Kent had sunk into a chair and he pinched his fingers across his eyelids, unable for a moment to proceed.

"Wh—what is it, old man?" he whispered at last. He tried to ask it in a normal tone.

He saw Addison Kent lift his head, saw his lips open—saw him stiffen in his chair, every nerve alert, gaze fixed unwinkingly across the room! Following the direction of that silent, intent regard he saw stealing beneath the hall door, visible through the open doorway of the room in which they sat,—the white edge of a sealed envelope!

In three bounds Traynor was across the room. He yanked open the door, levelling his automatic. Then he dashed out into the hallway and there followed a scramble of footsteps down the stair.

"Please! Please, Mister! I didn't do nuthin'. Honest to Gawd! I didn't."

"I'm not going to hurt you. Cut out that kicking, you young brat! Get up there!"

"I didn't do nuthin', Mister," pleaded the piping voice again. "A man give me a 'V' to bring that letter here—a motorcycle cop, with goggles on. How's I to know—?"

Half dragging the ragged urchin to the doorway, Traynor paused on the threshold. Then with a cry of alarm, he released his hold on the boy's collar and sprang towards Kent's chair—towards

Kent with the torn envelope at his feet and a sheet of paper quivering in his hand; Kent, white-faced and speechless!

Traynor fairly snatched the paper, his eyes racing over what had been written there with a lead-pencil:

"Addison Kent—

"They say one good turn deserves another. You saved my life to-night. You are on the right trail. Why do you not follow it? O'Carrol is within your reach.

—Alceste."

Weakly Traynor sat down in the nearest chair, wetting his lips. "W—well, I'll—be—d-amned!" he stuttered.

Without a word Kent got up, crossed to his desk and pulled open a drawer. He took out two extra clips of cartridges and passed one of them to Traynor.

"See that you have a full magazine in that gun, Tommy."

A sudden calmness possessed Kent now. He sat down at the desk, drew the telephone towards him and gave a number.

"Is that Police Headquarters?— Can you tell me if Lieutenant Fargey is anywhere around?— Off duty, you say? Has he gone home, d'you know?— Yes, I want to find him immediately. Thanks, but I want to see him personally— No, it's all right."

He rang off, waited a moment, then called up the nearest garage where he ran a monthly account.

"Hello, George—Addison Kent at the Annex—I want speed to-night. Send Crawford, if he's available— Yes, right away."

Traynor jumped to his feet.

"Where are we going?"

"Bob Fargey lives with a private family in Harlem. At present they are up state on a farm and he is baching it. We are going to the house."

"And after we pick up Bob—then what?"

"Then, Tommy, we are going to interview the real murderer of Henry Radcliffe and learn the full truth."

"O'Carrol?"

"O'Carrol."

As the car bore rapidly across town Kent fell silent. Traynor, keyed to highest tension, could hardly repress the desire for loquacity; but the novelist's face was mask-like and he refused to talk.

"You will know all presently—if we are not once more too late." He leaned forward. "Step on her, Crawford! I'll pay the fines."

The purr of the powerful motor rose to a roar as the speeding car took the turn into Lexington Ave., on two wheels and cut straight away northward towards High Bridge Park. At that hour the streets were deserted and when they swung the final corner of their mad journey there was only one light visible in the row of ancient houses—a light in an upper room.

They stopped in front of it. Kent sprang out and hurried up the walk to verify the number. But there was no need of that; for a head appeared at the open window and against the square of light they recognized Lieutenant Robert Fargey himself. He was in his shirt-sleeves.

"Hello, there! That you, Kent? What are you doing over here at this hour? Who's that with you?"

"Traynor—just the two of us."

"What do you want?"

"I've come for you, Bob, because—"

"So? Well, the door's not locked. Come right on up." His head and shoulders disappeared.

Addison Kent's hand was extended to grasp the brass knob of the front door when with an involuntary gasp he recoiled against Traynor who had followed up the steps. At the same time there reached the latter's ears a dull, muffled explosion from within the house.

Through the door, leaping for the stairs, pell-mell upward they went. Traynor saw Kent enter the lighted room,—saw his set, blanched face turn as Tommy reached the open door. An acrid odor struck his nostrils—

Then he shrank in dismay. Across the table in the centre of the room was sprawled the inert form of Fargey.

Suddenly alert, Traynor swept the room with the muzzle of his own weapon.

"O'Carrol? Alceste? Watch out! They're here! This is their work!"

He looked up wonderingly as Kent laid a gentle hand on his shoulder.

"Alceste's work—yes, indirectly." He nodded to the table. "The search is ended, old man. O'Carrol and Fargey are one!"

28
FACE UP

Tommy Traynor felt a momentary nausea. Dazedly he leaned against the wall. Fargey! Bob Fargey, whom he had known so long and intimately! The shock of the revelation left him speechless. A quilt had been dragged off the bed in the corner and lay on the floor beside the table with its silent burden. He watched Kent unroll it and pick from its folds the police automatic.

"He wrapped it around the gun in order not to have the whole neighborhood coming in here to see what was the matter," Kent explained as he pointed to the bullet-holes in the quilt.

A manilla envelope, fat with folded papers, caught his eye; he saw that it was addressed to himself and marked "Personal." A glance at those freshly written foolscap sheets was enough to establish the document as a written explanation of Fargey's tragic act. Kent sat down on the edge of the bed and began to read, passing each page to Traynor as he finished it.

"Dear Kent," it began. "When you read this I'll be away, solving the One Big Mystery. I have a hunch to-night that things are not breaking right for me and that the end is near; for, of course, I will not be taken alive. I saw to-night that you suspect the truth and word has just reached me that the 'lunatic' has escaped from the straitjacket—got clean away; I know for sure now what I strongly suspected at the time without knowing why—that that guy was Alceste himself. My big mistake was in not pinching him on the spot but that blue-eye business had me guessing for fair. Alceste will 'get' me sooner or later for to-night's work, as you will understand better when you have finished reading this. I intend to roll the bones to the last, though, as I have from the first in this thing. If the luck goes against me, I've no kick coming and I ain't squealing.

"There's some things I'd like you and Tommy Traynor to know about. Tommy was always fair and I think you are, too. I want to put it up to you and perhaps you'll be able to think more kindly of me. If you can't do what I ask about this thing, that's all right. Do whatever you think best.

"I killed Henry Radcliffe *by accident* when I fired into the room *at the woman*. I swear that this is the truth, so help me God! I had no quarrel with that poor gentleman. God forgive me! I even thought that I was saving his life when I fired at that cursed hell-cat; for they were struggling for the little gun in Radcliffe's hand and she was getting the best of him, being strong as a horse in spite of her gray hair. I saw red at sight of her and lost my head completely. Just as I pulled the trigger they swung around and he got the bullet I intended for her. He crumpled up in her arms and she didn't see me. I beat it.

"You know now she was the Countess Marinelli and you know what happened at the château over in France years ago. Yelland told me about Mrs. Radcliffe's history. I never was much for believing in Fate and all that, but it's mighty queer how things turn out sometimes, ain't it? To think that that poor little woman was mixed up in this thing like that and me not knowing it. I didn't see her that night of the dance at the château; I's out in the grounds with the Countess at the time. I wouldn't have recognized her anyways, for she must've changed a lot. To think that she was an eye-witness of that duel—right on deck and me talking to her and not knowing it and she not knowing me! I've changed a lot myself and even the Marinelli woman didn't know me till I showed her a scar she recognized and she saw I knew the facts.

"Well, anyways, you know I had reason for hating her; if she'd stayed away from the United States everything would have been different, but when all that past I'd been trying to forget was raked up and flung in my face— But let me tell about the duel. My father and I were estranged but God knows I bore him no ill will. I did not know it was him I was fighting that night. I'd arrived late that night from Paris and didn't know who was on hand at the Countess's party. She took care not to let me know about my father and she arranged the whole thing with the cunning of the Jezebel she was. She was mixing around pretty free in politics and I knew she was in the pay of the German Government; what I didn't know was that she'd sold some information to Russia and that my father knew of it. He belonged to a brotherhood of Irish patriots that were mixing up in things they had no business to; it was that we had quarrelled over, him and me. The Countess had been trying to get me to act as go-between for her in another little matter and she thought if she could get something on me, she could make me do as she wanted. So she arranged it to use me as the means of silencing my father, who had threatened to tell what he knew against her. She was a fascinating woman when she wanted to be in those days and I was young and foolish—a devil-may-care young blade and no mistake. She had my father on a string, too, and in our masquerade costumes and masks neither of us knew the other. She got us into the fight over an alleged insult and—you know what happened.

"I hid for a few days in a village of charcoal burners not far away, working as one of them and blackened well. Then as nothing happened, I got over my first scare and planned to work my way to some seaport where I could ship as a stoker on a vessel bound for America. I had often thought of going to the United States and it seemed the safest place for me. I had no trouble getting away; the police didn't seem to be on my trail at all.

"Once on this side of the ocean, I went West and buried myself in a mining camp for a while. I changed my name and altered my appearance as much as possible and after a while I began to get a new slant on things and began to fit right in as an American citizen. I made lots of friends and it was through one of them that I got into police work; it seemed a good line to take to keep posted and get first warning of any trouble coming my way from France.

"But nothing like that happened and I finally drifted to New York and joined the Force. As the years went by I came to forget the past like a bad dream and I lived for my work and was happy. I tried to do my duty and if I do say it myself, my rapid promotion is the proof that I succeeded. I liked my work and it came to mean everything to me. Nobody can say that Bob Fargey was not a good citizen of the United States. Things went along fine until two weeks ago.

"Then I got a bad jolt. I got a note one day, signed with the secret symbol of the Brotherhood of Irish patriots to which my father had belonged. The man who wrote it asked me to meet him in a certain cheap cafe on the East Side and, of course, I went. It was this Doc MacMurrough. He was pretty keen on faces and I'd met him in the old days with my father; he'd recognized me on the street, or thought he did. The family resemblance was strong enough for him to start looking me up and he wasn't one to overlook any bets. He knew all about what happened at the château. How he found out I don't know; but he knew and had gum-shoed around on my trail. I tried to bluff him, but it wouldn't work and what he had to tell me got my goat right off the bat.

"He said he was my friend and a sworn enemy of the Marinelli woman. He gave that as his reason for approaching me. She had come to the States after a bad mix-up on the Continent—her old game of double-crossing somebody. You can't do that in spy-work over there without getting knifed some dark night. To make a long story short, MacMurrough told me that she had brought along with her my *dossier* and intended to use it against me for her own ends as soon as she located me. When I asked him how he knew this he told me of Roger Levering who was a close friend of his and who had it in for his aunt. He said that they were staying with the Radcliffe's at Hillcrest and suggested that with Levering's help it would be a cinch to go through her papers in the safe and destroy the evidence against me, if I cared to take the risk. He was only passing the tip as an old friend of my father's; for he said he realized that I had been duped by the woman and was not responsible for the death of my father.

"This man, MacMurrough, was as smooth as they make them and he seemed so sincere about it that I didn't tumble to his game then. I thanked him and said I'd see. The more I thought it over, the more important it seemed for me to destroy those papers; with them out of the way I could give the Marinelli woman the laugh and pinch her if she got nasty. Later I met the two of them at the same place—MacMurrough and Levering. Levering pretended he was afraid to assist in stealing the document, but MacMurrough pointed out how easy it was. All he had to do was to get the combination of the safe and borrow the key to his aunt's deposit-box; I would slip in when the coast was clear, open the safe arid the box, take out the papers I was interested in, lock everything up again, hand him back the key and that was all there was to it. Levering agreed to do his part then.

"But still I hesitated. I asked for more time to think it over. Then I learned through MacMurrough that 'Mrs. Saint-Anton,' as she called herself, was about to have me traced by a private detective agency and I got desperate. I went out to Hillcrest that very night, dressed in old clothes. I had no intention of attempting anything so rash as murder, let alone that of Henry Radcliffe. I didn't dream that he was connected in any way with the events at the château. I went out to the house with the one idea of getting those papers which she held against me and destroying them.

"Levering had been warned by MacMurrough to watch out for me and he was waiting. He let me in through a window into the library. He had the combination to the safe and it was while we were trying to open it that we heard the voices up in Radcliffe's room, raised in anger. We were both scared somebody might come down to the library and Levering sent me up the fire-escape to see what was doing.

"As I say, I saw red at sight of her after all these years—the cause of all my troubles, still trying to do me injury and prevent me living my new life in peace. I wrapped the bottom of the window curtain around the little gun Levering had pressed into my hand as I slipped out the library window—the woman's own pearl-handled automatic, as it turned out—and fired.

"When I saw the terrible result of that shot I came to my senses mighty fast and slipped along the fire escape to take a look in at Traynor's window to make sure he hadn't been wakened. He was sitting up in bed! I just had time to swing over the rail and hang from the grating in the shadow beneath when he came out. I was thankful that the moon went under a cloud just then. I could hear him talking to himself and knew he hadn't spotted me. As soon as he went inside the room again, I dropped quietly to the ground and beat it back to the library.

"When I whispered to Levering what had happened he gave me one awful look and called me all kinds of a damned fool. I handed him back the little gun and I saw a devilish look come into his eyes. He told me then that he saw only one way out of the mess. It was the woman's gun; he had stolen it out of her trunk in order to be armed for this occasion. He proposed to obtain a gold pencil she owned and write the accusation on Radcliffe's shirt-cuff; then, if I could arrange to get myself detailed to the case, between us we could cover my tracks very nicely. He admitted having no love for her and while the scheme was devilish, I wasn't exactly crazy with love for her myself. It seemed the only way out and we arranged it that way.

"Just as we were trying the combination on the safe again we heard someone coming downstairs and just had time to hide behind a bookcase in the corner when in came Miss Radcliffe to try and find the combination to the safe in the desk. She had the case of pearls in her hand and took it away with her again. I was sweating pretty freely about then; things were getting mighty risky and I was anxious to get the papers and beat it.

"As soon as I had them, we locked everything up again and I got away O.K. I didn't tumble at that time to the big game Levering and MacMurrough were playing—not even when I learned about the robbery next morning. I didn't suspect Levering until Sunday night, after I heard about this here Alceste being loose—from Lamont—and found out that the pearls were gone, too. I began then to size things up and felt sure that the whole thing MacMurrough and Levering had in mind was to get me into a position where I couldn't say a word no matter what they tried to pull off—where they could even call on me to help them cover up their own tracks in these jewel robberies. They had everything planned. It was MacMurrough who faked the 'phone message that got Traynor off the scene Sunday morning.

"I was wild when I saw the mess I'd got myself into—and the disappearance of the shirt-cuff didn't help matters so's you could notice. I didn't think there was one chance in a hundred of recovering it and I began to wonder if Levering was stringing me and hadn't written the message at all. I tried to locate MacMurrough; but he'd made himself scarce.

"Then Sunday night Levering slipped me the good word that he'd found the cuff. We know now he listened to Mrs. Stanton—Mrs. Radcliffe—telling Lamont in the summerhouse Sunday night and beat it down to the Stokes place to get the Japanese box. That all seems clear enough.

"Well, things seemed to be coming my way then. We arrested the Countess and once I had her safe in jail I began to work on her. We had one sweet little session at last, all by our lonesome, and when she learned who I was she gave right up. She knew I had her at my mercy and that so far as she was concerned there was no mercy coming to her. She asked me to let her cash in in her own way and that suited me down to the ground. She was scared to face the music; for if she was extradited, she knew a firing-squad would line her up against a wall. She preferred to pass out as 'Mrs. Saint-Anton' and I agreed to it if she'd sign a paper, relieving me of all responsibility. I managed it so that the paper she signed was a confession to having killed Radcliffe. That completed the case very happily for me.

"I was so pleased with the way things had turned out that I began to think the luck would hold good if I played another round with Levering and MacMurrough. I wanted to redeem myself and show those two crooks that they couldn't get away with it with me on the job. By this time I was pretty sure Levering was Alceste himself. Then when Thompson turned out to be a Scotland Yard man and had the tip on where they were hanging out, I was sure I had them where I wanted them. With them out of the way I could close the book on the past altogether and go on as Bob Fargey without fear of future trouble.

"You know what happened to-night. We got MacMurrough; but Alceste escaped. I made my big mistake when I horned in on the roundup. I should have laid low and let somebody else get the credit of the capture; but I thought if I could pull it off it might satisfy even you, Kent, that I was on the level. Alceste ain't going to rest till he gets me for going after them: I ain't going to be surprised if he follows me here and tries to get me before morning.

"If neither you nor him shows up and I come through the night, I've got one chance left—to get Alceste before he gets me. I've got every exit from the country blocked from Headquarters and on the lookout for him. His description has been wired everywhere. But I have a hunch it ain't any use, that sort of thing, where he is concerned. He'll find a way of his own for beating the whole machine.

"If the game's up, I'm satisfied to leave Alceste to you. If anybody can get that devil, Kent, it is you. I warn you against him. He is the most dangerous crook I've ever known and the cleverest. If I don't find Satan at home when I call, it will be because he's still on earth and has got away from you.

"There's only one favor I have to ask and you may think it funny for me to ask it. But the name of Lieutenant Bob Fargey is clean, old man, and I have a great hankering to leave it clean. It is the one good part of my life—this that I have lived as a respectable citizen of the United States. I am well thought of at the Central Office. I am known all over the country and my standing in the Force is ace high. You can help to keep it so if you will allow the Radcliffe case to ride as it is. Nobody at Headquarters, in the newspaper offices, or the public at large—will fail to accept the case as solved by the suicide and 'confession' of the wicked woman who has been responsible for my downfall. The facts herein set down are known only to you and Traynor—and Alceste.

"If you can let me have a first-class funeral it is all I ask. I would like lots of flowers—as many as possible—and as many bands as you like—the more the merrier. Pick out the finest casket you can get; there will be money enough for a tip-top funeral. I am enclosing a list of the lodges to which I belong and no doubt they will all want to march as well as the boys on the Force, of course. I have written out some dope for the newspapers and perhaps Traynor will be good enough to see to this end of it and get good big type into the headings.

"I enclose also a signed statement to account for my suicide to the public—worry over the state of my health—incurable disease and so on. It should fill the bill all right.

"That's all—except that I have a hunch this Alceste is a German secret-service agent as well as a jewel thief and that he had two objects in coming to the United States. One of these was to pick up a few choice jewels; the other was to carry out the death penalty decreed by the *Wilhelmstrasse* against the Countess Marinelli. I happen to be the goat who served his ends. If I find that as a spirit I'm able to help you get Alceste, in the interests of humanity you can count on me!

"Well, boys, so long, both of you! I hear an auto coming—somebody hitting the high spots. It may be you. If so—I'm ready. Well, so long and good luck!

Your former friend,

Dermod O'Carrol,

—or, as I prefer it—

Robert Fargey,

Detective-Lieutenant."

Silently Traynor shuffled the last sheet of foolscap into its place and handed back the document to Addison Kent with a shake of the head.

"Poor Bob!" he murmured.

Kent slid the papers back into the envelope and put it into an inside pocket.

"It is not for us to stand in judgment, Tommy. If only we could have prevented this!" For a moment he stood, looking down at the inert form. "We can at least see that he has his big funeral," he said quietly.

With a sigh he turned away to the telephone on the wall at the head of the bed to notify Police Headquarters.

Then the receiver of the instrument jerked from his hand as he started at Traynor's excited shout behind him.

"Kent! Quick! He's still alive!"

In one bound Kent reached the table. He placed his ear over the heart and straightened up, his face pale, his eyes alert. They lifted him over to the bed and Kent sprang to the telephone.

"Give me the nearest hospital. Quick!"

29
The Gauntlet

Traynor tossed his hat onto the desk and felt for a cigar as he dropped into the nearest chair. "How's the arm coming along?" he asked cheerfully.

"Fine, thanks," smiled Kent through a cloud of tobacco smoke. "Anything new?"

"Not a thing. It looks as if the beggar has got clean out of the country. Headquarters has been everlastingly busy the past three days but everything they've followed up has failed to give a trace of Alceste."

"And Fargey?"

"Doing nicely. They tell me we can see him for a little while this afternoon. I've ordered the car. How are things at Hillcrest?"

"Rose is very happy with her mother, Ad. And she— I never saw anyone respond so quickly to a change as Mrs. Radcliffe has. She's actually got color in her cheeks."

"I am glad to hear that," nodded Kent with pleasure. "I suppose our friend, Lamont—"

"Oh, the Boss is out there half his time," laughed Tommy. "I never see him now without a flower in his lapel and I am getting suspicious that he is putting his hair up in curlers at night! What a strange ending this whole thing has come to!"

A shadow crossed Addison Kent's face. His jaws knotted for a moment.

"The ending has not been reached—yet," he said grimly. "The end will never be reached—until we have Alceste behind the bars. I feel that I have failed, Tommy,—failed miserably!"

234

"You're crazy!" cried Traynor, surprised at the despondency in his friend's voice. "Buck up! How can you say a thing like that? Isn't it something to have brought happiness to Rose and her mother—happiness out of tragedy? That was your work—"

"It might have evolved without assistance from me."

"What's the matter with you? You ran the mystery right out of the case. Fargey got away with nothing."

"Fargey was but a pawn in the game, Tommy. The real criminal has escaped. Has Lamont got back his jewels?"

"What're a few jewels? Nobody cares whether they are recovered or not! At least, neither Rose nor Lamont is worrying over it and I know darn well I'm not. We're concerned with other things more important. Rose and I are to be married—after a bit. So congratulate me, old scout."

"I do, indeed, Tommy," smiled Kent as he reached out and shook hands. He dropped back with a return of his despondency. "Nevertheless, I wish— Don't you see that Alceste has played with us at his own sweet will—all of us? Is he to get away Scot free? Apparently so. Even the definite tip that brought things to a head— came from Alceste—that note about O'Carrol's whereabouts."

"But you knew it was Fargey. What made you suspect him, Ad? Frankly, it was the surprise of my life."

Kent smoked in silence for a while before he replied.

"Not any one definite thing but a number of things, taken in conjunction with one another," he said thoughtfully at last. "His absolute certainty that 'Mrs. Saint-Anton' was the criminal—even before the shirt-cuff—was found was out of keeping with the evidence to justify it. His refusal to admit any other hypothesis and his manner when he made out his case against her indicated to me a degree of animosity which pointed to something outside his official position in the case. Then at the inquest the sudden complacency which he exhibited, following the disappearance of the pearls, struck me as strange. His excitement over the arrest of the woman and the manner in which he seemed to gloat over it set me wondering. The way the shirt-cuff came to light so suddenly in a trunk that should not have been overlooked in the first place and the wording of the message itself—pointed to a frame-up of some sort.

"Then there was the 'ghost' phase of the case—so outré and unusual that one would naturally have expected the keenest investigation of its significance. Yet Fargey paid scarcely any attention to it—compared to the other evidence—and he even was anxious for you and Levering to help him keep it out of the newspapers. He was afraid of uncovering something that would upset his case against 'Mrs. Saint-Anton,' I gathered; certainly he had no justification for his assumption that she must be the one who played the part of the 'ghost.'

"Meanwhile, my own investigations led me afield to the discovery of Mrs. Stanton's participation in events on the night of the murder and a strong suspicion of Levering's complicity in the crime. I began to wonder if he might not be Alceste himself, even as I suspected that Mrs. Radcliffe was still alive. Then followed the discovery of the chess-cipher message to Levering, introducing .an unknown quantity—O. C. I was sure O'Carrol was our man as soon as I heard Mrs. Radcliffe's story of the night at the Château du Vieux Pont and that it was the woman he intended to shoot, not Mr. Radcliffe.

"Then came the suicide of Fargey's prisoner and her 'confession.' I felt sure that something was amiss. I could not square this development with all the facts. I began to wonder about Fargey— to wonder if he was in league with the gang somehow. I got Donovan to help me quietly to look him up and discovered a few interesting things about him; among these was the fact that on the night of the murder Fargey did not reach home until four o'clock in the morning and was off duty at the time. Where had he been? I recalled that you were startled by sight of the moonlight on his face when he and Lamont stepped into your room from the fire-escape; if any significance attached to that incident, it must have been Fargey's face you saw because Lamont's status was established clearly enough by now. I at once asked myself if Fargey could be O'Carrol and could find no good reason for refuting the possibility. It fitted from every angle.

"I was not sure of it until I watched him at work during the raid on MacMurrough's place. I felt then that he was in desperate straits and surmised what afterwards proved to be the fact that he was seeking to save himself by a *coup de maitre*. I believe now, though, that Bob was merely playing for a show of weakness from Alceste—that, as he said, he was only bluffing and had no intention of shooting the man on the bed. Any way—"

He paused as a knock came on the door and the afternoon's mail was flopped in on the hall floor. Traynor stepped out and picked up the letters.

"Anyway, it didn't take Alceste long to strike at Fargey through me, did it?" Kent shuffled the letters and sliced one open. "He is the most unscrupulous, cold-blooded, daring— What the devil now!"

As he read the letter a glint of anger came into his eyes. His cheeks flushed and at last he hit the desk a resounding thump with his good fist and jumped to his feet.

"Read it, Tommy. By the Eternal! did you ever see such gall?"

Traynor began to laugh. It was a simple little farewell note from Alceste, no less, postmarked from a little town up-state and written on parlor-car stationery with the words "En Route" printed at the top:

<blockquote>

"Addison Kent,
Minaki Annex,
New York City.

My Dear Kent:

By the time you get this I'll be out of reach. I regret that pressure of business compelled me to cut short my visit; but I hope that some day I may enjoy your further acquaintance. You stimulate me and I know that I shall miss you.

You have given me the run of my life, old top. In terms of chess, shall we call it 'Stalemate' rather than 'Checkmate?' Some other day we may play another game perhaps? *Quien sabe?*

</blockquote>

I am sorry that I could not remain to attend Lieutenant Fargey's funeral. I am sure it must have been an imposing sight. However, I have ordered some flowers sent. I am solacing myself with the hope that some day I may have the pleasure of attending yours.

Auf Wiedersehn, my dear Kent,

Roger Levering (Pro Tempore)

but always your own

Alceste."

Kent turned from the window, slapped Traynor's hat on that grinning individual's head and picked up his own.

"Our taxi is waiting. Come on. Let's go and show it to Fargey. It ought to help him to get well."

They found the lieutenant waiting anxiously to see them. Traynor experienced a stab of pity at the tense eagerness with which he tried to read their faces as they entered the private room where he lay. It was his all that was at stake. His head was bandaged and it was something of a shock to see him so white and weak from loss of blood. He smiled faintly when he read the letter from Alceste.

"Ain't that guy the limit?" he commented.

Kent drew a chair alongside the bed, reached into his pocket and took out the envelope that contained the closely written sheets of foolscap.

"You will want to know what I intend to do about this, Fargey," he began at once. "That is easily demonstrated." He began to tear it up deliberately into little pieces and put them into his pocket. "As soon as I get home I intend to burn these scraps to ashes—personally."

"You—" He could not articulate for a little while but watched the tearing process with fascination. "You are going to give me—another chance?" he whispered at last in disbelief.

"All the chance in the world, old man."

"I—don't deserve it, Kent," he faltered. "I can only promise you that you'll never find me doin' anythin' to make you regret it. I— I've been a damned fool! I—"

"You are entitled to your own opinion, of course," smiled Kent. "None of us is perfect, you know, and a lesson well learned is usefulness multiplied." He took his hand gently. "You've had a bad dream, as you said yourself, and the best thing to do about bad dreams is to forget them as soon as possible. I feel that your greatest service is yet to be done. There is still—Alceste!"

He stood up.

"That's right, Bob. We need you on the job, you know," grinned Traynor cheerfully as he shook hands.

Lieutenant Fargey could not speak. The hot tears were welling from his eyes. But he raised his hand weakly—at salute.

They left him so.

THE GOLDEN SCARAB

FOREWORD

In presenting to the public a second chronicle from the somewhat intimate records entrusted to me by my old newspaper friend "Mr. Addison Kent," I have been led to select the case of *The Golden Scarab* for a number of reasons. Chief of these, aside from its timeliness, is the fact that it brought Kent once more in contact with his old enemy "Alceste," in rather a remarkable way which bears directly upon certain startling material in my possession for possible use at some future date. Also, I have received from readers of *The Gauntlet of Alceste* so many requests for the further history of this gentleman's exploits that I am left but little choice in the matter.

It has been my endeavour to adhere closely to the actual records, sufficiently strange in themselves. The assistance of Mr. Arthur Weigall, late Inspector-General of Antiquities, Egyptian Government, Member of the Catalogue Staff of the Cairo Museum and Officer of the Order of the Medjidieh, is gratefully acknowledged. In his volume *Tutankhamen* (Thornton Butterworth, Limited) he relates an actual experience of his own in connection with the mummy of a sacred cat, discovered in the Theban necropolis in 1909 by Lord Carnarvon; the incident is so analogous to the adventure which befell Addison Kent that I have taken the liberty of drawing upon some of Mr. Weigall's impressions and data in order that the portrayal may be accurate.

H. M.
Toronto, Canada.

243

1
Out of the Mystic East

Mr. Richard Malabar, late of the London *Daily World*, had not dallied with hazards in the ports of the Seven Seas without learning to be discreet. He was well aware that in all metropolitan centres are certain districts where at times the passing stranger does well to hold steadfastly upon his way; where blindness and deafness may be even imperative if one is to continue the enjoyment of fine music and beautiful sunsets. New York's polyglot East Side was hardy the place for experimental interference, if simple kindness could be so misconstrued. Nevertheless, in the early evening of this day in late summer—

A curt command brought the taxi to a sudden stop at the curb. Richard Malabar stepped out, his polished malacca cane hanging from his left forearm as he smoothed the yellow gloves on his sinewy hands and strode around the corner into the nearest side-street.

"Good evening, officer. What seems to be the matter?"

The Italian owner of the fruit-cart stopped gesticulating. The ragged urchin whom he held by the collar ceased squirming. The little girl with the Cinderella hair and the comically smudged face allowed one big gray eye to peek over a grimy fist while her sobs became less demonstrative, and she held closer to the policeman's coat-tail. Patrolman Tierney turned a quizzical Irish eye upon the newcomer in the sudden lull that had come upon the noisy group.

"Tony says thim two kids has tuk foive oranges and t'ree bananas widout payin' fer thim," he explained. "He's afther wantin' me to put in a gin'ral alar-rm to Headquarters to call out the reserves an' pinch the little divils as danger-rous characters!"

Malabar looked at the "dangerous characters" with a twinkle in his eye.

"Desperate thieves, eh? What did you steal them for, son?"

"Please, mister, we didn't steal 'em," piped the thin-faced boy hopefully. "We just took 'em. The kid sister was hungry, see? We hadda git eats!"

"A case of economic pressure, officer," smiled Malabar. "With your permission, I shall proceed to dispose of the case against the prisoners by settlement out of court. How much do five oranges and three bananas come to, Tony? Well, here is your money."

He called the newsboy over to him and pressed a bill into his hand.

"You and your sister go and dine at the Waldorf, old chap. What did you say your name was? Spud? Well, away you go, now!"

He shook hands with Patrolman Tierney, cleverly parting with another bill in so doing, and in a moment had vanished around the corner into his taxi.

To Richard Malabar, much travelled cosmopolite, the incident but served as an after-dinner mint to the excellent meal he had just enjoyed at a little Hungarian restaurant. He liked to dine in odd corners, and he leaned back in his seat well content. For the sight of Spud and his sister had brought back a vision of his own childhood woes. Poor little beggars! The smile which banished the haunting melancholy from his clean-cut face unlocked for a moment the golden personality that underlay the habitual mask behind which he was accustomed to retire from the world. Before he was more than a few blocks away his mind was back among the problems that obsessed him—problems gray cloaked in gravity.

At last, with a shoulder shrug of impatience, he dismissed them and directed his thoughts to the evening before him. The taxi was speeding for the comfortable quarters of Addison Kent, popular novelist and young man of good looks, health, wealth and fame, who lived in Minaki Annex, just off Riverside Drive. During the past two weeks Dick Malabar and Addison Kent had grown very close to that deep sort of friendship which transcends the mere companionship of kindred, bachelor spirits. And to-night they were to spend the evening together out in Westchester.

Malabar had first met the novelist some years ago at the Press Club in Wine Court Alley, London. Then the stories and articles of this hard-working Canadian newspaper youth were just beginning to attract attention in various magazines. The mutual liking between the two young men might have ripened rapidly into friendship if the journalist had not been called away on one of those overnight commissions for his paper which frequently took him on long and difficult journeys. Now, meeting Kent again in New York after the lapse of the years, Dick Malabar had found him riding the crests of the literary seas with a success which would have upset any young man not well ballasted with a sense of humour. And as their friendship grew, Malabar had been delighted to find that his own hobby, criminology, was likewise Kent's; to find the author's bookcases filled with rare books and his filing cabinets stored with a more complete collection of newspaper and magazine clippings than was available in any newspaper "morgue" or even at Police Headquarters; to find in Addison Kent's keenly trained mind a match for his own upon almost any subject.

The novelist greeted him jovially when at last Malabar reached the apartment. Kent had dined with his misguided publisher, he said, had delivered the new manuscript and his worries were over for a while.

"Are one's worries ever over?"

"Well, if that's how you are feeling, you need a tonic, my boy," laughed Kent. "I wish we were going out for a livelier evening than we are likely to have with the worthy Professor; but I guess we are in for it, Dick. Caron has been 'phoning again to make sure we would be on hand and that—" He broke off abruptly. "Anything gone wrong, old man? You appear to possess all the expansive merriment of a conscientious undertaker at a rich man's funeral!"

The gravity upon Malabar's face remained unrelieved for a moment as he stood regarding the novelist intently. Then a slow smile dispelled it.

"A bit of a wash and I am ready for the worst your professorial friend can do to us."

"That's George, signal-honking for us out front now. It will take us about an hour to run out."

"Right-o!"

Professor Emil Caron, the noted Egyptologist and archæologist with various letters after his name, had arrived in New York just two days ago. Because he was a close personal friend of Mr. Armaund Lamont, the well-known Fifth Avenue jeweller, silver-smith and collector of antiques, and because Addison Kent had received a special request from Mr. Lamont that he look after the French savant upon arrival, Kent had met the liner at the dock. Professor Caron had been confined to his berth with sea-sickness all the way across the Atlantic, and was in a highly nervous state. It was fortunate for his peace of mind that the novelist was there to ease through the Customs the cherished possessions of the ex-cited little Frenchman, or he would have gone to the asylum for the insane direct from the boat, instead of to the Westchester man-sion of his friend Lamont. Even as it was, there was enough fuss over certain odd-shaped cases and boxes to make Kent heave a breath of relief when the ordeal was over.

Professor Caron was by way of being something of an author-ity in archæological circles. He was bringing with him to America quite a collection of antiquities for distribution among various museums. Most of these had been consigned direct; but not all. The careful transfer of the "luggage" had required the personal supervision of the gesticulating owner, whose English failed him utterly under stress, and whose French was so voluble that at times it outran even Kent, who prided himself on his proficiency in that language. However, the novelist had done everything possible to facilitate the Professor's adjustment to his new surroundings and was rewarded by the genuine gratitude of the little man.

It would take a day or two to get unpacked and settled, he had explained, but the very first guest to be invited to this most mag-nificent home must be Mr. Addison Kent. Had he not had warm eulogy from his great friend Lamont?—the very warmest praise of

Mr. Kent and his very great abilities? Nothing must interfere. He must come and Professor Caron would be honoured to show him things he would be interested to see, and to tell him things that would amaze him—some very great secrets which on no account must he repeat.

"You have been so very good, Mr. Kent, to help me like this. I may have still greater need of your help, and it is well to prepare, is it not? You will come?"

Even had Kent not been interested in the subjects encompassed by Professor Caron's special hobby, he would have found it difficult to refuse. But he was greatly interested in such subjects and a little intrigued by the Frenchman's manner. He knew, too, that Dick Malabar had been in Egypt, and the mention of the fact brought an immediate invitation from the Professor for Malabar to come also. A friend for whom Mr. Kent could vouch—what could be more pleasurable?

Following a double wedding, Armaund Lamont and his bride, accompanied by Thomas Traynor and his bride, had gone abroad on an extended honeymoon tour. It would be some time yet before they returned, Kent knew; but the letter he had received from Lamont spoke in highest terms of Professor Emil Caron. Indeed, Lamont's confidence was best expressed in the fact that he had placed his newly acquired palatial home in Westchester at the disposal of the Professor for whatever length of time he chose to stay in New York. The place had been closed for the summer after the decorators had completed their work, and had been left in charge of Mokra, Lamont's Algerian butler, with the gardener to look after the grounds. This visit of a guest meant the hiring of a chef and kitchen help; but these details had been arranged by Lamont's office manager.

"I wonder what the little Professor has in store for us this evening," Kent remarked as they neared their destination. "He spoke as if he had some surprise or other up his sleeve. Aside from that, I must warn you, Dick, that Lamont's house is full of queer and rare things, picked up in odd corners of the earth. I think some of them will interest you. Lamont's confidential man is an Algerian—quite a character in his way. And Caron has brought with him a Nubian servant whom he picked up somewhere 'east of Suez'—a big, brown animal of a man who could draw good money as a Silent Slave in a leopard girdle in one of these Western stage spectacles of the Very Far East. He'd look great, posed on the marble steps of the Caliph's palace against a Maxfield Parish ultramarine sky, arms folded to bulge the biceps, a figure in bronze with a spot-light playing— Why, say, the fellow must be fully seven feet tall!"

"Oh, come now! come now!" chuckled Malabar.

They presently rolled in between the huge stone gateposts of the Lamont estate and curved up the avenue between trees and shrubs that circled the lawns to the great brownstone house, perched high above the Sound. Evidently the noise of their car had apprised the Algerian servant of their approach, for the great iron-grilled glass doors swung open to them before they could press the electric bell. Mokra himself stood there—a tall, dignified figure in immaculate black and white—and welcomed Addison Kent with a smile of recognition which seemed to consist largely of perfect teeth, startlingly white in contrast to his swarthy skin.

As he took their hats, gloves, canes and light overcoats, close to his heels stood the finest Persian cat Malabar had ever seen—a big, coal-black one, whose great golden eyes regarded the visitors with a calm stare of indifference A regular snob of a cat! He seemed to know that his fur was long and silky, that the red ribbon around his neck was very becoming to him and that he belonged to the aristocracy of Catdom. As Mokra preceded them down the wide hallway so did the cat, hugging close and picking steps with infinite grace across the polished floor.

"What a beauty!" Malabar admired.

"Lamont thinks a lot of him," Kent smiled. "He's captured no end of ribbons. Name's Aristophanes— 'Toph' for short."

"Ah, a humorist! That accounts for his solemnity!"

In the passage beyond the great staircase suddenly they were confronted by a giant figure. He appeared before the heavy velvet hangings that curtained the archway towards which the butler was leading them. His advent was so unexpected and he was of such startling physique that both guests halted involuntarily. Recalling

Kent's description, Malabar identified him at once as the Nubian who acted as servant or bodyguard, or both, for Professor Emil Caron; while he may not have been seven feet tall, his bulk seemed to tower over them—almost to threaten as he stood with folded arms, frowning at the Algerian in silent disapproval. In very truth, all he needed was a leopard skin about his loins, gold hoops on his ears, and a drawn scimitar to complete the impression of *Arabian Nights* theatricality

In the fleeting tableau Kent and Malabar were aware of Mokra drawing back, half in fear, half in resentment; of domineering contempt that crossed the brown face of the Nubian like the shadow of a sneer; of the black cat with back arched! Then the Nubian was bowing and holding aside the curtain for them to pass, while Mokra was smiling and politely assuring Mr. Kent that their host would be found in the library beyond.

2
THE WHISPER OF THE AGES

Professor Caron was half-way across the big room, eagerly greeting them even before he was close enough to shake hands. He had awaited their arrival with the impatience of an enthusiast who requires only an intelligent audience to make him happy. A little man of spectacles and the stooping neck of a student, as if he had spent many years in peering and prying for Knowledge in a never-ending game of Hide-and-Seek. And, like so many men who devote their lives to restricted fields of intensive investigation, he lacked complexities; to a degree, the world even ceased to exist for him outside of his own particular orbit. He knew that Addison Kent, being a literary man, was a fellow-student, and he soon sensed the fact that Kent's friend belonged in the same category. It pleased him greatly to be able to converse with them freely in his own language about his work, and to feel that their interest was genuine, their minds competent. He beamed upon them, therefore, with an enthusiasm so unaffected that it was almost childlike.

The great room in which they lounged, comfortably ensconced in deep leather chairs, was a harmony in luxury. The walls were lined with bookcases and various antiques, with here and there a valuable painting. The floor rugs were costly. The furniture was massive, particularly the round library table in the centre; it must have been eight feet in diameter, and was curiously carved and inlaid. As his glance roved the room, Dick Malabar's face showed approval of the artistic taste with which Mr. Armaund Lamont had arranged everything.

251

Noticing this interest, Professor Caron graciously suggested that presently they would make a tour of inspection. In addition to Mr. Lamont's most interesting pieces there were some things of his own which they might like to see. He had assembled them on an upper floor—in his own most beautiful bedroom, to be exact. It was there that he had unpacked his treasures, including the mummies.

"Mummies!" echoed Malabar, amused. "Hardly bedroom companions, Professor!"

"I sleep with them around me; for then I know that they are safe," he explained ingenuously.

"There's an idea for you, Kent. Write a story about the theft of a mummy, though I'm blest if I know how you would go about stealing one, or what you'd do with it after you got away with it!"

"It is not the mummies, Mr. Malabar, but the things that are buried with them. Some of these antiques are very beautiful and very valuable. In this great city are many wealthy people who would pay big sums—collectors, you understand." Professor Caron smiled a little uncertainly in mild reproof. "Robbery of the royal sepulchres was common in ancient Thebes; for, as you know, it was the Egyptian custom to bury with the dead much jewellery and great wealth in gold, silver, bronze and precious stones."

"Desecration of a tomb, I understand, was a very serious offence," prompted Kent.

It was. Professor Caron explained at some length just why it was so serious. To begin with, the ancient Egyptians believed in a life hereafter, and that to obtain everlasting life it was necessary to preserve the embalmed body. They believed that the spirit dwelt in the tomb with the body for some three thousand years before it was summoned to the Judgment Hall of Osiris, the god of the Dead; there the heart was weighed in the balances along with the Symbol of Truth, and so found wanting or vindicated. They believed that the spirit required food and comforts, and that is why embalmed food was placed in the tomb, along with many objects used by the deceased in his daily life. After three thousand years the jackal-headed Anubis came to carry the soul to judgment, and great pains were taken to make a comfortable and happy home. Certain things were inscribed on papyri to assist the deceased in repelling the attacks of demons. Hunting scenes and other activities in this life were faithfully depicted in the tomb in order that these decorations might remind him of his past exploits on earth and his *ka*, or genius, thereby be maintained. Many ceremonies were performed and services recited, and mortuary temples were built near the tomb where the spirit could go, after coming out on the east side to greet the sun, and where the friends of the dead could offer their devotions.

"So, you see, the safety of the tomb was a serious matter," concluded Professor Caron, "and was the subject of much thought by the Egyptian kings and their great men. It was the despoiling of tombs that led to the abandonment of the pyramid idea in favour of rock-hewn sepulchres, and it took many years, thousands of workers, and great wealth to prepare some of the great tombs of the Pharaohs. Every precaution was taken to house the dead securely and secretly, and to preserve the funeral furniture and other comforts for the spirit. If a mummy were disturbed, and its tomb destroyed, it would be both without name and homeless. Sometimes terrible curses were inscribed to frighten away robbers; for some thieves are very bold indeed."

Alas, yes! Nothing was safe from a bold thief. Professor Caron went on to describe some of the known tombs of the Pharaohs. Five hundred feet into the hillside, then down into the bowels of the earth for one hundred and fifty feet or more these ghouls who pillaged the tombs had to go. In the tomb of Sety I, they first went far down a long flight of steps; then came a passage to another flight of steps; then another passage to another flight of steps; then another passage into a room that expanded into a large hall with four huge columns supporting the roof. With echoing footsteps, the thieves had to cross this hall to more steps, leading downward still into another long passage. This in turn revealed more steps down into two more passages, ending in a large hall of columns with four rooms opening off it. Then down more steps they came at last to where the mummy lay in its sarcophagus.

"A regular palace underground, through which the spirit was thought to be roving loose, mind you! And, all the way down, the walls covered with sculptured and painted gods and demons of the Underworld, and the figure of the king stirring up the wrath of the deities! Nothing but silence and mystery in that deep place, gentlemen, and your thieves coming along with flickering oil lamps, casting dancing shadows—bold, is it not? No, nothing is sacred to bold thieves! Nothing is safe!"

"These curses you refer to, Professor Caron—the stories one hears about the revenge of ancient spirits upon those who disturbed them—do you put any stock in that sort of thing?" asked Kent with interest.

"There are many strange things that man does not understand," mused the little Frenchman, stroking his gray goatee reflectively. "It is well to keep an open mind on all things, my young friend. But these curses are not very plentiful and were for frightening away robbers."

"But the curse of the Pharaohs has come to be known all over the world from actual cases where harm has followed the meddlers."

"Why should harm come to anyone who entered ancient sepulchres to preserve the dead, not to destroy?—to renew their memory for posterity?" argued the Professor. "Even taking them seriously, they refer to robbers; but these actual occurrences of which you speak—usually there is a rational explanation for whatever happened."

"Not always," contradicted Malabar. "I knew a man who came into possession of a little bronze lamp—"

"Aladdin had one like it, and it brought him great wealth and happiness when he scratched it."

"The man I knew took sick—and died," declared Malabar solemnly.

"Pooh! pooh! Come, gentlemen, we must not grow sombre. I could recite many such stories; but let us go upstairs and I will show you one of these famous curses, inscribed upon a scarab."

As Professor Caron had intimated, his bedroom was commodious and elegantly furnished in keeping with all the other appointments in this house of luxury. A small sitting-room opened off it. Alongside the entrance to this room two cases stood on end, enclosing figures swathed in bandages; the mummies were not exposed to view, but the shape of the ancient bodies immediately identified them. Upon entering the room, however, the gaze of the visitors became focused almost involuntarily upon the startling wooden figure of a large black cat, which sat near the window.

"That case has never been opened yet; but it contains the embalmed body of a cat, wrapped in bandages like these other mummies. The Egyptians, as you know, regarded the cat as part household pet and part deity; it was a very sacred animal and, of course, poor pussy had to go along with his master! Now here, gentlemen—"

"Sacred to Bast, the Lady of Bubastis, wasn't it, Professor?" Malabar tapped the wooden figure with his finger-nails; it was hollow. He stood regarding the sombre image with interest. The light shone on the smooth, thick coating of pitch with which it was painted.

"Yes, yes—sacred to Bast," nodded Professor Caron. "Now if you will come over here to the table, Mr. Malabar—"

"What's this stuff that makes its eyes glare so? By Jove, Kent, look at the way those yellow whiskers bristle!"

"They used obsidian, rock crystal or coloured paste for the eyes," supplied Professor Caron, a little impatiently. "Now, here I will show you—"

"I remember reading something to the effect that when a cat died the whole household went into mourning and shaved off their eyebrows," volunteered Addison Kent. "I think it was Diodorus—"

"Yes, yes—Diodorus," agreed the Professor. "The same writer records a case where the Egyptians slew a Roman who had accidentally killed a cat— Now here, gentlemen, is the scarab I mentioned; it was found on the breast of the mummy on the right over there, and this is how the so-called curse reads: *'Who trespasses upon my property the sun god shall punish him. I will leap upon him as a wild beast upon his prey.*'" He chuckled. "Doesn't look as if there was much leap left in him at this late date, eh?"

They examined the large scarab with interest while Professor Caron rattled on: "Nothing was more highly revered by the Egyptians of old than the sacred beetle—*scarabæus sacer.* 'Khepera' (He who turns) they called it in ancient days, symbolizing the return of the sun each day, and representing the everlasting progress of life. The likeness of the beetle was made into amulets and placed upon the mummies to ward off evil. It was made into signet rings and worn by the living, being prepared as a talisman by the priests of the different temples. This sign of immortality was constantly before the people, and was used in the Government offices, bearing the Pharaoh's cartouche—the oval in which his name was inscribed—and was worn by soldiers going into battle and, in fact, by the people at large for good luck.

"That hole you see was where the gold wire passed through—to hang it around the neck of the mummy. I have seen many finer scarabs than this; the colours have faded badly. Scarabs were not in general use before the middle of the twelfth dynasty, but they were quite plentiful by the time of Amemhot III, perhaps most plentiful in the reigns of Thotmes III and Rameses II, because these were the longest reigns. This one belongs to the eighteenth dynasty; it is interesting and valuable on account of the curse—"

"And it was worn by that mummy against the wall there, you say?" The eyes of all three sought the silent figure as Kent spoke. "Who was he, Professor?"

"He's a long way from home," commented Malabar.

"Yes, gentlemen, and a long time dead," smiled Professor Caron. "His name was Sethutnakt, and he appears to have been the High Priest of Amon-Ra. See, here's his photo; it will not be necessary to unwrap him to give you a look at him. In the reign of Rameses II—"

An exclamation from Richard Malabar interrupted him. The journalist was pointing to another photo which Professor Caron held in his hand. It was also the photo of an exposed mummy—the most sinister of grinning faces; the mouth was open, revealing gleaming teeth; the hollow eye-sockets stared.

"An ugly customer, eh, my friend?" Professor Caron smiled with a hint of condescension at their evident repulsion. "That is the other one, over there by the door. I cannot tell you much about him as he is one of the nameless who lost his tomb, or, rather, he never had a tomb, because he died with his sandals on, out in the desert somewhere on some expedition to the breccia quarries. It is my opinion that he came to his end by foul play. His body was dug up from the sand by accident, mummified by the sand and sun in the Nubian desert; in that dry air exposure will mummify naturally."

"But he is all bandaged up—"

"The same as Seth? Quite so. We wrapped him up very carefully, for he is an odd and valuable specimen, and will be welcome in one of your American medical colleges. A vicious-looking person, I admit. But he has not bitten anything for some thousands of years!"

"You do not know who or what he was, then?" asked Kent.

"No. He may have been a great noble in his day in the palace of the king. He may have strutted in gorgeous raiment with all the pride of a peacock. But his day is long since done, and I sometimes think he is laughing at himself! That is what I call him— 'The Laugher.'"

Professor Caron had stepped half-way across the room towards the mummies while talking, and now he turned and started back to the table, chuckling to himself.

From the high ceiling of the room there suddenly fell a large segment of plaster. It landed on the floor with a heavy thud—in the exact spot where he had been standing as he spoke!

3
THE FINGER OF FEAR

I

Through the thinning dust Kent and Malabar exchanged quick glances; but Professor Caron continued to smile. He merely raised his eyebrows and shrugged his shoulders, remarking that it looked as if friend Lamont would require to see to his plumbing somewhere.

"Then you do not believe—?"

"The fall of plaster is undoubtedly due to some such simple thing as a bathroom leak, or, perhaps, a seepage from the roof at some time or other. Come, come, gentlemen! Association of ideas—that merely. We have been discussing this matter of ancient spirits exerting malevolent influence, and what more natural than that you should attach special significance to this simple incident? You must remember, however, that we are not robbers of tombs, and if one is reverent—"

"But you did not speak reverently a few moments ago, Professor, and look at that plaster!" pursued Addison Kent quizzically. "That might have injured you severely; perhaps it would have killed you! Why should it fall just when it did and just where you had been standing?"

"Pooh! Coincidence!" And again the little Professor shrugged shoulders with an air of indifference which, Kent fancied, was not quite genuine; in spite of himself, the Frenchman was disturbed and was trying hard to conceal the fact. "You cannot frighten me, my friend. We archæologists could tell of many strange coincidences; but we have not time for foolish superstitions in the great work we are doing."

"Yet I know of instances where these 'coincidences' brought sickness and death," chimed in Malabar, rather enjoying the situation.

"So? Well, maybe, my friend. But I am not afraid. I have told you that these curses were but to frighten robbers from the tomb in order to preserve the mummy and the tomb from desecration. The threat of dire calamity meant only additional protection, and we do not believe the things the ancients believed. You see how it is? We— Ah, Kellani! Just some plaster that has fallen from the ceiling. Everything is all right. We shall be going back to the library directly, and you may have this mess cleaned up then."

Kent turned to find the silent Nubian in the doorway, regarding them with strange steadfastness. His tumid lips seemed to be muttering some voiceless prayer while his large black eyes, half shuttered by bronze eyelids, were fastened unwaveringly upon Professor Emil Caron. His scant beard, worn underneath the chin like that of the *Wawa* sculptured on Egyptian temples, disappeared among the powerful muscles of his neck and throat as he lowered his great, frizzle-haired head in obeisance.

"Allah is great! A command has been given to be obeyed, sidi." Another long look and abruptly he backed out of the doorway and was gone.

The sudden appearance of the huge brown servant on the threshold, following the thud of the falling plaster, was entirely logical; but something in the tone of the Nubian's solemn voice, something in his look— Kent glanced sharply at his host and was startled at the sudden change that seemed to have come over the savant. His face showed pallor—or was it plaster dust? He was running one hand nervously through his scanty white hair, while the hand that rested on the edge of the table—Kent thought that it trembled slightly.

"I say, Professor, can you open this thing for us?" Dick Malabar was standing once more in front of the figure of the black cat, passing tentative fingers over the smooth surface, looking in vain for some indication of an opening. He half turned in surprise at a sharp ejaculation of annoyance from Professor Caron, who hurriedly crossed the room.

"No, no!" came his petulant refusal. "Away from there, monsieur! You must not touch that! Come away, please! I cannot open it yet. It has never been opened and there are many photographs to take of the different stages of the unwrapping—for the official records, you understand. Please, you must not touch it!"

His agitation seemed out of proportion to the simple cause. The journalist stole a look at Addison Kent behind the Professor's back and grinned cheerfully. It seemed to Kent that Malabar was taking a satisfaction in provoking their host that almost approached discourtesy, and he frowned and shook his head.

"We will go back down to the library, gentlemen, if you please. But first—"

He ran ahead of them to the doorway and looked out. Then, unexpectedly, he drew the door shut carefully and placed a finger on his lips for silence. He crossed the room quickly and, from the entrance to the bathroom, beckoned them mysteriously.

"Whisky and soda, if you have it, Professor," grinned Malabar.

But when they had followed him into the bathroom and this door also had been closed carefully, they were astonished to find Professor Emil Caron extending for their inspection a large leather travelling-case in which were disclosed his safety razor and other toilet articles. He picked out a fat silver-plated case which he proceeded to open; it contained a large round cake of pink soap, perhaps six inches wide and three inches thick.

"Is this part of the exhibit—?" Malabar looked at Addison Kent quickly; for Kent had pinched his arm sharply, and there was an intentness in the novelist's face that commanded silence.

"It is my special bath soap, scented with jasmine from the Souk-el-Attarine at Tunis." Professor Caron spoke in a voice that was scarcely above a whisper. "I want you to note it carefully. See, I have divided it in the middle and hollowed out a cavity. Presently I will show you what I intend to hide in this simple cake of soap and then you will understand. Please, I am not crazy! I did not bring you here to-night, Mr. Kent, just to show you mummies and discuss matters of antiquity. I am in grave trouble and I need your help.

"We will go downstairs now, gentlemen, and when you have had some cakes and wine you must make your excuses and leave this house as soon as possible. No matter how greatly you are astonished, please control yourselves and do not speak loudly. You think me a very strange host, no doubt; but it is best to be careful when danger lurks, is it not? What I show you must not be seen except by you, and what I tell you is for your ears alone. Come, time passes too quickly."

Without waiting for comment he led them out to the landing, and as they descended the stairs the little Frenchman was chatting animatedly of his belief that the much-discussed land of Ophir, mentioned in the Bible, was located at the southern end of the Eastern Egyptian Desert and why he thought the old workings there must be identified with "King Solomon's Mines."

II

It had been partly for the purpose of discovering proof of his theory regarding the location of the Biblical Ophir that Professor Emil Caron had penetrated deeply into the unknown wastes of the Upper Egyptian Desert. The great silver Nile, with its narrow strip of fertility on either side, was known to the tourist; but the hills of granite, sandstone, or limestone that for the most part walled it in were bare, and few there were who had dared the arid steppes that stretch endlessly beyond to the shores of the Red Sea. A half-dozen foreign Egyptologists had ventured along some of the known ancient routes in search of buried records—Lepsius the German, and Golenischieff the Russian, for instance. The explorer Sweinfurth, and Bellefonds Bey, Director-General of Public Works in Egypt under Mohammed Ali—these had surveyed and mapped certain sections, while a few prospectors had gone hither and yon. But, for the most part, it was a lost land, peopled with ghosts of ancient and forgotten days, given over to the sovereignty of the desert sun, which glared upon endless sands that forever shifted under hot desert winds—a land of slinking jackal and circling buzzard.

Into this trackless region of hazards and uncertainties had the camels of Professor Emil Caron rocked away, daily plodding deeper towards the mirage-haunted horizon and daily leaving farther behind them the security of law and order and human habitation. But, with his mind upon hieroglyphics, and his soul expanding with absorbing enthusiasm for the life of other times and peoples, the little savant had concerned himself but slightly with the desert dangers of his day and generation. So that presently he had awakened to find himself in the midst of an adventure which very nearly had cost him his life.

Seated once more in the library—beside wine and cakes upon a silver salver from the grand mosque at Kairouan—he held the undivided attention of both his guests. After serving the refreshments, Kellani, the Nubian servant, had been dismissed for the night. Nevertheless, Professor Caron continued to speak in lowered tones and with suppressed excitement.

"You will find it hard to believe what I have to tell you, gentlemen; but I assure you that every word of it is true. Strange, indeed, are some of the secrets that lie buried in the sands of that great land of mysticism and ancient traditions. If only I might persuade myself that it was all just a dream! Alas! that I cannot do."

He passed his hand nervously through his thin hair and glanced furtively about the room before proceeding. He would not weary them, he promised, with the details of his search among the rock inscriptions at the breccia quarries of Wady Hammamat, nor discuss the white granite of Um Etgal or the alabaster quarries or the mountains of Gebel Dukhan where the Romans quarried the famous imperial porphyry. At Rizk Allah in the Wady Khashab topaz mines were worked under the Ptolemys and, until the conquest of Peru, the only emerald mines known were located in the hilly Zabara district in the Wady Sikait. Enough just to say that the country was known as a land of riches in olden days, and many expeditions at one time and another had sought its treasure; inscribed

upon the rocks were the records of chief architects, master build-
ers, artisans, scribes, ship-captains, etc., of the ancient dynasties.
He had found much to interest him, and had made voluminous
notes as he studied the rocks. Time ceased to exist for him, and he
was content to wander about indefinitely.

Not so the cameleers he had hired, however. They grew anxious to get back to the Nile country, and began to give trouble. All
arrangements for the caravan had been looked after by Kellani,
the Professor's newly acquired body-servant, and it was the Nubian
who undertook to pacify them from time to time by promises of
doubled rewards. Professor Caron paid little heed to the discon-
tent of the guides or to the heated arguments that took place around
the camp-fires at night; all Arabs were great liars, and these thiev-
ing rascals had been utterly spoiled by tourist bakshish and were
never satisfied. Then one fine morning he and the Nubian awoke
to find themselves alone in the desert; with the men had gone the
best part of their supplies, camels and equipment.

It was little use to rage up and down. There they were! It was
not long before their predicament became so apparent that they
grew very serious over it. They conned their supplies anxiously;
the deserters had left them two camels, two small tents and barely
enough food to last them for a week. But it was the water problem
that worried them. Professor Caron was helpless and forced to rely
upon the Nubian; Kellani did not profess to be a desert guide. The
only thing they could do was to follow the tracks of the fleeing deserters and to pray that these would not be obliterated by the shift-
ing sands before they reached a well.

After journeying for a day without catching sight of anybody
they pitched camp despondently. Even the Nubian failed to hide
his worry as he hobbled the camels with thongs so that they could
not get up and wander away. For during the day they had somehow missed the tracks they had been following, and Kellani confessed that they were lost. However, he proceeded cheerfully
enough to knead dough upon his burnous, spread in front of the
fire, and to bake it on the embers. Allah willing, they would find
water to-morrow if it were so written.

But they did not find water the next day, or the next, or the next. Their camels surged onward, ever onward under the hot sun over sand marked only by desert creatures—the wiggly line where a lizard had made passage, the four prongs of a wagtail or a vulture's footprint, the short jumps of the jerboa, the light padding of jackal or fox and, once or twice, the heavier trail of a hyena crossing the tracks of a gazelle. The diminishing water in the goatskins grew grey and warm; it acquired the flavour of goat and tar. They drank sparingly in spite of the glutinous condition of their mouths and throats, hoarding every drop, more precious than diamonds.

It was Kellani's idea to give the camels their heads in the hope that instinct would lead them towards water. Their general direction appeared to be south and east towards distant hills. In time they came in under the shadow of these hills, and about sundown found themselves in a strange valley where the wind indulged in antics among the rocks, causing mysterious whisperings to waft about as the drooping travellers penetrated the dry watercourse.

A sudden cry from the Nubian startled Professor Caron out of the stupor into which he had slumped, and he found Kellani pointing excitedly to sheep-tracks. It was the first sight they had had of any sign of human beings; for where sheep were would be at least a solitary and ragged Bedouin—and water somewhere near! Even the camels, ordinarily impervious to hastening influences, seemed to arouse themselves to the excitement of the moment and followed the sheep-tracks willingly.

Then, without warning of any kind, a sharp command to halt rang out, and in the wink of an eye the two camels were surrounded by a band of swarthy and rough-looking Arabs, brandishing guns. They seemed to rise from the very ground. It was evident to Professor Caron that the ambuscade had been planned deliberately, and that from the moment the travellers had entered the valley they had been watched. Forbidding as these men were, and threatening though their attitude seemed to be, both the Professor and his servant welcomed the capture; for they were exhausted, and their tongues were swollen with thirst. Any relief was better than none.

They were led triumphantly into camp. When they had been given water to drink, and had recovered sufficiently to take stock of their surroundings and their captors, Professor Caron realized that he had stumbled upon what appeared to be the secret retreat of a band of brigands. Although mostly garbed like Bedouins, he saw that this cut-throat aggregation comprised several nationalities, and he might have trembled for his immediate safety but for the fact that their leader was a man of some education, who spoke French with a slight German accent. This man assured the little Professor that no harm would befall him if orders were obeyed.

He even appeared to know something of Egyptology. At any rate, he was greatly interested in the Frenchman's notebooks, and asked many questions—in fact, became enthusiastic. He introduced himself as Ludwig Von Strom, and appeared to welcome the opportunity of discussing these things with Professor Caron; long after his men were wrapped in slumber they had sat, conversing of archæology.

The next day the discussion had been renewed, and finally Von Strom had brought out from his personal effects for Professor Caron's inspection a roll of discoloured papyrus, and asked him if he could decipher it. To his utter amazement, Professor Caron discovered it to be, apparently, the inscription of a scribe of the temple in the reign of Rameses IX, about 1124 B.C., dealing with the systematic robbery of the royal sepulchres by an organized gang of thieves. It appeared that this scribe had been the only one to escape the wrath of the ruling Pharaoh, all the other members of the conspiracy having been discovered, brought to trial and put to death. He alone, Horishere, through false testimony, had escaped, and later had found his way to the secret place where the ghouls had buried their ungodly treasure. There he had gloated over his wealth, only to find that a wall of the unused tomb in which the treasure was hidden had collapsed and sealed him in beyond hope of escape. He had spent the interval, while awaiting death by starvation, in writing this, his confession. It was, the victim believed, the vengeance of Osiris, the god of the dead!

Amazed, excited, puzzled, Professor Caron had questioned the German closely as to where this document had been found and how it had come into his possession. At first Von Strom was reticent, but finally he claimed to know where the tomb was located and the treasure of Osiris buried. He had guarded his secret jealously against the day that it might be shared safely with some man of great learning in these matters, some Egyptologist of established reputation. Perhaps this meeting was "Kismet!"—as the Arabs say. Perhaps Professor Emil Caron was the very man, sent to him across the desert to this out-of-the-way valley by the gods themselves! If certain conditions were complied with, he might decide to take Professor Caron to the lost tomb and show him this treasure of Osiris that had lain buried deep beneath the sands for thousands of years. Then Professor Emil Caron could give the discovery to the world and win fame as well as fortune.

"Gentlemen, what was I to do?" Professor Caron paused in his recital and looked at them eagerly. Red spots burned in his cheeks, and his eyes were glittering with excitement. "These very tomb-robbers' trials, mentioned in this papyrus, already are known to us in fragmentary fashion—from the Abbott Papyrus which was discovered in 1857 at Thebes; from the Meyer Papyrus in the Liverpool Museum; from another fragment in the museum at Turin, and so on. When I tell you that they make mention of this very scribe of the temple, Horishere—do you not see, gentlemen, how important this document might be? Do you not see that with it I should be able to amaze not only America, but the whole world? Would you have investigated it further if you had been me?—at any cost?"

Professor Caron relaxed in his chair and eyed first Addison Kent, then Richard Malabar, as if for traces of scepticism.

"A fine story, my friends, eh?" be chortled. "A clever tale, is it not? You do not believe, perhaps? You do not—"

He sat up in his chair with a start, a finger upraised for silence. Into his eyes leapt a sudden look of fear.

"Hush! What was that sound! Did you hear nothing?"

4
THE SCARAB

I

They shook their heads. Nevertheless, Professor Caron got up quickly and went to the library windows, examining them one by one, and carefully drawing still closer together the heavy window-drapes. He came back to them on tiptoe, leaning towards them eagerly.

"A fine story, gentlemen—if it were only true!" he whispered.

"You mean—?" comprehended Kent.

"This papyrus of Horishere—I soon recognized it to be a clever fake!"

"And the buried treasure?" suggested Malabar.

"Ah yes, the treasure! That is different."

You have seen it? Personally?"

"Yes!" he whispered, again glancing nervously about the room. "That is why I am in such trouble now. Wait! I will show you something."

In silence they watched him go straight to the fine safe which Armaund Lamont had installed in his library behind a panel of wainscoting. Although nothing of great value was kept outside of the burglarproof vaults down town, the fact that Lamont had entrusted the combination of this library safe to his temporary guest was yet another proof of his complete confidence in the French savant. They watched with interest the process of opening the safe. Professor Caron finally accomplished it after many references to a little black notebook which he carried on his person.

He lifted out and transferred to the library table an oblong parcel, neatly wrapped in stiff brown paper. It was well tied with heavy twine and generously daubed upon the folds at each end with blue sealing-wax. Carefully the Professor got one of these ends open and drew off the outer wrapper like a glove. Working more rapidly now, he unfolded the inner layers of paper, revealing at last a sandalwood box. Producing a small key from his pocket, he unlocked the box and took out the contents, wrapped in white tissue paper. When this was removed, an oblong case of purple velvet was in his hand. Under their noses he finally snapped it opened with a dramatic gesture.

"Voilà!" he exclaimed with the pride of a connoisseur.

Kent and Malabar both started back in astonishment, then bent eagerly forward with subdued cries of admiration. Lying on its satin cushion was a beautiful scarab of pure gold, so exquisitely wrought in delicate design as quite conceivably to belong to an age of lost arts. Neither of the two marvelling guests had ever beheld anything like it before.

With a hand that shook in eagerness while his eyes shone with excitement, Professor Caron picked it carefully from its resting-place and turned the beautiful gold beetle over on its back.

They gasped. Speechless, they stared. Imbedded in a cunning setting lay a magnificent ruby, so large and pure it was breath-taking. It was carmine red with a slight bluish tinge—the colour which the Burmese compare to the blood of a freshly killed pigeon—"pigeon's blood red." The great stone caught the rays of the light; it lay shining and palpitating like a pool of blood! They could not take their eyes off it!

At last Addison Kent freed himself from the spell and stared at the smiling Frenchman with a sober face.

"Priceless!" he murmured. "And it is this which you are proposing to hide in your—upstairs?" He pointed to the ceiling.

"Assuredly. See, I shall remove it now and put back the empty case, re-sealing the outer wrapping. A burning match or two should soften the wax sufficiently."

"Professor Caron, it is not safe," protested Kent.

"You must not risk such a gem as that here—not even for a single night." It was Kent's glance now which roved anxiously about the room. "I want you to let me telephone and provide for its safe removal to a deposit box—now, to-night. I can arrange it."

But Professor Caron demurred. He had a reason for wanting it beside him for a little while. It was quite safe because nobody knew that he had it—except them; he had taken them into his confidence as an additional precaution. If by any remote chance his plans were interfered with, they—his friends—would know where to find the ruby and would be able to take charge of it according to his direction. They were alone, were they not? And Monsieur Lamont had provided this room with excellent blinds and drapes—

Addison Kent rose and stepped quickly across to the portières which screened the archway. His movement was sudden and silent. When he thrust his head into the hall he was relieved to find it empty; for he had fancied a movement of the heavy curtain. It must be just that his imagination had been keyed to special activity by the evening's surprises, he thought.

Turning back into the room, his glance fell upon Richard Malabar. The journalist was passing the scarab to Professor Caron with a hand that trembled visibly. All levity was gone now from Malabar's demeanour. Kent saw that he looked strangely excited.

II

"Professor, this so-called 'treasure of Osiris' you have been telling us about—" Malabar cleared his throat, a trifle impatient of his huskiness. "You say you have actually seen it?"

"Yes, I said that."

"This German, Von Strom, took you to see it?"

"Yes."

"To one of the unused tombs of the Pharaohs, where it was buried?"

"To an old and hitherto undiscovered sepulchre—yes. It was completely covered by the sand—deep down under the sands—hewn in the living rock."

"Was it located where the other discoveries have been made—in the Valley of the Tombs of the Kings or the Valley of the Queens?—somewhere in the ancient Theban necropolis? Where was it located, Professor?"

"That I cannot tell you, Mr. Malabar. The secret of its location was carefully preserved by the German. I was blindfolded. We travelled for a great distance. But I do not think it was anywhere near other discoveries. It was not as elaborate as a royal tomb, and had been intended for some lesser personage."

"Blindfolded! Hm-hm! Did this bandaging of your eyes take place when you set out from this valley where the wind whispered among the rocks and where you encountered these brigands, or was it later in the journey that such care was taken?"

"From the first, Mr. Malabar, I was blindfolded."

"Then you do not even know where this wonderful valley is to be found, let alone the tomb where the treasure is buried?"

"Alas! That is so, gentlemen. You must accept my statements" He looked appealingly at Addison Kent.

"Of course," nodded Kent.

"And are we to understand that this remarkable scarab you have just shown us—?" Malabar hesitated. "I am not asking these questions idly, Professor Caron. I am tremendously interested and only want to clear the air, as it were, of what appears a little confusing to me. This scarab, now. Are we to understand that it was a part of this ancient, buried treasure, taken from tombs of old by ancient robbers? Or did you purchase it from somebody? If so, what fabulous price did you pay for it? Just how did it come into *your* possession, Professor?"

It was their host's turn to hesitate. He stared at his inquisitor dubiously. He wet his lips, shrugged his shoulders.

"It was part of this treasure, was it?" persisted Malabar. "You found it at this lost tomb?"

"Yes."

"I have been in Egypt, Professor Caron. I know a little about Egyptology—not that I have given it the study you have, of course; but I know a little." Dick Malabar smiled in deprecation. "I know a great deal more, however, about precious stones. You surely are not asking me to believe that this beautiful ruby in its unique golden scarab setting is an antique, Professor!"

"No, no, Mr. Malabar—not an antique, of course. It is a cut gem of a much later period."

"Exactly. Yet you say you found it! Professor, do you realize that that ruby is almost the size of a pigeon's egg? Do you know that such large stones are very scarce? Even a fine, deeply coloured ruby of three carats is a rarity. One of nine carats is worth over £6,000. Do you realize the weight and value of that scarab stone? Rubies of that size are not left lying around carelessly. They are known—and *traced!*"

"Yes, yes, that is so, Mr. Malabar. The King of Ava was said to have a ruby, mounted as an ear-pendant, the size of a hen's egg!"

"The largest ruby found in Burma weighed 1,184 carats. Gustavus III of Sweden had a ruby as big as this one you have just shown us; he presented it to Catherine II of Russia."

"That was in 1777. Yes, I know about that."

"That ruby disappeared, Professor, long ago, and its present whereabouts is unknown. It has never been seen since."

Kent tapped Malabar's arm.

"Is it possible that this scarab stone—?"

"It may be the identical gem. Who knows? But whether it is or not, its discovery by Professor Caron as part of this so-called 'treasure of Osiris' proves that this buried treasure is not the loot of ancient ghouls but of modern thieves! He admits that the papyrus shown him by this German was a fake—"

"I think, Dick, if you will just hold your horses a bit, the Professor can explain everything," remonstrated Kent gently. "Am I right, Professor, in surmising that you merely have been leading up to the things you really wish to confide to us?"

Professor Caron, who had been fidgeting in his chair for some time, nodded and threw a grateful glance. His face was flushed with excitement, and it was evident that he was in an extremely nervous state. He was breathing rapidly. His hands fluttered uncertainly from his knees to the arms of his chair and back again. He dropped his voice so low that they had to lean forward to catch what he said.

"Not a word must you breathe of what I have to say," he whispered hoarsely. "You have seen me close the safe on that empty package, after heating the sealing-wax upon the broken end; it is as if it had never been touched. This jewel in my waistcoat I shall hide as soon as you leave this house. I am in much trouble, Mr. Kent, and I seek your help because Mr. Lamont told me all about your great abilities in the detection of crime. He told me of your dangerous encounter with that most dangerous of all—that gentleman thief of thieves. You, at least, understand, and bear with me because you know that it is not possible to be too careful where Alceste is concerned, and I—"

"What!" exclaimed Malabar sharply. "Alceste? Where does he come in?"

"Hush! Hush! Not so loud, Mr. Malabar, I beseech you!"

"But Alceste is dead!"

"That is correct, Professor. He was cornered in England by the police and committed suicide," nodded Kent, as Professor Caron turned to him in surprise. "Rather a tame ending for such a clever international thief; but it is the only sort of finish to the kind of game he played. His capture was bound to come sooner or later. The official record of his death is on file at Police Headquarters. There is no question about it."

"Suicide!" murmured Malabar thoughtfully. "He was not the sort to be taken alive. He would at least have the satisfaction of turning out his own light."

"Well, well," pondered Professor Caron. Then his face renewed its former expression. "Dead he may be—then I am very glad of that—but, gentlemen, his evil lives after him! Of that I can assure you. He has left a legacy of evil—" A shudder seized him, and he dropped his voice still lower. "Have you ever heard of a strange secret organization in the East, called the 'Order of the Golden Scarab'?" he breathed anxiously.

Addison Kent doubtfully shook his head. Dick Malabar leaned closer, his keen, intelligent face full of eagerness.

"Go on, Professor. Tell us about it," he urged.

"I will tell you. Yes. I—I—"

"Go on, then! Tell it! Tell it!" Malabar reached out and grabbed him by the shoulder. "In Heaven's name, what's the matter with you? TELL IT!"

But Professor Emil Caron's tongue seemed to be sticking in his throat. His eyes opened wide in sudden fear. His face went as white as chalk.

"Mon Dieu!" he gasped. "Look! Look!" He pointed shakily. "Take it away! *Quick!*" He shrank, cowering, in his chair.

Both Addison Kent and Malabar sprang to their feet and turned in alarm.

Across the broad expanse of the huge round library table there crawled slowly, steadily, a great ugly black beetle!

5
UNTIL TO-MORROW

I

With curiosity they leaned over the insect. Kent finally captured it and held it in the air with its legs clawing.

"I say, how do you suppose that thing got in here?—on that table?"

"Flew in through an open window, probably," smiled Kent, amused. He stepped across the room, opened one of the French doors and tossed the beetle outside. "Or, if you think it is getting rather late in the season for June bugs, Dick, and if you note further that not a single window in this room is open, let me suggest this explanation: It flew in through an open window during June or July when the decorators were at work and was a prisoner here ever since."

"And has been sitting up on yon curtain-pole till, becoming dizzy from the fumes of that pipe of yours, it fell from its perch and landed upon said table." Malabar chuckled. "How about it, Professor? Why all the excitement?"

But Professor Caron's chair was empty. He had slipped from the room, and even then was coming in from the hall, carrying their hats, coats, gloves and walking-sticks.

"You must go at once!" he decreed anxiously. "Please do not think me discourteous. I feel that it is best, gentlemen."

"But you did not finish telling us—" began Malabar, in protest.

"No, no! Not to-night, please. Not in this house! Not now!"

274

"But you were going to tell us—were you not?—until this harmless bug— Why did it frighten you so?"

Professor Caron drew himself erect with some dignity.

"You ask too many questions, Mr. Malabar. It is the failing of the journalist, is it not? I shall answer nothing. It is enough for me to express the desire that we defer all further conversation upon these matters."

"Certainly, Professor, if you wish it," apologized Malabar quickly. "I cannot tell you how much I have enjoyed this interesting evening, and I only hope that I may have the privilege of meeting you again soon—"

"By all means—to-morrow. Perhaps, Mr. Kent, we might take that drive you were good enough to suggest the other day. If you will call for me, we can spin away somewhere in quiet places, and then I promise to reveal to you everything that is on my mind."

So it was arranged. Professor Caron himself escorted them to the door. There was nothing for them to do but to take their sudden dismissal in good grace. They might smile at the whims of their host; but there was no question that he had been greatly upset by something. Keen as their curiosity was to know what lay behind the savant's strange fear, they forbore to question him further, especially as he promised to gratify their curiosity the next afternoon when they went motoring.

"I want you to feel that you can call upon me at any time for any help I can give, Professor Caron," assured Addison Kent as he shook hands warmly. "You have given us an interesting evening, for which both of us are very grateful. I would be remiss in my duty if I did not ask you once more to let me provide a place of safety for that wonderful ruby. Will you not change your mind and let me arrange it—to-night?"

"No, no! Everything is all right. There is no hurry. It will be safe, never fear."

"I am well acquainted at Police Headquarters, Professor. If you are at all nervous, it would be a simple matter for me to have a couple of good plainclothes men stationed—"

"The police! Oh, no, no, no! Please, Mr. Kent, do not worry, and do not tell anyone what I have shown you or told you. To-morrow afternoon I shall explain everything. Thank you all the same. And now, gentlemen, *au revoir*—until to-morrow."

With iron-grilled finality the great glass doors of the Lamont mansion forthwith closed behind them.

II

Once away from the big house and its grounds, both occupants of the car drew in the fresh night air with relish and relaxed upon the cushions. Neither was inclined to talk at first; each was busy with his own thoughts.

"Well, how do you feel now?" ventured Kent at last.

"As if I'd been down the rabbit-hole!" growled Malabar.

"To Wonderland with Alice?"

"No. To the cave of the Forty Thieves with the evil spirit of Alceste!—a cave littered with dead men's bones! Damn Caron and his mummies!"

"Careful, Dick! We don't want to run into an accident before we get home!" warned Kent cheerfully. "Personally, I enjoyed it. The Professor interests me. Strikes me you are on the trail of a devilishly good story for your paper when you get back into harness."

"Your choice of adjectives is admirable."

"Devilish?"

"Hellish, perhaps, when we get to the facts. You don't suppose he was just frightened by that bug, do you? It's what lies beneath. That thing carried some warning to him by suggestion. The man was in positive terror. I tell you, Kent, I don't like it!"

"This 'Order of the Golden Scarab'—is that what you are thinking of?"

"Yes—and thinking hard! The East is the home of the secret society and the birthplace of more intrigue, more devilment—! It would be meat and drink to Alceste! 'His evil lives after him,'" quoted Malabar.

He gave Addison Kent a strange look, as if his mind were busy with half-forgotten horrors, and as they passed a street light the novelist noted how pale he was.

"Pshaw! Dick, you take it too seriously. Funny, though, that Alceste's trail should cross in such an unexpected quarter. I wonder how Caron—that ruby—it's the most beautiful stone I ever looked at, I think."

"Deadliest poison plants often bear the most vivid flowers," remarked the journalist sententiously. "Entrancingly beautiful women sometimes prove most dangerous."

"Another way of saying that the golden scarab is at the bottom of Caron's trouble?"

"Yes."

"In what way?"

"God knows!" replied Malabar in a low, tense voice.

"Well, there's no use in idle speculation when we'll know all about it to-morrow afternoon. Let's forget it until to-morrow."

As they turned through Times Square on the way to Richard Malabar's hotel, the clock recorded the midnight hour.

III

The first rays of the morning sun were warming the closed window-blinds of Minaki Annex when Addison Kent was awakened by the jangling of the telephone beside his bed. Responding sleepily, he was surprised to recognize the voice of his old friend, Detective-Lieutenant Donovan, of the Bureau. At first he did not grasp what the voice was saying; but presently he was very wide awake indeed. For Lieutenant Donovan's calm matter-of-fact tones were entirely out of tune with the startling nature of his words.

"It's a queer lay-out, Mr. Kent, and I thought it was something that would interest you. The police were called in an hour ago. The place is out in Westchester—Lamont's new residence. The servants are frightened half out of their wits; I can't make head or tail of it. There's a friend of Lamont's, a Frenchman by the name of Caron, stopping there. He has died very suddenly in the night!"

6
"No Inquest is Necessary"

I

Detective-Lieutenant Donovan greeted them with evident relief. His recent promotion had been won solely upon merit, and he took his work seriously; hence he had found this futile hour at Westchester a poor beginning for the day, and therefore irksome. Word had reached the nearest precinct over the telephone; in response to the butler's frightened call a plainclothes man, accompanied by a constable, had been despatched to the house. The detective's report had been turned in to Headquarters, and Lieutenant Donovan had come out to substantiate it. But beyond the fact that the two "blacks" were frightened and upset, and that the "collection" upstairs in the bedroom was a queer one, he could see no reason for calling in the police. Everything was in order. The man had just died suddenly as he sat in his chair, down in the library, sipping a glass of port and reading a book. Apparently, it was a straight case of heart failure. Nevertheless, he had thought it best to advise Addison Kent—if only because the thing had happened in Lamont's house; also, he had summoned Dr. Crossley, the medical examiner.

All of which was exactly what Addison Kent had forecast to Dick Malabar on the way out. Donovan's telephoned description of the details had prepared him for this very attitude of the police. Coming so closely upon the heels of their evening with Professor Emil Caron, his sudden death naturally carried special significance to the two friends; but the police would base their conclusions upon

278

the cold facts as revealed by their enquiry. Malabar agreed with Kent that this was just as well, and they decided that if nothing were missing—in short, if the golden scarab were safe in its hiding-place—it would be best to let things take their course. With the police off the scene, there would be better opportunity for a quiet and thorough investigation, unofficially.

In accordance with their prearrangement, therefore, Malabar presently slipped out of the library and went upstairs to the bed-room. He was gone but a few minutes and, upon his return, Kent was relieved to catch his signal that the golden scarab with its wonderful ruby was safely hidden inside the cake of pink bath soap, as planned by Professor Caron the evening before.

The body of the late savant was sitting in a comfortable arm-chair at the big round library table in the centre of the room. Its position was entirely natural, the head pillowed on one arm, as if he had dropped off to sleep while reading the book which lay open before him. Nothing had been disturbed, and it was like this that he had been found by his Nubian servant. On a silver tray stood a wine-glass and a decanter; there were soda-biscuit crumbs on an empty plate and some more on the surface of the table. The face of the dead man showed the calm repose of a sleeper; it was as if he had fallen asleep quite naturally, and had slept away into another world.

"There is a safe—" began Addison Kent.

"I have not overlooked that," smiled Donovan, stepping across to it and touching the spring that moved the panel in front of it. "You see, it is locked and shows no marks of having been tampered with. Everything is in order, Mr. Kent."

"The servants?"

"I have questioned them all closely. There's a big buck valet, who came here with the Frenchman; the others all belong to the place. The butler, as you know, is that Arab fellow that Mr. Lamont has had so long in his employ. Then there's a gardener, who looks after the grounds—a Scotsman, named Sandy MacLean; he's been with Lamont quite a while, too, and his honesty sticks out all over him. These two were alone here, looking after things till Mr. and

Mrs. Lamont get back from Europe. Lamont bought this place not long ago, and the maids and all the rest haven't been hired yet."

"Then you've discovered nothing suspicious that would indicate anything unusual?"

"Not a thing. There's a chef and his assistant in the kitchen. They were hired on here just a few days ago from the caterer's—the Laidlaw people—but they seem to be O.K., for I called up Laidlaw's and these men have been with the firm for some time."

"Nobody heard any sound in the night?"

"No. Every one of them was dead to the world—slept right through."

"You said the butler and Professor Caron's man were both frightened. Did you find out the cause of that?"

"That don't mean a thing, Mr. Kent," declared Donovan with conviction. "You know how it is with a black when anything sudden like this happens; they go right up in the air. They're scared stiff of being haunted and carry rabbit's feet and all that bunk. Don't know's I blame 'em for gettin' the woollies, either, in this big house after dark and those coffins upstairs— Well, here's the doc at last, and we'll soon know if there's anything wrong."

Dr. Crossley, the medical examiner, arrived in a mood that matched the first five letters of his name. He was a very busy man with a morning so fully scheduled with places to go and things to do that he was in an exceptional hurry and cross because he was hurried. He listened carefully, however, to the detective-lieutenant's repetition of the situation, after which he proceeded with an examination of the body. He went upstairs to look over the "collection" of antiques, and came down, pulling on his gloves.

"Interesting, very interesting," he commented with a slight smile. "I think what is needed here is an undertaker, Mr. Kent. The police appear to have been called in just because a negro servant thought the place was acquiring too many dead bodies, ancient and modern! Professor Caron was quite elderly, as you note, and appears to have passed away quite naturally. In my humble opinion, no inquest is necessary. Nothing missing, everything as it should be—you understand?"

"What time did death occur, doctor?"

"About two o'clock this morning, I would say—about six hours ago."

"And the cause of death?"

"Mm—natural, quite natural. Seems to have slept right away. No sign of any abnormality. Heart weak, evidently." He picked up a small round bottle from the table. "This was found on his person, lieutenant?"

"Yes, doc—in his vest pocket," Donovan replied.

"Digitalis, Mr. Kent. As you perhaps know, it is a heart treatment. He probably went off very peacefully—while sleeping. No relatives here, I understood you to say? So, we can't question them as to his past state of health and so on. Well, it is hardly necessary."

"Is there anything exceptional about the pallor of the face, doctor?" asked Kent.

"No, I don't think so. He is in a sitting posture. The blood drains out of the arteries into the veins, of course; but he has not been dead long enough for post-mortem staining to have set in, except in the legs perhaps. Well, I understand you were acquainted with the deceased, Mr. Kent. You will look after all the arrangements, I suppose. Here is my card, if there is anything further I can do. I am in a great hurry this morning, and if there's nothing else—?"

"That's all right, doctor. Everything will be attended to, thanks."

Five minutes later the medical examiner's runabout was speeding south, and the heavy doors had closed on Detective-Lieutenant Donovan and his men.

II

As soon as they had gone, Addison Kent's manner altered. He turned upon Malabar.

"Now, let's get at it, Dick. Come upstairs and show me that ruby first." When the golden scarab lay once more exposed in his hand he drew a deep breath. "Beautiful! Beautiful! Many murders have been committed for less precious prizes. To begin with, I am going to hustle this down town into a safety-deposit box; we cannot feel easy till that is done."

"I've found out something about this sacred cat," offered Malabar, stepping over to the grotesque shell in which the mummy was enclosed. "These shells are usually in two longitudinal halves, sealed with adhesive gum and the whole thing thickly coated with pitch. Run your finger along there. Look closely."

"I see what you mean. Appears to have been resmeared," Kent confirmed. "This shell has been opened since it was found in its original state. Not very recently, though."

"Perhaps not. But why did Professor Caron pretend that it has never been opened? Why was he so nervous last night whenever I went near this thing? You must have noticed how he chased me away from it."

"He said the cat had not been unbandaged and had to be officially photographed in the process," Kent dismissed. "What we want to make sure of, as soon as possible, is whether this is a natural death or not. I am not satisfied of that yet. Come on down to the library."

On the big round library table were spread the articles which Donovan had found upon the person of the dead man, together with a pencilled inventory. Kent glanced at the list briefly, then picked up the little black notebook which contained the combination of the library safe. With this in hand, he proceeded to turn the dial slowly, and presently the door swung open.

Malabar joined him, peering inside. Last night they had watched Professor Caron replace the sealed package, after abstracting the golden scarab. There had been nothing else in the safe except a file of correspondence. The novelist and the journalist looked at each other now mutely. The sealed package, containing the empty velvet case, was gone!

"He may have changed his mind after we left and removed it," Malabar speculated.

"The answer to that is in front of you, Dick. Look at that correspondence file. Quite evidently, it has been rummaged hurriedly. The professor was too systematic to leave it in a mess like that."

Malabar made no further comment, but stood aside and watched with interest while Addison Kent proceeded to make a minute examination of the big room. It was not every day that one was privileged to observe a "Super-Detective" at work—one of those "Master Minds" one reads about—picking up such tiny clues as threads and shoe-buttons, and therefrom, by process of ratiocination, arriving at the Terrible Truth! But here was the creator of such exaggerated fictional characters himself at work on a real investigation! Here, forsooth, was an author who joked about his own characters yet was personally attempting practical results in deduction! If Dick Malabar had not had a great respect for Kent's abilities, he might have indulged in cynical amusement; as it was, he watched with sober interest.

It was little things for which Addison Kent was looking, apparently, but he did not go about whining like a hound on a keen scent and making strange grunts and noises or anything like that! He was merely the trained observer, silent and methodical, thorough. He did get down on his hands and knees, however, once or twice, and he did produce a magnifying glass before he finished! A spot near the big library table seemed to interest him; for he spent some time in close scrutiny of the very thick pile of the immense plain taupe Axminster rug, finally placing a chair directly over it in order that it might not be disturbed. In a far corner of the library he also paused a while. The surface of the library table came in for a careful examination. He took the stopper out of the decanter and sniffed at the wine; he held the solitary wine-glass to his nose.

The body in the chair next received attention. After studying its position, he looked long at the wrists of either hand, passing his fingers lightly over them. He removed one of the house-slippers with evident interest and carefully felt the silk-clad ankle. The neck, also, he felt gently. He seemed puzzled; but said never a word.

When he had finished by examining the telephone and tracing the wiring, he sat down, thoughtfully filled his pipe and lighted it. He smoked for several minutes.

"I am far from satisfied, Dick. But if this is a murder, it is a diabolically unusual one. Call in that Nubian servant, and let's hear what he has to say."

III

Kellani was far from at ease as he stood before them in the presence of his dead master; but it was impossible to tell from his manner whether his diffidence was due to anything more significant than the natural superstitions of his race. He was not of the Nubas, but of the Barabra, he informed them as he drew himself to his full height—from the Nile country.

"By which he means that he is not a slave or the son of a slave," volunteered Malabar in English. "The Nilotic branch dislikes the term Nuba because the pagan Kordofan Nubas were supplied to the Sudanese slave markets for years. He will be Mohammedan, but not fanatically so."

Kent nodded as he studied the giant figure before him. He was glad to have Dick Malabar beside him; if the man's French failed him, the journalist could come to the rescue with his knowledge of dialects.

"You know, of course, that the death of your master is a very, very serious matter, Kellani," Kent began carefully. "In this country the police are very quick to ask many questions when a man dies suddenly. We must know exactly what happened, and it will be best for you to tell the truth—all of it. You understand, Kellani?" Slow inclination of the head signified that he understood. He covertly shifted his position so that the body at the library table would not be within his line of vision so disconcertingly.

"When did you see your master alive last?"

Not since the night before, was the answer. After the gentlemen visitors had gone the master had summoned him to bring more wine to the library, where he was sitting up, reading books. When Kellani had taken in the tray he had not been needed further and had gone to bed.

"And you went straight to sleep, I suppose?"

"Certainly. That is why men go to their beds."

"And you heard no sound—no loud cry or other noises?"

"No, I heard nothing, sidi. The ears of Kellani go to sleep with the rest of his body."

"What time was it when you awoke in the morning?"

"At the hour of the first prayer."

"Just before sunrise—at daybreak, eh? And you came down here to the library right after that? Was anybody else in the house up at that hour?"

"No. It is a habitation of dogs and sons of dogs!"

"He's not calling you names, Kent," interpolated Dick Malabar hastily, as he noted the look in the novelist's eye. "It's a slap at Mokra."

Kent nodded appreciation of the fact; but he continued to eye the Nubian keenly.

"Why did you come down to the library so early, Kellani? Professor Caron was a guest, and it was not your duty to look after the house, was it?"

"I am my master's servant, and my master would have no other attend to his wants."

"But your master was supposed to be asleep upstairs, and it was much too early for him to need you. Why did you go to the library at that hour?" persisted Kent.

"There was the tray and wine-glass to take away, and some dusting—"

"*Glass*, did you say?"

Again the slow inclination of the frizzled head.

"And you found him dead at the table, just like he is now? Look, Kellani!"

Kellani looked, hesitatingly. His gaze did not linger, but shifted uncertainly. Plainly, he was ill at ease.

"In the presence of your dead master, Kellani, I demand that you speak nothing but the truth," impressed Kent solemnly. "Are you telling us the full truth?"

"By the pupil of this eye! yes, sidi. By the beard of the Prophet—!"

"Why have you hidden the second wine-glass?" demanded Addison Kent sharply.

"There was only one wine-glass. By Allah! only one."

"You are lying!" cried Kent, jumping to his feet suddenly. "There were two! You served two people in this room early this morning—your master and the man who called to see him after midnight!"

"Yes, sidi," admitted the Nubian, shrinking from the accusing finger. "That is true."

"By Jove!" murmured Malabar.

"Well? Go on—explain! What about this visitor?"

Badly frightened, Kellani told in his broken French of the stranger's arrival shortly after midnight. The lights were out, and Mokra and the others had retired. Professor Caron, however, still sat in the library, reading. The caller had not rung the door-bell, but had tapped on the glass of the French doors that opened from the library directly upon the tiled portico outside. Professor Caron had admitted the late visitor himself, through this library door. He had summoned Kellani almost immediately, ordering refreshments served. That was all Kellani knew about it.

"Who was this man? Had you ever seen him before?"

"No. I did not know him. I knew not his name."

"What happened after that? How long did the stranger stay?"

That, Kellani was unable to say. His master had sent him off, to bed, and he had gone there obediently, leaving the two gentlemen alone in the library.

"About the wine-glass—why did you hide it when the police came?"

His master had warned him that nobody must know of this midnight interview; that was why he had removed the second glass and said nothing. Always he was his beloved master's obedient servant, even as he was now theirs.

"Rather an unusual hour for a social call," mused Kent. "What did this man look like? Was he a small man, like Professor Caron?"

"Yes, a very small man, sidi."

"The truth, Kellani!" warned Kent sternly. "Again, I have to correct you! The man was a big man, powerfully built, strong! Was he not?"

"Yes, a very big man, sidi."

Addison Kent looked over at Dick Malabar helplessly, then rang for the butler.

"I would advise you to pray earnestly six time to-day, Kellani. Allah is great! Ask him to grant you wisdom other than the wisdom of the serpent. You may go."

As the Nubian strode to the door with alacrity, he almost collided with Mokra. The butler twisted quickly to one side, hastily thrusting out one arm, his hand closed except for the first and third fingers; it was as if, thereby, he would ward off some power to injure.

"See that!" whispered Malabar to Kent. "You note that he is resisting 'the evil eye'? Mokra belongs to the Kabyles—pure Berber stock—the original Numidian. Racial jealousy! Trouble brewing there, Kent."

IV

Mokra was agitated. Fear, anger, superstitious dread—all were written in his dark, heavy-boned face and anxious black eyes that looked restlessly about him. It was a more intelligent face, a more trustworthy face than that of the stolid Nubian who, so willingly, had just left the library with its silent sleeper and magic inquisitor who knew the answers to his own questions!

As Richard Malabar had intimated, Mokra was of the pure Berber race that was in North Africa before the Arabs came—of the Haratin or "Black" Berbers of the southern slopes of the hill country. Also, he had belonged to the Zouaves and had fought for France, earning honourable discharge. Long association with such French gentlemen as his present benefactor, Armaund Lamont, had enabled him to become proficient in European ways. His spoken French was not the atrocious pidgin tongue which the Arab attempts. From his Berber blood he derived a natural attachment to home life and habits of labour, which the Arab lacks; but to this had been added the influence of his army training and the polish of long services He was a loyal, faithful and efficient servant.

Addison Kent smiled at him. He had known Mokra for some time, and was aware of the confidence which Lamont reposed in him.

"You do not like Kellani?" he encouraged.

"May Allah slice him in pieces! Do not believe anything he says, Monsieur Kent. His tongue is without bones, and it moves in whatever way he chooses."

"I quite agree with you, Mokra. Did you hear anyone moving about inside the house last night?"

"No, monsieur. I went to bed early, and I slept very soundly. I heard nothing until roused by that son of a slipper in the morning."

"What time was that?"

"Not long after sunrise, monsieur."

"You missed the prayer at *fodjeur*, then?"

Allah forgive him! He had not slept so soundly for years. It was a *djinn* that had carried him away!

"Did you have anything to eat or drink before retiring?" asked Kent quickly.

"Only a glass of milk and a piece of cake, monsieur."

"The glass from which you drank—it has been washed?"

Assuredly. Mokra had washed it himself. He was not the "dirty dog of a Kabyle" which that mule of a fellah had called him. Allah demolish him! No Mussulman washed oftener than Mokra!

"I understand it was you who telephoned for the police. Why did you do that?"

"Because that whelp of the devil—that *fellah* with the eyes, ears, nose, teeth and tail of a dog's dog—!" Mokra paused, conscious that the excitement into which his words were leading him was out of place. "He said he would cut out my heart, monsieur, and I was afraid to be alone with him. I required some shiny buttons for him to see. That was why I called the police to come."

"Did you know that Professor Caron had a visitor here in the library last night after we left the house?"

No, Mokra had not known that. He was surprised.

"Kellani did not tell you?"

"No, monsieur."

"Very well, Mokra. That will be all just now—unless you have something to ask, Dick?"

"No. We'll ring if we need you again, Mokra."

As soon as the butler was out of the room, Malabar leaned forward eagerly. "That is true about the man calling here in the early hours of the morning? You were not just inventing it to test Kellani?"

"Hardly, Dick," smiled Kent. "It is as true as the evidence written in this room."

V

"Come here and see for yourself. Whoever poured the wine did so with an unsteady hand; if it was Professor Caron, he was agitated by the presence of the caller at that hour, and if it was the stranger himself, he was probably already under the influence of liquor. One of the glasses overflowed slightly on to the tray. You can see the mark of the two glasses quite distinctly, and you note that one of them had a larger base than the other."

"But that is not all, of course. Here on the surface of the table—stoop down and you will get the light on it just right—the mark is quite plain. A very big man has leaned his weight upon his hand there. The fingers are outspread, you note. A man with a hand like that must be over six feet and built to powerful proportions. He wore gloves and was careful not to remove them while in this room—a fact that is suspicious."

"That is why the impression is somewhat indeterminate, then," commented Malabar with interest. "What else?"

"Over here in the corner— You may have noted that in the corners of any room, covered by a carpet or large rug like this, the pile is scarcely worn, but is of its original thickness. He evidently stood here for some time—perhaps while he held forth at some length upon the object of his visit. Note the size of the marks made by his feet. They match the hand."

"How do you know that these marks were not made by the feet of Donovan or one of his men—the mark of the hand, too, for that matter?"

"Because none of the police wore gloves, and because the police are not equipped with golf boots. You can see the impression of the rubber studs plainly. The boots were brand-new—perhaps purchased specially for this nocturnal visit."

Dick Malabar rubbed his chin reflectively and slowly nodded his head.

"This man, then, stole the sealed package from the safe, you think?"

"Either he stole it or it was handed to him by Professor Caron, but I doubt the latter."

"You mean—?"

"Professor Caron was bound, hand and foot! The marks on his wrists and ankles are not very noticeable; but they are there. What puzzles me is why the visitor removed the Professor's slippers."

"Wh-what?"

"In replacing them he put them on the wrong feet—the right slipper on the left foot and the left slipper on the right foot. Look for yourself. I tell you, Dick, something damnable happened in this room in the early morning hours; but what? What?"

He took a pace across the room and back, head bent in thought. He paused at the table and idly picked up the two-ounce bottle of digitalis that had been found in the deceased's vest pocket.

"We know that the Professor was in terror from something or other, Kent. The fact that he hid the ruby shows that he was afraid of this very visit, doesn't it? It does not look well—the whole thing. Everything points to foul play—"

Malabar paused at an exclamation from the novelist, who was staring at the little round bottle in his hand.

"You are right, Dick, and here is some more evidence under our very eyes. I am going to telephone my friend Doctor Harvey, and have him analyze this stuff. I believe he will find the contents of this bottle inert; for digitalis is not active after eighteen months or so. The label shows the date of manufacture to have been over two years ago."

"Which means—?"

"That this bottle was planted in Professor Caron's pocket by the murderer to suggest treatment for a weak heart; that his death is not due to that."

"How was he killed?"

"It is not going to be easy to find that out."

"When the man who came here discovers that the jewel case is empty—that the golden scarab is missing—"

"It was that he was after?"

"Undoubtedly. He will come back here for it."

"And waste no time in doing so, I would say."

"I expect him to make another attempt—possibly to-night."

"What are you going to do?" Malabar looked up eagerly.

"When the gentleman calls to-night," stated Addison Kent quietly, "we shall be here to receive him!"

7
PORTENT!

I

The day grew oppressively hot and humid for the time of year; but that did not lessen the detail with which it was crowded for Addison Kent. There were cables to send to Paris and to Armaund Lamont in Switzerland. An undertaker took charge of the body of the late archæologist after Kent's own doctor had viewed it. Doctor Harvey carried away with him the bottle of digitalis, and also the spoonful of wine that remained in the glass upon the tray, promising to complete his analysis and report before night upon the desirability of an autopsy.

The thing which Addison Kent had planned to do first of all that day, however, had been erased from his programme through the arguments of Richard Malabar. Whoever was after the golden scarab, the journalist pointed out, was hardly likely to be alone in his quest. Professor Caron had intimated that nobody knew he had the gem in his possession; but this was disproved by the visit of the man who had walked off with the sealed package out of the safe. And, if one man knew of the ruby and its whereabouts, there was no telling how many more might be aware of the prospective "haul" and be on the watch. Whoever were after it certainly would be keeping a sharp eye open for its removal from the Lamont residence. Not only might it be dangerous to change the location of the jewel at the present moment; to do so might also defeat Kent's very purpose in taking up temporary quarters in the Lamont house—to surprise the thieves in a second attempt to enter the place in search of the scarab.

"I am satisfied that the fellow who came here has confederates, Kent," Malabar declared with conviction. "They may be only hired 'look-outs,' set to keep close watch on this house and the movements of its inmates. This is big game, remember, and well worth big effort."

"You have some suggestion to offer?"

"Yes. I advise keeping the golden scarab right here—for to-night, at least, or until the enemy have shown a lead which we can follow up. I believe with you that they will try to enter the house sooner or later, thereby providing us with our opportunity. But they will do that only if they believe the ruby is still here."

"That sounds reasonable," agreed Kent. "Would you put it back in the same hiding-place, then?"

"I've thought of a better place—better for our purpose, that is. Let us bait a trap, as it were. You will sleep in Professor Caron's bedroom—in his bed—while I occupy the sitting-room that opens off it. There is a davenport, if I remember rightly, or we can fix up a cot of some kind."

"And where will the golden scarab retire for the night?"

"On the breast of one of the mummies. It will tuck out of sight, quite nicely, inside the bandages. That is the last place whoever is after it will be liable to look for it. They will have a natural tendency to shy away from the mummies and—"

"Remember what Professor Caron said last night, Dick: 'Nothing is safe from a bold thief! Nothing is sacred!' Remember the thieves who penetrated the tombs of the Pharaohs in ancient days. Nevertheless, I think your suggestion is a good one; for, if we get them inside that bedroom and fail to nab them, we deserve to be licked!"

"That's my idea exactly, old chap. We'll take turns in standing guard. I shall take the first watch—say till three or three-thirty a.m. Then I shall wake you for your trick. Is that agreeable?"

"Perfectly."

So it was arranged. Evening found Kent and Dick Malabar installed at the Westchester mansion, to the great relief of Mokra. It was evident that the butler had been afraid of being left alone on the premises, even although the solid Scotsman—Sandy, the gardener—had quarters above the garage, scarcely a stone's-throw from the big house. The removal of the body from the library and the arrival of Kent and Malabar afforded the simple Algerian much comfort, and only the presence of the Nubian prevented him from being entirely happy. As it was, he felt pretty cheerful, and went about the laying of the table in the dining-room with an assurance which finally sent the late Professor's manservant, sulking, to his room in the servants' wing.

All day long the coastal stations had been flying storm signals. At sundown thunder-clouds were shouldered high in the heavens, mountainous, black.

"Looks as if we were in for a bad storm before morning," was Kent's comment as he glanced at the sky. They had come out on the portico after dinner for coffee and cigars.

"The worse the better," responded Malabar, smiling a little at the paradox. "Under cover of the Stygian darkness and the uproar of the warring elements, the determined enemy crept stealthily upon the sleeping fortress—all that sort of thing!"

The air seemed to hang like a pall, sultry, pocketed, dead. Out on the highway the sound of motors rose to a passing hum—died away. From the river persisted the staccato of a launch, strangely loud, and somewhere the dull beat of turbine engines.

II

"The telephone wants to talk with you, Monsieur Kent, if you please," announced Mokra from the library doorway.

"It was Harvey, Dick," Kent informed as he came back to his chair. "As I expected, that digitalis is inert—an old bottle of it, entirely useless."

"You think it was placed in Caron's pocket to mislead?"

"I'm sure of it. He was no more taking treatments for his heart than I am! Whoever planted it has run across the bottle, standing on a shelf somewhere; he suddenly conceived the idea and acted upon it without noticing the old date on the label. That much is clear."

"What about the wine?"

"There is a slight trace of chloral hydrate, but not enough to do any harm—not more than would be required for a sleeping-draught."

"That is strange. Does Harvey recommend an autopsy?"

"He does. We ought to have a report on that to-morrow; but I doubt if they'll find anything to prove that a murder has been committed."

"Yet you are convinced—?"

"I am waiting for the report of the medical experts."

Sandy MacLean passed with a light ladder on his muscular shoulder. He nodded to them and grinned.

"Everything snug for the night, Sandy?" called Kent.

"Ay, that it is. We'll no be needin' the sprinklers, Ah'm thinkin', sir." He paused to wave a hand at the sky. "Them clouds wull be gaein' lawn-waterin' the nicht." He went on towards the garage, wagging his head wisely.

"I asked Sandy if he had noticed anybody banging about the place during the day," remarked Kent.

"And—?"

"The answer is 'yes,' Dick. He saw two young fellows hanging about suspiciously, off and on, all afternoon. They were looking in at the gate, and once he caught them lounging on the grass, behind some bushes. He chased them off about their business. He had some tools stolen out of the garage not long ago."

"What did I tell you?" There was a note of satisfaction in Malabar's voice. "Well, let them come!"

"You had better see that you have a full clip in your automatic when you go on duty. You're sworn in as a deputy now, remember. If you have to, don't hesitate to shoot."

"I only hope we are not taking all these precautions for nothing," was Malabar's prayer.

"It will not be very difficult to approach the house, anyway"—and Kent indicated the surrounding shrubbery— "or to get inside, for that matter."

The grounds of the Lamont estate stretched away into the gloom, the boundaries lost in the darkness, except for the gleam of lamps on the posts at the foot of the driveway, where the heavy iron gates were closed and locked for the night. There was a light standard near the garage, while two lamps glowed dimly in their frosted globes on either side of the *porte cochère*. In every other direction the shrubbery afforded concealment.

III

About ten o'clock Addison Kent decided to turn in for a few hours' rest. He left Malabar amusing himself in the billiard-room. But it was some time after he was undressed and in bed before the novelist could get to sleep. Long ago he had mastered insomnia by sheer mental control; but to-night his mind seemed full of vagrant thoughts. He blamed the failure of his efforts to relax at first upon the fact that it was not his regular bedtime; but perhaps the presence of the automatic and the electric torch under his pillow, with all that they signified, had something to do with it.

Or was it the strangeness of his surroundings? He was not accustomed to a bedroom in which mummies in their coffins stood on guard! That grotesque black cat—!

In spite of himself his eyes kept wandering in the direction of the upright cases. He felt uncomfortable in their presence—nervous, as if about them hung some malignant spell, an aura of malevolence—!

Rather sharply he took himself to task. Was he a child, glancing apprehensively over his shoulder in fear of the Bogy Man? Nonsense! These rumours of malicious spirits exerting evil influences—why, the dried-up bodies, enclosed in those upright cases by the door there, were over three thousand years old—harmless as the dust of the ages! As poor Caron had said, just last night: "Why should they harm anyone who sought to preserve their memory, who—?"

Just last night! Professor Caron was alive and well then. He had stood right over there. Kent could see the smile on his face. Right in this room—just last night! This was Caron's bed! Up there was the place where the plaster— "I will leap upon him like a wild beast upon his prey!"

"Damn!" Kent punched the pillow irritably into a more comfortable position and kicked off the sheets. "Now, go to sleep, and be quick about it!" he apostrophised. "You've got to be up in less than five hours!"

Fitful blue light played into the dark room intermittently from the distant storm that was brewing. It would be sure to break in the night sometime, and if he did not get to sleep before that happened, the storm would keep him awake if nothing else did.

Queer how the cold blue light that came and went caught the shine of the pitch on the wooden figure that was the cat's coffin, sitting over there by the window. It gleamed on the rock-crystal of its staring eyes. He would not have much difficulty in imagining that the grotesque creature was winking and grinning at him—!

Deliberately, he turned his back upon it—and propped himself promptly on an elbow. For, out of the darkness from the opposite side of the room—! He shut his eyelids impatiently; but when he slowly opened them again—!

Without removing his stare, he fumbled for the light switch— and could not locate it. There was no mistaking the fact that two great eyes—real eyes—were glowing at him out of the dark—great, burning orbs like live coals!

Kent shut his eyelids once more and found, upon reopening them, that the glowing fires were gone from the spot. With a breath of relief he sank back on the pillow, but jerked up again instantly. They had not disappeared! They had only moved to another spot, where they still blazed at him in the darkness!

He stretched out an impatient arm for the light switch, found it and flooded the room. There was nothing to be seen at the spot!— not a thing!

Sheepishly, he snapped out the light and rolled over. After a while he dozed—slept. So that he did not hear the first low, distant rumble of thunder—like the mutter of approaching menace.

8
A House of Terror

I

CR-RASH!

Spasmodically, Addison Kent sat up in bed, blinking, only half awake. The first thing that was borne in upon his sleep-blunted brain was the fact that a terrific electrical storm was in full blast. Thunder-claps cracked overhead like exploding cannon. Lightning in long, vivid flashes for the moment lit the room like day—a moment of dazzling brightness, then utter blackness. The roll of the thunder rattled the windows in their casements. The rumbling was incessant. The rain was coming down in torrents, and he could hear the trees lashing in the gale that swept them.

Then suddenly Kent was wide awake as he caught again the glow of those two malignant eyes that had stared at him before. The balls of fire glowed from the far corner of the bedroom, low down, near the floor. In the next lightning-flash he got just a glimpse of something crouching for a spring!

R-ripple!—Crack!—ackle! came the thunder. He fumbled beneath the pillow for his automatic and sprang from the bed. Something struck him on the chest, as if launched from a catapult, and he went over backwards. He felt sharp pains as the clawing, yowling creature scratched the coat of his pyjamas to ribbons!

With a yell he fought it off. He leaped to his feet. In another flash of lightning he saw a dark form dashing away into the interior of the house. He lost sight of it before he could fire at it.

He ran to the wall at the head of the bed and slithered his hand about in search of the light switch. The button snapped under his thumb; but the room remained in darkness. The fuses were blown—probably throughout the whole house!

What had attacked him? He pawed the pillow till he got hold of his electric torch. He turned it on, playing the beam across the floor to the corner without finding there anything to indicate an answer. He swung the disk of light to the corner where the mummy of the Egyptian cat—!

With an involuntary cry of astonishment, Kent strode across the room to investigate. The coffin-shell, in which the mummy of the sacred cat had been so securely sealed, lay on the floor in two longitudinal halves!

The cat was gone!

II

Bewildered, Kent swung on his heel. A long, wicked flash of lightning dazzled him, and what he saw in that brief illumination of the bedroom brought a cry of horror to his lips.

He levelled the beam of his torch. The lid was off the coffin of the mummy on the right-hand side of the doorway! The linen strips in which it had been swathed were unwrapped—torn away! They hung in streamers from the upper portion of the shrunken brown body of the mummy!

It was "The Laugher," as the Professor had nicknamed him! The open mouth, the grinning teeth, the sunken sockets that had shocked Kent and Malabar the evening before in the photo they had seen—here they were now in horrible reality, glaring and gleaming back at him in the lightning's eerie blue flame!

"Damnation!" cried Kent in amazement.

But it was not in fear that the exclamation escaped him. He ran to the bed, almost in panic haste, slipped on his tennis shoes, grabbed his bath-robe from the back of a chair, snatched his watch from beneath the pillow and forced himself to approach the dire figure. Anxiously he played the beam of his torch about that awful

face, down the naked brown breast, around on the floor—everywhere! For it was upon the breast of this mummy that he and
Malabar, just a few hours before, had concealed the golden scarab
beneath the bandages!

And the appalling truth was that the priceless ruby, in its golden
scarab setting, had completely disappeared! It was gone!—successfully stolen!

III

For a moment Addison Kent stood there, dazed by the discovery. Automatically, he glanced at his watch. It was nearly three
o'clock in the morning.

Then his brain began to function. The thief, or thieves, had
broken into the house. They had been in this room—with him lying
there on the bed! It could not have been very long ago. They had
come under cover of the storm, and he knew by the intensity of it
that it was at its height right now. The thief could not be far away—
might be in the house still!

He cast the beam of his light into every nook and cranny of the
big bedroom. He looked under the bed, the only place that appeared
to offer concealment. He shut off the light as he cautiously approached the door that led into the sitting-room.

It was Malabar's duty to be on guard for half an hour yet. He
had not wakened Kent. Why hadn't he? Where the devil was he?
This thing had been done right under his nose!

Raging inwardly, the novelist nevertheless very carefully
entered the sitting-room, first flashing his torchlight into every
corner. Nobody was there. Malabar's cot was empty—had been unoccupied. Where was he? Perhaps he had been eliminated by the
thieves!

As this thought took possession of Kent he grew suddenly calm.
There was no telling what dangers lay before him in that great
house of darkness. He must investigate. Automatic in hand, ready
for instant use, and with jaws grimly set, he crept from the bedroom and made his way out into the upper hallway.

He reached the banister and peered over into the wide hall downstairs. The glare of the lightning came and went; it gleamed on the clusters of ancient weapons that hung on the walls, here and there, flashing from halberd and battle-axe, broadsword and shield, with cold fire; it shone on the suits of armour in the corners—shone and went out, shone and went out. The lower hall appeared to be empty.

Where was Mokra? Where was Kellani? Was he alone in the house? He listened long and carefully; but he soon realized that the infernal reverberations and roar of the storm effectively drowned out all ordinary noises. He doubted if even the bark of an automatic would be heard with that pandemonium going on.

As he drew back from the banister, his heart skipped a beat. Again he saw those fiery eyes glowing at him in the darkness of the upper hallway. They were approaching him now! Tense, he waited, his gun advanced.

Then he lowered it with an inward laugh at himself as a huge black ball of fur rubbed softly against his leg.

"Meow!" greeted Aristophanes lonesomely.

IV

Satisfied that the way was clear, Kent slipped noiselessly down the carpeted staircase. He did not show his light, and he held his automatic ready; but nobody was in the lower hallway.

Nor in the library, when at last he reached the archway and slowly parted the portières that hung there. He advanced into the room, and with the idea of catching a glimpse of the grounds at the next flash of lightning, he made his way cautiously towards the French doors that opened upon the tiled portico. He flung the heavy partly-drawn window drapes aside, and as the lightning came he flattened his nose against the glass and, with his hands at the side of his face, peered out.

He started back in. astonishment. He was staring straight into a face on the opposite side of the glass!— the face of someone who, in turn, was trying to see into the room where he stood!

Quickly he dodged to one side. But there was no gun-play. In the lightning glare he saw the figure out on the portico recoil in equal surprise. He saw the look of terror in the wide-open eyes. As the head turned, he caught a glimpse of the face and gasped amazement.

It was a young woman who stood there! Just for a moment she stood—a young woman in a mackintosh, dripping wet! The hood of it was over her head. Raindrops gleamed on fluffy hair where it protruded. Then the glare went out, and everything was black. By the time he could get his electric torch into play— she was gone!

And, even in that dramatic moment, Addison Kent realized that it was a very beautiful face.

V

He grabbed the door-knob, struggling with the catch. The bolt stuck!

In exasperation he dashed for the front door; but, by the time he felt the blast of the wind and rain, he had given up all hope of overtaking her. Like a frightened deer she had fled.

A woman! What was she doing there in a storm like this? In no period of calculation had he allowed for the possibility of a woman thief appearing upon the scene!

Up and down the portico he raged. The wind tore at his bath-robe and flapped it about his wet legs, to which his soaked pyjamas were already plastered. Outdoors, the uproar of the storm was deafening. The tall bushes were bent almost to the ground by the boisterous gale; they tossed about like maddened creatures. The turmoil of the thunder was incessant, while the torrential rain was drummed in gusts against windows and went swishing along the ground. It drove in slanted sheets; in the blue blaze of the lightning it looked like pelting silver.

Kent ran around the house to the rear, in the direction he imagined the girl would take. But she was nowhere in sight, and he swore impotently. He ran along the garden walk that ended at a small gate in the high brick wall which skirted the rear of the garden—

and stopped with a jerk as a blinding sizzle of lightning seared the sky, followed instantly by a terrific rip of thunder.

For, on top of the garden wall, loomed a huge figure! Just a glimpse of it he got—a big man in a felt hat, the brim hanging limp about his ears, shedding rain!

Blackness! Glare again! The man was gone! Blackness! Glare!

"Dick!" shouted Kent at the top of his voice.

Skirting the wall, white shirt-sleeves vivid in the bright flare, one arm extending his police automatic, ran Richard Malabar in pursuit of the man on the wall!

VI

Kent dashed after him. By the time he got to the spot, Malabar had disappeared. Kent shouted; but his voice was torn to shreds and tossed away on the fling of the storm. He stumbled about in the shrubbery for a while, but failed to see further sign of pursuer or pursued.

There was nothing for it but to go back to the house. He could accomplish little out there in that maelstrom with no definite objective. He began to wonder what had happened to the household—the servants. Where was Sandy?

He stopped at the garage and shouted several times without response. There was no light in the garage. The lamps were all out on the driveway and about the grounds. The house was lost in darkness, except when the lightning flares limned it, a glisten of streaming windows.

Kent let himself in at the front door and stood, listening, in the hall. After the hurly-burly without, it seemed almost quiet indoors now.

"Mokra!" he called. "Kellani! Ho, you Mokra!"

But there was no answer to his shouts.

Then he thought he heard a sound at the kitchen entrance and went cautiously towards it. He heard a stamping of feet, a gruff oath, the scratch of a match, the yellow flicker of a candle—then shuffling footsteps, advancing along a passage.

"Air ye a' recht, Maister Kent?" came Sandy MacLean's anxious enquiry.

He was coming along the kitchen corridor, the candle throwing a grotesque black shadow of him on the wall.

"The dommed fuses hae blown oot an' Ah'm thinkin'—"

He stumbled. The burring voice was silent. Then Addison Kent heard his low-breathed, horrified exclamation.

"What's wrong, Sandy?" he called, hurrying into the passage. The beam of his electric torch preceded him.

It was Mokra! He lay sprawled across the narrow corridor. He had been struck from behind, and the haft of the knife protruded from his back!

The two men stared at one another, their faces blanched in the uncertain light. The din of the storm beat about the house with fury unabated.

Upstairs, in the bedroom of the late Professor Emil Caron, the mummy laughed in silent fixity as the cold weird light came and went on its awful face.

9
Missing!

Addison Kent's look was grim as he stood up from examination of the Algerian's body. Here, at least, was no room for doubt. It was murder in the first degree—cold-blooded, treacherous, a stab in the dark from behind! These men with whom they had to deal were ruthless. No woman's hand could have driven that powerful blow; the knife had been wielded with vicious force.

"I swear to you, Sandy, that whoever has done this shall pay for it!" vowed Kent bitterly. "He was a faithful, loyal fellow—Mokra—and, by Heaven! they are not going to get away with a crime like this. I am going to begin by searching this house from cellar to roof. You have a supply of new fuses in the garage? Well, go for them while I'm getting dressed. I want lights at once. And bring a lantern with you."

"Aye, sir. Ah'm thinkin' a hurricane lamp—?"

"The very thing! Get it! Every minute counts. Hustle!"

There was a quality in the tone of the command that sent the gardener outside on the run. He was back in a remarkably short time and soon had located the blown fuses and replaced them.

"Turn on every light in the place as we come to it," ordered Kent. "We'll start in the cellar; but first—"

He glanced about the kitchen. An empty peach-crate stood on end in a corner, and he picked it up. He lifted down a dish-pan from a nail above the sink. Crate and pan in hand, he made his way to the front door and out on to the portico while the gardener switched on the library lights and drew the window-drapes aside, so that the light streamed out on the tiles.

As Addison Kent expected, he found several wet and muddy footprints; the marks of new rubbers were distinct—the small, narrow footprints of a woman. He covered the clearest of the imprints with the upturned pan and the shallow peach-crate. The marks were close enough to the windows of the library to be protected to some extent by the overhang of the roof; while the rain was still coming down heavily, it was not driving in against that side of the house.

"Now for the cellar, Sandy," directed Kent with satisfaction.

A draught of cool, damp air struck their faces as they descended; one of the cellar windows was wide open. The windows swung inward on hinges; the hook of the open window was in its eyelet on the joist overhead. Sandy swore that every cellar window had been closed when he made his rounds.

"You can see where it has been forced, of course." Kent pointed, then waved the gardener back as he made a close examination under the ray of his electric torch. "See if you can rustle me a couple of small boxes, Sandy."

One of these he turned upside down on the cement floor directly under the window; the other he passed through the window and upturned alongside the torn screen, which had been unhooked and thrown aside.

"Golf is a great game, Sandy," commented Kent irrelevantly.

"Ay, sir," agreed Sandy MacLean solemnly.

"Let's try the first floor now."

The novelist went systematically through every room without finding anything of importance apparently. It was not until they reached the bedroom he had occupied on the second floor that he showed particular interest.

"I should think there must be some good bargains in golf outfits at this time of the year, Sandy. Noticed any bargains lately?—boots, for instance?"

Sandy did not answer. Sandy was not there. He was not within earshot. In fact, he was not on the second floor at all. He was down in the dining-room at the buffet, pouring from the decanter which stood there a glass of whiskey, swallowing it neat. He had need of it; for one look into that bedroom—one look at that mummy—! With reckless generosity he played host to himself by pouring out a second man-sized drink. Thus fortified, he marched doggedly back upstairs, the look of fighting ancestors upon his rugged face.

"It's a braw, bricht, moonlicht nicht, the nicht!" he chanted, testing his speech as advised by Harry Lauder. "Hoots, lad! Noo, ye maun bring on the de'il himnsel'!"

In the servants' quarters they found the chef, sound asleep in his bed and snoring. Kent awakened him, without sympathy, to thunder, lightning and murder; but he might better have left him to his snores for all the information he could give, as it was evident that the fat Gaston would have slept through the battle of Waterloo and probably could be awakened only by the smell of something burning!

Not so his assistant Henri, in the bed alongside, however. The youth had his head buried in the bedclothes, and when these were pulled away, it was a wide-awake and startled young Frenchman who blinked at them in the bright light. His face was pea-green and he looked positively ill; at each peal of thunder he quivered in fright. The storm had awakened him, he said; he was always terrified like this in a bad storm.

"Where is Kellani? Have you seen him? Where's his room?" demanded Kent brusquely. "Come and show me."

The room the Nubian had occupied was at the end of the upper hallway. There was no need to ask questions; it told its own story of hasty departure. The drawers of the dresser were open and empty. Discarded clothing was littered here and there, and an old suitcase in the corner was half packed, as if the owner had been interrupted in his preparations or had decided suddenly not to hamper himself in his flight.

Addison Kent's face was stern as he considered. It had not been the Nubian he had glimpsed on the wall; for the face of the big man had been white. Mokra! There was bad blood between Kellani and Mokra. It might well be that the Nubian had done the deed. He belonged to a treacherous breed. Dick Malabar had said—

By the way, where was Malabar all this time? He ought to have returned to the house before this! Suddenly concerned, Kent turned to the gardener.

"We must search the grounds thoroughly, Sandy, at once. Mr. Malabar is out there somewhere, and he may need us. You fellows go back to bed, and be sure that neither of you attempts to leave without permission. Come on, Sandy."

The first fury of the storm had lessened considerably. The rain was pelting down still, but the velocity of the wind had fallen off, and the intervals between the lightning-flashes and the following thunder-peals lengthened steadily. The high brick wall at the foot of the garden, where Malabar had been seen in pursuit of the figure on the wall, was the logical point from which to start the search; but, of course, the deluge of driving rain had obliterated all footprints from the sward and had puddled the softer ground hopelessly.

Nevertheless, Kent sent the gardener off to the left while he went to the right, and they quartered back and forth, examining every piece of shrubbery and every stretch of lawn. The beam of the novelist's electric torch was like a finger, probing in the dark, and as the search progressed without discovery of any clue to what had taken place out there in the storm, Kent's anxiety grew. He was fast reaching the conclusion that Dick Malabar had carried the pursuit outside the grounds altogether, when he heard a halloo from Sandy, and saw the signal swing of the hurricane lamp, down at the foot of the driveway.

Kent joined him on the run. Sandy was pointing to a huddled heap near one of the big stone gate-posts, and Kent ran forward with a mutter of fear as the light revealed mud-stained shirt-sleeves.

Malabar was lying, face down, in a small puddle, his head just out of the water. A red gash was visible where his wet hair was plastered to one side, and Kent turned him over anxiously. There was a great bruise on his forehead; his face was scratched and bleeding; his shirt was ripped in several places, as if bullets—

"Dick! Dick!" cried Kent, shaking him gently by the shoulder. "Thank God!" he breathed as he noted the flutter of the eyelids. "Quick, Sandy, we must get him to the house as fast as possible."

Malabar opened his eyes.

"Ch—cheerio!" he murmured.

"How badly hurt are you, old man? How are you feeling?" asked Kent as he made a hurried examination for bullet-wounds without finding any.

"Top—top-hole!" came Malabar's voice weakly. "Beggar got— clean away!"

He fainted. They carried him quickly towards the house, bright now with illuminated windows.

10
PLUS AND MINUS

I

Richard Malabar's escape might well be considered to savour of the miraculous. He had been fired at several times at close quarters—point-blank, he said—and his bullet-torn shirt provided powder-stained evidence. He had come through unscathed, except for the bruises, cuts and scratches—painful, but not at all serious. With a raw beef poultice bandaged across his forehead, he lay back in an easy-chair in front of the library grate, sipping a stiff toddy while he eyed the flaming coal. The sudden drop in temperature that had ridden in on the back of the storm made the fire welcome in the coolness of the dawn hours.

For it was almost daybreak. The rain was over. All thought of further sleep had been banished from the Lamont residence while its inmates awaited the arrival of the police. Addison Kent had telephoned a full report to Inspector Lowry, Chief of Detectives. Already Police Headquarters had ordered a drag-net for the missing Nubian, and confidently hoped to have him brought in within a few hours. It would not be easy for one of his exceptional description to escape notice very long. Every underworld haunt where sanctuary might be sought would be combed, Kent knew, for two men of giant physique—one brown, one white.

As he had listened to Malabar's account of what had happened, the novelist had marvelled at the simplicity with which the theft had been accomplished in the face of the precautions taken to prevent it. It seemed almost as if Fate had conspired against them. If

Malabar had turned out the last lights earlier and retired to the sitting-room for his vigil; if he had not stepped out on the portico for a breath of air; if he had not felt the need of stretching his legs by taking a final turn around the house to make sure that everything was securely fastened!—

He had not reckoned on the closeness with which the house was being watched or the boldness of the thieves. Apparently they had spied upon him as he sat, reading, in the library; no doubt, they realized that he was on guard, and when he had gone outside for a moment they bad been quick to seize the opportunity of eliminating him. He had not known what struck him. When he recovered consciousness he had found himself in a far corner of the grounds, tied to a tree, hand and foot, with a gag in his mouth!

As simply as that the way had been cleared for entry. When the storm broke and the deluge of rain had revived him, Richard Malabar had fought the nausea of dizziness from the blow on his head, and finally had succeeded in loosening his bonds. His first instinct had been to get back to the house for his automatic, find out if Kent was all right and see what the thieves had accomplished. He let himself in through the French doors of the library.

"Very foolish of you to have gone outside unarmed, Dick," had been Kent's comment.

"It never occurred to me that they would be on hand at that early hour. It was not yet midnight. Yes, it was a fool thing to do."

By the time Malabar had secured his weapon, which was in the side pocket of his coat, the storm had been in full blast. He was about to start for the stairs to see if everything was in order—

"Had you done so, things might have been— Well, never mind. Go on."

"But, Kent, it was right then that I saw the bally fellow in the flopped hat. I saw him in a flash of lightning, making for the bushes from the direction of the house. He had the tail of his coat wrapped around something, and tucked up under his arm—"

"The mummy of the cat!"

"—and I went right out again after him"

"Through the library?"

"Yes."

"Leaving the door slightly ajar behind you?"

"I th-ink so."

"Otherwise, being a spring lock, you would have locked your-self out."

"Quite so."

"I wonder who closed it after you. When I came down and tried to get out through that door in a hurry, I found it not only closed but jammed so tightly I couldn't budge it."

"Hold on, now! I am not so sure that I left it open. I seem to remember giving it a yank to shut it as I sprang outside. No doubt it slammed shut behind me. There was such an uproar going on you couldn't hear a thing, and I was thinking only of stopping my man before he got away."

Apparently the thief realized that someone was after him; for he had hidden in the shrubbery and for a time had not made a move. Malabar had stalked him, and had been rewarded at last by sight of his quarry, making for the garden at the rear of the house. The man was clambering the wall by the time the journalist had got within range; but at the first shot dropped back and opened fire on his pursuer.

The duel had been fought out with only the lightning to reveal the whereabouts of each opponent. They had ducked about and stalked each other for some time, and had come together unex-pectedly at the foot of the driveway. Malabar was unable to say whether any of his own bullets had found their mark; certainly, they had not stopped the final onslaught of the desperate giant. Each had emptied his weapon by the time they had come so sud-denly to grips, and out of the dark the man had dealt Malabar a blow with the butt-end of his gun on the forehead. That was all Malabar had known until Kent had found him.

The awakening had been a very humiliating one for Richard Malabar when he had been told that the priceless golden scarab was gone and Mokra murdered. He seemed still dazed, and had refused to believe until Kent had shown him the evidence. Malabar then had clenched his fists and knotted his jaw muscles in angry mortification.

"They've made a bally monkey of me, Kent! I had no business going outside the house; I should have gone on guard up in the sitting-room, as we planned. It was upon my recommendation that we kept that ruby here—! I say, I wonder that you don't give me hell for the jolly old mess I have made of the thing! I shan't put up any defence, if you do; because, don't you know, there is nothing to say." He squared his shoulders. "Fire!"

Addison Kent smiled.

"If nobody ever made mistakes, Dick, the world would be a pretty unprofitable place for some of us. Forget it! I am to blame for risking the golden scarab in the first place. It is for me to re-cover it and get to the bottom of this whole affair. Cheer up, now! The first skirmish goes to the enemy; but the fight is only starting. And I have an idea that we shall find it not without interest."

II

Kent gave the fire in the grate a poke or two, drew up a chair opposite the despondent Malabar and cheerfully proceeded to fill and light his pipe. The journalist studied the other's keen face for a moment, noting the lines of determination, the firm mouth, the square chin.

"Would you mind telling me just where we are to head in?" he asked dejectedly. "Outside of the fact that it looks as if Kellani killed Mokra, and may have taken the scarab when he fled—I confess that is about as far as I can get, Kent."

"I'm afraid that is not far enough, old man. If you dismiss it so simply, you eliminate the man who attacked you—"

"No. He was outside, waiting for the Nubian to hand over the scarab and the mummy of the cat—in league with each other and all that sort of thing. I say, what about that cat business, anyway? Why should they want to steal a thing like that, do you suppose?"

"How do you know it was stolen? How do you know there was any mummy of a sacred cat inside that case? The thing sounded hollow when you knocked on it, didn't it?"

"By Jove! Yes, it did."

"And it had been opened some time ago—since its original discovery. It was resmeared with fresher pitch along the joint, you remember?"

"Then why should they smash it open like that?"

"How do you know that it didn't just burst open of its own accord?—change of atmosphere, humid weather, wood swelling?"

"Come to think of it, why not?" agreed Malabar, with interest. "The thing may have been empty without Professor Caron knowing it. Then you eliminate the cat, to start with?"

"I did not say so, Dick. But the cat seems to have worried you from the first, and I suggest the possibility so that you can clear it out of your mind as a triviality or, at least, of secondary importance.

"Let us lay down the facts, as we know them. Professor Emil Caron, a gentleman of standing in the archæological world, comes to New York with certain antiques for distribution to American museums. I receive a letter from Armaund Lamont, asking me to look after his guest, who, forthwith, is installed at the Lamont residence. He seems anxious to see me, and hints that he has a special reason for this; later, when we call on him, he states openly that he is in trouble, and that he seeks my help because Lamont has told him about my alleged ability in the detection of crime. He even mentions the name of an infamous gentleman cracksman, Alceste, with considerable apprehension—says that even though Alceste is dead, his evil lives after him; then he asks us if we ever heard of the 'Order of the Golden Scarab,' a secret society or something of sort in the East. He is proceeding to tell us what is on his mind when he becomes frightened by something—"

"The sight of a beetle, crawling on the table!"

"—and ends by refusing to say anything more at that time and in that place. He promises, however, to give us his full confidence the next day, and practically dismisses us.

"Prior to this, he has shown us a large and very valuable ruby, set in a golden scarab of exquisite design, removing it from a sealed package in the library sale and resealing the empty case. He has prepared a quixotic hiding-place for the gem, and refuses to have it removed from the house to a place of safety. We do not know how it came into his possession, except that he got it at some buried tomb in Egypt, the location of which he does not know, he having been taken there, blindfolded, by a German named Von Strom.

"The Professor has told us a strange story of becoming lost in the wastes of the Upper Egyptian Desert, and of encountering unexpectedly this Von Strom, the leader of a nomadic band of brigands. Caron is shown what purports to be a genuine relic of ancient Thebes—a chronicle, written upon papyrus in Egyptian hieroglyphics, dealing with ancient treasure buried in a lost tomb. The Professor deciphers it, but is suspicious of its authenticity. Nevertheless, he pretends to be convinced, and allows himself to be taken to this tomb and shown this buried treasure by the German.

"Again we are at a blind end; because, undoubtedly, Caron intended to reveal to us why he believed the document was a fake, and it is evident that it was because of what took place between him and the German at the hidden tomb that Professor Caron was in the present trouble to which he referred, and on account of which he was seeking our aid.

"That much seems clear. But while we are waiting for our second interview with the Professor, at which the full matter is to be laid before us, the unforeseen happens, and he dies suddenly in the night. That effectually silences him, and leaves his half-told story clouded in mystery.

"Subsequently, we discover that Caron was visited that night by a stranger, who was secretly admitted to the library by the Professor. This stranger took away with him the sealed package out of the safe. We surmise that it was the golden scarab he thought he was taking. In the morning Caron was found dead. The scarab we find, safely hidden, on the premises. Foolishly, we allow it to remain in the house to trap the thief, whose return we anticipate. He comes back, he succeeds, he vanishes—and so does the gem! I think that about covers it, Dick?"

316   HOPKINS MOORHOUSE

"Yes, and what I want to know is this: How did this man know where to look for the scarab? He must have had a confederate inside the house."

"Undoubtedly."

"The Nubian?"

"I think it very likely."

"He spied on us in the library, then—when we were with Caron."

"I think that Professor Caron was afraid of that very thing."

"Kent, the Nubian threw that beetle into the room," cried Malabar, with sudden conviction.

"Quite likely," smiled Kent. "And, if so, does that suggest anything else to you?"

"That the thing was a message—a warning?"

"Yes—from this 'Order of the Golden Scarab' perhaps."

"Oh. I say! They were both members! What?"

"And it was Kellani who looked after the hiring of the cameleers and all the preparations for the Professor's expedition into the desert. And it was Kellani who argued with them around the camp-fires—"

"I know," nodded Malabar. "I know what you are getting at. The thing was prearranged!"

"Exactly. Professor Caron was duped from the first. The guides deserted when the word was given, and instead of being hopelessly lost, the Nubian led the Professor to the valley where Von Strom awaited him."

"He was one of the German's own gang?"

"Yes. And instead of being his master's obedient servant, as he stated so unctuously, he was virtually his master's warder—to see that he obeyed instructions and carried out whatever damnable purposes Von Strom had ensnared him to accomplish here in America!"

"By Jove! Kent, I believe you have hit the nail on the head."

III

The novelist raised his hand in a gesture of protest.

"It is never wise, Dick, to nail down a lid until sure that everything is in the box or to rope a trunk until it is fully packed. In the

detection of crime, shrewd guesswork and even pure chance often
play a part. I doubt if any great criminal investigation, conducted
by the finest police organization in the world, was ever worked
through to a successful conclusion without the investigators, at
some stage of the enquiry, thanking their 'lucky stars' for some
fortuitous turn of circumstance—some discovery that was purely a
'piece of good luck.' Preconceived theories are just so many handi-
caps to start with; the tendency is to try fitting the facts to the
theory instead of the other way about. There is nothing more mis-
leading than the by-paths of false premises."

"But when you have a straight case of addition and subtrac-
tion—seven and seven are fourteen every time."

"Except when $7+7=x-y$," corrected Addison Kent. "It is the unknown quantity in any equation which must be established."

"Mathematical truths are beyond dispute, I always thought,"
ventured Malabar doubtfully. "For instance, if you accept the first
axiom of Euclid—that 'things which are equal to the same thing
are equal to one another'—"

"Then I must not misapply it. Otherwise, I will be proving to
you that red is a colour and blue is a colour; therefore, each being
the same thing, red is blue!"

"Oh, but you cannot mix red and blue that way because—"

"If you mix them, you will get purple."

"I certainly shall—purple in the face in a minute! What are we
arguing about, anyway?"

"There is no argument. Even the mathematical Mr. Euclid had
to establish certain things as facts before he could prove his problems. That is exactly what has to be done in this situation we are
facing. We are hanging Kellani without evidence in court. We both
feel sure that he killed Mokra; but, unless the Bertillon expert from
Headquarters finds his fingerprints on the handle of that knife,
we have no proof to offer."

"The motive is clear enough; he and Mokra hated each other.
Also, he has made a getaway."

"Granted. It is quite legitimate for us to cast about in the dark
for clues, and it is because I want your angles on the situation that
we are reviewing the possibilities. But we must not forget that it is

facts we are seeking. I merely point out that we do not know yet that Professor Caron did not die from natural causes and, if that were so, might it not alter greatly our attitude toward his whole story? Perhaps the Egyptian sun affected his brain, and the queer story he told us will become nothing more than a hallucination."

"All I have to say to that, Kent, is to suggest that perhaps we did not see the golden scarab or the ruby, and perhaps it has not been stolen, and perhaps the Nubian is upstairs now, sleeping like a little child, in his bed, and—finally and completely—perhaps I have no bump on my head as big as a goose-egg! But I am forced to contend that some things transcend imagination!" Malabar groaned.

"I think we may admit the bump on your head as an established fact," conceded Addison Kent gravely.

"Well established!"

"Also, there are one or two other facts which the night has brought to our threshold for consideration." Kent paused deliberately to give the fire another poke.

"What are you referring to?" asked Malabar, intrigued by something in the novelist's manner.

"You were not in a condition to observe closely when we carried you in here, Dick. You probably did not see the dish-pan out on the portico. Ordinarily, I do not put much stock in footprints—"

"Footprints!"

"Yes. You did not know that we had a beautiful young woman visiting us during the storm, and—"

"What!" It came from Malabar explosively. He sat up in his chair with a jerk.

"She looked in at the glass doors there, just as I looked out. I saw her quite clearly in a flash of the lightning. In fact, we were within a couple of feet of each other."

"Oh, the devil!" gasped Malabar with a note of exasperation.

"It's a fact, Dick. Come out and see the neat mark of her rubbers."

When they re-entered the library, Richard Malabar sank into his chair again. In his amazement he had hurried outside to examine this fresh evidence of further complications, and apparently the effort had set his head whirling. His face was white, and he closed his eyes weakly.

"All right—in a minute," he reassured. "Awful crack I must have got—from that bounder."

IV

The dizzy spell lasted but a moment, and presently Malabar was questioning Kent eagerly. What did the woman look like? She was young? Was she beautiful? What did she do? Had Kent followed her? Where did she go? What under the sun was she doing out in such a storm at such an hour? In fact, for one who openly had confided to Addison Kent that he was not interested in women in the slightest degree, Mr. Dick Malabar seemed to be surprisingly thirsty for information.

"I did not know that you had a romantic streak in you, Dick," said Kent in amusement.

"Rot!" denied Malabar. "But, good heavens, man, the thing is so— Well, it is like one of your own novels!" he finished amusedly.

"The question is: what connection had this girl with the theft that has taken place?"

"None whatsoever!" Malabar declared emphatically. "I refuse to have it spoiled by anything so sordid. I prefer to think of her as a beautiful young lady whose car broke down, somewhere on the neighbouring driveway, and who was seeking help. And, instead of gallantly coming to her rescue and proffering help, you frightened her away!"

"Seriously, though, Dick—"

"To let her get away like that!" Malabar reproached. "Our stars were not in the ascendant this night! You realize that she's gone, do you not?—vanished? You will never see her again. You cannot go all over New York, examining the rubbers of every pretty girl you meet. There must be a thousand girls wearing new rubbers of that exact size and shape."

"That is true," admitted Kent. "I do not put much stock in footprints as being of practical use, as I said before. I make use of them in fiction, legitimately enough, because there I can make it snow or rain whenever the need arises, and read a whole book of misdeeds out of the tracks conveniently left for my detective. But I am not foolish enough to try that sort of thing in this case. The fact of the matter is that most footprints look alike, and very few people walk so flat on their feet as to make distinct impressions. I covered those marks outside, chiefly to convince you of the lady's presence.

"However, once in a while a footprint carries some significance, even in a real case, Dick. We learned a little from the footmarks over there on the corner of the Axminster rug—that the man who visited Professor Caron wore golf boots."

"I fail to see the significance of that."

"Perhaps not in itself; but it remains for me to tell you that in the soft earth, close to one of the cellar windows which Sandy and I found wide open, I have under cover of a box a very perfect print of a large golf boot with every stud showing distinctly. And up in the bedroom—in the corner where the mummy-case of the cat stood—there is a second clear imprint of the same boot."

"Well, by George! That proves conclusively that the same man who visited Caron is the thief who got away with the golden scarab to-night and—eh? Why, it is as clear as—"

"Mud!" finished Kent. "In fact, the very clearness with which the muddy tracks have been made prove differently."

"That it was not the same man, you mean?"

"Yes. I measured very carefully the marks on the rug and made a drawing of them. The new footprints are three sizes smaller, for one thing, and for another, the rubber studs on the soles are a different make altogether!"

Malabar stared blankly. He rubbed his chin in perplexity.

"I fail to see that that proves the point, Kent," he objected. "The man may have changed his boots. Lots of men wear boots too large for them, or too small."

"The imprints have been too carefully placed to be genuine!"

11
"Miss Rockwood, of the *Mercury*"

The electric call of the front-door bell rang loudly through the silence of the great hallway.

The windows were bluing with daylight. From the distant kitchen came the sound of an egg-beater in a bowl and the aroma of coffee.

"Donovan," murmured Kent as he arose to answer the summons in person. In the vestibule he switched on the lights.

But it was not the police. Kent paused in surprise before opening the outer doors; for through the grilling he saw the tailored figure of a young woman, standing upon the tiled threshold. She turned at his approach.

"I have called to see Mr. Addison Kent," she began. "I understand he is here. Inspector Lowry said—" She hesitated, then smiled brightly. "Perhaps I have the honour of addressing Mr. Kent?"

The novelist bowed politely, conscious of a lyric quality in the well-modulated contralto voice that was particularly pleasing to his ear. He held the door open for her to enter, which she did with a murmur of thanks.

"I really must apologize, Mr. Kent, for intruding upon you at such an unusual hour; but in my profession no distinction is made between night and day when the call comes. May I introduce myself? I am Miss Rockwood, of the *Mercury*."

A newspaper woman! He might have known! He eyed her doubtfully; but before he could say a word, she had sensed his hesitation and had smiled at him. It was a smile of unusual appeal, and

the charm of it affected Kent strangely. He did not want to talk to
any newspaper representative. He did not want to hand out a story
to the Press before the police investigation. Whatever possessed
Lowry—! Yet he found himself smiling back at her.

"You see, Mr. Kent, I live out here in Westchester, and my paper called me as soon as they heard. The *Mercury*, as you know,
has a reputation for enterprise."

"But, my dear Miss Rockwood!" protested Kent, at last finding
voice. "This is such quick work that I am afraid it defeats itself.
We hardly know what has happened ourselves. The police are not
here yet, and until they take charge it would be inadvisable for me
to give you particulars of robbery and murder—" He noted her sudden alertness at the word. "How much did Inspector Lowry tell
you?"

"I only know that there is a good news story here, and that I
was told to get enough of the facts for an extra. Who has been
murdered?"

"Come into the library, Miss Rockwood," suggested Kent. "I
must ask you to wait until the police arrive. They should be here at
any moment now."

As he held aside the portières Kent saw her hesitate when she
caught sight of Richard Malabar in front of the fireplace.

"Allow me to present a fellow-journalist, Miss Rockwood—Mr.
Richard Malabar, of the London *Daily World*. Do not be alarmed
by the bandage; for he bears a charmed life—" He paused, suddenly conscious that she was paying no attention to him. He looked
at Dick Malabar, who had risen to his feet in evident embarrassment, a slow flush coming to his white face. Kent beamed upon
them.

"Not *the* Richard Malabar—the famous correspondent? Oh, Mr.
Malabar, this is a very great pleasure to me—to—to find you alive
and well and to meet you. Some of us here on the New York papers
have missed your articles for some time past, and a rumour got
into circulation—that you had been killed by bandits in Morocco
somewhere— You know how such rumours travel."

She sat down in the chair which Malabar drew up for her without taking her eyes off him—large, lovely brown eyes. Kent felt the fascination of those eyes. They were remarkable. In fact, as the novelist stole the opportunity of studying the visitor more closely he needed nobody to inform him that Miss Rockwood, of the *Mercury*, was a very beautiful young lady with a special charm of her own. It was not hard to imagine that with such personality and evident gifts she must be successful in her chosen work; yet his inability to recall where he had met her before made him feel annoyed with himself. At some social function or other, no doubt; but where? His memory refused to answer.

"You are not badly hurt, I hope, Mr. Malabar. You must tell me what happened. I want to know all about it, please. I would have telephoned; but the storm must have interfered with the wires somehow, for I could not get the connection, and was told the telephone here was out of order."

"The wires were cut, Miss Rockwood," Malabar informed her. Now that his first embarrassment had worn off, he seemed eager to talk to her—as eager as she was to listen. He looked across at Kent with a certain defiance in his grin.

"I have just told Miss Rockwood, Dick, that we cannot possibly give out a story for publication until the police arrive. It will be all right for her to remain here until the police take charge and get her story from them."

"But what a waste of time, Mr. Kent!" she protested. "I am quite willing to promise not to use the information Mr. Malabar gives me until the police confirm it. Is my promise not acceptable?"

Kent was conscious of a challenge in her smile as she turned the full appeal of those fascinating eyes upon him. There was amusement in them, and it required Malabar's understanding grin to stiffen his resistance.

"I have always been taught from earliest youth, Miss Rockwood, that only half of the letters in the word 'beauty' can be used in 'duty.' I fear that Mr. Malabar in his weakened condition— Why not ask me the questions you would ask him?" he bantered.

"Can a writer of popular fiction be trusted to handle facts?"

Kent acknowledged the thrust with a lift of the eyebrows.

"Judging by what one sees in the newspapers!—" came his countering drawl; but the sentence did not require finishing. Besides, with the utmost daring Dick Malabar had suddenly leaned over, captured one of the lady's little gloved hands, and patted it reassuringly.

"The events of the night, Miss Rockwood, naturally have upset my friend Kent. You will make allowances for him, I am sure. He used to be a newspaper man himself; that's how he got cynical, and ever since then it is his constant delight to obstruct honest, hard-working newspaper folk like you and me and prevent them from carrying out their orders. Now, get out your notebook and I'll tell you just what happened to me, and if he objects to us sitting in front of this nice fire, we will go outside and I will tell you what I know out there."

During this surprising speech the girl turned impulsively towards Kent, and again he was conscious of her eyes. Any resentment he might have felt at Malabar's assumption of authority was utterly submerged in the realization that she had allowed Dick to fondle her hand for a moment. She actually seemed to *like* it! To his further disturbance, Malabar proceeded at once to give her an account of his night's adventure which varied not a jot from the actual facts as Malabar had related them to Kent. He did not attempt to spare himself; rather, he enlarged upon his negligence. He glanced at Kent once or twice, but the novelist's head was turned resolutely away; if Malabar were playing for her sympathy and thought that Kent was going to come graciously to his rescue with words of deprecation, he was sadly mistaken. Let him take the blame! He was to blame! It would look fine in print! Serve him right!

But as the recital progressed and Kent stole a glance at Miss Rockwood scribbling notes with her gold pencil, he failed to discover any abatement in her evident admiration. In fact, the pair were becoming so absorbed in each other that neither paid any further attention to him, and he began to feel foolish and a little piqued. He knew that she was eager to get the story, and that she would not abuse the privilege of this advance information. Her promise was perfectly good, as his own would have been in like circumstances. He had only succeeded in appearing boorish! He felt strangely awkward and angry with himself for feeling so.

He glanced across at her again. Her neck was beautifully formed. The tailored costume she was wearing was becoming; it suggested the elegance of a perfectly developed and sylph-like body. There was a strength of character in her round, delicately modelled chin. The profile of her straight nose, the softness of her mouth with its suggestion of the sentimental without weakness, the proud carriage of her head—here was quality as well as beauty, refinement as well as daring. What a girl for a heroine in his next book! he thought as he studied her.

Then he realized, all at once, that Malabar was removing the bandage to show her the bruise on his forehead! He saw the solicitation in her expressive eyes; he heard her little gasp of commiseration, and caught the womanly tenderness in her low-spoken words. She reached over impulsively and patted Malabar's hand.

Addison Kent quietly stood up and left the room. He was not wanted. He was completely out of it. Maybe if he had had a sore toe to show like Tom Sawyer!—or was it Huckleberry Finn? *Where* had he met this girl before? One thing was certain: he was going to see that he met her again—just the two of them. Nonsense! What was the matter with him, to be going on like this? It was just that he was interested in her as a type to study—for story purposes. Type? No, hardly that. She was in a class by herself.

So he told himself as he wandered towards the kitchen quarters. The fragrance of coffee was very appetizing, and he would have Gaston prepare a nice breakfast-tray and bring it into the library beside the fire. Perhaps she would be glad to join them in a cup of coffee at least. On second thought, why not take in the tray himself when it was ready? That was why he had got up and left the room, wasn't it?—to be a thoughtful host? She would appreciate it, he felt sure, and he fussed about in the dining-room, carefully selecting the finest tray-cloth and napkins—the daintiest cups and saucers he could find.

"Get a move on, Gaston. We have a lady guest for breakfast, and she's famished. Are the eggs on? Toast done? Good!"

Finally it was ready, and he wheeled in the wagonette triumphantly—and nearly upset the whole thing. There was nobody in the library but Dick Malabar!

"Where is Miss Rockwood?"

"She left a moment ago—out the library door. Said she had to telephone her paper right away—"

"But, great Scott, man! She didn't have to go out to do that! Didn't you tell her we had the cut wires repaired now, and that the 'phone here was working again?"

"Well, by George! I am a silly ass and no mistake!" cried Malabar, his face twisting in disgust. "I clean forgot that for the moment!"

"Hmph!" grunted Kent. "You say she went out this way? What was the idea? Why didn't she use the front—?"

He stepped across to the French doors with a quick stride. He opened them and went out on the portico.

"Hey!" called Malabar. "Shut the door! The breakfast is getting cold!"

"Come here!" snapped Addison Kent, so sharply that Malabar started. "She stepped in that little mud-puddle there. And here is an almost perfect imprint of her left rubber at the edge of the tiling." He pointed. "Compare it with this imprisoned footprint under the dish-pan."

"By Jove!" ejaculated Malabar. "Identical, eh?"

"In size, shape—even the crisscross marks! Brand new rubbers!"

The look on Dick Malabar's face was a study in comical dismay.

"You think—? Oh, rot!" he cried. "Fancy Miss Rockwood out in that bally storm and looking in through those glass doors at three o'clock in the morning! You cannot expect me to swallow that, Kent. Preposterous!"

"I told you before that I did not put much stock in footprints. Rather an interesting similarity, though."

Malabar searched his face keenly as they re-entered the library; it was mask-like, with a touch of grimness about the mouth.

"Look here, Kent, remember what I said a while ago: there are a thousand women in New York, wearing new rubbers of the same size and shape. You'll have to examine the feet of a thousand—"

"No. Only nine hundred and ninety-nine now!"

He wheeled the wagonette alongside the two chairs in front of the fire.

Malabar chuckled.

"This cures me of any ambition to be a 'Sherlock Holmes'! Too much worry over a lot of little things that do not lead anywhere. Wait till I tell this to Miss Rockwood as soon as she gets back—"

"She will not come back here," asserted Kent seriously.

"What? When she is through telephoning? Don't be an ass!"

"And when the police get here we shall find that Inspector Lowry did not send the lady to us at all—has never met her, in fact. That is why she departed so hurriedly."

"Are you crazy?"

"What is more, when we presently call up the managing-editor of the *Mercury*, we shall find that there is no 'Miss Rockwood' on his staff!"

Malabar stared at him.

"Do you mean it?"

"Absolutely."

For Addison Kent thought he knew now where he had met her before. A certain poise of the head, the straight nose, the haunting familiarity—it was undoubtedly the girl in the hooded mackintosh who had peered through the glass doors in the midst of the storm about five hours before!

"You are all wrong, Kent," scoffed Malabar, with a laugh. "I shall continue to believe in Miss Rockwood. She's a mighty attractive girl. Charming!"

"Hmph!" Kent looked at him steadily. "She certainly pulled your leg, my boy!"

"Our leg," corrected Malabar complacently, his mouth full of toast.

"Try hard not to be an utter fathead!" growled Kent, as he poured coffee into two of the three dainty cups.

12
THE FRIGHTENED FACE

I

Two weeks sped by. It was a busy time for Addison Kent, and an interval of disappointments for the official police so far as making any definite progress in their search for the murderer of Mokra was concerned. Although many notorious underworld haunts had been combed and certain marked denizens thereof had gone through a grilling at Headquarters, not a single trace of Kellani, the huge Nubian servant of the late Professor Caron, had come to light. The big city had swallowed him as completely as if he had ceased to exist. In fact, the police machine having failed, the belief was growing on Centre Street that the river was the place to look for him.

The newspapers were tiring of the case. At first they had revelled in its possibilities, playing up in headlines the sudden death of Professor Caron in the Westchester home of his friend Lamont—making much of the mummies and antiques he had brought from Egypt, and of his notable record as an Egyptologist and scientist. But the inquest upon the slaying of Mokra had been exceedingly short and disappointing, owing to the lack of evidence and the scarcity of witnesses. Similarly, the enquiry into the death of the archæologist had led nowhere, and the medical evidence of the autopsy was full of learned medical terms that boiled down into the fact that Professor Caron was undeniably dead—probably from natural causes. The doctors were in disagreement on some points; but that appeared to be the prerogative of doctors, anyway.

As Addison Kent listened to the evidence, he marvelled at the skill with which the coroner refrained from asking questions that were liable to upset the mere formalities. For official reasons the police desired to keep certain facts from the public for the present. Neither Kent nor Malabar were afforded opportunity for telling all they knew, even had they been so disposed. Their statements had been made without reserve to the police; but no mention of the valuable ruby which had been stolen, nor of the story the late savant had told them, nor of the nocturnal visitor to the library— none of these things found their way into the newspapers. Even the details of what happened on the night of the storm were very incomplete and centred upon the flight of Kellani. Kent was allowed to tell how he was awakened by the storm and with Sandy, the gardener, discovered Mokra's body; but all reference to the big man who had stood on the wall was carefully eliminated from Malabar's story.

Of course, all this was done in order that the work of the police investigation might go forward unhampered. It suited Addison Kent perfectly; but he had never been more impressed with the farcical nature of this preliminary legal formality by means of which the law established the fact that a man was dead and "person or persons unknown" had killed him!

The results of the autopsy in the case of Caron interested Kent greatly. As he closely questioned his friend Dr. Harvey, in the latter's office, the novelist's mystification grew. There seemed to be something queer about the whole thing.

"You say, Harvey, that there was evidence of anæmia of the brain. Just what do you mean?—that it was a chronic condition?"

"No, not chronic—if by that you imply that it had been a constant condition, extending over a period of time. It is my contention that the anæmia was forced, though what would bring that about in this case I cannot imagine."

"Forced!" echoed Kent thoughtfully. "You are telling me, then, that there should have been more blood in the brain than you found. Would not the fact that he was in an upright position?—"

Dr. Harvey shook his head with a touch of irritation.

"That is what the others seemed to think, but I know better," he affirmed. "I disagreed on that point positively. The blood does drain out of the arteries after death. Quite true. But not enough for the brain to press against the skull—"

"You found that in this case?"

"We did—at least, *I* did. I stick to that. Nor does the upright position of the body account for the engorgement of the splanchnic bloodvessels of the abdominal area and—"

"Their condition was abnormal?" asked Kent quickly.

"Decidedly so. You have studied anatomy, Ad., and you will recall the fact that the splanchnic vessels are easily dilated; they act as a blood reservoir. After eating, for instance, more blood is required by the digestive organs—but I need not go into all that."

"Did you find the stomach full of food?"

"No. It was almost empty."

"Then the swollen bloodvessels were not due to the natural digestive processes?"

"No. That is what makes the condition so puzzling to me. Kent, I am blest if I can account for it! I never saw anything like it before. Even the vessels in the legs were dilated!"

"Abnormally?"

"Yes."

The novelist pondered, his brows drawn in a frown of perplexity.

"I understand the chloral hydrate found in the stomach was not enough to cause death?" he offered at length.

"Not at all. He had had a normal dose—only enough for a harmless sleeping-draught."

"Then, what *was* the cause of death?"

"Brain anæmia; ruptured bloodvessel; some kind of stroke—take your choice! But if you ask me what brought it about—frankly, I do not know!"

"There was nothing organically the matter with him, then? No heart trouble or anything like that?"

"Not a thing!"

"Thanks, old man." Addison Kent held out his hand and reached for his hat. His lean, tanned face was thoughtful. "What you tell me definitely confirms a suspicion I have been entertaining. Now I am positive that Professor Caron has met with foul play. But, until we can discover the diabolical manner of it, the fact cannot be proved. And until it is established that a crime has been committed, the murderer could dine with the District Attorney and the Police Commission without a qualm. It is the damnedest thing I ever bumped into! Well, so long! Keep you posted if there are any developments."

II

From Dr. Harvey's office Kent swung past the Knickerbocker and made for the subway kiosk. He wanted a word with Inspector Lowry, Chief of Detectives at the Bureau. As the train roared away with him, however, his thoughts switched back to the beautiful young woman who had stepped into the case out of the storm. Where was he to place her in the tangle? As he had surmised, Inspector Lowry knew nothing of her; neither did the *Mercury!* Never before in his life had Addison Kent been so completely baffled, so keenly absorbed in a girl for her own sake; but when he allowed his mind to dwell upon the appeal of her personality, he was brought to a rude halt by the facts of the case. The two did not fit at all, and the result was a double-barrelled interest—professional on one hand; entirely personal on the other!

He and Malabar had argued about it for half an hour. She certainly had bowled old Dick right off his feet! He persisted in refusing to admit that "Miss Rockwood" was anything but a jolly fine girl, and he didn't care a tinker's damn whether she was really a newspaper woman or not, or whether she had looked in through every glass door in New York in the middle of every bally storm that had blown along for a year or more. So far as he was concerned, she could make a regular habit of it, and he would still say that she was all *right* and probably had good reasons of her own for everything she did, and it was nobody's bally business!—

Regarding Miss Rockwood, there was no sane argument in him. Malabar could be as reckless as he liked and be as big a fool as he liked; but, decidedly, it was Kent's business to find out who this girl was and why she had masqueraded as a member of the *Mercury* staff and why— She must have had some reason for spying upon them at that early hour of the morning. Had she forgotten something when she came to the house in the storm and returned to find it? Was she concerned in the theft of the golden scarab? If so, that theft having been successfully accomplished, why did she run the risk of coming back on the scene right on the heels of the robbery?

On the other hand, if she were not in league with the gang, what on earth was she doing there at that hour under such weather conditions? Her motive must have been a strong one, and Kent was entirely at a loss to find the answer, whip up his imagination as he might.

He had been afraid to make his questions to Lowry and the *Mercury* other than casual for fear of arousing too much curiosity. He would follow a lone trail in his search for the girl, he decided. Where could he pick it up? It appeared to be a hopeless quest.

III

He emerged from his absorption in the problem just in time to leave the Underground at the Canal Street Station. He made his way up the stairs and turned into Centre Street, where was to be found the old brick-and-stone structure of the Criminal Courts building, joined to the Tombs Prison by the Bridge of Sighs, and where also was located the gray stone Police Headquarters. Towards the latter building he directed his steps.

Inspector Lowry greeted him with a very-man-we-want-to-see heartiness. Kent was popular at Police Headquarters; it was generally known that he stood high with the Commissioner, the District Attorney and the Washington authorities. A well-thumbed set of the detective novels he had written was to be found in a reading-room bookcase. The practical work he had done for the Bureau at different times was appreciated, particularly the fact that Addison Kent was always ready to step aside and allow the police to take most of the credit for the work he did. In his hob-nobbing about he had made friends in every department of the service.

But just now the inspector was glad to see him because Jerry Donovan had been trying to get Kent on the telephone all afternoon to inform him that they had decided to raid a certain place upon which suspicion had fallen in the hope of discovering a clue to the disappearance of Kellani.

The Café Belgique on lower Third Avenue was a cheap restaurant which sought to cover its deficiencies by a gaudy show of ornate front. As an eating-place it was not as clean as it might have been nor was the food uniformly well cooked. The class of patrons for whom it catered, however, did not appear to be over-particular in regard to these things, which were overbalanced by the smoothness of the dancing floor, the excellence of the jazz orchestra and the general gaiety of the place. The cabaret, the police knew, was merely a blind for the real business carried on—upstairs, at the back of the café, where were hidden various questionable devices by which one might lose as much money in an evening's play as one happened to have available.

This fifth-rate gambling dive was run by a shifty-eyed individual of doubtful antecedents, known as "Singer" Lieb, who stoutly maintained at all times that he was a Belgian. A police raid upon the Belgique was no new thing; whenever the police were at a loss, a strong-arm squad descended upon Singer's place on the chance of netting somebody who was "wanted": for odd were the fish who glided in and out of the troubled waters of this notorious "joint." More than once had gunmen of rival gangs demonstrated the quickness of their trigger-fingers upon the premises. It was no "showplace" for curious visitors, seeking underworld "sights." It was the real thing!

Kent indulged in a slow smile, therefore, at mention of "Singer" Lieb, so called because of his habitual sing-song flow of talk when presiding over a gambling game which required announcement of its movements. Singer was a tin-horn who in his day had toured the fairs with various crooked wheels of fortune; he had been confidence man, race-track tout, shell-game artist and whatnot in his younger days. Now that he was fat and bald and "wealthy," he played for bigger stakes in equally questionable ways on the edge of the underworld. The fact that the police had decided to raid the Belgique indicated to Addison Kent how completely at a standstill was their investigation.

For nearly an hour the novelist and the inspector were closeted together. When the interview was over Kent went straight to his rooms in Minaki Annex, just off Riverside Drive; he remained there the balance of the afternoon, going through his mail and poring over certain volumes and folders from his very complete files. He studied his medical charts on anatomy for a while. The street lights were on when he finally took a bus, sitting lost in a world of his own all the way down town. He came back to realities in time to transfer to a taxi at Forty-Second Street, and dismissed it at a point on lower Fourth Avenue. He walked briskly around a corner or two, and vanished somewhat suddenly from sight down a flight of steps to a basement entry where a crude, half-hidden sign announced that S. Pomereski cleaned, pressed and repaired while you waited.

"Good evening, Porn," nodded Addison Kent to the lean, white-faced, big-nosed Polish proprietor who sat cross-legged, plying his needle industriously.

The shop was empty, and the novelist passed on through the curtains that shut off the back apartment, where Pomereski promptly joined him.

With the dropping of his needle and thread, the Pole seemed to acquire new personality. His eyes gleamed with interest as Kent threw aside coat and vest. He bustled in and out with various garments, exhibiting the enthusiasm of an artist. For that was what Pomereski was—an artist in transformation, a master of theatrical make-up, but as well a past master in the art of street disguise so clever that it could stand the closest scrutiny under the strongest light.

And of all his patrons this handsome young man was his favourite, his confidant and friend of long standing and proven worth. For S. Pomereski had not always been S. Pomereski the tailor. He spoke several languages; he was one of the most valued lieutenants of Mr. Addison Kent on occasion.

"I will have none of this theatrical clap-trap," Kent had stated in the beginning of their association. "We'll leave the wigs and false whiskers, grease-paint and all that to Monsieur Lecoq and the pages of Gaboriau. I want only *natural* appearance, a change of expression—watch my face!"

And at the demonstration of facial mobility Pomereski's eyes had shone with appreciation and understanding. He was an artist, and here was a client after his own heart.

Perhaps half an hour after Addison Kent had entered the inconspicuous little tailoring shop, there departed a nondescript young man of very ordinary appearance, somewhat shabbily dressed in a wrinkled and grease-spotted sack suit which at its best had been a cheap "hand-me-down." He walked with a slouch of fatigue, as if he had trudged many blocks that day, looking for work. His hair was uncombed, and his neck none too clean above the greasy collar of his coat.

Opposite the Café Belgique, over on Third Avenue, this tired and hungry individual came to a hesitant halt and looked across at the brightly lighted and garish front of the restaurant. His hand came slowly from his pocket, and he counted the coins on his palm with anxiety. Finally, having watched for a pause in the flow of traffic, he crossed the street, noting as he did so that a taxi was drawn up at the curb, directly in front of the entrance to the café. It was empty, but no "vacant" sign showed on the indicator.

Kent crossed the side-walk, and as he stepped into the entrance he almost collided with a young woman who was hurrying out. He felt her staring at him intently. Just for an instant he looked her full in the face; then she had brushed past him quickly, was across the intervening space and into the taxi.

The slam of the door galvanized him into action. He started to run towards the taxi, but was too late to stop it as it spurted off up the street. He stood at the curb for a few seconds, staring after it uncertainly. Then he saw the girl's face peering back at him through the rear window—startled, anxious.

Kent's eyes roved quickly about him. There was no taxi in sight which he could hail; but on the opposite side stood a shabby little Ford runabout, and he darted across to it, blessing his good fortune as he heard the low beat of the running engine. The owner had just disappeared through a shop door nearby. There was no time to explain; so Kent slid in behind the wheel, planted his feet into position, and was off in pursuit.

For that frightened face at the rear window of the taxi—those wide-open eyes!— In spite of the heavily rouged cheeks, the gaudy clothes, the giddy little hat, Kent recognized her!—recognized the same startled look that had been indelibly printed on his memory in a long flash of lightning. It was the girl of the hooded mackintosh who had looked in at him out of the storm! It was the "Miss Rockwood" who had posed as belonging to the *Mercury* staff!— dressed now like a chorus girl in some cheap burlesque show!

With a thrill of elation, he stepped on the accelerator and gave chase.

13
A Gentleman in an Awkward Position

Addison Kent pulled the runabout around a corner on two wheels just in time to see the white body of the girl's taxi flash out of sight, two blocks distant. It had gained on him down the comparatively quiet street into which he had just turned, and with horn honking he sped along as fast as the little runabout could go. The driver of the taxi knew his business, and, urged by his fare, no doubt was making for streets where there was greatest freedom from traffic congestion. Unless Kent could catch up with him before the chase resolved itself into a test of speed, it would be hopeless; for the taxi could outdistance him on a straight-away stretch. Kent's one hope was that the pursued would be held up somewhere in a temporary blockade of traffic

As he turned the next corner, therefore, he peered ahead anxiously, and was elated to note that he had gained. The white taxi was just a little over a block ahead now; but, even as he was congratulating himself, he heard a traffic policeman's shrill whistle and saw the cab dart forward again, boldly passing between two trucks, dodging in and out in an effort to get to the front before the whistle blew again. Kent realized that he himself was going to be stopped by that next traffic signal, and he instantly put on his brakes, backed around the corner and fairly flew down the side-street to the parallel avenue. Up this he turned and made steady progress.

He had this manouvre to thank for the sight he presently caught of his quarry, crossing less than half a block away. The driver

337

seemed to be trying a similar move. Then he saw the white cab pull in to the curb unexpectedly; the girl stepped out and walked rapidly away. The taxi swung out again and was gone.

"Thinks she's given me the slip," chuckled Kent, as he brought the runabout to a standstill on the side-street, jumped out and went after her on foot.

It was soon evident that the girl was anxious to make sure of her escape, however; for she turned every corner she came to, and once she crossed the street and doubled back on her trail, slipping into a dark doorway and remaining there for some time, watching passers-by. It was fortunate that Kent had divined the stratagem in time to get under cover or he would have been discovered. At last she seemed satisfied, and started out again, still laying a zig-zag course which presently brought her to a cross-town car-line. With a sharp glance over her shoulder, she boarded the first surface car that came along.

Kent hailed a taxi and trailed along at a safe distance. When she left the street-car, he dismissed the cab and was not half a block behind her when she stopped at a corner and was joined by a man—large, heavily built, dressed in rough tweeds and wearing a loud purple tie. The man raised his hard, black hat, and they appeared to greet each other like old friends.

Kent puckered his lips in a soundless whistle and got as near to them as he dared. He could not overhear what they said, and he was rather relieved to see them bid each other good night and go in opposite directions; for he did not like the looks of the man. The girl turned back and passed on the opposite side of the street. The novelist strolled casually across and followed discreetly, wondering what she had said to her uncouth acquaintance and where she was going now.

He was not long left in doubt; for presently he realized that their course along Eleventh Street was bringing them directly towards a district of second-class apartment houses on a curving street in the neighbourhood of Seventh Avenue. He was not surprised to see her mount the steps of a large apartment house, and it was with some satisfaction that he waited to follow and obtain the address; no doubt this was the end of the chase.

He was about to step boldly across when he was disconcerted to observe the big man in the tweed suit and the purple tie come striding around the nearest corner and make for the apartment house, entering without hesitation. Kent lost no time in getting after him, and was rewarded by the sight of the girl shaking hands with him. Together they entered the elevator, fortunately with their backs to the entrance, and they did not observe him on the outer steps.

He backed down, perplexed. What should he do now? He strolled a few paces on the side-walk, gazing up at the front windows, floor upon floor of suites. For a moment he was convinced that he had made a mistake in identity—that she could not be the girl he sought; that perhaps, after all, this was a cheap little actress, meeting her "gentleman friend" by appointment. Yet he shook his head impatiently. He had a strong memory for faces, and it was not often that his intuition was at fault. No, he was not on any wild goose chase, no matter how appearances might point.

What name would she be using here? Without that knowledge, he could not enter the place and boldly locate her. They must not see him, and it looked as if there was nothing for it but to stay outside and wait till they came out, a rather unpromising prospect. Unless—

Unobserved, he slipped around to the rear of the place and surveyed the building anxiously. With two exceptions the windows of the rear suites were lighted. One suite on the ground floor was dark, and another, directly above it, on the fourth floor— Even as he looked, the light came on, and with satisfaction he saw the unmistakable figure of the girl as she pulled down the blind.

What luck! He had them located! Still, what good did that do him? He stood there, watching that oblong of light, four floors up, and turned over the possibilities. He might enter the building through the front, go up to the fourth floor and reach their very door; but then?— Was he justified in eavesdropping, even allowing that he could hear their conversation? What was this man to her?

The huge shadow of the subject of his speculation just then moved into the yellow oblong of light. The fellow was standing there, legs outspread apparently, and his arms raised in angry gesticulation. For all Kent knew, this "sport" might have the girl in his power and be threatening her! Manifestly, it was his duty to get into a position where he could be of assistance to her, if she needed him.

The fire-escape captured his attention now. Could be negotiate it without being seen? If he could get up to that window—

He was underneath it in a couple of strides. The reflection from the lighted windows was all he had to risk; the dim globe above the tradesmen's entrance was around at the side. Here at the back was an area of clothes-lines, stretching across from each suite to pulley-wheels which were fastened in a blank brick wall of the neighbouring building. There was a possibility that the janitor might come out or that some tenant might begin manipulating a clothes-line. Well, he would have to chance that. His greatest danger would be in passing the lighted windows on the second and third floors.

The first platform of the escape was twelve feet above his head; but, by standing on a huge ashbin, he was able to reach a ground-floor window-sill and from there swing off to the grating and pull himself up. It took muscle; but he managed it without noise and sat down to remove his boots.

With these in his hand he crept cautiously and slowly upward. A noisy wrangle that was going on in the second-floor suite favoured him, and with redoubled care he edged past the third-floor windows. In each case luckily the blinds were drawn, and he climbed soundlessly, although his heart nearly stopped beating once as he almost stepped on a saucer of milk, evidently set out for the family cat!

At last, with a deep breath of relief, he found himself on the platform at the fourth-floor window. He almost exclaimed aloud in the joy with which he noted that the blind had not been pulled down all the way; there was a crevice of light showing at the bottom of it, and he would be able to see into the room. For a moment he lay at full length beneath the window, scarcely daring to breathe; he must make sure that his passage up the fire-escape had not attracted unwelcome notice before he risked the shadow of his head against the lighted window.

But nothing happened. A man came out somewhere below, whistling a jazz tune, and pottered about, his boots scraping on the granolithic pavement; he went away again, still whistling. A door banged in the basement. A cat in the area was meowing, meowing. A window opened somewhere, and loud voices reached him in heated argument, mingled with the blare of a phonograph, playing "Mamma loves Papa!" Then the window slammed shut again, and these sounds were cut off.

Very slowly he raised himself to his knees and looked into the room. The girl was standing on one side of a small table near the centre, talking rapidly in a low voice; he could not distinguish a word she was saying, but he could see that she was making some sort of earnest appeal to the big man. The latter was listening with head to one side and a smirk twisting his coarse, wide lips, while his eyes never left the girl's face; those eyes in their smallness seemed lost in the gross expanse of his beefy countenance. The bulging muscles of the thick shoulders ended in a short bull neck. At the edge of his blonde hair a wen protruded from his forehead. Teutonic was Kent's prompt appraisal as he took in every detail with instant antagonism. He would know this person again whenever and wherever he saw him.

The novelist's ear already was pressed close to the window; but the musical murmur of the girl's voice was still indistinct. If only the window were raised a fraction of an inch!— But he dared not experiment; his position was too precarious, and the least sound would lead to instant discovery.

Then, unexpectedly, a sharp exclamation reached him, startling him beyond measure. It was loud with astonishment and came from the big man involuntarily—just one word; but it set Addison Kent's pulses wildly, madly racing.

"*Alceste!*"

Kent's eyes clung eagerly to the streak of light beneath the blind. His ears strained to catch what followed.

"*Ssh!*" warned the girl with sibilant anxiety. She glanced quickly towards the window, then upward to the suite above, while the watcher held his breath.

With a quick nod of approval her visitor acknowledged her wisdom and obediently lowered his voice. The expression on his face was an open book of excited interest in something the girl had been saying. There was sudden craft and a mingling of suspicion in the small animal eyes. He plucked a pencil from his vest pocket and held it out to her, at the same time reaching into an inside pocket and withdrawing a huge brown leather wallet, fastened by a rubber band. With a quick pull he yanked this off and opened the wallet, fumbling among its papers with thick fingers. Presently he threw one of these out on the table and watched while she proceeded to draw a little sketch upon the blank side of the sheet.

Addison Kent looked hungrily at that wallet, fat with papers. It fascinated him. What might a search of it reveal? They had brought the name of a notorious international thief into their conversation! What did these people know about that old enemy of his? There was only one "Alceste"—one who had borne that dread name in the underworld—and now he was dead and buried! But "his evil lives after him" poor Caron had warned, and—could it be that this girl, this man, were connected in some way with the theft of the golden scarab? The girl had been on the scene during the storm! He felt sure he was not mistaken in her identity. And this brutal hulk of a man—what if he, too, had been there? The man he had glimpsed on the garden wall had been big, at least. Was it possible that the clue to the whole thing was inside this room—within ten feet of him?

The thought set his pulses hammering and parched his throat. Breathlessly he watched—noted the extreme interest with which the fellow was following the movements of the pencil in the girl's hand—noted the forgotten wallet, pressed by the left hand against his thigh, gradually tilting as he leaned farther forward across the table—saw the bits of paper that slipped out and fluttered to the floor beneath the table.

"Good! That's enough, mademoiselle. I believe you now!"

It came boomingly in excellent French with a slight German accent. The big man and the girl were both laughing—with relief, Kent fancied, in the case of the girl. Her companion's laugh was entirely one of comradeship as he shook hands heartily, picked up his hat and stepped towards the door. He made an elaborate bow over her hand, which she permitted him to raise to his lips.

He was gone. Kent sat back and considered. Should he hurry down and follow the man or should he wait and get those pieces of forgotten paper under the table? Very likely the fellow would be gone by the time he got down and around to the front of the building. He looked under the blind again; the girl was yawning and reaching for the light switch. The light in the sitting-room went out and a moment later came on in the adjoining bedroom. He got a glimpse of her passing into the bathroom beyond and the door closed behind her.

That decided him. The opportunity was too good to miss—if only the window-catch were not fastened!

He pushed at it gently and firmly and thrilled as he felt it give. His fingers were soon under the bottom of the window, and very quietly and carefully he raised it. Warm perfumed air flowed upon him. After a hasty survey he put one leg over the sill and in a moment was standing in the room.

On hands and knees he crossed the intervening space to the table, and his groping fingers soon located the fragments of paper. He thrust them into his pocket and rose to his feet.

"Don't move!—except as I tell you! Up with your hands! Quick!" The snap of the electric switch brought a flood of light. "Now, you may turn around!"

Addison Kent slowly turned, his hands above his head. The girl, tense and cool, was standing within a few feet of him. In her hand was an automatic, pointed steadily, straight at him!

14
A Lady in a Predicament

"How do you do, Miss Rockwood?" Kent grinned at her cheerfully. "We appear to be constantly meeting, 'face to face' as they say in the novels!"

"You followed me, then?"

"Evidently."

"I thought I had got rid of you—"

He smiled as she lowered the automatic and restored it to its holster, slung under her arm, inside her waist. Slowly his arms came down from their elevation.

"I cannot tell you how anxious I have been to meet you again, Miss Rockwood."

She eyed him coldly.

"You seem to be very sure of yourself, Mr. Kent."

"May I return the compliment, Miss Rockwood—at least, I hope it is a compliment. I am glad to see that you do not deny your identity."

"Why should I?"

"Your role this time is so—so different," he suggested.

"So is yours, Mr. Kent—entering a girl's room through the window! Excuse me while I wash this stuff off my face."

Before he could think of anything to say, she had calmly turned her back upon him and walked into the bathroom, deliberately closing the door behind her. He sat down on the nearest chair, twiddling his thumbs, his eyes crinkling with appreciation of her equanimity. Then he remembered that he was in his stockinged feet,

344

repossessed himself of his boots and put them on. She rejoined him presently with the thick rouge no longer disfiguring her cheeks.

"Am I looking more like my real self now?" She turned her glorious eyes upon him; but there was no coquetry in their depths— only a patient boredom.

"Decidedly," he approved. "Now, if I only knew who that real self was—" He looked at her appealingly.

"I introduced myself when I saw you last. I am Miss Rockwood—" She paused at his look of disappointment. He was shaking his head reproachfully.

"Not 'of the *Mercury*,' please! You see, Pulver—the managing-editor of that reliable paper—is a very old friend of mine, Miss Rockwood!"

"How interesting!" Her brows arched with polite attention.

"He denied all knowledge of you!" continued Kent regretfully.

She looked at him steadily for a moment, then shrugged her shoulders.

"It seems too bad to have a good story spoiled like that, does it not?"

"Yes? But there are always others to tell. I am wondering what new one you are going to tell me now!"

"What do you mean, exactly?"

"Surely you need not quibble with me, Miss Rockwood! You know to what I refer—your running away from me this evening, your make-up, the man in your room!"

"You seem to be taking a lively interest in me, Mr. Kent!" she retorted with analytical eyes.

"I do, indeed!" He spoke with an intensity that surprised himself.

"I am afraid I am not going to tell you much. There is not a great deal to tell."

"Oh, but I wish you would, Miss Rockwood!" he urged impulsively. "I really want to believe in you—very much."

She glanced up quickly at his earnestness, and as she studied his serious face—handsome in spite of the smudge on one cheek, so artfully placed to fit the clothes he wore—she dropped her long lashes suddenly and coloured.

"What is it you wish to know?" she asked.

"Who was that man who just left this room?"

"If you were listening at the window, Mr. Kent—as I have no doubt you were—you heard nothing, at least, that would suggest any interest on my part in the man—other than in a business way."

"I saw him meet you on the street. I did not like his looks. He seemed to be a rough specimen, Miss Rockwood. I did climb the fire-escape, as you intimate. I felt that I might be of service to you."

"So kind of you!" she murmured. "If you heard all that was said it will not be necessary for me to tell you so much." She smiled at him innocently.

"Unfortunately, I heard very little. The window was closed—" He stopped short, realizing the blunder of his admission even as he spoke.

"All I can tell you about the man, Mr. Kent, is that he is a danger to someone I love—"

"Another man?" It was blurted out before he thought. He metaphorically kicked himself!

"Yes." Then she added quickly: "But do not misunderstand me, Mr. Kent. I have no time for love affairs."

Kent realized all at once that his intense question and his feeling of relief at her reply indicated a susceptibility that was both strange and disconcerting. He took himself in hand sharply and cleared his throat authoritatively.

"I have no desire nor any right to pry into your personal affairs; but there are some things which I want you to clear up for your own good."

"Yes? What are these things you wish to know?"

Kent took a breath and ticked them off on his fingers as he enumerated.

"I want to know all about that man who just left you—who he is, what he does for a living, if anything, and so on. I want to know why you meet him so secretly and go to such pains to throw me, your sincere friend, off your track to-night. I want to know why I find you masquerading like a cheap actress and frequenting a place

like the Belgique. I want to know if you ran away from us at Westchester because you were afraid of the police!—

"Understand, I am your friend, trying to help you. I want to
know why you passed yourself off as a newspaper woman in order
to call at the Lamont residence—what the object of that early morning visit really was. I want to know what you were doing there,
even earlier that same morning—in the middle of that terrific electric storm when you looked in at me through the glass doors of the
library—at nineteen minutes past three a.m., to be exact. It is important that you explain your actions that night in some detail,
Miss Rockwood; as you know, there was a murder committed and
a very valuable gem stolen. If I am to help you, I must have your
full confidence; otherwise, the situation is liable to become very
awkward for you.

"You note that I am not accusing you of being connected in any
way with what took place that night at the Lamont residence; I am
hoping for an explanation most earnestly, Miss Rockwood—one
that will satisfy the authorities. At the same time, you must admit
that your actions to-night scarcely remove you from suspicion; that
is why I must have a complete answer to all my questions regarding this man who was with you. While I did not hear all of your
conversation with him, I did overhear enough to require explanation; it is better that you make that explanation here and now to
me, as a friend, than to make it under other circumstances which
might not be so—well, let us say, comfortable."

"You would hand me over to the police?"

Through it all she had sat quite silent, listening to the arraign-
ment with a faint smile; but the smile was gone as she asked this
sudden question, reading his face intently.

He shook his head.

"That is something which need not be discussed, Miss
Rockwood. For one thing, you are much too sensible to force an
issue when the way out is so simple."

"Simple!" She laughed shortly.

"Yes—the simple truth," he urged gravely.

"Is there anything that you have left off your list of questions, Mr. Kent? Please make it complete, so that I will know exactly what ground you want covered."

"Yes, there is another item—a big one. I heard a name mentioned in this room by your visitor—a name that stands for everything that is bad—the name of a notorious criminal, known to the police of Europe as well as America. I refer to Alceste! I want to know how that name came into your conversation. What do you know about Alceste? You imply that you were having a business interview with this man here in your room. I want to know why you brought the name of Alceste into it. I want to know exactly what either or both of you have to do with—*the Order of the Golden Scarab!*"

The novelist leaned forward as he spoke, his keen eyes seeking penetration of her expression. Slowly and with significant emphasis he enunciated the last six words. But she looked back at him blankly, a little frown of puzzlement on her brow. The words apparently meant nothing to her.

"Are you trying—to frighten me, Mr. Kent?" A smile started uncertainly at the corners of her pretty mouth, then dodged back again. "You are so terribly solemn!"

He reached impulsively for her hand, and she suffered him to pat it reassuringly.

"Pardon me if I seem too serious, Miss Rockwood; but it is a very serious situation for me as well as you, and I want you to clear it all up for me. Do not be afraid to confide in me fully; I really do want to be your friend."

She gave a breath of relief and smiled at him brightly.

"Very well; but it is such a long list of things—! It is going to take much longer than I thought." She glanced down at her exceptionally short skirt and looked at him with a delightful twinkle in her eyes. "You will be good enough to excuse me for a few moments while I get into some decent clothes, Mr. Kent? Then if you would let me make you a cup of tea?—"

He thrilled with the allure of her.

"Delighted!" he smiled back at her, and at once she left the room. "Great!" he exulted to himself as the door of the bedroom closed.

Everything was going to be all right, he felt sure, and was conscious of a pronounced feeling of relief. No girl who was guilty could behave as she was behaving. There would be an adequate explanation of all the mystery that had surrounded her in his mind. Malabar had been right in his blind loyalty to her. "Charming!" he had said. She was—and more!

"If Dick could only see me now!" he chuckled. "Well, it's my turn!"

Then he gazed in sudden dismay at his grimy hands and eyed his spotted, wrinkled clothes with distaste. He straightened his dirty collar and his threadbare green tie, brushed futile fingers down his soiled trousers, and decided that when she came out he would ask her if he might wash.

His eyes took in the sitting-room, every detail of it; but he was not impressed. The pictures on the wall were cheap prints; the furnishings, while adequate, had a used look, and the room somehow seemed severe. It lacked those little feminine touches which he would have associated with the apartment of a girl like Miss Rockwood. If this were her home—

He impatiently dismissed the thought that obtruded. It was true that this place seemed to fit the character she had been playing that night, rather than the well-dressed, perfectly poised "Miss Rockwood" who had paid the early morning call out in Westchester. It was hardly likely that she would have two homes! It was hardly likely—

He fidgeted in his chair and cleared his throat loudly. He wished she would hurry. Women were so confoundedly fussy about their clothes and how they looked! If all the hours they spent in front of a mirror, preening and fooling around!—

A glance at his watch apprised him that fully ten minutes had gone by. He got up at last and tapped diffidently on the bedroom door. There was no response. He tapped again, louder.

"Miss Rockwood!" he called. No answer. "Oh, Miss Rock-wood!"—louder this time. Still no reply.

He wondered for a moment if she had fainted or anything like that. He listened; but could hear no sound of running water nor any movement beyond the door! It was then that Addison Kent began to realize the truth. After another loud knock on the door, he turned the knob and opened it, calling out to her as he did so.

He swung the door wide. The bedroom was empty. He strode across to the bathroom door and rapped on it sharply. Not a sound! He opened it then. The bathroom was empty! He looked in the clothes-closet; not a stitch of wardrobe! It was empty!

A door at the end of the bedroom caught his eye, and he made for it. When he opened it he found himself looking out into a cor-ridor. He could see the elevator shaft at the far end.

"Well, I'll be damned!" He snapped his fingers in annoyance.

He went back to the sitting-room for his cap, let himself out of the apartment and made for the elevator. The manager of the build-ing had quarters on the ground floor, and was much surprised to find himself being questioned very fully in a voice of authority, backed up by a police badge.

"The apartment was rented yesterday by a young woman—a Miss Rockwood, of—of—"

"Of the *Mercury?*" Kent smiled grimly.

"That's it! She said she was a newspaper reporter. Yes, the *Mercury*; I remember now. She rented that furnished apartment for just one night, and as it was vacant—"

"What? For just one night?"

"Yes. But she had to pay something to get it," assured the man-ager, wagging his head sagely. "We ain't givin' nothin' away here! Nor we ain't trustin' *nobody!*"

"You are an exceedingly wise man," commended Kent.

15
Mr. Addison Kent Takes Off His Coat

I

The young man in the greasy cap who slouched off down the street exhibited no outward sign of the fires of resentment which smouldered within him. If there was a hint of hardness about the set lines of his mouth, it was no more than the usual handwriting of Poverty's private secretary, Ill-Luck. He turned into the first decent-looking restaurant he came to and ordered a full-sized steak; when it was placed before him he attacked it with the relish of hunger.

As he ate, the novelist's mind was busy with the scenes through which he had just passed—the uncouth man, the refined girl; above all, with Alceste. What did this strangely assorted pair know about that clever crook who, upon another occasion, so nearly had written "Finis" to the career of Addison Kent? The introduction of his name into their conversation held some significance, if he but had the wit to grasp it.

Yet Alceste was dead, officially and completely—and buried! Scotland Yard had said so, and Scotland Yard did not make many mistakes! The New York police had welcomed the news. So had the police of Europe, no doubt. There had been an exchange of congratulatory telegrams. Kent had accepted it without question. Only his friend, Armaund Lamont, the wealthy Fifth Avenue jewel expert, had shaken his big head doubtfully.

What was it Lamont had said one time about this unique cracksman? "He is here—there—nowhere! Jewels, rarest of gems, always the precious stones that he takes, and nothing else! He knows the fine ones—always the very finest he takes. The police run after him like hens after food. But he is always—gone! He has wings! He sinks under water! He buries himself in the earth! He strikes, disappears, is dead, forgotten; then, when least expected—*voilà!* he is alive, takes what he wants and is gone again! He is *le diable!*"

They had smiled at the excited Frenchman at the time, Kent remembered; but the subsequent events had been far from a smiling matter. Dead and forgotten, then alive again when least expected! Was it possible—? Kent shook his head in smiling scepticism as he lingered over his coffee and ashed his cigarette on the edge of the saucer. Yet, if such an unheard-of thing could be true— if Alceste, by some necromancy, should prove to be alive and here in New York!—then indeed would the situation become suddenly fraught with unimaginable dangers to everybody concerned, but particularly to one named Addison Kent, his sworn enemy!

The novelist sat for a while, head bent, absorbed in these speculations. When he looked up he was startled to see a man, wearing dark-coloured glasses, gazing in at him through the restaurant window. Impelled by something—a flash of something untoward— a flicker of subconscious warning—Kent half rose from his chair and reached for his cap.

At his first motion the man was gone, and the author sat down again, feeling foolish. Was the mere thinking about Alceste enough to raise visions? Surely he had not got to that point—seeing things! Some hungry loafer, attracted by the food displayed in the window! He had come along just as Kent had decided that, supposing Alceste *could* reappear in New York, he would have to wear smoked glasses to hide those telltale eyes of his; the operation Dr. Mac-Murrough had performed upon them would make it doubly necessary now for Alceste—if he were alive—to conceal his eyes. No wonder those dark glasses on the loafer at the window had startled Kent for the moment!

Laughing at himself, he felt in his pocket for a match, and his fingers came in contact with the three bits of paper he had picked up from beneath the table where he had seen them slip from the big man's wallet back in the apartment. The girl had not noticed them, or she would have questioned him. With a gleam of interest he now smoothed them out on the table. All were irregularly torn scraps of print—two from a newspaper and one on the better grade of paper used by illustrated magazines. The two newsprint fragments he laid to one side after a brief glance—one a patent medicine advertisement, the other a typical sporting-page report of a boxing bout.

The tearing from the magazine page was more interesting. It was evidently taken from an article upon aviation, and this paragraph explained that flyers doing stunt flying keep their eyes fixed in the cockpit or on some designated point in order not to be confused by the revolving landscape.

"Three blanks—a bad draw!" muttered Kent resignedly, as he idly turned it over and began to read what was on the other side.

He leaned suddenly forward, reading eagerly, and a thrill shot through him. He brought his fist down on the table with a thump that made the dishes jump. He felt the texture of the paper between thumb and forefinger.

"S.C. Book—45 lb. stock," he appraised. He studied the type face. "There's an article I must find and read."

He shoved from the table. At the door he paid his check and departed without waiting for change. Outside he hailed the first taxi he saw.

All the way back to Pomereski's he sat lost in thought. He scarcely spoke to the Pole as he changed into his own clothes. He took the Third Avenue elevated and was roared northward through the city. At Minaki Annex Mrs. Madden, his housekeeper, heard him unlocking the door of his apartment and came across the hall from her own quarters, following him in.

"There was a gentleman called to see you this evening, Mr. Kent. He seemed very disappointed you were not here and wanted to be let in to wait for you—"

"You know the rule, Mrs. Madden."

"I do, sir. I did not let him in, of course. I told him I did not expect you to return for some time."

"Did he leave his name?"

"No, he would not do that—said he wanted to surprise you as he was an old friend of yours and happened to be in town—"

"An old friend? Where from?"

"That he did not say. He would give me no information about himself. He said he would call again sometime."

"What did he look like, Mrs. Madden? Can you describe him?"

"Well, the only thing that made him any different from ordinary was his glasses. His clothes were neat and well pressed. He was wearing dark-coloured glasses as if he had something the matter with his eyes."

"Dark glasses!" echoed Kent with interest.

"Yes. I couldn't make much of his face on account of them and the light being kind o' dim in the hall. I put the mail on your desk, sir, as usual."

"Thanks—and, Mrs. Madden!" She turned at the doorway. "On no account whatsoever are you to let anyone into this apartment during my absence. Yes, I know you know that and I am not finding fault, of course. I merely want to impress it on you that just now, particularly, it is vital to adhere to that rule. Don't open this door for anybody—not even for the police or the President of the United States!"

"Yes, sir, I understand. Is there anything I can do for you, sir? You have dined, of course?"

"Yes. No, there is nothing, Mrs. Madden, thanks—except to see that I am not disturbed for an hour or so."

He toyed with the paper-knife on his desk for a few moments after the door closed. Dark glasses again!—an old friend—from out of town—who could it be? Impatiently he called Inspector Lowry on the private wire which connected the apartment with Police Headquarters.

"Jim, this is Kent talking. Jerry's expecting me to show up at the Belgique to-night; but I find I can't make it. Tell him to keep an eye open for a big German—blonde, beefy, wen on the forehead— a little lump. Have him brought in without fail, if he's there. I'll

stand behind whatever charge Donovan lays. Tell him it's important; I'll explain when I see you.

"And, Jim, listen. Have your file clerk turn up that Alceste dossier—right now, please; I'll hold the wire. Run through the last of
the Scotland Yard correspondence and let me know if there is any
mention of the measurements of that man they buried as Alceste—
his height and so on. Eh? No, I haven't gone crazy! Never mind, I
want to know."

As he waited with the receiver to his ear, Kent tried to recall
the announcement of Superintendent Brownlee, of Scotland Yard,
concerning the death of Alceste. With the police of several countries co-operating to capture him, this notorious cracksman had
had the temerity to revisit England. He had been cornered at last
in a lonely cottage on the edge of a moor and, when escape proved
impossible, he deliberately had set fire to the place and committed suicide. Upon his charred body the police had found such articles
as his watch and a tin case containing various papers which identified him beyond question as the famous Alceste for whom they
had sought so earnestly for a long time. A tame ending for all his
cleverness, but the only sort of finish to the kind of game he had
played!—a brilliant mind, gone wrong! It had been, so patently,
the thing that Alceste would do—commit suicide rather than be
taken to stand trial—

"Hello! Yes? Not a thing, eh? No, it's all right, Jim, thanks.
That's all just now. I'll call up later after Donovan gets back. So
long."

Kent reached for the code book and proceeded to write out a
cablegram to his old friend, Inspector Arthur Thompson, of Scotland Yard. His face was grave as he put in a call for a messenger.

II

The next twenty minutes Kent spent searching through his files
for magazine clippings which compared in paper and print with
the particular bit of paper which was intriguing him. At length he
slipped on his overcoat, picked up his hat and hurried out, knocking

on his housekeeper's door and handing her the cablegram for delivery to the messenger.

His destination now was the Lambs Club. As he expected at that hour, he found his publisher, Charlie Baxter, in his favourite corner of the lounge. Baxter laid aside his newspaper and judiciously felt the fragment of paper which Kent placed in his fingers.

"I make it 45 lb. S.C., Charlie. What magazine would you say that was from? I think I know; but I want to be sure. Note the type face and the spelling of such words as 'fixt' and 'prest'—*Literary Digest*, isn't it?"

"That's what I'd say. Why all the excitement?"

"No excitement. Everything calm and serene. Just want to read the article of which that's a part."

"Well, Cowan's here somewhere. Why don't you ask him? He might recall—"

"Good!"

"Hey, come back here! I want to talk shop a minute. We'll have the proofs of that new jacket to-morrow—"

"See you later, Charlie. Don't hold me up just now."

Cowan was a member of the *Digest* editorial staff, and Kent located him playing snooker pool. He tapped the bit of paper reflectively when the novelist had explained the situation.

"Can't say offhand," he frowned. "We publish so many items about aviation in the course of a year and, for all you know, this may be out of a back number—away back. I don't seem to remember—but that doesn't signify. I'd say it was *Digest* print all right, but— Leave it with me, Kent, and I'll see what I can do to locate it in the morning—or are you wanting it to-night? Have you tried to trace it through the *Reader's Guide* at the library?"

Kent did not need to go to the reference library for a copy of the *Reader's Guide*; he had one at home. But his own very comprehensive files would provide the shortest route to the information he sought; he did not pay clipping agencies for nothing, and now that he was sure of the magazine from which the item was torn, the search was narrowed. Under the subject of Aviation, with

its various sub-classifications, there was a formidable array of folders which bulged with data.

He returned direct to Minaki Annex and settled down to the
task of sorting and reading. Without the title of the article or the
name of the author, it promised to be a weary search; but fortune
favoured him, and it was only a little while before his eye encountered the actual paragraph which had aroused his interest. It was
in the review of an article in the New York *World* by an Army Medical officer concerning the speed at which human beings could fly
through the air and live. As Kent read it carefully, his elation grew.

"By the Lord Harry!" he ejaculated.

He reached for the telephone and, after a few moments' delay,
got connection with the Lamont residence out in Westchester. Dick
Malabar, however, had been out all evening and had not yet returned.

Kent grabbed his hat and coat, switched out the lights and for
the second time that evening hurried away from his apartment.

III

As the result of a specially cabled request from Armaund
Lamont in Switzerland, Addison Kent continued to live at the
Lamont mansion in Westchester, although over two weeks had
elapsed since the tragic happenings which had first taken him
there. The residence of the wealthy jeweller was full of valuables,
and Kent could understand how disturbed Lamont must have been
over the sudden death of his guest, Professor Caron, and the murder of his trusted servant Mokra. He naturally would feel easier in
his mind if he knew that a friend in whom he had utmost confidence was actually upon the premises until he returned home.
There was no reason why Kent could not meet the request, and he
had agreed, particularly as Dick Malabar seemed quite content to
remain with him for company.

Nothing that would add to their comfort had been overlooked.
Lamont's office manager, Dunlop, had *carte blanche* instructions.
Under Gaston's skilled direction, the cuisine was all that could be

desired. He had promptly discharged Henri, his assistant, for incompetence and had a new man in the kitchen. Dunlop had also hired a new butler, who seemed entirely competent, and altogether the menage was highly satisfactory.

When Richard Malabar returned late that night, however, he was not prepared to see the mansion bright with lights. There was evident activity in the kitchen quarters; the lights were on, and he could see busy figures coming and going. Through the dining-room windows he saw with amazement that the butler had the table set with snowy linen and an array of silver and crystal; It could mean only one thing—a supper-party. As he let himself in Malabar heard a strange pounding emanating from the library.

Overcoat still on and hat in hand, the journalist paused in the archway and looked into the room with increasing astonishment. The place was topsy-turvy seemingly. The huge round library table that had stood in the centre was in three pieces; one of these had been backed against the far wall, another segment on the opposite side of the room, while in the middle—

"My word!" cried Malabar at last. "I say, Kent, what the devil are you up to?"

For Addison Kent, in his shirt-sleeves, lay sprawled on the floor at full length—on his back with his head out of sight beneath the centre portion of the table. He hunched out from beneath this and looked up with a cheerful grin.

"Just in time, Dick, to give me a hand before our guests arrive." He got up, dusting his trousers.

"What's it all about? What guests?"

"Well, there'll be some medical men and Fraser of the Metropolitan Museum—who took charge of Professor Caron's collection for his estate, you remember—and then there is Inspector Lowry, Chief of Detectives at the Bureau; he's bringing along one of his Bertillon experts, and I expect Detective-Lieutenant Donovan will be here also. Dunlop, from Lamont's office, is coming—and—oh, yes, Doc. Harvey, of course."

"What's happened?" Malabar's blue eyes were alive with quick interest.

"You'll know all about that presently. You may have noticed, Dick, that all evenings are not of the same size; this happens to have been one of the large ones—the largest evening I have met for quite some time—

"Now, don't stand there staring! They'll be here in a minute. Give me a hand with this table; I want to get it together again before anyone comes. Get busy, man!"

16
And Startles an Audience

I

Half an hour later Addison Kent was facing a small but intent audience in the library of the Lamont residence—an audience which had assembled at that unusual hour only upon the novelist's urgent request. That he had not called them together merely for social intercourse they were well aware. They waited with the keenest interest for him to speak.

"In the early morning hours of the twenty-seventh of last month, gentlemen," he began, "there occurred in this very room a thing so hellish as to be almost past belief! The annals of crime are replete with examples of transcendent cunning; but I propose to uncover to-night something entirely new—a crime so simple in its ingenuity, if I may be permitted the paradox, as almost to defy detection. But for the good fortune which attended me this evening it very likely would have been added to the long list of undiscovered crimes. I shall prove to you conclusively that Professor Emil Caron, on the night in question, did not die suddenly from any process of nature, but was foully murdered in this room!

"Before proceeding with the demonstration of how the crime was consummated, I must ask the medical gentlemen present to bear with me while I draw your attention for a moment to a few scientific truths which are pertinent. I would ask you to consider the subject of motion and the reactions of the human body to movement. The subject is one which is occupying the minds of those interested in aviation tests. You may recall that Lieutenant Williams, of the Navy, who won the Pulitzer Trophy races with a speed of 243.67 miles an hour stated that in turning the pylons he 'went out cold'—that is, he lost consciousness temporarily. This is by no means an uncommon experience of aviators in stunt flying, and more than one novice has been killed while attempting air stunts because of this temporary vertigo in making sudden turns at high velocity. With the maximum speed which may eventually be attained by human beings in the air we are not concerned. I do wish, however, to lay before you the causes of this temporary dizziness experienced by stunt flyers.

"If I appear to assume the role of a professor of anatomy, talking to pupils entirely ignorant of the subject, I crave the indulgence of you professional doctors, and would be grateful for your correction if I make any misstatement of facts with which you long have been familiar. Circulation of the blood in our bodies by means of heart and bloodvessels is controlled by nerves; so that the bloodvessels contract or expand according to the amount of blood required in any particular part of the body at any particular time. Our digestive processes, after eating, call for a special supply of blood; similarly, when we are undergoing special mental activity the brain telegraphs for more blood. The splanchnic bloodvessels in our abdomen are specially elastic and easily dilated as a blood reservoir.

"If we lie down or stand up—whatever position the body assumes—adjustment of blood circulation takes place immediately. If we jump too quickly from our beds to an erect position, we feel dizzy and things blur before our eyes because sufficient blood has not yet reached our brain for the sudden change from the horizontal to the perpendicular. Riding in a fast train which hits a curve to the left, our bodies sway to the right—the direction in which the train had been travelling; if before the train curved, we had leaned to the left, our bodies would have been pulled to an upright position. This is due to what is known as centrifugal force. It is to overcome this recognized force that railroad tracks and automobile speedways are elevated on the outer side at the curves to avoid accident; it is because of this centrifugal pull that aviators bank their machines in making a turn.

"But while these precautions offset the centrifugal pull upon the vehicle of travel, they do not prevent that pull upon the human body and its fluid content. Aviators, though strapped into their seats to keep their bodies in place, experience the pull upon their blood, which rushes into the easily enlarged splanchnic vessels of the abdomen and even into the legs; this creates a condition of anæmia, as you medical men call it, in the brain—a lack of blood which causes vertigo and loss of consciousness, as experienced by Lieutenant Williams.

"Equilibrium, gentlemen," continued Addison Kent, "is a complex matter which we human beings with our wonderful bodies are accustomed to accept without analysis. Our bodies automatically adjust themselves in constantly changing relationship to space. Eyes, ears, skin, muscles, joints and tendons—from all of these we derive impressions; so that instinctively we know whether we are standing or sitting, where our legs and arms are, in what direction we are moving and whether our head is tilted to one side or not.

"Our common experiences of motion are those of the horizontal plane or, as in riding in an elevator, the vertical plane. Circular movement, however, human beings experience only to a minimum extent. Some of us are more susceptible to the reactions of motion than others; the up-and-down pitch and the side-to-side roll of a boat, for instance, will make some of us seasick more quickly than others. In passing, I wish to draw attention to the fact that the late Professor Caron was confined to his berth all the way across the Atlantic because of sea-sickness, proving that he was extremely sensitive to motion.

"It is hardly necessary for me to pursue the line of thought further. The part which our ears play in the matter of equilibrium we may leave to disputing physiologists, whose opinion is divided as to the functioning of the endolymphatic fluid in the canals of the internal ear. Suffice it to say that it is possible to establish a condition of motion which would have fatal effects upon the delicate organism of the human body.

"May I cite the experiments of Dr. Garsaux, of France, in this connection? He rotated on a wheel a number of dogs at speeds varying from four to six turns per second— I beg your pardon, Dr. Harvey?"

"Go on, Kent! Go on!— Nothing! Only I see what you are leading up to. Splendid!"

A murmur of approval ran round the room, and with a smile the novelist continued:

"Dr. Garsaux found that only a few of the dogs survived the experiment. In some cases the brain had been injured through pressure against the skull. The autopsies showed brain anæmia and *an engorgement of the vessels of the abdominal area!*

"Gentlemen, I use the very words which my friend Dr. Harvey used in describing to me the condition which he noted in the autopsy that was performed upon the body of the late Professor Caron! It was Dr. Harvey's opinion that this anæmia of the brain and the engorgement of bloodvessels was forced, inasmuch as there were no digestive or other conditions to account for it. He was not prepared to state at the time what could have brought this about, for he was justifiably perplexed.

"It is the cause of that condition which I have been fortunate enough to discover, and which I shall now proceed to demonstrate. I have to inform you that the late Professor Caron was killed in this room by application of the principle of centrifugal force—killed by dizziness!—sustained brain anæmia, forced with astounding ingenuity. He was murdered as deliberately as if he had been stabbed like the Algerian butler Mokra, or as if he had been shot through the heart!"

II

Disregarding the effect of this startling announcement upon his audience, Kent stepped forward and laid his hand upon the library table.

"How was this fiendish thing accomplished? Take a look at this cumbersome piece of furniture. As a library table it is unique— entirely adequate, although somewhat unwieldy. You note that it is very substantially built—rather a striking affair. It is one of the most highly prized antiques in Mr. Lamont's collection. But it is not the table as you now see it which makes it so valuable; it is what it conceals. This is merely the outer shell. All right, Dick, if you will be so good as to take hold of the side next you—"

With Malabar's assistance Kent pulled the table apart, turned a screw beneath and wheeled aside the two larger segments. There remained a centre section, oblong in shape, upon a solid pedestal. Kent had loosened the screws before the guests assembled, so that he and Malabar were able to lift off the top and side panels of this centre section in one piece. Revealed now was a huge and solid-looking roulette wheel which brought the guests out of their chairs with exclamations.

"I regret that I am unable to detail the history of this remarkable contrivance, gentlemen. I believe it has quite a history, and I am sure that if Mr. Lamont were here he could entertain you for some time with its story. I believe that Mr. Lamont regards this roulette wheel as one of his most cherished possessions because of its history; for undoubtedly it was one of the first roulette wheels constructed in France a very long time ago, and there is no other just like it. I had heard of its existence but had not seen it, and it did not occur to me to look for it in concealment here until this evening when my mind was directed along certain channels, as presently I shall explain.

"Note that the wheel's rim is of solid steel and that it turns as part of the wheel itself, unlike the improved type of roulette wheel, which turns within a bowl, as it were. Note also that the pedestal upon which it finds a solid base is likewise of metal and that, cumbersome though it seems, the wheel revolves very easily. As nearly as I have been able to discover in the brief examination I have given it, this wheel revolves upon a conical pin in a smooth socket. It is really a large spinning-top. You note how fast it travels and how long the motion is sustained when I give it a single twirl with my hand. It has been recently oiled for use. Driven by an electric motor, you can imagine how efficient an instrument of death it became in the early morning hours on the twenty-seventh of last month."

A babel of questions arose, and Kent waved his guests back to their seats.

"If you will let me finish, gentlemen, I will be glad to answer any and all questions. Upon and under the rim of the wheel I find marks which could only have been made by the screw clamps which were used to hold in place the board upon which the body of Professor Caron was laid. As you may remember, there was a trace of chloral hydrate found in his stomach, but only enough for a harmless sleeping draught. This was administered to him in the wine which he drank; so that he was entirely helpless and could offer no resistance. I like to think that he did not know what was happening to him—that he was already unconscious when he was bound to the board, hand and foot, and was whirled to his death without either terror or pain.

"I have been unable to locate the board which was fastened in place across the wheel; no doubt it has been destroyed. A hole was bored in it—as proven by the sawdust I have collected in this envelope—so that it fitted over the central pin, which helped to hold it in position. It is likely that Professor Caron's body was laid out horizontally with the head at the exact centre and the feet extending outward and that a weight was placed on the opposite end of the board as a counterbalance. An electric motor was used to spin the wheel at the required velocity; I have located unmistakable traces of this and also of the transformer used to convert the current. With the doors closed the subdued hum of motor and wheel would not be noticeable; in fact, I doubt if it could be heard at all in the servants' wing, where the only persons in the house at the time were sound asleep.

"That is how the deed was done, gentlemen. The traces of it were easily obliterated—the table top put back in place, the transformer removed from the wiring, the motor taken away, the body of Professor Caron placed in his chair at the table as it was found the next morning—with an open book before him as if he had fallen asleep while reading and had passed away quite naturally. The murderer even placed an old bottle of digitalis in the vest pocket to suggest that his victim was in the habit of taking treatments for a weak heart. No doubt the murderer let himself out of the house early that morning, hugely satisfied with his own cleverness.

"And, gentlemen, but for this fragment of paper which I hold in my band, we might never have known the truth!"

III

The novelist looked around at the intent faces of his audience as he paused. Every person in the room was listening eagerly to this amazing revelation. Inspector Lowry and Detective-Lieutenant Donovan were leaning forward, completely absorbed; Addison Kent was unfolding for them a case which would become renowned in police circles if only the police could bring the guilty person or persons to trial. The doctors sat with "Quite so" expressions of approval upon their sober, professional faces.

"You are naturally wondering how I stumbled upon this truth," Kent went on. "As a student of anatomy, my mind has been busy with the problem revealed by the autopsy; but it was this bit of print—torn from an article in the *Literary Digest*—which set me upon the right track. This article, I may say, proved to be a review of another article which appeared not long ago in the New York *World*—written by an army medical officer, Major L. H. Bauer, Commandant of the School of Aviation Medicine at Mitchell Field, Long Island. In it Major Bauer predicts that the human element must be taken into account as limiting increasing air speeds, even if mechanical difficulties are overcome; in fact, it is his argument which I have presented in outlining the effects of motion upon the human body. His article even makes mention of the experiments of Dr. Garsaux, of France, and it is the paragraph dealing with these experiments which I hold in my hand.

"This clipping—or rather, it is torn out roughly from the *Digest* page—came into my possession this evening in a manner which may provide a clue to the identity of the murderer and perhaps lead to his immediate apprehension. The man from whom I got this excerpt had the clip-it-out-and-save-it habit and carried around with him all manner of clippings of things that had interested him; it may prove significant that in the present instance the part of the article which he preserved was this paragraph giving the details of the Garsaux experiments. This, of course, is something for special conference with my friends of the police who are present.

"Also, I shall make no more than passing reference to the fingerprint clue which I have discovered upon the mechanism of the roulette wheel. That is something for the Bureau of Criminal Investigation and Mr. Smythe, the Bertillon expert, who is with us. It is enough for me to say merely that this clue has led me to make some enquiries which point to immediate action on the part of the police.

"How the murderer came to know of this concealed roulette wheel we have not learned yet, but that he had an accomplice in the house is certain. That would seem to indicate premeditation. From facts already in possession of the police I would say that the motive will be found linked to certain past events in the life of the late Professor Caron. I am at liberty to divulge nothing further until I have had opportunity of conferring with Inspector Lowry and Lieutenant Donovan.

"This much only I can add by way of warning to you all. The criminals who could conceive and carry out a deed such as I have described are dangerous in the extreme, and inasmuch as this case grows deeper the further we go with it, and the establishment of Professor Caron's death as murder in the first degree is likely to bring things to a head very quickly—because of this I must ask each and every one of you present to-night to keep secret what I have told you and shown you, for through such secrecy only will the police be able to work unhampered.

"So impressed have I been by these discoveries, and some others which I may not mention, that I am being led to a conclusion which at first seemed an impossible one. I have cabled Scotland Yard for verification of my suspicions, and if the reply is what

I expect it to be—then, gentlemen, I must doubly warn every one of you to forget that you have been present here this evening and to be on your guard constantly. For this case will assume new and positively dangerous aspects for everyone connected with it! The hand of Alceste—"

"*Alceste!*"

Inspector Lowry was on his feet. Detective-Lieutenant Donovan gripped the arms of his chair and leaned forward with eyes narrowed. Richard Malabar, startled and suddenly alert, half rose—then dropped back in his seat, his face troubled and anxious. For of those present these three realized most fully the significance of that dread name.

"Kent, what do you mean?" demanded Lowry. "Do you mean to say that Alceste has a hand in this affair?"

"I am beginning to believe so, inspector."

"You say that, knowing as well as I do that the police records show that crook to have been dead and buried for nearly a year!"

"You have only the word of Scotland Yard for that."

"The word of Scotland Yard is not a thing to be passed over lightly."

"Granted, inspector. But neither is the ingenuity of this Alceste. Your own records at Headquarters Contain ample evidence of the lengths to which this paranoiac will go; we had a visit from him—you recall the Radcliffe case, of course? His sojourn in America, I believe, proved very profitable and, in fact, altogether enjoyable to him; he left us with considerable regret that he was obliged to cut short his stay!"

"I had nothing to do with that case!"

"He walked away scot-free, inspector, by undergoing a painful eye operation—a special tattooing process—which changed the colour of his eyes! I mention this merely to show that in a tight corner the man's wits are at their best. Scotland Yard is sincere enough in the belief that the charred body they buried was all that was left of Alceste—as indicated by the evidence found upon the body. I earnestly hope they are right."

"But you doubt it?"

"Yes!"

"The evidence found was conclusive."

"The more conclusive it was the more I would doubt it. It is no new thing for evidence to be left around conveniently for the police to find. Until I have the measurements of that body Scotland Yard buried, and have checked them against the true measurements of Alceste, procured by me personally and now in my own files— until then I shall be unable to free my mind from the growing suspicion that Alceste merely has added one more smart hoax to his list!"

"And is alive to-day?"

"Very much alive to-day!"

"And here in New York?"

"And here in New York!" repeated Kent with conviction.

"Will someone kindly lead us in prayer?" suggested Dick Malabar, attempting to relieve the sudden tension in the room.

But his levity fell flat, and he welcomed the butler's announcement that supper was served.

17
THE GAME GROWS DANGEROUS

I

Richard Malabar paced about the library restlessly, his brows gathered in concentrated thought. It was nearly three o'clock in the morning. The supper guests had gone; but neither Malabar nor the novelist felt like retiring. The night had been too full of surprising interest to leave them otherwise than wide awake.

"You look worried, Dick. What's on your mind?" questioned Kent at last, slipping his pen into his breast pocket and closing his notebook. "I thought everything went off very nicely, didn't you? Everybody seemed to be duly impressed—"

"Impressed? Of course they were impressed! Who wouldn't be? It was a marvellous bit of work; but instead of complimenting you, I am going to give you my frank opinion, whether you like it or not."

"Well?"

"Kent, you are a damned fool!"

"Well?"

"The thing that impresses me about this whole business is the personal danger into which it is heading you!" Malabar's lean face was full of concern as he stopped and laid a hand on the author's shoulder. "My dear old fellow, take the advice of a friend who has knocked about the world a great deal more than you have, and drop this case right now! It is a matter for the police. Let them handle it. For God's sake keep out of it! I have no fondness for funerals, and I certainly do not want to be buying flowers for yours! That's what it is going to mean if you go on with it!"

"Oh, I don't know. I have at least a fifty-fifty chance of buying a lily for the other fellow!"

"Why not go up to Canada after big game?" persisted Malabar. "We've talked about it enough. Let's do it. You go on ahead and make the arrangements, and I'll join you within the week—as soon as I have disposed of one or two business matters here. What do you say, old chap?"

"You mean well, Dick; but it cannot be." Kent smilingly shook his head. "It would never do to disappoint Alceste after he had come back all the way from the dead!"

"Oh, damn Alceste!" cried Malabar irritably.

"Then, there is the young lady—"

"I thought so! You are going to remain here and risk your life for a woman of the underworld!—"

"That'll do, Malabar! We'll leave her out of the discussion, if you please! You noted that I made no mention of her to-night?"

"It was sporting of you," conceded Malabar, "but—"

"I'm telling you straight that her connection with this affair must not reach the police, no matter what happens to me. You understand? I mean exactly that, and, as a friend of mine, I expect you to keep quiet, Malabar!"

"What are you going to do if—"

"There is to be no 'if' about it. I am going to get her! It may take till Christmas; but I am going to get her myself!"

"You lose sight of the possibility that Alceste may have some-thing to say about it, Kent. By the way—those measurements you have on file—I am curious to know how you will spot the gentle-man if he does turn out to be alive. How will you know him?"

"He is about three inches shorter than you are, Dick. His eyes originally were blue like yours: but lacked the expression that goes with a warm-hearted personality like yours; he was the coldest proposition imaginable—a man devoid of soul, and it showed in his hard eyes. You read up the Radcliffe case, didn't you?"

"Yes, I was interested in it because of your connection with it."

"Well, then, you will remember that Alceste escaped from the police in a daring manner, fooling them by changing the colour of his eyes from blue to dark brown by a special tattooing operation, performed by his accomplice Dr. MacMurrough, who was shot and killed by the police while trying to escape from the house in which the pair were cornered over on Long Island.

"Tattooing of the eye is done on the cornea in front of the iris; so that it would mark those eyes of Alceste for all time to come. I fancy he will find it a handicap for the rest of his days; for while the pupils of his eyes in a dim light will dilate as usual behind the cornea, he will have but the fixed orifice left in the tattooing through which to see. Under a strong light the pupils of his eyes will contract to pin-points, and it is then that he would be easily recognized by the tiny rim of blue that will show about the pupil— the original, natural blue behind the artificial colouring on the cornea. Do you follow me? Well, that is why Alceste will require to wear glasses that conceal his eyes—probably smoked glasses of some sort."

Malabar smiled and nodded his head.

"I see. It would appear, then, that you are not the only fool-hardy person in the world! Well, I don't wish you any bad luck, old boy; but I still think the wisest thing you can do—"

"Is to go to be—*ed*-uh!" yawned the novelist.

II

As Addison Kent had predicted, action by the police followed close upon his demonstration of how Professor Caron had been killed. The thumbprint he had discovered upon the socket of the roulette wheel was clearly defined in oil—a small, almost woman-ishly slender thumb—and if not the tell-tale mark of the murderer himself, it was at least the mark of an accomplice—the mechanic who evidently had assisted in fixing the wheel, attaching the motor and so on. Reasoning that the murderer must have had an accomplice in the house, it had only required elimination of all thick-thumbed inmates to send Kent straight to Gaston, the French chef, with searching questions in regard to the discharged Henri, who, at the time, had acted as kitchen help. The young man, as Kent remembered him—cowering under the bedclothes in fear of the storm the night of the robbery—had been of slight build. From Gaston Kent had learned that Henri was ambitious to become an inventor, and had been for ever tinkering around a motor in his room, experimenting with an improved attachment for which he hoped to secure a patent!

From the moment the Bertillon expert reported that the thumb-print on the wheel and a thumbprint found in Henri's room were identical, the drag-net was out for the former cook's assistant, who seemed to have vanished since his dismissal the week before. Then Donovan discovered that one of Singer Lieb's croupiers likewise was missing suddenly, and on a lucky inspiration he put Smythe to work on a thumbprint of the "St. Boniface Kid," with highly sat-isfactory results; for the thumbprint of Singer Lieb's missing crou-pier, who had presided over a roulette layout in that worthy's gam-bling "joint" on the Bowery, was identical with the thumbprint found on the roulette wheel at the Lamont residence!

Here was something definite at last! At once Singer Lieb was on the carpet again at Headquarters, and the police redoubled their efforts not only to locate the St. Boniface Kid, but to find Kellani, the vanished Nubian manservant of the late Professor Caron, and also to unearth a certain large blonde man with a wen on his fore-head.

But their search proved singularly abortive. Although care had been taken to keep from the newspapers any inkling of Kent's dis-closures, it was Donovan's opinion that the news had leaked into underworld "grape-vine" channels. Even before this—on the night Addison Kent had found his scrap of paper—so peaceful and se-rene had the police found things at Singer Lieb's place that the intended raid had been postponed. Apparently due warning had been given by somebody. It looked suspicious.

A period of watchful waiting followed.

III

It was during this lull that Addison Kent quietly disappeared from his customary haunts. The mail accumulated on his desk in the apartment at Minaki Annex, and enquiry of Mrs. Madden, his housekeeper, would have elicited the information that he was "off on a holiday trip." Even Richard Malabar could have given no information as to his whereabouts, had any enquiring friend sought the novelist, while the only information obtainable at the various clubs to which he belonged would have consisted of three words—"out of town."

But the comings and goings of a popular author among the exclusive clubs which he frequents are lost in the kaleidoscopic affairs of a metropolis—of no more consequence than the arrival of a new tenant in a cheap tenement a few streets south of Washington Square. And the comings and goings of a young plumber, looking for work, are even less to be noticed in a great city—as inconspicuous as the greasy peak of his cap, or the spots on his "hand-me-down "clothes, or the smudge on his cheek. Departure of the one; arrival of the other—what matter? The world is full of authors; it is fuller still of young men out of work!

The despondent young mechanic who had ordered a full-sized beef-steak in a restaurant over on Seventh Avenue a week before, and who had departed without waiting for his change, was still job-hunting without success. It must be confessed, however, that his method of looking for work was somewhat unique, inasmuch as he spent most of his time—had anyone taken the trouble to follow him about—haunting cabarets and pool-rooms, chiefly in the Bowery district. Strangely enough, also, he seemed always to be able to pay for the food he ordered, although often he merely picked at it without appetite. Once or twice he had left hurriedly before his order could be served, paying for it at the door and complaining of not feeling very well.

These sudden exits in pursuit of possible leads, however, had not advanced Mr. Addison Kent one step forward upon the quest which lured him. At the end of several days he had uncovered not a single trace of the girl who had flaunted him or of the massively built man, to meet whom she had hired a special apartment for one night. The sum-total of his perambulations had been to attain the toleration of a few doubtful characters who would as soon use their "black-jacks" on him as not, if it were made worth their while.

True, he had learned a few things at first hand about bootleg-ging operations—which just now, as never before, appeared to occupy the attention of gangland—and about the "hijackers" who were finding it extremely profitable to rob the bootleggers of their illegal gains. Gunmen bragged openly enough of the "jobs" they had "pulled" ashore or afloat, and Kent heard tales of bloody fights that had been waged by the boldest of the hijackers outside on the open seas, beyond the limit set by the Supreme Court as the "dead-line"—the distance from the American shore which liquor-carry-ing craft must stay to avoid seizure under the Volstead Act.

Some of these sea-fights were almost past belief. Vessels of "Rum Row" had been the stage for violent gunplay between rival factions, comparable only to the most desperate clashes of old-time pirates! The coroners were reporting an astonishing number of "floaters" as the result of these battles, and Kent was quick to sense the undercurrent of unrest and suspicion that was abroad in the underworld. The bootleggers were living in terror of the hijackers, and the hijackers who preyed upon them were in mortal fear of each other; hates and jealousies were leading to treachery, which in turn was breeding new feuds constantly.

All of this was very interesting to Addison Kent as a student of criminal psychology. It was interesting to know that Prohibition had provided the gangsters of New York with such a golden oppor-tunity for predatory descent upon the bootleggers, who could not call upon the police for protection because they themselves were outside the law in their very profitable undertakings. It was inter-esting to speculate on the length of time which must elapse before the gunmen hired by the bootleggers for protection and the gun-men who turned to hijacking would exterminate each other.

Interesting, certainly. But was it going to help Mr. Addison Kent find Miss Edith Rockwood, "of the *Mercury*," or the man with the wen who carefully kept a record of how Dr. Garsaux, of France, had killed dogs scientifically by spinning them on a wheel?

It was this question Kent was asking himself as, with neck hunched in the turned-up, greasy velvet collar of his old overcoat, he swung off Broadway into Astor Place. His pace slackened as he advanced. It was not difficult for him to maintain an air of listlessness with the realization that probably he was looking for the proverbial needle in a very large haystack.

And supposing he did find her, what was he going to say to her? What was he going to *do?* Well, he would give her one more chance to answer that list of questions he had put to her the night she had calmly walked out on him and left him to whistle for his answers! What he would do would depend upon her. Confound her! She was a deceitful crook, hob-nobbing with criminals of the worst type! It looked like that, and he was trying all the time to believe in her and help her. Why? Just because she was beautiful? What was the matter with him that he should be so obsessed by a girl no matter how beautiful?

He crossed the street and went on down the Bowery. It was after eleven o'clock, and back on Broadway the theatre crowds were surging out and making for the popular eating-places. The novelist had as his objective the Casa Loma Cabaret. It was over in a quieter section, several blocks away; but it was worth the walk, for it was fairly clean, and they served a rarebit there that was not half bad, while the coffee was excellent.

Shortly after turning the next corner Addison Kent threw a swift look over his shoulder and swept both sides of the street behind him with a keen glance. He saw nothing to justify the intuition which warned him; yet he was almost positive that someone was following him!

IV

The Casa Loma was not as crowded as he expected to find it, and he had no trouble in getting a table in a corner which commanded a view of the front entrance. On either side of the dancing-floor were ranged boxes, or small compartments, partitioned from each other and designed to seat two couples; the balance of the long room was an open restaurant, the space filled with round tables. Kent had chosen a table at the end; so that with his back to the partition of the first compartment he was well placed to observe without becoming conspicuous.

He gave his order to Tony, a waiter with whom he had scraped acquaintance during the past few days, and allowed his careless glance to rove through the room. The Italian trio at the upper end—harp, violin and piano—was getting ready to play; but the tuning was lost in the general chatter and laughter. Then Kent forgot everything else but the two men who had just entered and stood near the door, eyes flitting from table to table. One was thin and tight-lipped, with deep-sunken eyes; the other had a thick neck and a flat nose and looked like a professional prize-fighter. A single quick glance assured the novelist that their faces were entirely unfamiliar to him.

As the new arrivals advanced in response to Tony's lifted finger, Kent became suddenly absorbed in close scrutiny of the menu card. He kept the menu in front of his face until the men were seated—in the very compartment alongside his table. He did this on impulse; for he had no reason to believe that the pair were interested in him. In fact, it was soon apparent that they were absorbed in each other's confidences as soon as the waiter left them. Their voices were pitched too low for Kent to hear what they were saying.

Tony had brought him his rarebit, and he was well started on it when above the mumble of conversation in the neighbouring compartment he caught mention of a name that keyed him to instant attention—the name of the St. Boniface Kid! With jaws motionless and head back against the partition, he strained his ears. With growing satisfaction he caught the name of Singer Lieb. Then, in a pause of the music:

"I tell you de Kid's gotta beat it! The dicks is onto him, see? Dis here big guy wid de lump is a friend o' Singer's an' everyt'ing's hunky. Get me? Dere's a skirt—a friend o' Wasserhaus—dat's de big guy, see? An' I'm to meet de bunch in half an hour, an'—"

"Can it, Kayo! This ain't the Grand Central an' you ain't callin' trains!"

That was all Kent could hear; for the voices again reverted to a mere mumble and the orchestra was playing again. But Kent finished his rarebit with an elation which he was careful to hide.

Unhurriedly he got up at last and put on his coat, called his waiter, paid his bill and sauntered leisurely past the groups of laughing men and women to the front entrance.

Once outside, he walked briskly for a block, crossed over to the other side of the street and came back until he stood nearly opposite the entrance to the Casa Loma. In a dark doorway he waited and watched. When the two men he had overheard came out he intended to follow them; it looked as if they might lead him straight to the very quarry he was seeking.

Not far down the block a taxicab was drawn up at the curb while the driver refreshed himself at a lunch-counter. Carefully Kent studied the street.

V

There they were now, just coming out! Would they walk or ride? If they got into that taxicab—it was the only one in sight! Ye gods! that was exactly what they were going to do. And there was the chauffeur, just coming out from his coffee and doughnuts!

Anxiously Kent scanned the street both ways for some vehicle in which he could trail them. Not a thing he could hail! Was he to lose this opportunity—the first that held promise of definite results?

He stared out at the taxi, his eyes on the rear of it. Would he be able to hang on behind? The men were climbing in now.

Then just as Addison Kent was about to make a clash for it, to his great joy around the corner up the street came a ramshackle brass-bound limousine of ancient vintage with a bearded driver in front. The impression the novelist got as he ran out into the street was that here was some old Jewish merchant, all dressed up and returning from a joy-ride—an unprepossessing old codger who apparently had been the guest of bootlegging friends.

"Follow that taxi just ahead there!" Kent commanded brusquely. "I'll pay well. Here's a V in advance, and there's another coming if you keep 'em in sight."

Without more ado he yanked at the door and leaped inside the closed body of the limousine, shutting the door behind him with a solid slam. But the driver had no intention of disputing the gifts of the gods; the money was in his hand, and with a jolt the car lurched away so suddenly that Kent was pitched bodily into the back seat. He only laughed with relief. What a godsend this old "bus" was! And the fact that he had found it unoccupied—what luck!

Eagerly he peered ahead through the front glass and saw the taxi turning out of sight. His man was right after it, however, and soon it was in full view again, less than a block ahead. Fine! Kent picked up the speaking- tube and cautioned his driver to keep his distance.

"Twenty bucks if you do this job right," he encouraged, and, with a wave of the hand to signify that he heard, the owner of the commandeered car bent over his wheel.

For perhaps ten minutes they twisted and turned at a moderate pace in the wake of the taxi. Kent continued to sit forward, watching for the first evidence of alarm on the part of the pursued; but the occupants of the car ahead did not appear to notice that they were being trailed, and no effort was made either to dodge or to speed away.

Kent's head presently gave a little bump against the glass through which he was looking. It bumped a second time and almost subconsciously he realized that he felt drowsy. This was no time to fall asleep! He roused himself impatiently. What a stuffy old "boat" this was! He blinked foolishly—then grew conscious of a peculiar, penetrating odour that sickened him!

Snf! Snf! He sniffed at the thick, sweet air and with a thrill of alarm realized what it was.

Chloroform! But where?—how?— Then he saw it—in the roof of the car—a dark, wet patch, spreading rapidly and dripping—raining! Drops were failing upon his head, his shoulders!—

The windows of the car were tightly closed—all of them!—heavy plate-glass windows! He reached for the handle of the door as the pungent fumes beat at his senses—the handles had been removed from the inside!

He snatched the speaking-tube and shouted—at least he thought he shouted! Two glittering evil eyes looked in at him through the glass in front!

Trapped! Frantically he put his shoulder to the door and tried to smash a window with his fist. The fumes grew overpoweringly strong! He fought to get out his automatic—head singing, senses reeling!—

The automatic was in his hand. With a last desperate effort he raised it and tried to pull the trigger; but the weapon fell from his paralyzed fingers and everything went black!

18
THE MAN IN DARK SPECTACLES

Many miles away waves were booming on a rocky coast. Boom! Boom! Boom! No, it was the surf hissing up a gravel beach—pebbles swishing back in the undertow. Boom! Boom! Boom! Boom! Boom! Boom! Ah, he had it now—a voice talking—a heavy bass voice talking, and a lighter, quieter voice answering? That was it.

Very slowly Addison Kent came back through a dream valley to realities. He tried to open his eyes, but he felt too weak and sick. He could feel a cool draught on his face. It was heavenly, and he gasped it in—life-giving, blessed air.

"—came damn near finishing him!"

"Which would have been a matter of great regret, *mein herr*, I admit," said the more unctuous voice. "But it looks as if the pleasure of doing it yourself in your own way was not to be denied you after all. Ssh! He is coming to."

Through half-closed lids Kent slowly examined his surroundings, feigning semi-consciousness as long as he might. He lay prone upon a dirty floor. The walls were bare and none too clean; they furnished no clue to the nature of his prison. For that he was a prisoner was evident; his hands were tied together behind his back, and his ankles also were bound. Recollection came slowly but steadily to him, and as the full memory of the circumstances which had brought him to this pass took possession of his mind, the nausea he felt was not all due to the anæsthetic. A sickening apprehension of impending menace held him.

What a fool he had been! How easily he had been lured by the deliberate conversation of the two men in the café! How opportunely the ramshackle limousine had come along just when he needed it—a carefully prepared trap to capture him, with spring-locks on the doors, handles missing on the inside, windows specially thick-paned and compact! And in his blind eagerness to follow the men ahead he had noticed nothing! What a fool! With chloroform, a gallon of it maybe, in a rubber container right over his head to drench him at a single rip—one pull on a string by the driver out in front— Was that how they had done it? Well, how it had been accomplished did not matter now; it had succeeded! Knowing the resourcefulness of the men with whom he was matching wits, he should have been on his guard!

He groaned in self-condemnation—then opened his eyes in an access of interest. A huge face—a beefy, red face—was bending over him; but it was the lump on the forehead upon which his gaze fixed. It was the big man with the wen for whom he had been seeking!

The big face with its ugly leer was suddenly withdrawn and another took its place. As Addison Kent stared back in fascination a thrill prickled his spine. For he was looking straight into the face of a man in dark glasses, and the mocking voice in his ear was none other than the voice of his arch-enemy—Alceste himself!

"Ah, my dear Kent, welcome back from the Elysian fields," it purred. "I was afraid that perhaps you were too busy plucking flowers in the Garden of the Hesperides to return to this wicked world even to meet such a very old friend as I. That would have been very disappointing, eh?—after my old college chum here, Otto, had arranged a ticket straight through to the Pit of Acheron! It would never do to send you to Heaven when a special reception is being planned in your honour down in Hell, would it? I am so sorry to see you looking so ill; but you will soon feel all right. Let me help you to sit up—ah, that's better! Here is a cushion—there, is that comfortable?"

Kent shook off the dizziness that threatened him when he sat up. Then, as his brain cleared, every faculty sharpened to meet the desperate plight in which he found himself. For Addison Kent was quite aware that his chance for life in the hands of these men was pretty slim. He was completely in their power, and could look for no mercy. They were capable of anything! To bluff it out to the end—that was all that remained.

"Well, well! So we meet again, my dear old chap! Let us see, how long is it?— But that doesn't matter, does it? Much has happened. You knew, of course, that I had died over in England—ah, yes, very sad!— 'the lone couch of his everlasting sleep,' as Shelley puts it. I was glad to see that you were not as stupid as the police over that convenient event. Your cables from Scotland Yard—how nicely they confirmed your suspicions! Really, it would have distressed me greatly, my dear Kent, had you lost faith in me! You remembered that our last little game ended in stalemate, and that I had promised you another game, and you remembered that I always keep my promises. In many respects you are admirable! Sorry to say, though, that it will have to be checkmate this time, old fellow—business affairs, you know. They require so much of one's attention these days that one has to curtail one's recreation. So this will be the last time I can play with you, much as I should like to continue to amuse you."

Kent said nothing. His eyes fastened upon those sarcastically curling lips. The cap which was pulled well down on the forehead seemed ludicrously out of place with the immaculate evening clothes. A white silk scarf was around, the neck, the ends tucked inside the collar; in the loose folds of it the chin was buried deep in concealment. With the dark glasses covering the eyes, those smiling, moving lips were the only part of the face that seemed alive.

"By the way, I do not believe you have been formally introduced to Otto—a thousand pardons! Come here, Otto. Allow me to present a very old and esteemed friend, Mr. Addison Kent, the novelist— Herr Otto Wasserhaus, Kent, King of the Rum Runners! Even now his sea-going clipper, the *Albatross*, lies in the offing, laden to the Plimsoll marks—"

"*Ach himmel!* you introduce too much!" interrupted the German. "I am to meet you, Mr. Kent, so damned delighted! I have too much of you heard! So I invite you on board my ship and we take a little trip—*hein?*"

"I have not had opportunity of discussing the details, Otto; but I hope you are planning to treat Mr. Kent with the consideration due to a guest of his intelligence?"

"*Ach*, yes! We will not make matters mincemeat. *Nein!* We make the mincemeat out of him and feed the hungry fish!"

"Interesting, Otto, interesting; but, if you will permit me to say so, much too crude. Do you not realize that Mr. Kent is a man of learning? He knows all about a great many things—the circulation of the blood, for instance. He can tell you all about anæmia of the brain, Otto, and engorgement of the splanchnic bloodvessels, and why you get dizzy! He knows all about the up-and-down pitch and the side-to-side roll, and all about centrifugal force and—"

"*Du lieber Gott!*" cried Wasserhaus, his face paling. "You will please to shut up!"

The laugh of Alceste turned Kent's blood cold. There was a deadly menace in its tone. How had this devil learned—? Was it possible that a dictaphone—?

Like a bird fascinated by a snake he watched that mobile mouth. Every detail of it was being printed indelibly upon his memory— the shape of the lips, the irregular edge of the red membrane, the tiny indentation just below the centre of the lower lip—the teeth, and in particular one tooth that was revealed only when the mouth drew down at one side sneeringly—a tooth with a thin band of gold across its middle!

"One would almost think, Wasserhaus, that you were not quite sure of your prisoner—that in the back of your fat head was some wild notion that our friend here was going to slip through your fingers!" The voice grew instantly colder. "If I thought that, Herr Wasserhaus—I would take this whole matter out of your hands at once! Do you understand? This man must die! If you let him escape— you go straight to Sing Sing—and there they will sit you in a chair much wired and strapped—"

"*Ach*, you fool! Shut up! We kill him now and make sure!"

"I thought so!" sneered Alceste. "You would let him off with a mere knifing, would you? You have him here, tied and helpless, and you imagine yourself back in your father's slaughter-house, sticking pigs! Bah! Now, listen to me, you ass! This man has got to get what is coming to him, but nothing as quick and easy as that, *mein herr!* It has to be something slow and lingering! He has to be made to squirm! Do you hear? *Squi-irm!*"

"So-o?" The German grinned slowly as he rubbed the white bristles on his chin, and he looked at the other with approval in his evil little eyes that seemed almost lost in his bovine face. "*Ach*, that iss so, my friend! Squirm it iss—like worms! We drop nicotine in his eyes. Ha! Smart man, iss he? Well, we make him smart, the swine!"

"I must apologize for Otto, my dear Kent. I am sure you will feel as sorry for him as I do; but we must not be too harsh in our judgment. He has not had our opportunities for education—

"You promise, then, Otto, that if I leave this in your hands there shall be no hasty action? Get him aboard the vessel. Get him out to sea and then—eh? You promise? Very well. How soon can you run him out in the launch?"

"Before daylight the launch leaves."

"Splendid! Then I entrust him to your hospitality, Otto. But remember—no action here! It is too risky, and too much is at stake— You see, Kent, how solicitous I am for your welfare?"

Kent yawned deliberately.

"Pardon me," he apologized politely. "It is very kind of you, of course. Would you mind telling me where I am at the moment? You will concede a natural curiosity—not that it matters at all, but—"

"Forgive my thoughtlessness!" and there was a note of admiration in the suave voice. "I must ask you to overlook the lack of accommodation here, but we did not expect you quite so soon. The bareness of this room indicates nothing as to its location; but the dampness may have conveyed the fact that you are in a cellar, dear old chap—beneath a perfectly honest shop—Sprechenberg's—boots and shoes, clothing and so forth—in the heart of New York's most vicious section—"

"Not very far from the Café Belgique perhaps?" drawled Kent coolly.

"Excellent, my dear Kent! It is right back of this—over on the next block. Why, were you wanting a cup of coffee or something? How would this do?" and to Addison Kent's amazement Alceste drew from his hip pocket a silver flask, unscrewed the top and extended it solicitously. "It is bootleg liquor, but good stuff. You need have no hesitation in sampling it—eh, Otto? You would not refuse such a very old friend a farewell drink?"

"Farewell! *Ach!*" grunted the German in disgust. "You want maybe to kiss him good-bye yet!"

"That is decent of you!" acknowledged Kent gratefully as he returned the flask after a long pull at it. "It has bouquet."

"For you a big bouquet we pick soon!" leered Wasserhaus meaningly. "Come, we waste already too much time!"

"The Lord High Executioner speaks to some purpose. It is hardly likely that I shall see you again, much as I shall miss you. You are up to your old tricks of meddling in other people's business, Kent!" Again the voice had grown frigid, merciless. "This time—*God help you!*"

With a mocking bow he turned and followed the rum-runner out of the room. He stopped in the doorway, beckoning to someone, then stepped back inside, followed by one of the two men whom Kent had attempted to trail from the Casa Loma; there was no mistaking that brutal face.

"This is Mr. Kayo MacGonnigle, Kent—the coming champion at his weight anywhere in the world. He will sit at the top of the stairs here in case there is anything you need. That cushion you are resting on is off his chair, but he has kindly consented to let you have the use of it for the time being. If you want ice-water, or anything like that, just ring for it, and Mr. MacGonnigle will give you a new idea of service!"

With a loud guffaw MacGonnigle withdrew. The heavy door through which they passed closed. Kent counted the bolts thudding into sockets—five of them!—and the finality of the sound was ominous.

As his eyes travelled the bare walls of the low-ceilinged room, realization of his utter helplessness surged upon him. The place was empty—not even a wooden box to sit upon. There was but the one door, through which his captor had disappeared, leading up a short flight of stairs to the shop above. Not even a window— Yes, in the wall opposite, at the top, was an oblong window for ventilation purposes presumably, for it looked out on the dark interior of the open cellar. It was tight closed and, judging by the accumulation of dirt and cobwebs which grayed it, its existence long since had been forgotten.

Caught like the proverbial rat, with no more than a rat's chance of survival! Despondency settled upon Addison Kent like a heavy blanket as he lay stretched on the dirty, damp floor. His own careful preparations for his sojourn on the East Side precluded all hope of interference on the part of his friends; he was supposed to be away on a holiday trip somewhere, and no alarm would be felt at his prolonged absence for some time to come.

A holiday trip!—yes, an ocean voyage, no less!—a long voyage from which for Addison Kent there would be no return! They were going to take him away from here to a launch some time during the night, and the launch would run the gauntlet of the revenue officers somewhere along the coast and land him eventually on board a rum ship, named the *Albatross*, owned by the man with the wen—Herr Otto Wasserhaus. This much he had gathered from the conversation; the very fact that Alceste had been so careless in his talk in front of Kent indicated how sure he was that the prisoner could not escape!

Alceste never made mistakes—unless for a purpose! Was it intended to mislead him? Was that it? Those references to the electric chair at Sing Sing—the German's face had shown agitation in spite of himself! And then Alceste had mentioned centrifugal force!—

So interested did Addison Kent become in the speculations which opened before the probe of his keen analytical mind that for a space he forgot his immediate surroundings. Time passed—how long he did not know; as nearly as he could judge, it must be about midnight. Voices in heated argument occasionally came from a distant part of the shop overhead. Now and then there was a scrape of boots on the grit of the landing where the pugilist MacGonnigle sat on guard.

It was useless for him to strain at the cords around his wrists; it only increased the pain with which they cut into his flesh. He had been bound with practised hands, and there was no evidence of any loosening of those knots, no matter what pressure he brought to bear or bow he twisted. He was still weak from the effects of the chloroform—still a little sick; but the whiskey had helped. The nausea was passing, and if he husbanded his strength he would be a lot better by the time they came to take him to the launch—if they did not give him another dose of it then!

He lay inert, motionless. The unreality of it all out there on the Bowery—just a block away—the sidewalks were crowded with denizens who turned night into day. Even a few ragged urchins of the quarter still played about the pushcarts of the hawkers under gasoline flares; women of many nationalities in multi-coloured shawls talked and gesticulated in groups; swarthy-faced men, dapper-dressed gunmen, slinking figures out of dark questionable alleys rubbed shoulders there. Noise!—loud laughter, loud talk, giggling! Sibilant whisperings from the corners of mouths! Lights blazing in front of moving-picture theatres lurid with posters—lights glittering in front of garish establishments—tinny pianos banging away at jazz tunes, boisterous cafés with hurrying waiters in spotted aprons—life!—jostling, jumbling, noisy life!—just over on the next block!

The solitary gas-jet in the cellar room sputtered feebly to maintain its sickly flame. Addison Kent lay back with aching head pressed against the damp cool plaster of the wall and closed his eyes. The only sounds were the distant murmur of voices somewhere overhead and the occasional scrape of the guard's boots on the landing outside—that and the movements of a rat somewhere in the cellar beyond.

The movement of the rat was persistent, irritating. Then Kent heard a new sound—so faint as to be almost indistinguishable except to straining ears in the throbbing silence of that cellar room. The gnawing of the rat had ceased—had been replaced by a slight scraping sound, a dull faint rubbing sound, equally persistent.

It seemed to come from—where? The novelist turned his head and listened. His hearing was acute, and at last he located it; it was not under the flooring, but in the wall that faced him—no, not in the wall, but at the window near the ceiling!

Gaze riveted now, he lay still, breathlessly watching those dirty panes of glass. Was it to be ended here after all? Was someone presently going to shoot at him through the window? It would be easy enough! It would—

A spot on the glass? He had not noticed it a moment ago! Was it growing larger—widening? Yes! Slowly it widened, a black spot. Kent watched it, tensely. Then he saw something glisten in the middle of that spot from which the dirt had been rubbed—something that caught the light from the gas-jet—just a glint. A human eye! Someone, with extreme caution, was spying upon him!

Addison Kent wet his dry lips. He wanted to cry out, but made no sound. His pulse was hammering at his temples as his ears caught the faint scrape of the sash and he saw the right-hand edge of the window slipping outward. The window was being steadily and noiselessly opened!

Still he lay silent, fascinated. Now he could see the darkness of the cellar beyond beginning to show, a black streak—wider, wider—!

A face appeared, the lips puckered, a slim finger upon them, admonishing silence! With a little gasp, smothered in his throat, Addison Kent stared, breath bated. There sprang into his eyes a quick light of understanding, of wild hope!

He recognised that face—that smile of encouragement. It was *she!*—the girl who had flaunted him! the girl he had known as Miss Rockwood!—his elusive Lady of the Storm!

19
NAIDA

Obeying her signal. Kent slowly and without noise rolled across the floor until he was directly beneath the window; then sat up, knelt, stood erect. She had disappeared for a moment; but now he saw the end of a long narrow box being carefully eased over the sill upon her upturned palm, and at once he took a position which would enable him to receive it on his back. With hands tied behind him and feet fastened, the matter of balancing that box to the floor without sound was not easy. Finally, however, he managed it; but beads of perspiration stood out on his forehead before he finally sank with it to the floor and got it gently on its side with only the faintest of scratching contacts.

He stood up again, exchanging a cheerful smile for her delighted pantomime of approval. She held a jackknife in her hand now and motioned for him to stand on the box. This, again, was a process requiring slow and careful movement, and he heaved a breath of relief when at last he accomplished it.

Edging slowly through the window—head and shoulders, waist—she hung down towards him and in a moment had severed the cords about his wrists and pressed the knife into his right hand. The faint perfume of her hair thrilled him. Her anxious whisper was at his ear:

"Quick! There is not a moment to spare! As soon as you are able you must climb through this window. I will help you. There is an underground passage— Oh, Mr. Kent, be careful not to make a noise; but hurry!"

He was already chafing his benumbed wrists—rubbing them back to life and feeling. He got down off the box as soon as he had freed his ankles and, removing his boots, tiptoed noiselessly to the door. He could see nothing through the keyhole except the steps of the stair. A rustling of paper, however, indicated that Mac-Gonnigle might be reading a sporting extra.

Back at the window, he passed up his boots to her. They had left him the old overcoat he had been wearing, and now he quickly tied the sleeves of this into a fast knot and passed it up also. She divined his purpose at once and, twisting the coat into a roll, thrust it across the sill with the tied sleeves downward. Then, while the girl hung tight to the coat on her side, Addison Kent from the top of the box carefully put one stockinged toe into the loop of the sleeves for a purchase and gathered his muscles. He could reach the window with arms at full stretch, and, taking hold of the sill on either side of the coat, he slowly drew his body up until his head and shoulders were through the window.

He saw now by the light of the pocket flash in her hand that she was standing on a large packing-case. There was room for both of them upon it, and with her assistance he wormed cautiously through the window and slid down to it on his hands. She gripped his ankles, and he slipped over on his back soundlessly.

For a moment they both remained there, motionless, listening; but all that could be heard was their own breathing.

"Great!" he exulted in her ear. "You're a brick!"

She cautiously closed the window while his fingers flew at his shoe-laces. He got down off the packing-case and reached up for her; but she was already beside him, and he felt his hand caught in hers, pulling him gently forward. His pulses quickened at the touch of her fingers.

The ray of her flashlight danced ahead of them through the open cellar over a litter of empty packing-cases, excelsior, cardboard strips and general rubbish. She made directly for a pile of broken boxes in the far corner, leading him around behind this with a whispered word of caution. Then it was that Kent noticed a small opening in the masonry, barely big enough for passage. He crawled through at her direction and waited while she noiselessly lifted the lid of a packing-case across the opening behind her.

For a few rods they crept on hands and knees over what appeared to be the bricking of an old drain; then abruptly the girl got to her feet. He stood beside her and peered about with interest; but the dancing white disc served only to indicate a passage about a yard wide, stretching ahead of them between dark walls of dirt-encrusted brick. It sloped downward for a short distance, then twisted abruptly to the left, then to the right, as if to avoid some underground conduit or a sewage pipe.

"We can talk now," she intimated over her shoulder.

"This passage brings us out at the Belgique over on the next block, I suppose?"

"Yes. How did you guess that?" In her surprise she paused, turning the beam of the electric torch against the wall beside them and appraising him quickly in the reflected glow.

"The gentleman in the dark glasses—"

"Dryden? He told you about this passage?"

"Hardly!" smiled Kent. "Dryden, he calls himself, eh?"

"He comes occasionally to see Wasserhaus—some business associate, I believe."

"Miss Rockwood, how did you know I was back there—a prisoner?"

"I saw them carry you in."

"Where were you? What are you doing here? You cannot be a member of this rum-running gang or you would not be helping me to escape."

"I would not leave a yellow dog in the clutches of Wasserhaus if I could help him to get away," she responded bitterly. "This is no time for inquisitions, Mr. Kent!" she reproved sharply. "Come, we must hurry. We—you are not safe yet."

"In helping me you are running risks—"

"They would shoot both of us without a moment's hesitation!"

"Then why are you doing this for me?"

"Your life is in danger, Mr. Kent. I can hardly standby and see you murdered in cold blood, can I? Think of the disappointed public, waiting in vain for your next novel!" She smiled at him with attempted whimsicality, and he shook his head at her reproachfully.

"You ran away from my questions that other night, Miss Rockwood! I am here because I set out to find you. I want to help you in whatever difficulties you may be placed—"

"Then forget all questions—forget everything but escaping from here as quickly as possible! We are both in great danger! come!"

They went on again silently. Addison Kent closed his lips firmly on the crowding thoughts that clamoured for expression. She was right; it was no time for questions at the risk of their lives. At any moment his escape might be discovered by MacGonnigle, and, knowing of this passage, they would realize at once where he was and telephone Singer Lieb to block exit at the other end.

As if divining his thoughts, she spoke to him again in guarded tones:

"There is telephone communication between the shop and Lieb's private quarters; but I cut the wire!"

"You are wonderful!" he commended.

"The passage forks just ahead of us. The left branch finds outlet in a Chinese tea-shop—Loo Ling's—several doors down the street from the café; the other comes out in the basement of the Belgique—"

She clutched his sleeve in sudden alarm. At the same time she extinguished the flashlight. It was nothing more than a puff of air that smote their faces, but Kent realized its significance even as the girl crowded close to him and whispered in his ear:

"Someone coming! Quick! We must run for it—the left passage."

She had pressed an automatic into his hand, and at the comforting feel of it he drew in his breath and was after her. He put his arm to her waist and ran just behind her in the dark.

It was not far, and fortunately the passage was straight and unobstructed. She stopped him suddenly, and they listened. Above the thumping of the blood in his ears, Kent sensed rather than heard a slight sound ahead of them.

They were in motion again now, walking swiftly. The girl had taken his hand. He felt her pull to the left and turned after her into the branch tunnel that trended to the left towards Loo Ling's. He collided with her unexpectedly and felt her warm breath on his cheek as she warned for silence.

They were not a moment too soon. The sound of a softened impact reached their ears, followed by rapid footsteps. The footsteps broke into a run, and there grew along the damp bricks of the main passage a little glisten of light.

Kent crowded her deeper into the branch tunnel. She was wearing a bright-coloured sport sweater with scarf and tam to match, and, as he realized the hazard of the advancing light, he shifted his position to shield her from discovery. With his arms around her, they waited, motionless as statues, a blot of darker shadow against the tunnel wall.

The light grew—the beam of an electric torch, dancing, dancing. The running footsteps pounded towards them. Suppose the men should suddenly turn into their retreat! Kent gripped the automatic and poised on the balls of his feet for a quick whirl into action.

Passed! The runner had passed, and they were safe. The footfalls receded along the main passage. The girl had peered out beneath the novelist's arm as the man swung by, and now her bated breath drew in sibilantly. She moved gently for release.

Instead, Addison Kent's arms suddenly tightened about her. His blood was racing madly through his whole being. That dark tunnel, the running man, the danger—he had forgotten everything except that his arms were around this beautiful creature who had eluded him—his mystery girl! What mattered anything but that he had found her again?—but that he loved her madly! That was what was the matter with him—what lay behind his anxiety to help her— to keep her out of this infamous tangle of events in which she seemed enmeshed—to keep all knowledge of her from the police! He loved her! He knew it now! And it overwhelmed him!

"Edith! Edith!" His voice was low and vibrant. "I know you by no other name!"

"Mr. Kent! Are you mad?" She struggled to release herself.

"Yes!—for you! I do not know who you are—what your name is—what you are. But I do not care if only you will understand and believe that I love you, love you! You have grown to mean every-thing to me, and I am not going to let you run away again! Tell me who you are—where I can see you—your real name—"

"Please! Please, Mr. Kent!" she entreated in desperate anxiety. "That man who passed was the Badger—one of Berlin Harry's gang—the worst—"

His kisses stopped her.

"—worst gang of gunmen—hirelings of Wasserhaus! Something must have gone wrong!— *Please!*—oh, my dear, if you love me!—"

Again he kissed her fervently. Abruptly her arms went about his neck, and he felt her warm, moist lips on his in sudden sweet abandon. Out of that ecstasy he struggled with difficulty to his senses.

"Your name, dear—what is it?" he pleaded.

"I cannot—tell you!" She was trembling. "Oh, this is madness!"

"Your first name, then—at least tell me that!"

"Naida—that is all I can tell you."

"Naida!" he repeated tenderly. "Naida!"

"Quick, let us go! They have discovered that the telephone is out of order! The Badger has gone to investigate. They will be upon us in a moment!"

"You will come with me—now—out of here?"

"No, no!" she protested hastily. "I cannot. You must go alone. I will get out through the tea-shop. Don't worry about me. Quick! There is not a moment to lose."

"You will meet me later, then?"

"Later—when I can—I will send you word—when it is safe."

"Naida, listen! Are you quite sure you will be all right? I will not leave you here exposed to danger—"

"I will be all right—I know what to do—oh, if you would only hurry!" she implored.

"Promise me that if anything goes wrong you will get a mes-sage to me at once—to the Westchester address. Promise!" he in-sisted, his arm about her shoulders.

"Yes, yes, I promise. You must get out by way of the café. It is best to separate. Here, put on these glasses. They will think it is

Dryden, and you can slip through. You will have no trouble with the cellar door— Now, please, for your own sake—*go!*"

With one last embrace he pressed the automatic into her hand, turned and ran. At the fork in the passage she stood for a moment, casting the beam of her pocket flash to light him on his way. It was not far, and with the door in sight he waved back to her, and the light swung away as she darted for Loo Ling's tea-shop.

Kent reached the heavy wooden door which marked the entrance into the basement below the Café Belgique, and listened. It occurred to him that perhaps she in turn was waiting to hear the door close behind him; so he opened it cautiously and peered out. The cellar was in darkness. He closed the door with a little thud, and again crouched in the passage, one ear bent to catch any sound out of the cavernous blackness. Silence!—heavy, throbbing, complete. She was safe.

With a breath of satisfaction Kent slowly opened the basement door, slipped out and drew it shut noiselessly. For a moment he crouched to one side on the cement floor in the dark, listening.

Then his heart stood still! Loud and shrill rose the summons of a police whistle! Heavy blows of an axe and splintering wood!— the crack of a police automatic and hoarse shouts, followed by a growing tumult overhead—shrieks and yells and oaths and running feet!

20
The Police Close In

I

A door crashed open at the head of the cellar stairs. Pandemonium! A band of yellow light! *Slam!* Blackness again—blackness,
heavy breathing, tense whisperings!

Kent dodged across to a barrel and crouched, behind it. In the
momentary streak of light he had seen three dark figures scramble
down the stairs. The round disk of an electric torch floated about
the basement. Then feet scurried across the cement floor for the
entrance to the underground passage.

"Aw, dis is a swell joint—dis is!" a voice growled in disgust.
"Why'n't dey tip us off? Harness bulls! If de Badger hadn't got wise
to dat fly cop—"

"Close your trap, Nifty!"

"Well, wot's de lay? Dey ain't got not'in' on us! Why de fade-
away?"

"We ain't takin' no chances, see? Dem's de orders! Beat it!"

"Some snitch!—"

The passage door closed upon them. Berlin Harry's gang! Kent
knew them—notorious gunmen, every one of them! Hirelings of
Wasserhaus, Naida had said. Unarmed as he was, there was nothing he could do to stop them. No doubt the Badger had already
warned the rum-runner and Alceste!— She would be safely out
through Loo Ling's before this. He must get some of Donovan's
men around to that shop—

With these thoughts racing through his head, Kent was already stumbling up the cellar stairs. He yanked open the door at the top and burst out—right into the arms of a burly policeman.

"Here he is! Loot'nant, I got him!—ah, ye would, would ye!"

"Let go, you fool!" cried Kent angrily, plucking away the dark spectacles the girl had given him to wear. "Donovan! Quick! Get a couple of men down in the basement—there's an underground passage between here and Sprechenberg's shop right back of this, one block over! Hustle! The men you want are there, but they've been warned—"

A whistle shrilled. Detective-Lieutenant Donovan roared his orders and dashed after Kent, who was already making for the front entrance of the café. Side by side they ran around the corner with a section of the strong-arm squad at their heels. Kent glimpsed the patrol-wagon, backed up at the curb and crowded with a huddle of complaining humanity guarded by a knot of blue uniforms.

"For the love o' Mike, Mr. Kent! What were you doing with those glasses? We got a tip on a guy with dark specs and your friend with the lump on his forehead; so I pulled the raid—couldn't find you to let you know—"

"Didn't get him, did you?"

"We got *seven* of him!" exploded Donovan— "every one of 'em wearing black spectacles! What the devil!—"

"Save your breath, Jerry. Speed up!"

They swung the second corner and bore down on the Sprechenberg clothing shop, which was surrounded at the double-quick. The place was in darkness—not a chink of light showing anywhere—and the peremptory ratta-tat-tat of Donovan's pistol-butt on the door panels echoed hollowly. The door was locked, and in response to the detective-lieutenant's command, one of his men smashed the lock and forced an entrance.

The place was deserted. In the office a chair was overturned and a drawer, yanked from the desk, lay upside down on the floor, which was littered with bills of lading and invoices. The chair MacGonnigle had occupied out on the landing had tumbled down the short flight of steps. The door to the room where Kent had been held prisoner stood open, and as Donovan's flashlight scoured the bare walls, Kent gave a brief account of what had happened.

"Hello! What's this?" interrupted Donovan, striding abruptly back to the open door. "Something for you, maybe."

Over a wire nail in the middle of the door had been jabbed a folded telegraph blank, and straddling the nail hung a pair of dark-coloured spectacles—large round glasses in cheap rims with side-shafts that curved to fit the ears!

The paper was addressed to "Mr. Addison Kent," and the novelist knew what was in it before he unfolded it—another of those characteristic taunts of Alceste. He read it with a slight smile at the corners of his mouth, then passed it to Donovan without comment.

It was in bold, backhand script—evidently a disguised hand:

"My Dear Kent,

"Congratulations! You really interest me at times. I thought we had you ready for the sacrificial altar and that the game was played out; but apparently not! Well, better luck next time, old bean!

"I feel very sorry for you. So, with my compliments, I am leaving you my spectacles. Perhaps if you wear them you will be able to stop this blundering about. Hoping that with these you will be able to look the shining truth in the face and at last make some progress, believe me always, in youth and piety,

Your own
Alceste."

"What do you know about that!" cried Donovan in exasperation. "Maybe he thinks we're a pack of fools! We'll show him! He can't get away with that in this burg! Say, do you know what he did?—passed out specs like these to a dozen guys back there—Heaven only knows what he told 'em!—and when we bust the joint wide open, looking for a guy in black glasses we pinch *seven* guys in black glasses! And while we're doing that, he *takes his off* an' goes for a stroll!

"But this party ain't over yet; it ain't no more'n started, an' we'll show this bird— Come on, if you want to see the fun!"

II

It was no idle flare of disappointment, those words of Detective-Lieutenant Donovan. Ever since the night that Addison Kent had established the death of Professor Caron as cold-blooded murder, the police net had been drawing steadily tighter. Every outlet from the city was guarded, every known underworld haunt, liable to furnish a clue to the whereabouts of the three men who were "wanted," was under surveillance. Descriptions of the St. Boniface Kid, the big German with the wen, and of Kellani had gone out through official channels, and the story of the hunt reached the newspapers through City News Association bulletins from Police Headquarters; more than one ambitious young reporter was out "digging" for a "beat," while theorists at the Press Club held forth in comfort.

Now to this much-wanted trio would be added a fourth—now that Addison Kent's suspicion had blossomed into certainty; now that Alceste was known definitely to be loose in New York. To lay this internationally notorious cracksman by the heels would be a feather in Lowry's cap which that worthy inspector would spare no resource of the department to acquire. And behind the Bureau would stand the Commissioner, the District Attorney, the Washington Service itself.

Kent realized that Alceste's taunt was entirely personal—a mere gesture for the fun of the thing. He wanted to see some real progress made, did he? He might find his challenge accepted with results altogether outside his calculation! He could not win always, clever though he was; for pitted against him would be the cleverest brains of an efficient police organization, guiding the full machinery of its far-reaching resources. There were few well-known crooks within the confines of the city whom that machine could not lay hands upon at discretion; whose goings and comings could not be secretly detailed to Headquarters upon order. How long could Alceste hope to escape the drag of such an efficient fine-tooth comb? The one thing he had to rely upon was lack of description—double identities; who was he and what did he look like? But that was an advantage which could not last indefinitely; sooner or later someone who knew him would fall into the toils of the police and furnish a clue.

Who did know him? Kellani, the Nubian, who had fled the night of Mokra's murder? The police were satisfied that Kellani, if still alive, was not in New York, and their search for him had gone afield. Wasserhaus? Undoubtedly Wasserhaus knew something, and with the additional information which Kent could supply it would be a matter of time only before Wasserhaus would be doing his explaining at Police Headquarters—if he could be prevented from putting to sea in his rum-running ship, the *Albatross*. All that was necessary was to tail Berlin Harry and his gang; Wasserhaus was paying them well, no doubt, for protection from hijackers in his bootlegging deals. Berlin Harry, Nifty Dean, the Badger and the rest—all were known to the police, and through them it ought to be possible to get in touch with the German rum-runner, and even to discover the location of his vessel beyond the deadline.

The smoke curled from Addison Kent's pipe and shot in a blue stream from the corner of his mouth as he sat at a table in the deserted café and puzzled it out while waiting for Donovan.

Yet the problem was not as simple as all that. There was Naida to consider; at all costs she must be protected. Was he ready yet to make full report to Inspector Lowry? Not until he had seen her again and learned from her own lips the answers to all those questions he had asked her—not until he knew just how she fitted into the picture. That she hated Wasserhaus and was ready to work against him—was already doing so—Kent was positive. He was equally sure that when she was able to tell him everything, much of what now appeared confusing would be explained; not for an instant would he permit himself to doubt her no matter how incriminating the circumstances appeared.

And it did look as if the girl was in the thing up to her pretty neck! That was why he must not be in too great a hurry to turn the case over completely to the police; his work was not yet through, and he must continue independently until he had her story in full. He had realized this even as he had led Donovan through the underground passage and up into Loo Ling's tea-shop. It was evident that it was through this outlet that Berlin Harry's men had made their escape, and even as Donovan's squad searched and questioned the smiling Loo Ling, Addison Kent had kept silent about the three gunmen he knew to have passed that way.

For his discovery that Wasserhaus was a rum-runner and that these men were his hired gunmen had steered Addison Kent's thoughts along a new channel. It deepened the significance of information which had reached him that day through his own particular friend and underworld lieutenant, Pomereski, the Polish tailor. According to that astute barometer of secret activities, there was a big break coming in certain underworld circles—a carefully planned coup that was to set one Slipper Dagg and his following upon velvet cushions for the rest of their days—a break that was being nursed to fruition in the folds of secrecy. For Slipper Dagg was a gunman who was of the elite in gangland, and who took no back seat for Berlin Harry or any other rival; and of late the Slipper had carried a "deep heel" and so had every member of his gang.

"Hijacking!" had been Pomereski's terse explanation of this sudden wealth. "De Slipper's de King Pin of dem all, Mr. Kent, an' dere's de biggest break yet on de way."

Was there a connection between the plans of Slipper Dagg and Berlin Harry? Were those two notorious gangsters in collusion or at enmity? Was the cargo of the *Albatross* the stakes in the game, or, rather, were the hijackers preparing to descend upon the vessel after the cargo had been disposed of and walk away with the proceeds at the point of the gun? The possibility was at least worth considering; if the surmise should prove correct, Wasserhaus would have enough trouble on his hands to keep him busy for a while, and he would have to fight out his own battle without any possible appeal to the police for protection.

Another question: Was Alceste dipping into this rum-running game? It was profitable enough; but somehow Addison Kent could not bring himself to think that his enemy would get mixed up in anything so entirely outside his own line. It was too sordid—too far beneath that finesse which had come to be associated with the name of Alceste. He might know Wasserhaus—evidently did know him—might even have business dealings with him—

Wait! Might those business dealings concern other things than bootleg liquors?—a certain wonderful ruby, for instance?—the golden scarab itself? Was Wasserhaus the big man who had visited the Lamont residence the night the scarab disappeared? Was it he who had murdered Professor Emil Caron? What was it the late Egyptologist had said about Alceste:

"Dead he may be, but his evil lives after him." And then he had asked if they had ever heard of a secret Eastern organization known as the "Order of the Golden Scarab"! What was the connection? Always it came back to Alceste!

Kent shook his head impatiently. The thing was a muddle, or else he was not thinking as clearly as usual. His eye fell upon the two pairs of spectacles that the night's events had thrust upon him. They lay on the table before him now as he smoked—the glasses with which Alceste so brazenly had presented him and the spectacles Naida had given him. They were identical! "They will think it is Dryden, and you can slip through," she had said. How had she obtained them? Had she known that in wearing them he would be aiding Alceste to escape?

"Confound her! She's a witch!" He smiled sentimentally, remembering the moist sweetness of her lips. He could do nothing, he suddenly realized, until he saw her again and learned all she could tell him. It would simplify the whole problem. Once he knew her story, he could act intelligently; until then mere speculation was futile. His hands were tied hopelessly.

He looked up as Detective-Lieutenant Donovan joined him.

"Well, that's that! We're cleaned up here. Now for a snack at the nearest beanery and we're ready for the next point of call."

"And just where might that be?" enquired Kent with interest.

"The St. Boniface Kid!" There was a gleam of satisfaction in Donovan's resolute eye. "We've got him dead to rights—backed into a corner he can't get out of in a hurry. By daylight he'll be behind the bars!"

21
THE MESSAGE

I

The first gray finger of dawn was feeling into the sky above the East River when Addison Kent reached the side-door of Pomereski's tailoring establishment and noiselessly let himself in with his latchkey. He slipped upstairs to the room that stood always awaiting him and, after scribbling a note that he was not to be disturbed and pinning this to a panel of the door, softly shut himself in and turned the key with a sigh of weariness. Removing his boots only, he stretched out on the bed and in a moment was sound asleep.

It had been an exciting and fatiguing night. To be sent to the very borderland of death by an anæsthetic route; to be awakened to the immediate prospect of direst peril; to escape from this into the arms of an emotional ecstasy; finally to spend the rest of the night keyed to high pitch in a police man-hunt—all within a few hours! Little wonder that even the novelist's exceptional physique felt the strain—that he slept like a log!

Detective-Lieutenant Donovan's prediction had come true; daylight found the St. Boniface Kid in the hands of the police. Harried from cover to cover, deserted at the last by his "friends," the young French-Canadian from St. Boniface, Manitoba, had been driven into a corner. Hysteria more than anything else had led him to put up a finish fight against overwhelming odds; only "strict orders" to take him alive had saved him from being riddled with bullets. Even so, he had to be removed, unconscious, to a hospital

404

cot instead of a cell, and it would be forty-eight hours at least before he would be in condition for "grilling" at Headquarters. He probably knew who had murdered the late Professor Emil Caron, and his wisest course would be to turn State's evidence. Altogether, Donovan had every reason to feel satisfied with the night's work.

The afternoon was well advanced before Addison Kent awoke, greatly refreshed. For a while, hands clasped behind his head, he lay luxuriating in the feeling of well-being that tingled through his six feet of muscular manhood and allowed his mind to dwell upon his love for Naida. What a girl she was!—as clever and brave as she was beautiful! And she had risked her life to rescue him! She must care for him a little—no, a lot! She had not been able to resist his kisses, and oh, the tenderness of her when she had yielded him her lips! "Oh, my dear, if you love me!—" She had called him "my dear"!

His face sobered. Where was she now? If she were still in danger, how could he go to her? He was no farther ahead than before—did not know who she was or where to look for her—knew only that her first name was Naida! He should have insisted— Then his anxiety cleared as he remembered her promise to communicate with him as soon as it was safe—to send him a message if anything went wrong—

His eyes fell upon his neat tweeds on their hanger by the door, reminding him that it behooved him to get dressed and be about his business. For one thing he must call on Inspector Lowry. And he must get out to Westchester as soon as he had finished his business down town; supposing already she had telephoned him there!

He was across the room, fumbling for his watch, before he remembered that he had handed it to Pomereski to put in the safe. He went to the window and raised the shade; as nearly as he could judge, it must be after four o'clock. By the time he had had a shave and a good meal at a first-class restaurant over on Broadway—

Someone was talking in the next room—to Pomereski. Setting down the water-pitcher and pausing above the wash-basin, Kent listened. The tones were not so guarded but that he could hear an occasional sentence—something about "a dozen blue jerseys and a dozen sailor's caps." Pom was stocking sea-togs—drummer for some Yidd factory likely—

He plunged his face into the cold water with relish and scoured and spluttered. Dozen blue jerseys; dozen sailor caps—dozen jerseys; dozen caps—jerseys; caps! It was an idle refrain that kept time with the rubbings of the towel—an unattached thought—

The movements of the towel on Kent's ruddy cheeks grew slower and slower. Pomereski was not placing a buying order; he was being instructed to make delivery by someone who seemed very anxious about the dozen blue jerseys and dozen sailor caps. It was Pomereski, the confidential costumier of the underworld—not Pomereski, tailor and clothier—who was swearing by all the gods he knew that delivery would be made without fail.

"All you gotta do is tell de Slipper I say dey'll be dere."

Not long after the caller had departed Addison Kent was standing in Pomereski's little back office, receiving his gold watch from the safe. He eyed the pale little Pole in whimsical mood.

"So Slipper Dagg, with a dozen men disguised as sailors, is putting to sea, eh? Does he know where the *Albatross* is, or is he on a scouting trip? Take it from me, Pom, a lot of those jerseys and caps of yours will be gone for good—unless Berlin Harry— Say, are he and the Slipper on friendly terms?"

"You know t'ings, eh!" cried Pomereski, with a grin of admiration. "It's de big break, Mr. Kent—to-night—to-morrow—I dunno. It not good to speak 'bout. No, de Slipper an' Berlin Harry—dey too jealous 'bout each odder to be frien'. Dey fight—*pst-pst!*—tomcats!"

"Then, listen carefully, Pom. I know Slipper Dagg personally— that Acheson affair, you remember? I was able to get him out of a rather nasty hole that night, and I think he will remember me. I rather like the Slipper—for his sense of humour, I guess. Well, I want you to wish him *bon voyage* for me if it's the *Albatross*— It is? Well—this man Wasserhaus, who owns the vessel, deserves everything the Slipper can hand him, and inasmuch as the police are not concerned in the Slipper's seafaring ventures, I personally wish him luck. But warn him to watch out for Berlin Harry's gang;

Wasserhaus has hired them for protection. Tell him I told you to warn him, though probably he knows all about it." With a wave of the hand, he made his way out to the street.

Half an hour later Addison Kent was on his back, with his cheerful pink face obliterated by a creamy lather of shaving-soap. Half an hour later still, looking pinker and more cheerful than ever, he sat behind a disk of snowy linen and lifted the silver covers from sundry well-cooked and appetizing viands while an attentive and immaculate Swiss waiter hovered near to anticipate his every need.

And by the time the big hand of his watch had completed yet another half-cycle he was sitting at that same round table—cleared now except for a hammered-brass finger-bowl and an untasted *demi-tasse*—sitting there, staring at an entry which he had made in his morocco-bound notebook. His fat red fountain pen was still in his hand. The ashes from his cigarette feathered unheeded down his vest.

For upon Addison Kent's face was something very like consternation. And the colour drained slowly from his cheeks.

II

"Is—there anything I can get you, sir?"

"No! Just leave me alone!"

His voice sounded strangely dry and flat. He was unconscious entirely of the impatient gesture which banished the observant waiter to a discreet distance.

It was not what he had written—a simple entry of details—that disturbed him; it was the subconscious impression that welled upon him as he wrote—a stirring in the recesses of memory, as if what he were recording found echo somewhere in past experience—a sense of familiarity so elusive that it had required this mechanical tabulation to give it birth. Then out of it, like groping mental fingers suddenly closing, that gleam of intuition—that thought which crystallized as a blind conviction in the face of reason!

Deliberately he combated it—probing, analyzing, marshalling cold facts in review, weighing discrepancies. He forgot his surroundings—lost track of time. When finally he arose from the table the colour was back in his cheeks and an exaggerated calmness was upon him.

He went straight to a telephone booth and called Inspector Lowry, at Police Headquarters.

"If you can make it on such short notice, Jim, I'll buy you the best dinner in town. I want to talk to you."

"You're on!" accepted the inspector promptly. "I want to go over things with you myself. Seen the papers? Sitting pretty, eh? Say, before I forget, your friend Malabar was calling up this afternoon, enquiring for you—seemed tickled to death over the capture of the Kid. Where'll I meet you? Canadian Club, did you say? O.K. for— say, seven o'clock."

Kent put in a Westchester call and presently heard the voice of Gridley, the new butler at Lamont's.

"Is Mr. Malabar there, Gridley?"

"No sir, 'e's not at 'ome, sir. Is this Mr. Kent? Beg pardon, sir, but I was to tell you as 'ow 'e'd 'ardly be 'ome till rahnd abaht midnight, sir."

"Do you know where I can get in touch with him, Gridley? I wanted him to join me right away."

"Sorry, sir, but Mr. Malabar didn't leave no hother word, except as I knows as 'ow 'e's dinin' hout, an' I've taken the liberty, sir, of lettin' Gaston hoff duty for the night—"

"That's all right, Gridley. Have there been any telephone calls for me today? Any messages or letters?"

"No, sir. Nothink, sir."

Kent glanced at his watch. He hardly knew whether to be disappointed or relieved at the lack of any communication from Naida; if she had not yet found it safe to make an appointment to meet him again, it was no less evident that nothing had gone wrong sufficiently to justify the message she had promised to send him. Comforting himself with the old saying that no news was good news, he hurried out and swung along Forty-Second Street, past the library and down into the congestion of Broadway. He had just time to get in a call upon the management of the MacAlpine.

With the information he sought duly recorded in his notebook, Addison Kent was back at the Belmont, opposite the Grand Central Terminal, and stepped out of the elevator at the second floor into the select quarters of the Canadian Club just in time to greet his guest. It was evident that recent developments had put Inspector Lowry in good humour, and that he had arrived fully prepared to do justice to his dinner and to enjoy a quiet evening with the novelist in the comfort and seclusion afforded by the club.

The discovery that his host had dined already and proposed to content himself with a dessert in no way disconcerted the inspector's appetite or stopped his flow of reminiscence. He was there for the evening, and so interested did both participants in the succeeding private conference become that it was well on towards midnight before Addison Kent finally bade Lowry good-night and took an express for the Bronx.

He mounted the steps of the Lamont residence, key-ring in hand, but found Gridley still on duty and opening the door for him with a welcoming smile.

"Mr. Malabar is hin, sir!" he greeted, in what seemed to be an unnecessarily loud voice, and as soon as he had received the novelist's overcoat and hat he hurried ahead down the hall to the library, calling out: "It's Mr. Kent, sir!"

Kent smiled after him. Gridley certainly was beginning to lose some of his professional pomposity. Malabar's voice was in earnest conversation at the telephone; the disconnecting click of the instrument was simultaneous with Kent's first step down the hall.

"Hello, there! Back again, eh?" The journalist jumped up with extended hand. "Congratulations, Kent—St. Boniface Kid, you know. I read about it in the early editions—tried to get hold of you, but Lowry couldn't tell me where you were. By Jove! splendid work! When I read— I say, why are you staring at me like that? Collar on upside down or something?"

Kent's intent gaze remained upon him in silent analysis. Behind Malabar's exuberant manner was a nervous tension which defied concealment.

"What is the matter?" Kent asked quietly.

At once Malabar shrugged his shoulders and dropped into the nearest chair. The face which he presently raised was lined by unfeigned anxiety.

"I've had some awfully bad news, old chap," he confessed. "Just getting ready to take a train for Newark. An aunt I am rather fond of—just got word she's dying—serious automobile smash—" He stopped short, biting his lip in aggravation. His face whitened.

For in two strides Addison Kent had reached the library table and was stooping to pick up from the floor a piece of yellow paper, torn from an ordinary manilla paper bag. From where he had been standing he had seen the name at the bottom of that hasty message—boldly written in heavy black with what must have been an eyebrow-pencil. Kent's startled eyes raced over the lines:

> "W. knows truth. Held prisoner—73—3—top floor, rear—act quickly.
> "Naida."

III

"My God!" breathed Kent. "When did this come?"

"Ten minutes ago."

"How? Messenger?"

"Yes—a ragged newsboy."

Kent turned upon him, eyes blazing.

"And you—! You were trying to keep this from me? You were planning to sneak out of here without me knowing—that cock-and-bull yarn about your aunt at Newark!— By Heaven, Malabar! I'll give you just one minute to explain yourself! This message was for me, and I won't stand for!—"

"Message for *you!*" cried Malabar, in genuine amazement. "You are crazy! It is *my* message!"

"I tell you, it's *mine!* It's from Naida. She told me—" He checked himself abruptly. White with anger, his eyes narrowed. "Since when have you known her right name, Malabar?" he demanded sharply. "To you she was supposed to be merely 'Miss Rockwood'!"

Kent stepped quickly across to the other's chair, gathered the top of his vest into one fist and yanked him to his feet. Just as swiftly the journalist freed himself from that clutch with one sweep of a muscular arm.

"Keep your hands to yourself, Kent!" he warned in strident resentment.

They glared at each other.

"I want to know how far this thing has gone, Malabar."

"How would it be if you minded your own business!"

"That's what I'm doing!"

"You are not!"

"I repeat: Since when have you known her as 'Naida'?"

"Suppose I throw that question back in your face! When did she become 'Naida' to *you?*"

"Answer my question!" commanded Kent in ominously quiet tones.

"You answer mine!" retorted Malabar with spirit. "What right have you to question me?"

"I discovered only this evening that you have been meeting her—clandestinely—at your hotel!—"

"Well? And supposing I have?"

"Now I find you trying to double-cross me, your friend, by sneaking—"

"Sneaking! A mean word! I'll swap you one for it—snooping!"— and Malabar's mouth drew down sneeringly.

Addison Kent stared at him for a moment speechlessly. With an effort he controlled himself. His face was as white as chalk with rage, but his voice when he spoke was coldly calm. Like one in a daze be began to talk quietly:

"Since I left this house a few days ago things have been happening. I came in contact with the criminals involved in this Caron case—fact is, they had me in a tight corner from which I escaped only through Naida's intervention. The danger she is in now is due to that. She made me leave her down there because she thought it would be safer for her! She promised to send me word here if anything went wrong.

"So much for that. I have met Alceste! He is very much alive! They had me tied up, and he taunted me to my face. He was wearing black spectacles, and he had a cap pulled down over his forehead and a white silk scarf around his neck; in the folds of it he kept his chin well buried. All I could see was his mouth and the end of his nose, you understand; but I had a good look at them—"

He got slowly to his feet and crossed the room, thawing a white silk handkerchief from his pocket.

"Here, let me show you how he wore the scarf—around his neck—so!" He laughed a little. "No, up around the chin—that's better! And the beggar afterwards made me a present—of these glasses!"

As he spoke Kent held them upon Malabar's nose and leaned back in amused contemplation. Angrily Malabar struck them off, and they smashed on the tiles in front of the fireplace.

"There now, you've broken my souvenir, Dick!" protested Kent. He smiled. "Rather a clever disguise altogether, don't you think? Surprising how completely one can cover up the face, and how hard it is to recognize any single feature in detail when it is isolated from the rest."

"Don't be an ass, Kent!" Malabar at last found voice. "What has all this got to do— For heaven's sake, let's drop it! Let's go together and rescue that girl!"

"Ah, now you talk like my good old friend Dick Malabar!" cried Kent. "I knew all we needed was something to distract our attention until we both cooled down; hence the little demonstration. I was only going to add that one's memory is such an unreliable thing after all that it requires some definite reminder, such as—"

"Stop! Keep away from that drawer!"

Addison Kent's casually extended hand was arrested in midair. He moved not a muscle. For as the words pinged the room he divined, rather than saw, the lightning movement which accompanied them.

Even before he slowly crooked his head to look, he knew that Alceste's automatic was trained upon him point-blank!

22

A Mask is Removed

"Credit me with paying you the compliment of taking precautions, old bean," drawled the cool, insolent voice of Alceste. "You surely would not expect me to leave the cartridge clip in the magazine of the gun you keep in that drawer?—particularly when I have been rather expecting this show-down at any moment?"

He favoured the novelist with the condescending smile one might bestow upon a blundering child; but it was a smile of the lips only. Behind the levelled weapon were alert eyes, cold, hard. Kent met them with a strained look.

"You see, you have such an unfortunate habit of making a nuisance of yourself—a bad habit that has been growing upon you of late. I had decided it was time for us to part company, and was planning to leave our happy home this evening. That was why I instructed Gridley to tell you I would not be home before midnight; I hoped to be gone before you arrived, and had you given me another twenty minutes—but, pardon me—you may sit down, of course. I said—*sit down!*"

Obediently Addison Kent backed into a chair without altering the focus of his steady gaze. He spoke no word.

"Make yourself comfortable, my dear fellow. Now that you've put your foot in it, we may as well have this thing out and be done with it. There are quite a few things to say— I beg your pardon, but were you trying to speak?"

"You, Malabar! Of all men—*you!*"

413

"I do hope you are not going to indulge in sentiment and all that sort of rot, my dear Kent! Let us drop pretence. You did not come here to-night to greet your old friend Dick Malabar, you already suspected the truth when you stepped into this room. Your real object in provoking a quarrel over that message was to uncover proof of your suspicions—playing for a look at that molar of mine with the gold band around it! Very clever of you! But although you were about to reach into that drawer for your automatic—just to be on the safe side, as it were—you were none too sure of yourself. You are not sure, even now, that I am not playing a wild prank upon you!"

"I wish to God I could think so!"

"The intensity with which you say that betrays a degree of sentimentality which I find distressing in one who has so much cleverness to commend him. It is one of your weaknesses—"

"To have given you my honest friendship—to have trusted you— a weakness? What manner of man are you?"

"At least one who can keep his head in an emergency. Let us proceed to analyze this so-called friendship over which you are inclined to become maudlin. Let me put some straight questions to you, and I want straight answers. Is what I have surmised correct? Did you come here to-night, expecting and believing that I was Alceste?"

"Yes."

"Very good. You are sufficiently satisfied of that to pull a gun on me?—to hand me over to the police?"

"Yes."

"In spite of the fact that Dick Malabar's eyes are blue, with no sign of the tattooed brown which you expected had disfigured the eyes of Alceste for life? How do you account for that?"

"I do not know. It is one of the discrepancies which I cannot explain—unless the tattooing dye has faded—"

"Well, we may put that down as one point scored on you, my dear Kent. If you will recall, the tattooing operation performed by the late lamented Dr. MacMurrough was by a special process of his own which enabled him to perform the operation quickly. You apparently lost sight of the fact that intentionally he might have used a special dye which would fade out and leave no trace after the lapse of—say, some months. You should have known me better than to think I would ruin my eyes for all time to come, just to escape a momentary inconvenience. Yes, you were rather disappointing in that item!

"Suppose we try another. Take the matter of my height. According to your measurements of Alceste—carefully ascertained by you, I believe, on the former occasion of our meeting—measurements by which you seemed to set great store—well, according to those measurements, Dick Malabar is over three inches taller than Alceste! What about that? That, too, has been difficult to account for, has it not?"

"Yes—until I remembered that you stop at nothing to obtain your ends."

"Go on. You interest me greatly."

"There is an apparatus on the market for stretching the body, of course—a system of spinal treatment that allows the articular and intervertebral cartilages to expand. By gradually thickening the twenty-three rubber-like cartilages which act as cushions between the vertebral bodies in the spinal column, it is possible to increase the height by natural growth—a matter of approximately two inches. You could probably gain another inch or two through correction of posture."

"Capital, my dear fellow! Splendid! It took me just about six months to obtain the desired result, and it is permanent. When you pass maturity and your spinal shock-absorbers begin to wear thin, I recommend you to try a little systematic stretching; it will make a new man of you!

"So it was your concentrated study of my mouth the other night which gave you a glimmer of the truth, eh? I rather expected it would, you know; but it was a risk I was forced to run in order to duly impress my friend Otto."

"I—do not understand. I am in no mood for cryptograms!"

"Nor in any position to resent them!" reminded Alceste incisively. "There are so many things you do not understand! If I told you that Wasserhaus was so far from being any friend of mine that he was my worst enemy—not even excepting present company—would you believe me?"

"I have seen no evidence of it," said Addison Kent wearily.

"And if I told you that Naida rescued you the other night because I instructed her to do so, and that I kept Wasserhaus and MacGonnigle otherwise engaged while she did it—would you believe that?"

"*No!*"

"I thought as much! Which brings us back to where we started, you see—this wonderful friendship you have for Dick Malabar! If I put that friendship to the test by asking you to let bygones be bygones—by asking you to believe that things are often not what they seem—by pleading with you to trust in Dick Malabar, even though you now know him to be Alceste—what would you say? If I appealed to that wonderful friendship you throw at me as a reproach, and asked you to believe that in due course I could explain everything to your satisfaction—asked you to forget that I was Alceste and to join me to-night in the rescue of Naida—would you trust me, Addison Kent? Answer that! Would you?"

For a long moment the novelist looked at him steadily, seeking to fathom this new and unexpected tack, while the other watched him closely—studied every inflection of the tense face.

"There are some things which wound too deeply to be readily forgiven—some things which are beyond explanation," answered Kent at length, in a flat voice.

"Quite so! Your boasted friendship is but surface sentimentality, incapable of any acid test! Knowing me to be Alceste, you have room in your generous heart only for enmity!" There was a tinge of bitterness in the accusation.

"Alceste has placed himself outside the pale, Malabar—if that is your real name. My duty is clear before me—to hand you straight over to the police! How dare you expect any other treatment from me, you damned scoundrel! You—"

"At least we know exactly where we stand, old bean! Now, kindly drop all sentiment and let us proceed—"

"*Gridley!*" shouted Kent at the top of his voice. "*Gridley!*"

II

"A most unseemly bellow!" protested the mocking voice. "If there is something you are wanting, why not allow me to ring?" He reached out and pressed the push-button that summoned the butler.

Gridley was not far away, and he came on the run, checking his haste abruptly at the archway.

"Ah, Gridley, Mr. Kent wants you, I believe. It would be in order for you to sing for him that beautiful thing of Cadman's, 'Call Me No More'!"

For a moment only Addison Kent regarded the grinning servant; then he waved his hand hopelessly.

"Permit me to make you acquainted with a very good friend of mine. Kent—Mr. Bert Gridley, the well-known character actor. You have heard me speak of Mr. Kent, of course, Gridley. You might see that that rope of yours is handy. Much as I regret it, I find we are going to need it—what's that, Kent? Oh, I thought you said something!

"You will understand that we are quite alone in the house— just we three. Gaston was anxious to get off to-night to attend his grandmother's funeral or something, and I sent Sandy away with a letter which it will take him all night to deliver. About Gridley— the opportunity of having his companionship here was too great a temptation for me to resist when the vacancy occurred. He's really a splendid fellow—reliable, strong and *willing*—aren't you, Gridley? Alongside him, Barkis was a mere beginner in willingness! You will take good care of Mr. Kent when I leave, Gridley. Better go for your rope now and hang it over that chair—"

"It's out in the dining-room, Dick."

"Then, get it. *Sit quiet*, Kent! You are much too fidgety. I hope you are not planning to try anything foolish! I would strongly advise you not to!"

"What do you propose to do?—if I might be so bold as to enquire."

With smouldering eyes the novelist tallied the net result of his sarcasm—a faint, cynical smile at the corners of that mouth.

"Well, now, I have been considering. Inasmuch as you seem so anxious to rush me to the police-station, and as that is something which undoubtedly would interfere with my night's activities and my future plans—to tell you the truth, dear old chap, I thought we would tie you up tight to a chair in here in the library where it is so cosy and warm. Gridley will remain with you, of course, for company, and will keep the fire replenished so that you can gaze into the flames and conjure mental pictures to your heart's content— think out the plot of a new detective story, if you like. If you behave yourself, I have no doubt that Gridley will get you something to eat before morning, and perhaps he might even read you a bedtime story—"

Quick as a flash of light Addison Kent acted. Nothing was to be gained by attempting to secure the automatic from the table drawer; with the clip of cartridges missing it would be utterly useless. Equally futile would be any effort to overcome Alceste by sudden assault; for the powerfully-built Gridley would bring the fight to a termination no less sudden than unsatisfactory. A single chance only lay open—a slim one—of flight. If Kent could dodge out through the library archway without being shot down, there was a chance that he might reach the front door before Gridley reappeared. The pointing automatic was too great a risk to wrestle with the catches of the glass doors which opened on the tiled portico; he would be shot to pieces! No, the only chance was to duck and run for it—a dangerous hazard. With apparent weariness, Kent yawned prodigiously, stretching wide his arms and knotting his muscles. The moment his right hand came in contact with the little onyx table beside his chair his fingers darted for the neck of the heavy Venetian vase that stood upon it.

With that backward grip came his sudden forward leap—one single movement—the overhand fling of his arm that sent the vase hurtling through the air with the full weight of big muscles behind it—the cat-like side-spring which threw his body low and landed him half-way across the space separating him from the archway.

He did not wait to note the accuracy of his aim. The loud crash of the vase was in his ears as he lunged for the portières with a desperate energy which he had never surpassed in the wildest rugby rush of his college days.

"*Get him, Grid!*"

Through the archway catapulted Kent. To the left he dashed— down the wide hall where the polished floors and panelling caught the sheen of the lights. He wondered why Alceste did not fire. He was conscious of the startled Gridley behind him, near the arch- way, with a coiled rope in his hand. Then, just as hope was lending wings to his flying feet—just as he was straining for the vestibule—

Hiss-ss-ss-ss! Along that smooth, slippery, well-waxed floor, like a long black snake, shot Gridley's rope. The next instant Addison Kent was jerked on his face—flung prone with a force which whacked the breath out of his body!

23
"For You the Game is Ended!"

Like a roped steer the novelist was dragged ignominiously along the hall, feet first, through the archway into the library. Half stunned, he was placed on a straight-backed chair around which flew coil after coil of the lariat until he was pinned there, as helpless as if he were encased in a strait-jacket.

"'Western stuff,' I believe they call it," was Alceste's amused comment as he slid his automatic into his hip pocket. "Good work, Grid! Tie his feet to the front legs of the chair, and I guess we may come to the conclusion that the gentleman is in for the night and guaranteed a quiet evening at home among the friendliest of companions—oh, not you, Grid! I refer to good books—such as you see lining the walls of this beautiful room. It is hardly likely that Mr. Kent will be feeling any too kindly towards you for that nasty bruise on his head and—jt!—jt!—his lip is cut! Wipe that trickle of blood off his chin—ah, that's charitable of you, Gridley. You may go now and finish packing; I'll ring when I need you."

As he spoke he tapped the end of a cigarette vertically upon the silver case from which he had taken it. Carefully he inserted it in an amber mouthpiece, methodically lighted it and exhaled a cloud of blue vapour at the ceiling.

I warned you not to try anything silly, Kent. Perhaps I should have told you that Mr. Gridley at one time was a motion-picture star—the original 'Pinto Pete' in a series of famous cowboy pictures—and throws a lariat with the best of them. I don't know what your friend Lamont is going to say to you for smashing that rare vase of his! Just look at it! Aren't you ashamed of yourself?"

He lolled back in a big leather chair and regarded the prisoner quizzically. Then his eyes narrowed, and he leaned forward quickly.

"You fool! Do you think this is some five-o'clock tea-party? Lucky for you that Gridley's lariat got you, or I should have been under the painful necessity of potting you from the portico!"

Addison Kent rolled his head impatiently.

"Are you man enough to answer three questions truthfully?" he challenged bitterly.

"What is worrying you, dear boy?"

"Is that message from Naida genuine?"

"Why, of course it is!"

"Am I right in supposing that you claim to love her?"

"Yes, she is very dear to me indeed!"

"Then, in God's name, why are you wasting time here when you ought to be flying to her rescue? What happens to me doesn't matter; but for God's sake, go to her at once!"

There was no doubting the sincerity in the husky voice, the honest anxiety in his eyes.

"You believe me to be a—shall we say, rival? for the lady's favour? And, believing that, you would send me to her to become her hero?"

"Quit your everlasting gab! What do our differences matter when she stands in need of help? Good heavens! man, don't you realize that her very life and honour—" He paused at the other's raised hand, at the strange smile that warmed the face for a moment—the smile that for just an instant revealed the old Dick Malabar he had known with affection.

"You are worrying unnecessarily, old chap. Forgive me for not advising you at once that everything is being done for Naida that can be done at the moment. Already I have taken action—over the telephone—and she will be protected. She was removed from the address given in that note very shortly after she despatched it; so it would be useless to go there. I know where she is; you do not. I know how to rescue her in the surest way; you do not. But I cannot make the final move in the matter for a few hours, and I swear to you that I am telling you only the truth.

"With so much at stake you may begin to understand why I would have shot you down without hesitation had you escaped from the house! Affairs of which you have no inkling are coming to a swift and dangerous culmination, and I can brook no interference with my movements from you or the police!" Alceste paused, and the flinty lines repossessed his lean face. "Understand this, Addison Kent; so far as you are concerned the game is over; the pieces presently will be laid away in a wooden box and the chessboard folded on you. You are going to be put where your interference with me will cease. At last it is *checkmate!*"

"Must I remind you that a cut lip is hardly the right condition for laughing," drawled Kent contemptuously. "Your tragic theatricality is passable comedy; but when so long drawn out it becomes a boring performance. If you seek to entertain me, I am more interested in these affairs of which you say I have no inkling. I hope you are not going to tell me that you are going in for bootlegging! It would be so *déclassé* after your artistic activities in acquisition of the treasure of Osiris!"

"Ah, I can see that you are feeling better, my dear Kent," purred Alceste. "You ought to do more public speaking! Yes, it has been rather a pretty little game, although you have been too easily fooled for it to have been very exciting. Shall we hold a post-mortem on it? Would you care to have me point out your bad plays!"

"It was you who took the golden scarab ruby from the breast of the mummy that night!" accused Kent bluntly.

"Something you certainly should have found out long before this," admitted Alceste coolly.

"And the mummy of the cat—you stole that also?"

"Assuredly, old top! Inasmuch as the cat was the hiding-place for a fortune in precious stones—diamonds, rubies, pearls, sapphires and so forth—you would scarcely expect me to overlook it! Besides, had I not taken possession of these trinkets somebody else would have got them that same night."

"The man I saw on the wall in the rain, of course."

"Of course."

"Wasserhaus!"

"Gridley's lariat seems to have jarred some of the cobwebs out of your brain! Your perspicacity amazes me!"

"So your story of the supposed fight you had with the intruder out there in the midst of the thunderstorm—that was a pure fabrication!"

"As a writer of fiction you should be able to appreciate it."

Kent studied the sardonic smile of his enemy with disturbing realization of the extent to which he had been duped.

"We found you lying in a rain-puddle near the gates—Sandy and I—with a gash on the top of your head, a bad bruise on your brow and sundry bad scratches. At least your wounds were real!" declared Kent caustically. "You had to have an alibi; so you inflicted them upon yourself."

"Really, my dear fellow, the light of understanding is making you quite bright to-night! If you want to know, I bashed my head against one of the stone gateposts—ran at it full tilt like a jousting knight. It was a simple matter, of course, to shoot holes through my shirt with my automatic, and when you and the gardener arrived I promptly fainted. The only difficulty I experienced was to keep from laughing while you were lugging me to the house."

"It was typical of you who never do things by halves," muttered Kent. "Instead of trying to capture the big man, you passed the jewels to him—your accomplice!" He looked up quickly. "Why did you go to the trouble of faking those footprints outside the cellar window and again up in the bedroom?"

"A clumsy piece of work, I concede. I wanted you to think it was the man who had visited Professor Caron and left the imprint of his golf boot in the library."

"That was Wasserhaus!"

"Was it?"

"You know it was! You know it was he who killed Caron!"

"Excuse me, Kent! I know nothing about the murder of Professor Caron."

"Nor who killed Mokra?"

"I do not know."

"You lie!"

"I tell you, my hands are clean!" surged Alceste. He controlled his anger with an effort and reached abruptly for the push-button.

"What was Naida doing there that night?" demanded Kent suddenly.

"I believe you are the only one who insists that she was there at all!" was Alceste's surprising rejoinder. "Is everything ready, Gridley?"

"All set," replied the butler, who had just stepped into the room.

"At least it was she who called here early that morning, passing herself off as a newspaper woman."

"Yes, she called then to see if I was all right," answered Alceste coldly. "My time is up, and I am leaving you now. It is quite possible I may not see you again, Addison Kent. In parting I have only this to say to you: It is unfortunate that a man of your ability should mix so much folly with his cleverness. You should have stuck to your impossible detective stories and left actual police work alone. You are a bungler who succeeds only in making himself an annoyance. You have been a mere child in my hands, and I could have killed you times without number. But I chose to let you live in the hope that you would see the error of your ways and mind your own business! It was partly with the idea of studying you at close quarters and perhaps influencing you to drop your meddling in things outside your legitimate field that I used your acquaintanceship with Richard Malabar to work from the inside on this adventure."

"You did not play fair! You struck below the belt!" cried Kent furiously.

"Remember what I said about sentiment!" reminded Alceste in sharp reproof. "I have no stomach for friendship which will not stand the test of faith. You have chosen your own bed and you are going to lie in it. As for Naida—"

"As for Naida, she is mine! I do not believe she loves you!"

"Yours!" laughed Alceste. "Well, well! How pretty a conceit! You seem to lose sight of the fact that for you the game is ended, as I have already pointed out. Shortly after three o'clock this morning—it is now just 1.23 by my watch—a closed car will call here for you. Gridley will go with you, of course, to see that you are safely delivered at the other end of the journey. Every provision will have been made for taking care of you and preventing any further activity on your part. Meanwhile, you will remain right here, just as you are, with Gridley to see that you behave yourself. Much as I would like to loosen that lariat and trust to your word of honour—you would not give your promise as a gentleman, I suppose, to make no attempt to escape or communicate—"

"*No!*" refused Kent vehemently.

"Quite so. It is purely a matter of your comfort, dear old chap; but it is just as well. And now, I must go; but first, with your permission—"

He stepped across to the library table and from a drawer—the same drawer for which Addison Kent's hand had been reaching when Alceste stopped him—he lifted the automatic which the novelist kept there. Fascinated, Kent watched him coolly extract *a full clip of cartridges* from the magazine of the weapon!

"It is unfortunate that our automatics are of the same make and calibre, is it not? You see, old bean, you came in on me before I had quite finished my preparations, and my own gun was empty. So, if you don't mind, I will just transfer this full clip now and"— bowing elaborately— "bid you a fond farewell!"

At the archway he paused and bowed again. Then across the room drove the full-throated mockery of Alceste's laugh. And for Addison Kent it left an echo of derision and a sense of utter defeat.

24
The Dark Hour

The hush of the night hours mantled park and boulevard. Winding driveways were deserted; only at long intervals did a belated automobile speed loud passage through quiet streets or a footfall upon pavement knock onward with solitary emphasis.

The Lamont residence was in darkness except for dim light in one spot. The mellow chime of the huge old clock in the lower hall was followed by two slow strokes—whirr-rr-*boom-m-m!*—thirr-rr-*boom-m-m!* The momentary resonance rode arrogantly forth upon the stillness of the house; the stillness came back. In the library the coals rustled softly in the grate as the red heart of the fire settled closer to its thin bed of gray ashes. Through the great room restless shadows tossed, reaching blindly about the rich woodwork—miserly fingers which groped for elusive glints of firelight reflected upon polished surfaces. The heavy curtains were drawn across the French windows; but beyond the glass doors the dimly lighted library doubled itself indistinctly against the lurking blackness outside.

Two a.m.! One more hour of discomfort and monotony to endure! Shortly after three, Alceste had said, the car would call. Addison Kent found himself looking forward to its arrival with a degree of eagerness which he would not have thought possible. Any kind of action which would bring this torture to an end was to be welcomed. His limbs were growing numb from the stricture of his bonds. He had ceased to plead for relief; the callous Gridley sat slumped in a leather chair, feet sprawled toward the fire, lost in

426

the pages of a book while he abstractedly munched, munched, munched—*sslup!*—apples!

The champing of Gridley's jaws irritated Kent. The odour of the apples irritated him. The whole situation was getting on his nerves. He tried to doze; but thought was piling, coiling, in his mind, and for once he could not bring on that blankness which he had trained so carefully to answer to his call when he wanted to cease thinking and go to sleep. There was nothing for it but to mount the black beast that obsessed him and give rein.

The thoughts which swooped upon him in the bitterness of that dark hour were sable-winged. Defeat and derision jeered at him in the laughing echoes Alceste had left in his ears. Humiliation dragged at him. Self-reproach pointed a scornful finger. He had failed—miserably! As his enemy had said, for him the game was over, and he had lost!

The first ten minutes had been sufficient to satisfy him that there was nothing he could do except to await the will of his captors. Bound to the chair so securely, the hope of working free from the lariat with its Western hitches soon expired. If he moved, the chair would have to go with him. It would be possible to overbalance it; but what advantage would be gained by lying prone upon the floor? Even if it were possible to hunch along toward the telephone over in the corner, Gridley had taken care to plant himself beside it. To tumble on to the fireplace and burn the lariat somehow?—Gridley would be after him at the first move! Shout for help?—They were alone in the great house that stood back in its grounds, well away from the deserted highway. Use some pretext to get the butler out of the room?—Gridley was alert, suspicious.

So Addison Kent sat on, his head sagged in pretence of sleep; but behind his closed eyelids he was busily going over and over the situation from every possible angle and finding no loophole of escape! His memory retraced the conspiring hours which had led to this cul-de-sac—back over the entire stretch of events to that first night when he and the pseudo-Malabar had called upon the late Professor Caron.

Only a few weeks ago! Yet what a change! Professor Caron was dead—murdered! Mokra, Lamont's faithful Algerian butler, was dead—also foully murdered! The mummies and relics of the archæologist were gone. The golden scarab with its startling ruby was gone. Kellani, the Nubian servant of Caron—that silent brown slave out of the *Arabian Nights*—was a fugitive! "Dick Malabar" had vanished! Kent alone remained, and, according to Alceste, soon he too would be—gone!

What were they going to do with him? The closed automobile would arrive presently. Where would it take him?—to what fate? Was he to be spirited to some out-of-the-way spot and deliberately murdered like the others? Alceste had been free enough with his talk. How much of it was mere bluff?

Bluff! The man was a dare-devil! All through that tense scene between them he had sat there, smiling and bluffing, relying upon an empty gun to enforce his commands—aware all the time that if Kent had reached into that table drawer and possessed himself of the loaded weapon, the whole situation would have been altered in an eye-wink! Yet Alceste had made no move to eliminate the danger; he had been content to bluff it out, as if he revelled in hazards which another man would have hastened to avoid!

Or was it that because he was a past-master of psychology he trusted to mental control? For Alceste had not lied. He had not said that he had removed the cartridge-clip; he had merely *suggested* that Kent would hardly expect him to leave the gun loaded under the circumstances. He had been confident that Kent would accept the suggestion because no normal individual would act otherwise; to disarm an expected opponent was so palpably the thing to do, if possible. And, like a big fool, Kent had not reasoned clearly; he should have realized what was now very apparent: the fact of Alceste trying to stop him from opening the drawer was *proof* that the gun was *loaded!*

As the novelist's mind skipped back nimbly over the weeks during which Alceste had lived close to him under the guise of friendship, it was to marvel at the man's audacity. The masquerade at times had been edged with difficult situations which had been carried off in convincing manner. Not once had Alceste's

resourcefulness failed him or his sang-froid weakened. Even grant-
ing that the thing had been accomplished only by taking unfair
advantage of Kent's trust and friendship, nevertheless it had been
a daring venture, boldly piloted to success. Only by assuming an
identity which would be unquestioned by his enemies dared Alceste
return to New York. The heart of the enemy's camp he had chosen
as his safest retreat! He had forestalled suspicion by living and
working with the very man he most feared! That had required
nerve, and Kent conceded reluctant admiration.

The strategical advantages of the situation were at once apparent. Everything had played right into his enemy's hands! The visit
to Professor Caron, as Kent's sponsored friend, had put him at once
in touch with the object of his visit to America—the priceless golden
scarab ruby and the other jewels. To plan the theft had been easy;
it was Alceste who had suggested that the scarab be kept on the
premises instead of being placed at once in a safety-deposit vault—
that it be placed on the breast of the mummy, nice and handy for
him—that he should stand guard during the first half of the night!
No wonder he had said Kent was easy to fool and was nothing but
a bungler!

And with what consummate skill throughout the man had
played the role of Richard Malabar! To assume a warm, friendly
personality so foreign to his real self had required histrionic tal-
ent of a high order. He had made himself very agreeable, a charming
companion, a clever conversationalist, a man of taste and refinement! The kindly expression of his eyes—

Eyes! Not brown but blue! Alceste was not fool enough to ruin
his eyes for life! Of course not! Kent should have had sense enough
to suspect the truth—the use of a *fading* ink by Dr. MacMurrough
for the tattooing operation! And right over there in that chair the
impudent beggar had sat, calmly asking Kent how Alceste was to
be recognized if he did show up in New York, and never batting an
eye when Kent had explained in detail just why Alceste's "dam-
aged" brown eyes would require to be concealed behind dark-
coloured spectacles!—explained that Alceste was three inches
shorter than Malabar—

Something else Kent should not have relied upon—those carefully acquired measurements of Alceste on file at the Minaki Annex apartment! He should have remembered that this paranoiac stopped at nothing to obtain his ends—had once changed the colour of his eyes, had left charred evidence of his death to mislead Scotland Yard and, through them, make the world safe for a fresh start. A man who would knock his head against a stone gatepost to inflict wounds when wounds happened to be necessary to deceive—such a man would not overlook the advantage of increasing his height. It was so simply acquired by therapeutic stretching that Kent should have foreseen the possibility.

"It's just as he says; I have been the veriest child in his hands!" muttered the novelist in self-abasement.

"He has played with me at will from the first! He was meeting Naida—"

Naida! Wildly Kent's mind raced down this new avenue of surmise. In an agony he wrestled with the problem of the girl's part in the puzzle. Only for one heart-stopping moment did black doubt assail him; then he swept it aside impatiently. No matter what Alceste declared—no matter how appearances might point—he must believe in her. It was the one thing to which he clung. He *knew* she was all right—true blue. Those devils who had her in their power—any part she had played in the maze of events she had been *forced* to play. He must not allow crafty suggestion to mislead him a second time.

Those words of Alceste— "Affairs of which you have no inkling are coming to a swift and dangerous culmination!" What had he meant? Some drama altogether outside this Caron case?—a dire something, the evil roots of which reached backward into the past—into the East? Had it to do with that nebulous "Order of the Golden Scarab" which poor Caron had mentioned with bated breath? Alceste was involved in that somehow. "Dead he may be; but his evil lives after him!" had been Caron's comment—in the presence of Alceste himself! And Caron had been murdered within the next few hours!

Yet Alceste had denied angrily all knowledge of the murder, declaring that his hands were clean. Suppose that were true. Suppose Alceste himself were in the dark. He had been pale with worry that night when they rode homeward after their visit to the excited Professor. They had talked of Caron's evident fear and its cause; Alceste had admitted his belief that the golden scarab was at the bottom of it. In what way?

"God knows!" had been his solemn reply to that question.

But Alceste's mystification explained nothing. How had that magnificent ruby come into the Frenchman's possession? As with all such outstanding jewels, no doubt the shadows of dark deeds lurked upon the path it had travelled through time and distance. Here in New York it had come unexpectedly to light, and here in New York—almost immediately—its evil influence had been manifested. Had Alceste's interest in it been other than the mere theft of a valuable gem? Had he known it was on its way across the Atlantic and dared everything for some deeper purpose? And now the event—whatever it was—was coming to this "swift and dangerous culmination."

If it was an affair of which Addison Kent could have no inkling, what was the use in attempting to speculate upon it? He was travelling in a circle. Yet it intrigued him—worried him. Alceste was concerned in it; who else might be involved? Wasserhaus? Kellani? *Naida!* There was no telling what—no tell—

For a moment Addison Kent's thoughts came to a full stop. He sat there in blank astonishment, staring straight before him. He listened—listened for the slightest sound—listened for a repetition of the queer thing that had obtruded upon his vagrant attention. He was entirely alive to his immediate surroundings; for he was almost certain he had caught a slight sound that belonged outside that room.

Slowly he turned his head till he had full observation of Gridley. But that phlegmatic individual gave no evidence of having heard anything. He was still engrossed in the book—still munching apples. The plate was empty, Kent noticed, and Gridley's great teeth were just biting into the last red apple. No, *he* had heard nothing.

Yet Kent's ears were acute, and he was sure he had heard a sound out there on the portico somewhere—like the soft scrape of a boot upon the portico tiles—a heavy boot, placed with infinite caution. He watched the glass doors keenly, unwaveringly; but all he saw was the dimly red reflection—

No! Beyond that—out there in the blackness beyond—what was that point of light?—two points—three points of light—as if something out there caught gleam from the room? Scarcely breathing, he watched, watched. Then he realized that slowly these points of light were creeping closer and—in a moment—

His thrill of excitement increased. He knew now what it was—a pair of eyes and a row of white teeth beneath! But they seemed to be disembodied—to be floating in the dark without a face to make them human!

Then he saw the face! It was coming nearer. Presently it was being pressed against one of the little bevelled panes of glass. The eyes rolled as the man quickly surveyed the room within. And the face was swarthy—black—negroid! Upon the large head was an old hat such as seamen wear.

Astounded, Kent stared. He could not believe his eyes! Was he dreaming? Yet there was no mistake! *It was Kellani!*—the huge Nubian who had fled from the house the night Mokra was murdered—the man for whom the whole police machine had combed the city in vain!—Kellani himself, widely grinning now—grinning in at him and suddenly signalling him, warning silence!

25
Open Sesame!

I

Kellani!—alive and in New York!—back here at the very scene of the murder for which he was "wanted" by the police! They were searching for him everywhere. How had he escaped them? Why did he come here in the night to the Lamont residence, of all places? Was he friend or foe?

The sight of those large rolling black eyes in that negroid face out there in the dark had startled Addison Kent. It took him a few minutes to recover from the sudden thrusting upon him of an identity so unexpected and almost uncanny. From the first this mountainous bronze creature had seemed like some slave from the *Arabian Nights*—a genie—bizarre, theatrical. He had vanished the night of the storm as if upon a magic carpet; he reappeared now as if summoned from the air by the rubbing of a magic Aladdin's lamp!

After his first astonishment Kent began to think quickly. The friendliness of the Nubian's grin seemed genuine enough. At a glance he had taken in the situation, and it was evident from his actions that he intended to do something about it. Hence his warning for Kent to remain silent. The novelist waited, not a little curious as to the procedure Kellani would adopt.

The swarthy face had vanished. Not a sound revealed the presence of an intruder. The Nubian was familiar with the Lamont mansion, and it was likely he would attempt to gain admittance through a basement entry in the deserted servants' wing. In that case he might be expected to approach the library silently from the inside.

433

Kent yawned noisily. Without seeming to do so intentionally, he managed to shift his chair slightly, so that the archway into the hall came within his line of vision. At the movement Gridley looked up from his book and grinned across the white apple-core poised in his hand.

"Gettin' tired, Kent? We won't be on the move till about an hour from now, I guess; so there's time for another of those nice naps of yours. Say, those apples were great! You don't know what you're missing—"

"Might poke up the fire a little, Gridley, if you don't mind," Kent suggested.

"Not a bad idea at that," conceded Gridley as he rose, luxuriating in a satisfying stretch. "Beats all how cramped a fellow gets, just sitting, don't it?"

He stepped to the fireplace and with the brass tongs stirred the coals and added a lump of fresh fuel.

Kent threw a swift glance towards the archway. Yes, Kellani was there! Leaning out from the concealment of the portières, the Nubian flashed a signal which Kent answered with a nod of understanding.

"I have been studying that wonderful painting up there above the mantel, Gridley," he remarked in an intimate, interested way. "I've looked at that Turner many times; but I do not believe I fully appreciated it before. Perhaps the subdued lighting is just right for it. Come here. Take a good long look at it— No, stand over there and you'll get it at a better angle! I want you to tell me, now, if you don't agree with me that the colour tones of that sunset are simply marvellous. They seem almost the real thing, don't they?"

Flattered by the respectful tone in which Addison Kent was deferring to his judgment upon this artistic matter, Gridley cleared his throat importantly and stood with legs apart, gazing up at the canvas with his head inclined critically to one side.

But his judgment was never pronounced! Creeping with the stealth of a leopard, the Nubian crossed the intervening space— and was upon him! Not with a rush and a jump—just a quiet contact of his body against his victim's back, followed by a quick double twist which interlocked the two bodies in an immovable embrace.

Gridley was no weakling. His amazement, however, was so complete that for a moment he just stood there. Then when he summoned his muscles to action he found himself as helpless as if wedged in a vice. About his legs were twined legs more powerful than his; his arms had been drawn up behind his back and interlocked there as by a bolt of muscular iron. He could not move! He had been grasped in such a way that any increased pressure produced sharp, penetrating pain, as if a nerve centre were impinged. Perspiration stood out upon his forehead.

Then he saw the great brown hand, with fingers spread, advancing up his chest towards his throat, and he opened his mouth to voice his panic. But the fingers darted in, closing his windpipe in a throttling grip, so that only a mere gurgle escaped.

Kellani looked over his shoulder and grinned reassuringly at Addison Kent. There was so much calm confidence in that grin— the mahogany countenance was so impassive that for a little Kent scarcely realized what was happening. Gridley's eyes were protruding and his face had blackened before the novelist perceived that the man was being slowly but surely choked to death!

Kent's cry of protest was ignored. Kellani continued to grin. Not until the big body of the butler went limp did the Nubian remove his strangling clutch. With the untangling of the limbs Gridley's body slumped to the floor and rolled over inertly like a sack of meal.

"You've killed him!" gasped Kent, staring down in horror.

"No, sidi," murmured Kellani quietly, already busy with the knots of the lariat. "Soon the breath of life will come again into the son of a dog! There is need for haste, master."

II

He spoke in Arabic, a language Addison Kent understood better than he could talk. Kellani's French, on the other hand, was poor, Kent remembered, although the Nubian seemed to understand well enough what was said to him in that language. Between the two, they should be able to get along satisfactorily.

There was a lot of talking to do. Kent had many questions to ask, and Kellani seemed to evince anxiety that no time be lost. He already had lifted the unconscious Gridley from the floor to the chair Kent had just vacated and, using the same lariat, was rapidly trussing the plastic butler securely while the novelist stamped about the library, kicking his legs and swinging his arms to restore them to normal state. By the time Kellani's task was completed, Gridley was showing signs of coming back to a full knowledge of life's vicissitudes. The Nubian lifted the chair with its human freight as if it had been a roped bundle for a camel's back; he stood with it perched high on one powerful shoulder and looked enquiringly at Kent.

"Where do you want this viper put, sidi?"

"We'll stick him down cellar—in the furnace room—where he will be out of earshot," was the novelist's prompt decision, and forthwith the human package was transported there like a sack of apples and deposited with a thump.

"There is much to say, sidi, and many things to do before the coming up of the sun," Kellani began as soon as they were back in the library. "This night is possessed by deeds of black devils! Allah save us from evil! I have come far and by shadowed ways to bring you my message, master. I come from the Daughter of the Morning—from the Little Lady who is as beautiful as morning light across the sands. She bids you make haste to join her."

"What—what the devil are you trying to say?" puzzled Kent. "Where have you been hiding? On some vessel? Is that why you are wearing these sailor togs? How did you get here? What brings you?"

"Allah is great and good!" smiled Kellani. "I have been held in bondage, sidi. I have escaped by swimming through troubled waters. See, I have been very wet! The Little Lady, whose face of beauty is the reflection of a beautiful heart, was kind to me and helped me to escape. She sent me here to find you, master. She is known to you as Naida, and may Allah preserve—"

"What!" Kent seized the Nubian's great arm and regarded him with imperative eyes. "Naida! You say *Naida* sent you? You know where she is? Speak, man!"

"Her eyes that are like the morning star—"

"Speak!" commanded Kent impatiently. "Where is she?"

"—will be clouded over, sidi, unless we reach the ship before the day falls," finished Kellani composedly.

"The ship? What ship?" Then he knew! "You mean the *Albatross?*—Wasserhaus?—he has taken her there?"

"Yes, sidi, even so has it come to pass."

For just an instant Addison Kent eyed the Nubian keenly, searching the inscrutable brown face for possible trickery. But a few direct questions dispelled all doubts; Kellani knew the facts of Kent's narrow escape from his enemies through the underground passage with Naida—things which only Naida could have told him.

"Let me get this straight, Kellani. You saw her brought aboard the *Albatross* by Wasserhaus himself. You have been on that vessel ever since the night you ran away from this house. You had been seized by Wasserhaus and his gang because you knew too much, and you were taken out there for safe-keeping—locked up— a prisoner. Naida was considered safe, once on the ship, and was allowed to move freely about the vessel. She found out you were a prisoner and assisted you to escape. She sent you to me, and you got away from the vessel and were picked up by a tug and brought to the waterfront. There you boarded a river boat and came up the Hudson to a point above here, landed and came down to Westchester from the north after dark. Is that correct?"

"Yes, sidi."

"You know the location of the *Albatross* now?"

"Yes, sidi."

"And can take me there?"

"Yes, sidi."

"Why did you run away from here the night Mokra was killed? Do you know that the police are trying to find you, and that if they do, you will be arrested for—murder?"

The Nubian's eyes looked frankly back at him.

"I did not kill Mokra," he stated evenly. "I went away because it was so commanded and I was afraid, sidi, to disobey. Knowledge had not been opened to me then; but I have learned since." A flicker of hate gleamed in his eyes—and was gone again. "By the grace of

Allah, I go from here, master, to bring punishment upon the man
who killed Mokra! Time presses, sidi."

"And who is that, Kellani? Wasserhaus? It was Wasserhaus who
killed Mokra that night?"

"Yes, sidi. But the man's real name is not Wasserhaus. In the
East he is known as Von Strom—Ludwig Von Strom!"

III

As Kellani said, time was pressing. Questions would have to
wait. Action! Action! Tingling with the prospect, Addison Kent
sprang to the telephone. Already his clear-thinking brain was can-
vassing the situation swiftly—gauging the hazards, discarding,
deciding. The sudden turn of the wheel which had lifted him out of
dark despondency had elevated him to pinnacles of hope. Naida
had sent for him, and he was going to her! Youth sang in his veins
as he responded to the call.

In a fever of impatience he fumed at the delay in getting telephone connection. He wanted Pomereski, and he wanted him at
once. Pomereski might be asleep—might be out—might be— Ah,
the luck had changed! Pomereski's voice came over the wire com-
municating with the Pole's personal quarters—his bedroom.

Rapidly Addison Kent made enquiries and issued instructions.
No, Slipper Dagg and his men had not left yet; but they would be
starting in an hour from now. Yes, Pomereski knew where to find
him. Yes, Pomereski thought it could be arranged.

Kent swung from the telephone.

"The servants are all away, Kellani. Out in the garage—the Sedan—I'll drive it myself. It is the quickest way—and safest. You
can tell me the rest as we travel. Are you armed?"

With a slow smile the Nubian thrust a hand under his jersey
and produced a long dagger with a curved point. It gleamed wickedly in the fireshine. Kent shook his head.

"You'll need a gun. Wait!"

Upstairs to his room he raced, three steps at a time. He slipped
on a sweater, kicked off his shoes, pulled on his golf boots and

snatched a cap from a hook. He strapped on a loaded police automatic in its holster, thrust a spare revolver into his pocket and, with a large package of cartridges in his hand, plunged downstairs again.

Down to the cellar to take a look at Gridley! The butler had recovered consciousness, and glared sullenly up at him.

"Your friends will be along soon, Gridley. You will hardly be able to attract their attention down here. The servants will look after you later on. I am leaving a note for Sandy, who will hand you over to the police in due course. You are too full of apples to need anything to eat!"

He slammed the furnace-room door behind him and locked it. Out in the garage he measured the gasoline in the tank of the Sedan, scribbled a note to Sandy in explanation and pinned this to a post where the gardener could not fail to see it as soon as he opened the door.

A moment later they were rolling out between the stone gate-posts—and shot away with roaring engine splitting the night.

26
From the Valley of Whispers

The hands of the little clock under its tiny electric bulb beside the speedometer pointed 2.40. At 3.45 Slipper Dagg and his men would be putting out to sea. Fastest going by the shortest route to the rendezvous mentioned by Pomereski would eat up at least three-quarters of an hour. Twenty minutes' leeway—that was all!

Addison Kent stepped on the accelerator as they swung a corner into Westchester Avenue. They tore across Westchester Creek. At that hour the streets were deserted, and through Westchester Square they sped without a check. If a policeman stopped them, the novelist had only to show his badge; Kent explained this to the Nubian and instructed him to drop to the floor of the Sedan if necessary, and cover up with the plaid rugs. The danger of recognition was not great; but it was as well to take no chances of the delay which an argument would entail. They rolled swiftly over the Bronx Bridge and headed south-west towards Third Avenue at East Hundred-and-Fiftieth Street.

"Now talk, Kellani. I want the whole story of your connection with this man Wasserhaus, or Von Strom. Be quick!"

In the Nubian's large black eyes glowed quiet admiration for this friend at the wheel of the flying car—the man who knew how to get to places quickly, how to handle policemen, how to command the situation and bring them both out of all difficulties. The beautiful "Daughter of the Morning," as Kellani had named her, had said this gentleman was good and brave, and Kellani was glad

440

to obey him. With straightforward simplicity the brown giant from the distant Nile country told all that he knew.

Nor in the telling did he attempt to spare himself condemnation for the evil ways into which he had fallen through association with low companions in Cairo. He had drifted so gradually from one thing to another that he had come under the power of Ludwig Von Strom before he realized what it all meant—when it was too late to turn back; for Von Strom had seemed to take a special delight in bringing about Kellani's final subjugation. Perhaps he had coveted the Nubian's great physical development as an addition to the fighting strength of his robber band.

That was what they were, as Kellani soon discovered—brigands who waylaid and robbed and sometimes killed. As a mere recruit in crime the brown giant had not been admitted to the inner circle of his new associates; he had first to be tested and to prove his qualifications for such honour. So it came about that, as his initiation, the Nubian was assigned the task of getting Professor Emil Caron into the toils.

What Von Strom's object was in approaching the inoffensive archæologist, Kellani did not stop to enquire. He did as he was told—blindly, intent only upon pleasing Von Strom. His instructions were to obtain employment with Professor Caron, making himself so useful that the preoccupied little Frenchman gradually would come to rely upon him more and more for the execution of bothersome details.

So efficient had Kellani proved himself that by the time the Frenchman was ready to undertake his planned journey into the desert in search of rock inscriptions, the Nubian was entrusted with most of the preparations. This included the hiring of the cameleers and all caravan arrangements.

Von Strom had told him to bribe the guides to run off with all but two camels and most of the equipment, leaving Kellani and Professor Caron alone in the desert, to all appearance lost. Kellani had desert experience, and, while pretending not to know his way, he was to "wander" to a certain valley where Von Strom and his men would be waiting.

No harm was intended, the German had assured Kellani. It was merely that the leader of the brigands had important business to transact with the archæologist—business so very confidential that none must know of it. The clever lies he told were not discovered to be lies by the trusting Nubian until long afterward.

The valley which Kellani was to seek was difficult to find—a dire, far-off place of unknown voices which for ever whispered among the rocks—echoes which cried and groaned and fell suddenly silent, only to break out again in mad laughter. A place of terror in very truth when the blue shadows crept into the hollows while the barren hilltops stood out black against the red dusk— most terrible of all when the stars burned big and bright in the deep cavern of the night and bats fluttered and flopped, and gloomy owls hooted answer to wailing hyenas on distant ridges of the desert! Kellani had been to this Valley of Whispers once before, and he was afraid.

Yet he tried to find it. But for a time they had been actually lost; so that the supply of water gave out, and the last of that journey had been a nightmare for both Kellani and the archæologist. When only a drink was left in the goatskin water-bottle, Professor Caron had insisted upon Kellani taking it; Kellani was a big man who needed more water than a little man, he argued, and also it was upon Kellani that hope of rescue depended. In that extremity the two men—the white and the brown—had looked long into each other's faces, and it was then that there had been lighted in the breast of the simple Nubian the fires of an undying affection for the Frenchman who was at once master and friend.

More by good luck than anything else, Kellani finally discovered the right direction, and, half dead with thirst, they had reached the Valley of Whispers and had been taken to the camp of the brigands, where Von Strom hastened to allay the fears of Professor Caron by overtures of friendship. When they had rested and recovered from the effects of their experience, long talks took place between Von Strom and the Frenchman. Then one day the two of them rode away from the valley alone, the archæologist with a bandage over his eyes. Kellani was ordered to remain behind; but did so with some misgivings.

At the end of seven days both rode back into the valley, and Professor Caron's eyes were still bandaged, as if to conceal from him the location of the valley. Kellani was overjoyed to see him again. Where they had gone he did not know; it was enough that his master was back again, apparently in his usual good health.

Yet there had been a difference which, after a few days, began to puzzle Kellani. He thought that his master was afraid of something. There was a hunted look in the little Professor's eyes at times—a look which he hastened to conceal. Apparently he was in the best of spirits, and his merry laugh rang out in Von Strom's tent frequently. Nevertheless—

Then Kellani learned that his master was about to leave for America—that far-off country of which so much was heard from the American tourists who flocked about the bazaars of Cairo with so much money to throw around. To his great delight Kellani was told by Von Strom that he was to go along with Professor Caron to the wonderful new land far across the ocean. The news filled him with so much happiness that all things suddenly appeared good, and he only half listened to what Von Strom told him in secret regarding his special duties of watching that Professor Caron made delivery of certain things that were to be entrusted to his care.

After several days of preparation came the transfer of some strange bundles to the shores of the Red Sea, and one night they were conveyed in a felucca to an Arab dhow, which had waited off a lonely section of the barren coast. Silence and secrecy were maintained, for fear of revenue men; but no interruption occurred, and they finally sailed away in the dhow. Von Strom went along with them—to see them safely aboard the liner, he announced.

This did not take place for some time, however, as they had to beat down the coast. In leisurely and somewhat stealthy fashion they eventually reached their destination and took passage to America. All the way over Professor Caron had been ill with seasickness, and Kellani had noticed again at times the strange fear in his eyes, particularly after they reached New York. Kellani himself had begun to feel afraid without knowing why, and the sudden appearance of Von Strom upon the scene—calling upon his master in the middle of the night—had terrified him. Von Strom secretly had boarded the same liner after bidding them good-bye! Why? Kellani had become afraid of him.

Next morning he had found his master, dead. Kellani was sure that Von Strom had something to do with it, but in what way he could not understand. In this strange country the Nubian had distrusted everyone, and he had not been truthful when questioned by Addison Kent because in his fear he did not understand that Kent was the friend of his master and was only trying to find and punish the one guilty of his master's death.

Von Strom had come again the next night and had threatened Kellani with death if he did not do exactly as he was told. Von Strom was in an ugly mood, and ordered him to leave the house at once and join him. The Nubian had been afraid to disobey, and he had carried out instructions, only to be seized and chloroformed by the German's men and hustled on board a launch. When he came to his senses they were on their way to the *Albatross*, which was anchored well out to sea, off the New Jersey coast. Once on the ship, Kellani had been roughly handled and promptly locked up in the forepeak of the vessel, where he had been held prisoner and treated like a dog.

After Von Strom—or "Wasserhaus," as he was now calling himself—left the vessel Kellani had been more kindly treated by the crew in the matter of food; he had been allowed even out on deck to stretch his limbs, being taken back to the paint-locker whenever a boat approached within hailing distance.

Thus had the days lagged, until Von Strom unexpectedly returned to the *Albatross*, not long after sunrise, bringing with him the beautiful young lady. Through a grating Kellani had observed them, and from the closeness with which the German was watching her and the haughty manner in which she disdained his overtures, it was evident that the young woman was not there of her own free will. The captain argued over the arrival of this new passenger; but he was in the pay of Von Strom, and a cabin in the waist was allotted to her. She dined with the officers in the saloon and afterwards seemed to be allowed the freedom of the vessel, inasmuch as she could hardly plunge over the side and escape in broad daylight.

All that day activity on board had increased, as if the *Albatross* would up anchor shortly and put to sea. By this time Kellani had learned, among other things, that the vessel carried liquor in her hold, and from the air of expectancy aboard, he was satisfied that an effort to land this cargo was about to be made.

Under cover of the general preoccupation the Little Lady, who already had discovered him and had talked to him secretly through the grating, carried out her plans for Kellani's escape. Shortly after nightfall, when a lighter hailed them and drew in on the lee-ward side, she reappeared and slipped him a key which she had obtained somehow from the steward. During the confusion of trans-ferring cargo to the lighter, and while interest was centred on the "hams" of liquor-cases passing over the leeward side, Kellani had escaped, leaving the key on the outside of the lock, as instructed, in order that the Little Lady could secure it and return it to the steward.

Silently he lowered himself by a rope over the bow, where a sail had been stretched to hide the name of the vessel. He swam quietly along the windward side to the stern, where a quarterboat which the deck boys had been using while red-leading the hull still swung under the counter by a painter. To climb into this, cut adrift and float off into the heaving blackness of the water had required but a minute. Presently he had paddled far enough from the *Alba-tross* to unship the oars and start on his fifteen-mile pull for the shore.

When he set out it was still comparatively early in the evening. The sky was overcast, and after about an hour's steady rowing he was almost run down in the darkness by an inbound tug. The quarterboat had fouled a trailing cable from the stern of the tug, and Kellani had been quick to make fast to it; so that he had been towed in most of the distance, thereby gaining much valuable time.

Such was the Nubian's recital, prompted by occasional ques-tions from his interested auditor. He was unable to give Addison

Kent further particulars as to the plans of Von Strom or the activities aboard the *Albatross*, except to say that he believed the vessel would weigh anchor not long after daybreak. For what port she would lay a course he did not know.

"Am I to understand, then, that you have not known at any time, and do not know even yet, what it was that Von Strom entrusted to Professor Caron for delivery in New York, or where it was to be delivered?"

"I know not, sidi."

"Neither Von Strom nor your master ever made mention to you of the place to which they journeyed from this Valley of Whispers, or what happened between them to make your master so afraid?"

"No, sidi."

"Did you ever hear of the golden scarab, Kellani?"

"Yes, sidi. It is the sign of the secret council to which only the elect gain entrance."

"Sort of secret society?"

"Yes, sidi. In the East it is talked of only in whispers by a few who know of it."

"Why in whispers?"

"Because it deals out death, sidi, to those whose tongues become loose."

"Von Strom was a member; and your late master—did you ever suspect that he had become a member of this ring of thieves, Kellani?"

"No, sidi. He was a good man."

"Of course. And you are telling me the full truth now—not holding back anything because you are afraid to speak?"

"No, master. You are my friend, and I have nothing to fear. I have told you all I know. I seek only to avenge my beloved master's death."

"You are sure he was killed, then?"

"Yes, sidi. But how it was done—that I know not."

"By Von Strom?"

"His hand is red with wickedness! He is a shaitan!"

"A live beetle, Kellani—what does that mean to the members of this golden scarab society?"

"It is the warning of the death decree, sidi."

"Quite so. Did you know that a live beetle dropped off the table in front of your master not many hours before he was murdered—while we were visiting him, in fact?"

"No, sidi, that I did not know!" A sharp intake of breath was the only sign the Nubian made that he was disturbed.

"You did not—well, throw it into the library yourself, then?"

"By Allah, no! Does my friend think that Kellani is lying?"

"No, Kellani. But it is very strange—a large June bug on the table! Your master was badly frightened by it, Kellani."

"Allah have mercy! I do not associate with bugs, sidi! Does a servant who loves his master send him sentence of death? Allah! Allah!"

"It must have fallen from the curtains," nodded Kent thoughtfully. "One other thing is puzzling me, Kellani, and there is little time now for explanation so that you can understand why I ask these questions. Later I will tell you. Von Strom must have known there was a roulette wheel at the Lamont place; but how could he have found that out? You understand what I mean by a roulette wheel?"

"Yes, sidi—the spin of fortune by which men lose many *mithcals* of gold. I heard talk of it when the master met Lamont Effendi in Cairo—a roulette wheel not like those used now, sidi—very old but very strong."

"Ah, so that's it! Lamont told Professor Caron all about this wonderful old roulette wheel he had here in New York? And you reported this to Von Strom?"

"Yes, sidi. The devil's dog asked many questions about this meeting between the two gentlemen, and I told him what was said."

"Kismet!" muttered Addison Kent as he bent over the steering-wheel.

27
"Yo-ho-ho and a Bottle of Rum!"

I

The sea-going tug *Nancy B* churned steadily through the darkness, outward bound. The lights of New York threw a luminous penumbra in the sky eighteen miles astern, where Bartholdi's statue of "Liberty Enlightening the World" on Bedloe's Island held her tall torch against a thin mist that was drifting in from the Atlantic. Just ahead the white blaze of Sandy Hook Beacon smeared the black water at the entrance to the lower bay, and beyond Ambrose Lightship the ocean swell heaved slowly in out of the night.

Dawn was not far off, but as yet it was pitch dark and cold. The spray which occasionally flew at the bow as the tug dipped and rounded Sandy Hook Point froze where it struck. Except for her running-lights, red, green and white, and an occasional glow in the engine-room, the *Nancy B*, with a plume of black smoke trailing from her funnel, was but a shadow, headed south-west. With the stealth of a thief in the night she slipped to sea and vanished into the darkness that walled in every coast light from Sandy Hook to Fire Island.

Innocent enough her appearance—a tug setting forth to pick up an early morning tow. But beneath the tarpaulins, heaped so carelessly abaft the deckhouse, lay a shivering huddle of cursing humanity in blue jerseys and sailor caps—masquerade seamen— ten carefully picked gunmen from the New York underworld, friends of Slipper Dagg, eager to join in any mad hazard which promised sufficient return for the risk and discomfort. And piracy on the high seas—nothing less!—was the mission on which the *Nancy B* was tossing away into the blackness towards open water!

As Addison Kent watched the lean, alert face of the Slipper, standing in oilskins beside the man at the wheel, he marvelled. Addison Kent, forsooth! writer of popular detective stories, sometime associate of the Bureau of Criminal Investigation, friend and confidant of the Police Commissioner himself, of the District Attorney! Here was he on board this tug, companion of notorious gunmen, outward bound on an expedition that belonged in the repertoire of the late redoubtable Captain Kidd!

Madness! Under the excitement and strain of the night's events he had not realized fully into what he was heading. True, he had made it very plain to Slipper Dagg that his presence must not be misconstrued as offering either official approval or police protection in the lawless venture upon which Dagg and his men were embarking. The matter was entirely personal. He had explained frankly the urgency of his visit to the *Albatross*; he could not seek help through official channels without involving the young lady he was trying to rescue in an awkward tangle with the authorities. Forced to act independently and secretly, and knowing of the expedition which was setting forth for the very destination he must reach in the shortest possible time, he had asked merely to be taken along as a passenger who would attend strictly to his own business once aboard the rum carrier.

That had been how he explained it. And Slipper Dagg, wise in his day and generation, had listened with a faint smile at the corners of his wide, humorous mouth—had looked at the huge Kellani, just ashore from the very vessel they sought—had then studied his watch and grinned widely as he nodded assent. For he knew that Addison Kent would keep his promise not to interfere, and Slipper Dagg was not unmindful of past favours. Besides, if "the rib" was "wanted" and Kent was trying to save her from the police—that was enough!

A hand pulled at the novelist's coat-sleeve, and he found the Nubian beside him.

"We must reach the ship, master, before the day falls," spoke Kellani with a trace of anxiety. He pointed. "More over that way— and faster. We are still far from the ship."

Addison Kent's face cleared and his jaws set resolutely. This had been the only way to reach Naida in time, and it was not for him to hesitate, but to go through with it without questioning the means to the end. Naida must come first. He stepped forward and repeated to Dagg what Kellani had said.

Promptly the *Nancy B* swung off two points to starboard, and the rhythmic beat of her engine quickened to the signal for full speed ahead.

II

Braced against the side of the deckhouse, Kent pulled his sou'wester tighter upon his head, restless under the enforced inactivity. Out there somewhere across the tossing water in the blackness she was waiting—waiting for him—depending upon him— Naida! She had sent for him in the hour of danger and difficulty, and he was coming—coming closer to her with every throb of this fast, strong tug. But there was need for speed. God alone knew in what extremity he would find her or what the next few hours held in store

Pomereski had met them with oilskins and sea-boots. He had wanted to come along; but Kent had ordered him back. Following their raid on the *Albatross*, Dagg planned to be set ashore with his men opposite the scene of the operation; the gangsters would scatter, finding their way back to their New York haunts one by one or by twos and threes. So that, if everything went all right, Kent, Naida and Kellani could return safely on the *Nancy B* without attracting unwelcome attention.

If everything went all right? That was just it! On a desperate adventure like this any number of things might go wrong, and Addison Kent wanted Pomereski in reserve for emergencies. If the Pole did not hear from Kent by a given hour he was to report immediately to Inspector Lowry at Police Headquarters and start official action.

For there was Wasserhaus—Ludwig Von Strom—to consider. The man was a criminal of the worst type, who would hesitate not an instant to go to any lengths for revenge if the cards played into his hands. Out here at sea, beyond territorial waters, he could laugh at United States revenue cutters and coastguard boats. Boarded by modern pirates—hijackers—he would be free to fight with every gun at his command. The problem of bringing him within reach of the New York police on a charge of murder seemed insurmountable—unless Kent kidnapped his man without regard to complications.

But Naida first! Nothing mattered so much as her safety. If Von Strom had dared— Kent gritted his teeth as he fought torturing thoughts. Aboard that vessel there must be some real men who would not permit—good Canadian sailor men—men of Lunenburg—salt-bitten young Nova Scotian fishermen, long-limbed, fearing neither man nor devil, yet holding womankind in respect—Kent knew them, and he found solace in the thought that the *Albatross* was manned by such a crew. They would turn on the German and his gunmen if need arose—laugh in the face of any odds.

A Canadian vessel, the *Albatross*—steel coaster, 24-foot beam, 2,000 tons—chartered by Von Strom, *alias* Wasserhaus, upon the recommendation of Singer Lieb. That much Kent had learned from Slipper Dagg. Apparently the proprietor of the Café Belgique had joined the German in some sort of deal for this cargo of liquor which was being run ashore. But, aside from all financial speculations, Addison Kent knew that Von Strom's real reason for chartering the vessel was to provide a base from which to carry out the special object of the visit to New York.

Why had Von Strom followed Professor Caron from Egypt? Why had he killed the Frenchman? He had been after the golden scarab ruby and the other jewels, of course; but where did he stand in connection with those "affairs of which you have no inkling" which Alceste had intimated were coming to a "swift and dangerous culmination"?

Deliberately Kent drew mental rein. He had been over that ground already without result, and just now there were other things

to consider. The next hour or two would be crowded with very definite action—a serious fight between rival gunmen, certain to result in bloodshed. No quarter would be given on either side.

In his slow, humorous way, Slipper Dagg had admitted that he
and his men were gambling their lives on the issue. What concerned
them most was the strength of the enemy. Dagg mustered enough
men to take care of the rival gunmen unless, as he half suspected,
Berlin Harry was planning to "double-cross" his employer. In that
case, it would be quite within the possibilities that additional men
had been smuggled aboard the *Albatross* when the rum-running
lighter had gone out for its cargo of liquor.

"You mean that Berlin Harry would turn hijacker himself and
rob Wasserhaus after the money was paid over for the cargo!" Kent
had asked with interest.

"You've said it," the Slipper had confirmed tersely. "There's on'y
one guy that bird ain't double-crossin', an,' that's himself An'
knowin' him for what he is, I can't seem to see him sittin' around,
suckin' his thumb beside a hundred grand, when all he's got to do
is to reach out an' grab the dough!"

"But this man Wasserhaus—what about the crew?"

"Ain't likely they'd butt in on what ain't any o' their funeral.
An' out here on the blue an' boundin' deep there ain't nobody goin'
to holler' 'Cop!'"

"'One hundred grand'—you mean one hundred thousand dollars? Would there be that much money on board?"

"Thinkin' we was comin' out here for our *health?*" grinned Dagg.
"This ain't no piker's game o' penny-ante we're sittin' in on, brother
We takes our chances o' gettin' plugged; but not for a nickel! Why,
say, a hundred grand ain't more'n half what some o' these birds
sails away with. Figure it out. Booze is sellin' at fifty a case out
here on 'The Row,' and the guys runnin' it ashore gets another
twenty on top o' that. How many cases in a shipload? Say, I know
some guys—" and Slipper Dagg spoke feelingly of certain hijacking windfalls which were breath-taking.

For not yet had the magnitude of the trade in illicit liquor attracted the powerful cliques into whose hands it was destined to
pass; not yet had it been organized, systematized and financed for

protection on a scale which insured against depredation. The business was done cash down on the spot; huge sums changed hands at times, and quick fortunes were being made. With so much money lying around it was an opportunity for "stick-up" men which was too good to be overlooked; so that the hijacker, as he was called, was soon preying upon the bootlegger who handled the liquor, in spite of secret service men, Federal Prohibition enforcement officers, and all the machinery hastily organized to cope with the situation.

Desperate running fights between the opposing forces were of daily record in the newspapers. Across the Canadian border high-powered automobiles sped madly along the highways, heavily laden with liquid contraband, while automatic pistols spat death and defiance. Drivers of seized truck-loads were waylaid and knocked on the head. Trickery, treachery, open bribery and murder kept company with the penetration of the traffic from seaport to the farthest interior; liquor could be obtained by anyone with the price, anywhere, at any time. Lured by huge profits, "easy money," young men who might have hesitated to break a law which they respected were carried away by the "adventure" and excitement; there were always men ready to hazard the trip, just as there was always a supply of liquor off shore—just as always ships floated on water and grain grew in the sunshine.

At seaports "times" were "good." Poorest fishermen, oystermen and beachcombers were finding profitable employment unloading the "rum" ships. Volunteer excise men became easy victims of the "fixers" who accompanied the drivers of the trucks which loaded whiskey along the waterfronts. Powerful motor-boats with airplane engines equipped with special mufflers spent the day in isolated rivers and coves, tuning up for their trip to the nearest "Rum Row" in the night, ten miles outside the three-mile limit fixed by the Supreme Court as the deadline. Government patrol boats with sharpshooters on the look-out sought to intercept the rum-runners inside the prescribed area in their dash for shore.

It was warfare in grim earnest. Addison Kent had been aware of the conditions; but he had not realized fully the cold facts that underlay the newspaper stories. He remembered the vessel which had been found recently with her decks splintered by machine-gun fire and littered with rifle-shells, her cabins battered and disordered, her hold looted and a notebook found which recorded liquor sales—nearly four thousand cases, valued at $190,000. She had been raided by hijackers and her crew ruthlessly slain!

It was real!—as real as those murderous, callous gunmen aft within a biscuit toss of where he stood, even now crawling out from concealment of the tarpaulins and examining their weapons with muttered curses! It had been a night of unbelievable realities. What was to be the climax that awaited fulfilment within the hour?

And as the gravity of the situation was impressed upon him more fully, Addison Kent was thankful that he was on board this piratical tug—thankful that he was there to protect Naida from the dangers which were about to break loose on all sides of her. His face was set and resolute as he carefully examined his own automatic.

III

A light off the port bow! Dim, blurred through the mist it showed—the riding-light of some anchored vessel. At once aboard the *Nancy B* the tension grew—low-spoken orders, and all lights on the tug were obliterated; she changed her course slightly, slipping through the water with undiminished speed, merely a blacker shadow in the darkness.

"That'll be one o' them Gloucester fishin' smacks on Rum Row," Slipper Dagg vouchsafed confidently. "They carry two thousand cases apiece for a syndicate that has 'em under contract. We're due to be alongside them about now. Keep well off to the right, cap. There's a flock o' them schooners anchored within half a mile o' each other, an' they're layin' south right along the coast to about twelve miles east o' Seabright. We got to kick free o' them, an' the big bird we want ought to be off by itself a couple o' miles farther on."

It was evident that Slipper Dagg knew what he was about. He stepped aft to look over his gang, and Kent could hear him carefully emphasizing instructions. The deliberateness of the whole thing was appalling—vicious rats of the underworld, stealing in upon their victim to kill or to be killed—for a riffle of ill-gotten money! It seemed good to Kent to note the great bulk of the simple Nubian from the far-off desert spaces presently looming beside him at the rail.

"The day is not long away, sidi," muttered Kellani.

Kent peered eastward and did indeed imagine a faint change in the depth of the blackness.

"We are getting close to the *Albatross* now," he reassured.

"Yes, sidi."

"Kellani!"

"Yes, sidi?"

"Remember what I have said about Von Strom—the law must take its course. I want him—"

"Yes, sidi."

"*Alive*, Kellani! You understand? Answer me!"

"Yes, sidi."

"And we are not concerned with this murderous rabble. We keep out of the fight—unless attacked. We are here to rescue the Little Lady."

"May her day be blessed!" murmured Kellani.

They fell silent. It was quiet now on board the *Nancy B*; the only sounds were the swirl of the water at her bow and the dull regular beat of the propeller, churning under the counter. Time passed. Occasionally off in the mist a faint speck of light swam in view for a moment or two and passed astern. Presently the Nubian's hand touched the novelist on the shoulder, and over the port bow Addison Kent saw dim lights that floated slowly towards them out of the distance—a green light, a red light, a white anchor light on a foremast, a black mass of shadow that blotted out the vague grayness eastward.

The tug's propeller stopped, then resumed—a slow beat that was scarcely audible. It stopped again. Not a sound as they floated in the dark, lifting slowly to the ocean swell—nothing but the faint washings of the black water.

"His Nibs is sure about that sea-ladder bein' down, is he?" Kent was startled by Slipper Dagg's hoarse whisper at his elbow. "We'll stop right here an' send the skiff ahead to give her the once-over.

We got to put a crimp in the look-out before we can make a break, an' we got to work fast, believe me." He was gone in the dark before the novelist could reply.

Whisperings aft where shadowy forms clustered. The skiff that had ridden the comber behind the tug was drawn alongside. Three men stepped in, the painter was flung free and they vanished into the gloom.

During the wait that followed Addison Kent strained his eyes towards the vague outline of the *Albatross*, riding at anchor not far away; but all he could discern was a deeper blackness that bulked on the water. She was, he knew, a steel freighter of 2,000 tons—the usual type, with well-deck fore and aft, two steel masts, a single funnel and deck cabins in the waist; storage rooms in the forepeak and "fo'c'sle" quarters for the crew under the poop-deck astern. Kellani had described her adequately, and, according to him, a sea-ladder was down on the port side of the for'ard well-deck—left for the convenience of the men who were red-leading the hull and whose quarterboat Kellani had stolen while making his escape.

Kent listened; but there was no stirring of life aboard the vessel. It was almost uncanny. The crew? Asleep, of course—all but the morning watch—one man, probably, as she was at anchor. She carried a crew of twenty-five besides the captain—first and second mates, steward and mess-boy, a bo'sun, a ship's carpenter, four A.B. seamen, and two deck-boys; also there would be a chief engineer, a second and third engineer, an oiler, a donkeyman and eight firemen. Were they *all* asleep? Where was Von Strom and the Berlin Harry gang? And where in that black shadow was Naida?

In a fret of impatience Kent sought out Slipper Dagg.

"See here, Dagg—" he began.

"Close your trap!" whispered the Slipper fiercely.

Kent saw that the gunman was leaning forward, his anxious gaze riveted on one spot. Presently he drew back with a sigh of relief as three quick flashes of an electric torch winked in the darkness.

"They got'm!" came his exultant whisper. "All set, Ben! Easy now! Kick her straight past an' drift in alongside on the right."

"Keep close to me, Kellani," admonished Kent tensely.

Noiselessly the tug approached. The black bulk of the *Albatross* towered slowly in upon them.

28
NEMESIS!

I

The deckhouse of the tug was almost on a level with the after well-deck of the coastal steamer, and like shadowy wolves the hijackers swarmed aboard. They crouched by the bulwark while their leader received the murmured reports of the three scouts he had sent ahead. They had experienced no trouble in surprising the lone watch on deck. The fellow proved to be one of Berlin Harry's men, and had been more interested in what was transpiring in the engineers' messroom than in attending to his duties; they had black-jacked him without a sound while he looked through a port-hole into the messroom, and—

"What's the lay?" cut in Slipper Dagg impatiently.

"Dey's countin' de coin on de table an' de gang—"

"How many?"

"Fourteen, countin' de big guy wid de bump on his bean."

Dagg swore.

"An' the crew?"

"Beat it somewheres. De bunkhouse is empty—"

Addison Kent waited to hear no more. With a warning squeeze of the Nubian's arm he slipped away and, Kellani at his heels, lost no time in climbing the ladder to the waist. There was no sign of anyone about the engine-room deckhouse as they slipped past, and Kent was in a fever of anxiety. What was going on—had already happened? Where were the crew if their fo'c'sle bunks were empty?

It could not be possible that they had deserted the ship while Berlin Harry and his thugs—

"Go, Kellani! You know your way about. Search! Do not stop searching until you find some trace of her. Then you are to rejoin me here at once. Make haste! Hell's breaking loose in a minute!"

Beyond the engine-room two alleys divided the rest of the waist into three sections—officers' quarters and staterooms to port and starboard, while the centre comprised engineers' messroom, steward's pantry and stores, the main saloon and above that the bridge, chartroom and captain's cabin. The engineers' messroom was directly in front of Kent as he crept forward to look through one of the portholes which faced the engine-room deckhouse. The portholes were closed; but through the thick glass he could see clearly enough to take in the lighted room and its occupants.

It was packed with men, all craning their necks to look over one another's shoulders. At the table, directly under a swing lamp, sat Berlin Harry and Nifty Dean, absorbed in counting a litter of greenbacks into neat piles, each secured by an elastic band. So startling was the sight of that cluster of avaricious faces encircling that great pile of money that for a moment Kent's gaze was fixed.

Then his eyes roved eagerly in search of Von Strom, *alias* Wasserhaus. Even more startled, the novelist located him in a corner of the room, entirely ignored—trussed up by his thumbs to a beam in the ceiling

Only by standing on tiptoe could the German relieve the torture of his position, and it was apparent that he was suffering a physical agony that matched the mental distress of his financial losses.

For Slipper Dagg had prophesied well. Berlin Harry was running true to form—even now counting the loot—hijacking the man who had hired him to safeguard the very fortune which lay on the table! And it was because they believed that the German was holding out on them—had still more money in concealment—that they were ill-treating him in this diabolical manner.

Kent drew back from the porthole, thinking quickly. It was a matter of moments only before the Dagg faction would close in.

The opportunity of bottling up the enemy inside the messroom would be apparent at a glance to the keen-witted Slipper; but would Dagg stop at that, or would he and his men proceed to convert the messroom into a charnel-house by shooting down the helplessly crowded occupants in cold blood? It could be done easily enough through the skylight and portholes and at the single door that opened on the port alleyway; it would be wholesale murder! On the other hand, once let those desperate thugs of Berlin Harry out of that messroom and the decks of the *Albatross* would run red in a gun-fight to the finish! They must be taken prisoner somehow—disarmed—Von Strom must be captured. How? How?

There was Dagg now, creeping around the corner of the engine-room deckhouse on the starboard side, followed by one of his men! Another was sticking his head out on the port side. They were shadowy and indistinct in the growing grayness of the dawn. Kent started towards Slipper Dagg with warning hand upraised—

A stumble in the darkness on the port side of the engine-room deckhouse!—the sharp accidental discharge of an automatic pistol as the man went sprawling over the saddle-bunker hatch!—a bitter oath as Slipper Dagg leaped like a cat for the cover afforded by the saddle-bunker hatch to starboard!

It was on the knees of the gods now! One breathless moment of utter silence—then wild commotion in the engineers' messroom! The light went out. The door was being opened with stealth.

Addison Kent jumped for the starboard alleyway that gave him free access through to the for'ard well-deck. He had barely time to crowd in behind the heavy iron door. Automatic in hand, he watched through the crack.

II

Two flashes of red darted in the gloom; the bark of the pistols was like a single shot. The hijacker who had given the alarm inadvertently by stumbling pitched again across the saddle-bunker hatch opposite the port alleyway, and this time lay there inert. But he had got his man—the first to come out of the messroom; the latter lay in a huddle across the iron coping of the alleyway door-sill.

With an involuntary curse, the fellow crowding out behind him tripped over the body and fell headlong into the open. As he picked himself up in a panic, Slipper Dagg got him from a crouched position behind the starboard saddle-bunker; the shot spun him upright. Then he suddenly crumpled, his boots threshing a brief tattoo on the deck; he lay still.

Dead silence followed. The faint lap of the water against the sides of the vessel was audible to Kent's straining ears. Behind the iron door, eye glued to the crevice, he stood, tensed.

Again the report of Dagg's automatic was like the crack of a snake whip—three quick shots. *Smash!—tinkle!* That would be the glass of the nearest porthole. *Crack! Zut! Zip! Whi—i—ne!*—a fusillade in reply and a choked cry of pain from the direction of the starboard saddle-bunker! The hatch was not within Kent's line of vision; but he knew that Dagg or one of his men had been hit.

Silence once more—so complete that his ears throbbed. The water gently slapped. Somewhere aloft something or other creaked as the *Albatross* lifted to the slow ocean swell.

After an interval he caught a new sound—a slight rubbing as if someone very carefully were slithering along the wall of the engineers' messroom, closely hugging the shadow. There was the drag of a boot—a hoarse whisper, alarmingly close. With bated breath the novelist realized that the Berlin Harry gang were crawling out from the dangerous trap in which they had been caught like foolish flies lured by sugar to indiscretion.

Dagg's last quick shots, then, had been a bluff to cover his retreat to the after well-deck, where he had commanded his men to remain while he and two of the scouts reconnoitred the position. That must be it. The Slipper had seen the wisdom of getting his men under cover and the enemy into the open, because objects rapidly were becoming more distinct in the first cold blue of the daylight.

Not a muscle did Addison Kent move. His very life depended upon what happened in the next minute or two. Would these thugs search the alleyways toward the for'ard well-deck, or would they locate the position of the Dagg gang and concentrate aft? If they looked behind the door which concealed him, he could hardly hope to shoot his way through; he would be riddled!—

A sharp exclamation came from the direction of the port saddle-bunker where the unfortunate stumbler lay across the hatch cover. They had recognized him as one of Slipper Dagg's men, and a stream of blasphemy greeted the discovery. At the same instant the morning breeze brought a vagrant swirl of acrid black smoke curling in on them, and at once the tug alongside the after well-deck drew their attention.

A shrill whistle through a pair of fingers was followed by the shuffle of crowding feet and a murmur of hurried instructions. Kent saw the figures within his vision slink beyond the corner of the engine-room deckhouse on the port side. His tense muscles relaxed. With a breath of relief he passed the sleeve of his sweater across his moist forehead.

That had been too close for tranquility! It was not more than ten minutes since hostilities had opened; but it had seemed an age. The Berlin Harry crowd had not known who was attacking them. Where was the crew of the vessel? What was Kellani doing? He must waste no time— Ah! the battle had begun in the after well-deck!

The staccato of the automatic pistols was incessant now. Kent slowly swung the door—then hastily recovered it and crowded back behind it. Up the alleyway, against the oblong of light at the other end of the passage, he saw three black figures entering. They came towards him on the run, pistols in hand—some of the gang who had gone forward to investigate up the port alleyway and were coming back on the starboard side to get into the fight. It was to recall them that the whistle had been given.

Had they seen him? With finger on the trigger of his automatic, Kent crouched. The pound of boots echoed loudly in the narrow passage. Here they came! The novelist's quickened pulse seemed suddenly to stand still. They had stopped short just as they reached his hiding-place! His teeth set grimly—

A cautious movement—the creep of feet! Kent raised his automatic and watched the inner edge of the door like a cat, ready to pounce. At the first swing of that door he would fire and leap!—

"Aw, ain't nobody out dere but de stiffs, Badger!" complained a voice. "Get into de scrap!"

With a rush the trio was over the door-sill and leaping for the engine-room deckhouse. Again Kent's sleeve dried his forehead in relief. The pause had been merely for cautious survey of the open deck before them! The Badger, eh? He seemed fated to be crowding to one side in concealment while the Badger went past on the run! Not very long ago, in the underground tunnel with outlets at the Café Belgique and Loo Ling's tea-shop, it had been the Badger who passed while Naida—

Naida! He must find her without further delay. Quietly Kent closed the heavy door and bolted it. He turned and started along the passage towards the bow of the vessel—then halted with a jerk and quickly threw up the muzzle of his weapon as the oblong of light in front of him was suddenly blotted out—

"This way, sidi," reassured the even accents of Kellani.

III

Up on the bridge abaft the chartroom—in the captain's cabin with door barricaded and shutters closed, with the woodwork freckled and splintered by bullets!—

"My God!" cried Kent, aghast. He made for the bloodstained rungs of the ladder; but the Nubian reached out and pulled him back hastily.

"The night has been black with evil, sidi," he cautioned. "It is well to go slowly. If she be alive, she will shoot everyone who approaches by the ladder. Call out, master, and give knowledge of our presence."

"If she is alive!" echoed Kent thickly. "Naida! Hello, there! *Naida!* It is I—Kent—Addison Kent and Kellani! Thank God!"

The slats of a shutter had opened. With her glad cry in his ears, Kent fairly ran up the ladder, calling out to know if she was hurt. He could hear her tugging at the barricade inside. When the door finally opened he was there with arms outstretched for her—

But she was standing back, smiling glad welcome, cool and collected! It was unnecessary to ask if she was all right; that fact was apparent in her self-possession. The anxiety went out of Addison

Kent's hungry eyes as he looked—was reborn as he took in the disordered condition of the cabin and the bruises which clutching fingers had left upon that beautiful white throat—

"Naida!" He stepped towards her. "Thank God, we're in time!"

"I am almost out of ammunition," she laughed, and held out
her hand.

He grasped it and eagerly drew her towards him; but she held
back, looking beyond him expectantly.

"Where's Dick?" Then, as he did not answer, a sudden look of
alarm filled her beautiful eyes. "Did you not come together? Oh,
Mr. Kent, what has happened?"

Dick? It was Malabar she was asking for! Malabar she was anxious about! Had their kisses, then, meant so little? *Mister* Kent!
He was only a "Mister," while Malabar was "Dick." Sharply Kent
took himself in hand—and smiled back at her reassuringly as he
explained his presence and what was transpiring on the after well-
deck.

At once she was serious, practical. Rapidly she sketched for him
the story of the night—just the essentials for him to understand
what they must do. The hirelings of Wasserhaus had run amuck!
Shortly after midnight the lighter had gone with the cargo of liquor, heading out to sea; but more gunmen had come aboard to
join Berlin Harry in his plans to hold up the ship. They had
smuggled drugged liquor into the fo'c'sle and got the crew stupe-
fied. They had blackjacked the officer of the watch and overpowered the others. The first mate and the captain they had chloroformed in their bunks—

"And you?" urged Kent.

She had been awakened by Wasserhaus forcing the door of her
stateroom. The German had been celebrating and was half drunk.
There had been a struggle, abruptly terminated by Berlin Harry
and Nifty Dean, who had promptly seized Wasserhaus and carried
him off.

"It's all right, sister," they had assured her. "You're under our
protection. You stay right here."

But she knew the breed, and she had lost no time in gathering
her ammunition and fleeing to the captain's cabin, where she

barricaded the door and waited, automatic in hand. Later they had come back, and when she had refused all their invitations to come down and join them they had tried to force her. Not until she had wounded several had they left her alone, promising that they would attend to her in due course.

"What have they done with the crew? Pitched them overboard?"

"No, they've locked them up—down there in the storeroom. We must hurry and release them. Captain Head is a gentleman and—oh, come, Mr. Kent! Hear that!"

It was Kellani forcing in the small, tight door in the forepeak that gave access to the paint-locker. He stood aside with a silent bow as they joined him. The air that smote their nostrils was thick with nauseating odours—the stench of vitiation, the sickening sweetness of chloroform.

Kent waved Naida back, beckoned to the Nubian and plunged inside. One by one they brought them out into the open air and laid them on the deck, where Naida, with a bucket of cold water beside her, made hurried ministrations. Some of them were in worse condition than others; not all of them were unconscious. The second mate was able even to assist in reviving his brother officers; the fresh air quickly restored Captain Head and the first mate, although their faces were yellow with pallor beneath the tan of their weather-beaten skin.

"How long have they been in there? Since midnight? It must be well over six hours since the drugged liquor—"

Kent shook the shoulder of a burly young seaman who was sleeping peacefully, and watched his ready response with interest. The deck-boy sat up, blinking. He appeared to be wide awake, suffering no ill effects, and the novelist smiled up at the anxious-faced girl.

"Paraldehyde," he explained. "Its action is quick on the knock-out, but ends in natural sleep after a couple of hours, with little after-effects; it is used to quiet inebriates and in severe cases of chorea. If they had used chloral—"

He paused as the firing broke out with renewed vigour among the combatants aft. The noise brought most of the sleeping sailors to a sitting posture. The captain was on his feet now, his pallor rapidly giving place to ruddy anger as he administered some well-deserved kicks.

"Get up, ye blithering fools!" he commanded harshly. "Devil take ye if I dinna wallop ye m'sel' onless ye drive yon scum off the ship! Ochan, dae ye want to lay there an' be murdered? Dinna ye know there's a fight gaein' on?"

In a few words Naida had put the facts of the situation before Captain Head, and with kicks and blows and castigations he rallied his crew to full recovery. The steward, who had scouted aft, returned with the grave report that the gunmen had broken into the saloon and had taken the stand of small arms and all the ammunition. This was bad news; for even the officers had been disarmed, and without weapons they were helpless against the thugs. Even so, the mounting rage of the men of Lunenburg as they realized what had happened to them and their vessel would have carried them into the fight with bare fists had the command been given. They shifted uneasily while the officers conferred.

It was just then that a seaman stepped up and drew attention to a speeding launch which was bearing down on them to port out of the thin mist that narrowed vision upon the expanse of heaving water. All eyes watched the rapid approach of the small power-boat which was cutting the water in a streak of foam. The craft was equipped with mufflers; her engine gave out only a subdued vibrant hum as she came down on them at high speed. In the uproar from the after well-deck the new sound was scarcely noticeable.

Red dawn was in the sky, and it was Addison Kent who first caught the glint of the machine-gun, mounted in the bow of the oncoming launch. At his shout of warning everybody dropped below the bulwarks except Naida. She was too absorbed in peering eagerly at the stranger to heed anything.

Kent seized her and carried her bodily across the deck as fast as he could go with the idea of getting her within the shelter of the paint-locker. But at the door, she protested so vigorously that she struggled free and deliberately ran back to the rail. Before anyone could prevent it, she climbed up in full view, hanging on to the ratlines and waving her hand—

"Dick! Dick!" she called.

And at that Kent halted in his tracks. One quick glance satisfied him that it was indeed Richard Malabar who was standing up in the launch and waving back at her. He came up the sea-ladder, hand over hand, with the agility of a monkey. He was no sooner over the side than Naida threw herself wildly into his arms!

A bullet whanged against the steel foremast and whizzed overboard!

IV

"You appear to be having a little excitement aboard, captain," smiled the newcomer. "I regret that we are so late; but certain necessary formalities caused unavoidable delay. If it is not presumption, may I express the hope that we are in time, nevertheless, to be of service?"

"And who the devil are you, sir?" demanded the astonished Captain Jabez Head with a dignity befitting the other's unctuous diction.

"The gentlemen below, sir, are attaches of the British Embassy at Washington, and with your permission—" He stepped to the side with a beckoning gestures then glanced aft as a second stray bullet *zinged* off the foremast. "May I enquire, Captain Head, as to the position of affairs? Just before setting out we learned that you were liable to be boarded by hijackers, and we ventured to bring along some sawed-off shot-guns and two machine-guns—"

At that they surrounded him eagerly. Explanations were as brief and incisive as the occasion demanded.

"Allow me to present Colonel Wetherby and Captain Wilcox. We are here to arrest a man known as Wasserhaus, but who is really Ludwig Von Strom, wanted by the Egyptian Government upon evidence supplied by the British Secret Service, represented here by this young lady. The matter is before the Canadian authorities at Ottawa, captain, and everything is in order. First, however, you will want to stop that nonsense aft."

While the machine-guns and ammunition were being hastily hoisted aboard Richard Malabar slowly approached Addison Kent, who had listened dumbly.

"Ah, my dear fellow, there are times when you really do show some ability," was the suave admission with that mocking inflection of Alceste. "Your presence here ahead of me is indeed a delightful surprise, although you will hardly expect me to approve of your travelling companions. I trust you left my good friend Gridley in the best of health?—" A dig in the ribs!—a sudden grin! "Come to life, old top!" and it was the old Dick Malabar who now shook him by the shoulders.

"Wasserhaus—" began Kent stupidly.

"You can have what is left of him when I get through with him!" Malabar's face sobered quickly. "I say, I want you to keep out of this show. It is not going to amount to much; but I want you to escort my sister into that launch and take her out there beyond all possibility of stray bullets. God knows, she's run enough risks already!—"

"Escort—your—*what?* Your *sis—sis!*—" stuttered Kent.

"—*ter,*" supplied Malabar. "Bravest and best sister in the world, dear old bean!"

V

From a safe distance they watched the progress of affairs aboard the *Albatross.* The bitter fight between the rival gangs of gunmen was in full swing still; so completely absorbed were the feudists that they were entirely unaware of what had been transpiring in the fore part of the vessel. Events had moved so swiftly that the actual time which had elapsed since Slipper Dagg and his men had stolen aboard was short.

"Look!" exclaimed Naida. "No, over to the left—the man running. See, he's just starting up the ladder to the bridge! Isn't that Von Strom?"

The crew already had crept aft through the alleyways to take up position for the attack on the gunmen in the after well-deck; for the moment the for'ard well-deck was deserted. Kent picked up the binoculars from the plush seat beside him.

"Yes! Von Strom, with Kellani chasing him!" as a second figure came into sight, climbing after the first. "And I told him—!"

"I know Kellani's story," murmured Naida. "He has great cause to hate Von Strom."

"I told him he was not to take the law into his own hands notwithstanding—"

Captain Jabez Head's stentorian bellow through a megaphone was punctuated by a warning ripple of machine-gun fire. At the whistle of the bullets overhead a yell of dismay arose from the surprised gunmen. There was a wild scramble for cover from this new and unexpected menace.

"He is firing at Kellani!" cried Naida anxiously. "What madness for Kellani to expose himself in that way! He seems to be unarmed. He will be killed!"

"Possibly," was Kent's interested comment. "Kellani has that curved knife of his in his hand. I supplied him with an automatic; but evidently he has lost it or distrusts it—there! See that? There is method in his madness; he is deliberately drawing the other's fire—to empty the gun! God help that German if they ever get to grips! Here, take a look and see if you can make out what Von Strom is clutching in his left hand."

"It looks like—money!"

"That's it!—a huge bundle of greenbacks! In the general excitement trust him to think of the swag!"

Kent searched for a second pair of glasses, found them in a locker and focused them eagerly upon the *Albatross*. The machine-guns were in deadly action now; the rattle of them drowned out the popping of the German's gun.

At a cry from Naida the novelist switched his glasses back to the bridge just in time to see Kellani tumble behind the chartroom. In a flash Von Strom was off the bridge, sliding unseen down the ladder. With a breath of relief Kent saw the Nubian crawling cautiously on hands and knees, stalking his enemy.

Across the well-deck fled Von Strom. He was making for the ratlines and was half-way up the foremast by the time Kellani missed him.

Down the ladder raged the swarthy giant, looking to right and left like a black bloodhound who momentarily has been thrown off the scent.

Deliberately the huge German paused to level his pistol. He fired—and missed! He fired again twice in quick succession, then climbed madly upward as he felt the Nubian's nimble feet on the ratlines below him.

There was no stopping Kellani. On he came, hand over hand, the knife held in his teeth; in the red sunrise it gleamed athwart his dark face. Von Strom flung his empty weapon downward. Kellani merely turned his frizzled head as the pistol sped past his shoulder—and climbed without a pause.

The terrified German had reached the crow's-nest at the foretruck, which was as high as the ratlines went. Against the red haze eastward the steel mast etched thin and straight; beyond the foretruck it tapered to a mere black whip with the wireless yard near the top, a flimsy stick which seemed scarcely strong enough to carry the threads of the aerial. Below it the light yard from which the signal halyards descended to the bridge seemed flimsy also in its slimness.

Throwing one desperate glance aloft, Von Strom knelt at the foretruck and held out the great package of money. Ignoring this plea for his life, the Nubian climbed steadily closer. Again the German looked aloft; again he pleaded. He left the money at the crow's-nest and shinned up the mast till he got one leg over the signal yard. Once more the gesture of supplication!

At the foretruck Kellani paused to pick up the bundle of bills. Never before in his life had the simple Nubian seen so much money at one time in one spot, let alone actually held it in his hands. He took the knife from between his teeth long enough to throw back his head in open laughter. The attitude was eloquent of a magnificent derision.

Suddenly he hurled the money at the man above him. It struck Von Strom in the face and hit against the mast. The impact broke the bank-notes loose; they scattered and flew, the paper bills caught by the freshening morning breeze, which showered them in a cloud, fluttering, wobbling. Against the bright sky it was like a flock of black swallows which soared and dipped, sailed, dropped—down into the sea!

Hastily Addison Kent swung his glasses aft. The firing had ceased abruptly, and the captain was bawling through a megaphone. At that distance it was impossible to hear what was being said; but apparently the fight was over. The tug was pulling away at full speed!

Was there time yet to stop Kellani? Had nobody aboard noted the pair on the foremast? It was useless to shout—useless to attempt to speed in to the rescue of the German. Whatever was to happen would have happened before—

It was happening even now! Breathless, the watchers in the launch gazed helplessly at the drama. Von Strom was straddling the signal yard. He dared go no higher! Yet relentlessly the Nubian was climbing and reaching for him! Panic-stricken, completely obsessed by fear, the German began to back out on the signal yard, his full weight bearing upon the starboard guy that held the yard in a horizontal position.

The result was inevitable. Under the strain the guy snapped! Instantly the yard flew up on the starboard side and down like a pump-handle on the port side of the mast. Unprepared for that swift jackknife closing to the vertical, Von Strom spilled off backwards!

Like a plummet he plunged headlong to the steel deck below!

For a long moment Kellani gazed downward. Then he slid to the foretruck and stood erect, facing the east where the morning sun hung just above the horizon, a blood-red ball in the haze. Slowly and solemnly against that blood-red disk the Nubian's arm was raised aloft. Thus he stood.

And it seemed to the white-faced watchers that the silhouetted figure symbolized the fatalism of the East, which ever bows its forehead to the sands before the mystic decree of the stars and the wisdom of the Infinite.

29
THE SINGULAR TRUTH OF THE MATTER

I

Considerably more than the day's sensation was the arrival of the death ship *Albatross* in New York Harbour. As she sailed up the bay with her blood spattered deck and her bullet-splintered woodwork, the vessel herself was a sensation; for thus did her doughty skipper deliver her in confirmation of the remarkable story he had to tell the United States authorities. But when it became known that he brought with him eleven dead bodies and almost as many prisoners, mostly wounded; that among these were numbered some of the underworld's most notorious gunmen; that dead on board lay the self-confessed murderer of the late Professor Caron and of Armaund Lamont's faithful servant, Mokra—it was little wonder that the newspaper extras set New York agog! The fact, too, that the vessel had been taken in charge by representatives of the British Embassy from Washington, and that startling revelations might be pending concerning contraband liquor operations—here was splendid background upon which to spread lengthy and lurid descriptions of the battle at sea, rich in imagination!

It was a hectic day for all concerned, particularly for Mr. Addison Kent. He had reached the dying Von Strom just in time to get from him a confession of his guilt in the Caron case—that he was responsible for the death of both victims; but the German had passed away without revealing anything except the bare fact of his guilt. However, the details of the crime, as reconstructed by

Addison Kent, were substantiated by the statement of the St. Boniface Kid to the police; in every particular the novelist had surmised the truth. Only the motive remained a mystery.

To the best of his ability Kent piloted his friends through the tedious formalities and stood between them and undue annoyance by newspaper reporters, who clustered like flies around a honeypot. At the end of the day he was glad to relax, and he set out for Westchester with pleasurable anticipation of the quiet evening they had planned—just the three of them—Dick, Naida and himself.

And as they sat in front of the library fire after dinner it seemed to Addison Kent that he had never felt so completely contented. His cigar had never had such flavour and fragrance. The dinner itself had been a pleasantly cheerful affair—a conversational treat as well as a culinary triumph for the painstaking Gaston. The service—considering that Kellani was just being initiated to his new duties—had been quite satisfactory; he had the makings of a fine servant, Kellani, and Kent had sent the poor fellow into the seventh heaven of happiness by his words of commendation. But, even had there been cause for complaint, it is extremely doubtful if Addison Kent would have been aware of it—not acutely, at any rate; for in the presence of Naida Malabar!—

He looked across at her and smiled, and she smiled back at him—for no particular reason at all; they just smiled. She had managed to get some much-needed sleep during the afternoon and had awakened greatly refreshed. Kent thought he had never seen her looking so beautiful, although he had not seen her very often— never before in a dinner gown. She was positively stunning!

"Even to you, Kent, whose business it is to weave bright threads of romance on the loom of a soaring imagination—even to you the facts I am about to lay before you will seem well nigh incredible." Richard Malabar's tones were weighted with solemnity as be spoke without preamble; he had been sitting in silence for some time, staring at the grate and finding in the red coals long avenues of retrospection. "Yet I swear to you that I shall state only the plain, honest truth in every particular. Naida agrees with me that you are entitled to know the full facts from the very beginning, and they will be given you without reserve, in order that you may judge my case upon its merits. That is all I ask.

"It is fitting that my 'confession'—if such it can be called—should be made in this room, where so much has happened during the past few weeks. My life has been replete with sudden changes and more than an average share of hazards and excitements; it is no new thing for me to appreciate the extent to which circumstances alter cases or the swiftness with which those circumstances may occur. I think you will agree with me, however, that since last night—

"Last night, Kent, quite justifiably, you were prepared to turn me over to the police, knowing me to be a notorious crook, Alceste, whom you had every reason to regard as your most dangerous enemy and a man who was a menace to society! Last night my sister was defending herself behind a barricade at the point of a gun against a gang of thugs on board the *Albatross!* Last night the man from whom both of us had most to fear had Naida in his power, and with that weapon he had me at his mercy! Last night, in short, the stakes were on the table, and the ball was spinning in the wheel for a number of people!

"Do you begin to understand why I was forced to eliminate you from the game—as I thought—by leaving you tied up and guarded?—why I dare run no risk of police interference with my plans by exposure as Alceste? There was no time for lengthy explanations which, no matter how true, would be discounted and distrusted. I do not know whether you believe in a 'destiny that shapes our ends'; but after what happened during the night I do not see how you can help believing in it!

"For to-night—what a difference! Here we sit, safe and sound, and can talk of the thing calmly in the past tense! Von Strom is dead, his power to injure unjustly—gone! I am able to reveal the truth to you, and do so gladly, knowing that you will be fair in your judgment of the strangest predicament which an honest man was ever called upon to face. For, like poor Caron, I turn to you, Addison Kent, for advice and help. God alone knows what lies ahead!"

And Richard Malabar told his story.

II

Mud banks and nipah palms, wooded hills and beyond the jungle of the interior! Tall trunks of trees with giant creepers that matted overhead and shut out the blazing sun! Chattering colonies of monkeys in the tree-tops, and at the water-holes huge beasts of the jungle! Flat lands and miasmic vapours! Coral shores of islands, washed by a pea-green sea! Borneo! The Malay archipelago! India! The coast of Malabar! Pirates! Iniquities! Tropical storms! Wreckage, adrift in dangerous waters!

Waifs of the sea were Richard and Naida Malabar—lost children—little nobodies from nowhere!—washed ashore on the coast of Malabar, on the west side of India, after a severe tropical storm! They were found, lashed to a fragment of wreckage from some unknown vessel—the tiny baby girl tightly held in the arms of the unconscious boy. In spite of the best efforts of the kind whites who finally took the foundlings in charge, who the children were and where they came from remained a mystery. Without family and without name, they were given the name of the coast upon which they had been cast; they grew up under the name of "Malabar" in England, where they were sent by their foster parents to be educated.

The mystery of his birth remained with Richard Malabar through life as a tantalizing quest, luring him with beckoning finger upon a trail that had no end After leaving school the boy gravitated into journalism, which had for him a strange attraction; also it enabled him in the course of his professional activities to wander about the earth, always seeking, always studying—hoping that some day he would chance upon the answer to his question: "Who and what am I?" Mastery of languages came easily to him. His newspaper commissions took him into many strange ports. There he mingled with the underworld flotsam in the belief that in such surroundings he was most likely to find some derelict of the sea who had the information for which he hungered.

But it had been without avail. Thus, Richard Malabar, the British journalist, war-correspondent, world traveller, had lived his life, well and favourably known, the qualities of a gentleman inherent within him. And at times strange penchants and whims had obsessed him—a mad urge to be up and away to Somewhere Beyond—restless as the sea which had cast him ashore, figuring in many an adventure, broad-minded, talented, brilliant—a strange mixture of kindly impulses, keen enjoyments, artistic appreciations and spells of sadness and loneliness.

In the whole world was but one who knew and understood and shared—his sister, Naida. She was his *ALL* in love and tenderness. At all times he had safeguarded her—through those terrible beginnings of memory—those jungle years when they had romped together upon the sands and threaded dire tangled paths. He had taught her all his boyish skill, and together they had learned secret modes of communication; so that like children of the wild they had lived those first hard years—had lived by their wits!

Later, during schooldays in England, they had not seen so much of each other. The girl, however, had grown to young womanhood with an ingrained love of outdoor life and, in many respects, with almost a man's outlook. Delightfully feminine, she nevertheless had too much independence of spirit to be content with a "clinging-vine" existence. Like her clever brother, she had exceptional intellectual powers and abilities. It was almost foreordained that she should find in the British Secret Service the work for which she was so peculiarly adapted.

Then without warning had come that strange break in Richard Malabar's life, leading directly to the present trouble in which he was enmeshed. His paper had sent him to Morocco to look into a disturbance which threatened to develop into serious disagreement between the Riffs and the French. Having discharged this commission, he had drifted to Algiers, and there one night in a dark alley he was set upon by a band of thieves who coveted his purse, and received a blow on the head which laid him out in the gutter, where his assailants left him for dead.

And as good as dead was Richard Malabar the journalist from that night on! As if the earth had opened and swallowed him, he vanished. Even his paper, with all its great resources, failed to locate him and, after a year had gone by, regretfully ceased to regard him as "missing." Time passed. Even his sorrowing sister at last gave up hope of again seeing him alive.

III

North beyond Le Pas—north beyond Sturgeon Lake, where a trail across the ice led into the country of Canada's latest gold-fields—a crude prospector's cabin, banked with snow! Inside, blaz-ing logs in an open fireplace, and a grizzled "sourdough" stirring at a steaming pot! Across the single room another "old-timer," industriously mending a broken snowshoe! The skin of a huge timber wolf stretched on the wall, and a pack of pelts in a corner! Steel traps! Rifles! A line of drying socks! Samples of quartz! Mining tools! A coloured calendar!

Upon these things did Richard Malabar the journalist open his eyes. So did he return to his world—to the memory of his life, his sister, his profession—to the memory of sudden attack in a dark alley-like street in Algiers! He lay in a rough bunk, beneath red blankets—warm Hudson Bay point blankets—and wondered to find himself so. His head hurt, and he felt weak. As a man whose mind wanders in a fever, he talked of Arabs and desert sands and rebel-lion in the hills!

They brought him hot soup to drink and asked him if he felt better. They related to him strange things—that he had spent the night at their cabin three nights ago and had told them then that his name was Bob Elliott, and that he had been up at Rice Lake; that he was anxious to get away before the spring break-up made travelling impossible by dog-team; that he had left the next morn-ing with six huskies and a carriole; that he had met with an acci-dent—got off the trail and fell into a crevice, severely striking his head; that the noise of his dogs had attracted the attention of Bill Davis, who had turned aside to investigate and had rescued him and brought him to the cabin; that he had been lying on the bunk for many hours, unconscious!

But, strangest of all, the calendar showed that nearly two years had elapsed since that night in Algiers! Two years! He had sense enough to conceal from his rough but kindly hosts the sudden

problem which this startling fact threw at him. Behind closed eyes
his mind groped for the solution, and he strove to turn the pages
of memory for answers to the questions that throbbed upon him.
But there were whole pages missing, and he realized that for two
years his mind had been a blank as to his identity, and that during
that time Richard Malabar had ceased to exist and another had
taken his place!

Amnesia—a straight case of amnesia!—the thing he had so frequently read about in the news columns—men, through accident
or a sudden blow, losing completely their identity and wandering
away—sometimes for many years! It was a common enough experience, he knew. Many cases were on record of these wanderers
suddenly coming back to their former life and occupation—usually with memory restored by a second accident. That was what
had happened to him!

Bob Elliott! He had told these prospectors that his name was
Bob Elliott and that he had been to Rice Lake! Had he, then, become a mining man? Obsessed with an eager desire to probe for
information about this life that he had led during the interval, he
nevertheless obeyed the instinct which prompted him to conceal
his worry, and he said never a word of his trouble to his present
companions.

He was soon able to get up and move about. He awaited an
opportunity to overhaul his dunnage-bag without interruption; it
came one afternoon when both prospectors set out together to visit
their trap-lines. Eagerly Malabar examined everything that had
been in the possession of "Bob Elliott," and as the search progressed his perplexity grew, until at the last he had sat in a daze,
white-faced with apprehension, overwhelmed by what he discovered.

It was evident that he had not lacked the "means" to equip himself with a prospector's outfit which represented the best quality
that money could buy. In fact, among the first things he found were
several books of "traveller's cheques" in favour of several different names. To his amazement he discovered that the signatures

for all these names were in his own unmistakable handwriting! He got out a sheet of paper and signed them, one after the other, finding the signatures facsimile! "Robert Elliott," then, was but one of the names by which he had been known? That was strange!

But not as strange as what was to come! He found a secret pocket in the lining of the leather case in which his military brushes were enclosed, and the little lumps which had aroused his curiosity turned out to be diamonds!—a dozen of them, none of them exceptionally large, but all of them of pure water and valuable! He found no less than eleven keys to safety-deposit boxes in various cities of Canada and the United States! He found a booklet, entitled: "How to Increase Your Height"! He found certain other papers which mystified him, and a little amulet or charm of curious design—made of pure gold, wrought in the form of a scarab, with the Egyptian symbol of Osiris, the god of the dead, engraved upon its flat side!

Finally, carefully hidden away, he came across the little black book. It was small enough to go inside a cigarette case; but the information it contained was as dangerous as dynamite! On the surface it was innocent enough—a simple record of business transactions and general trade conditions; but, concealed cleverly within the report, was a cipher. Intuitively Malabar seemed to realize this fact and, having set to work to discover the key to it, was not long in learning the hidden information—secrets of criminal organization, passwords, records of theft—information which convinced the journalist that during the period which was now blank in his memory he had played the part of a magnificent crook!

Imagine it! He, Richard Malabar, late of the London *Daily World!* Where had he been? What had he done? With whom had he been associating? What was this secret society, the "Order of the Golden Scarab," to which he evidently had belonged? To what depths had he sunk?—what crimes committed? The police of New York, London, Paris!— Where was he to head in? Above all, was this criminal "throw-back" the result of some sinister strain in his blood?—out of the blank beginnings of his life? Or was his excursion into the criminal ranks but the natural result of the close study he had given for years to underworld types and criminal psychology—the drift of a mind which had suddenly lost its rudder?

Was ever an honest man placed in such a devilish predicament?

IV

After the first panic into which the discovery threw him, Richard Malabar bent every wit to the decision of what he must do. There must be no mistakes made. A single misstep and his fate might be sealed! He allowed his beard to grow during the time he remained at the prospectors' cabin, and he felt reasonably sure that the silent and unsociable man who finally came down out of the north country would pass unrecognized. At Winnipeg he found a room in a quiet lodging-house, and there settled himself to await an answer to the cable he had despatched to his sister Naida.

This cable he had sent in their own secret code. He told her that he was alive and well, but in grave trouble, and he must see her as soon as possible; either he would go to her or she could come to him. When her overjoyed reply reached him at last he found that she was in New York, where her work had taken her. This was highly satisfactory, and he wired her that he would join her there within a week.

They met, as arranged, and together went over the strange situation carefully. It seemed to them, then, that Fate was playing with them—treating them like pawns in a game, as indeed Fate had done in the beginning; for the work upon which Naida was engaged—the case which had brought her to the United States on behalf of the Egyptian Government—concerned the theft of certain valuable antiques from the museum at Cairo and the bold activities of a secret organization of criminals in the East, known to the underworld as the "Order of the Golden Scarab." She was in New York to await the arrival of a French Egyptologist of undoubted standing but known erratic tendencies—Professor Emil Caron. She had been assigned to keep an eye upon him in America, certain suspicion having fallen upon him in secret-service circles. According to the papers in her brother's possession, Malabar had had dealings of some kind with the very group of criminals in which Naida was interested!

Brother and sister had stared at each other in dismay! There was only one honourable thing Richard Malabar could do, of course—join his sister in an effort to get to the bottom of the situation; help her to recover for the Egyptian authorities as many of the stolen antiques as possible; run this "Golden Scarab" crowd to earth and, if he found out what his connection with them had been, do his best to redeem himself.

It was just at this time that Malabar had renewed his acquaintanceship with Addison Kent, immediately becoming interested in the work the novelist had been doing for the police. Their mutual hobby—the study of criminology—brought them together quickly in a common interest, and Malabar had been astonished to find that Kent had had an encounter with Alceste—a notorious jewel thief who had been creating something of a stir internationally in police circles.

In the little black book which Malabar had found in his dunnage-bag the name Alceste was mentioned several times in such a way that it seemed to be the name Malabar had used in his nefarious dealings during the blank period which he was now trying to penetrate. As he studied the Radcliffe case, in which Kent had encountered Alceste, Richard Malabar was conscious of faint stirrings of memory—an elusive sense of familiarity which made him wonder if he were indeed Alceste himself—the very man with whom Kent had matched wits!

What a dangerous position! How long could he hope to avoid recognition by a man as keen as Addison Kent? Very carefully he began to throw out questions—to lead Kent to talk of this Alceste—and there had been comfort in Kent's description of the cracksman as "a sardonic individual, Dick—the very antithesis of your own genial personality—three or four inches shorter than you. . . ." Malabar now understood why that booklet, "How to Increase Your Height," had been found in his dunnage-bag.

Then came Kent's casual revelation of the fact that at Police Headquarters Alceste was recorded officially as dead and eliminated! The novelist little knew the difficulty Richard Malabar had experienced in restraining himself at this tremendous news. It meant the removal of his greatest worry. He saw at once that as Alceste he had made a clean getaway from the burning cottage on the edge of the moor where Scotland Yard had closed in on him, and he was filled with thankfulness and a certain admiration for the diabolical cleverness of that other and sinister individual who had taken possession of him temporarily.

Later that same night, at the Lamont place in Westchester—when he heard Professor Caron's strange story and held the golden scarab itself in his hand—again Malabar had glimmers of memory. He realized that he was on the trail of important discoveries in connection with the case upon which his sister was working. After Kent had left him at his hotel he had rushed to Naida with the news, and to them both it seemed like a gift of the gods—the opportunity of getting Caron's story from the inside.

That, however, was not to be. The death of the Frenchman brought things to a climax more rapidly than was expected. From the first Naida had been positive that the Professor had been put out of the way by criminal associates. Already she had investigated the passenger-lists of all recently arrived transatlantic liners, and had got a lead which tallied with her official records—a description which had put her at once upon the trail of Wasserhaus, who was none other than the notorious Ludwig Von Strom.

The strategical advantage of her brother's position on the inside as Addison Kent's friend had enabled her to foil Von Strom in his second attempt to secure the golden scarab and the other jewels which, she was now satisfied, had been in Professor Caron's possession. Her brother's relation of the evening's incidents convinced her that the precious stones had been smuggled into the United States, concealed within the case which contained the mummy of the sacred cat. It was arranged, therefore, that they should act without delay, Malabar securing the jewels and passing them out to his sister, who thereupon would lose no time in placing them in official hands.

Not a moment too soon had they acted! In the midst of the storm Von Strom had arrived, and but for Malabar's promptness and Naida's presence on the scene to assist him, the German undoubtedly would have succeeded in the theft. Poor Mokra's interference with Von Strom had been something as unforeseen as it was unfortunate.

This, and Kent's subsequent establishment of the Frenchman's death as a crime, had complicated the situation by setting the police on the track of Von Strom. For Malabar and Von Strom had come almost face to face the night of the storm, and Malabar was sure that he had been recognized as Alceste. If the German fell into the hands of the police, he would not hesitate to direct them to Alceste—with fatal consequences to Malabar! On no account must the police record of Alceste's death be upset!

Von Strom's amazement at sight of him had been genuine. Apparently this organization of criminals in the East had known Alceste, and had likewise accepted the reports of his death. Knowing now that Alceste was still alive, there would be no doubt in the German's mind that Alceste had purloined the jewels Von Strom was after. It seemed likely that overtures would be made for a division of the spoils upon threat of a "tip" to the police. It therefore became imperative for Malabar to learn just what had been his former connection with the gang of which Von Strom evidently was a leader.

The dangerous task of cultivating Wasserhaus to find this out had been undertaken by Naida, and it was while she was engaged in this mission that Addison Kent had followed her. Now that things had assumed perspective, it was easy to see that what Malabar and his sister should have done was to take Addison Kent into their fullest confidence; but at the time the wisdom of this had not been so apparent. It had seemed best to run down the full facts first, Malabar playing a double role; for as Alceste he was able to move in underworld circles.

It was during one of his quick excursions after information that unexpectedly he had learned the plans for "silencing" Kent. To save the novelist it had been necessary for Malabar to appear as Alceste and, in front of Von Strom, pretend to gloat over the capture. It had been a risky thing to do; but, bearing in mind Kent's description of the cracksman's smooth, sneering way of talking, he had flattered himself that he had completely fooled the German, although he could not be sure of Addison Kent. With Naida's help, Malabar had got him out of the dangerous situation—only to find that Kent had indeed discovered who Alceste was.

But things had begun to happen so rapidly then that there was no time for explanations, even had the novelist been in a frame of mind to believe them. Von Strom had discovered that Naida was Alceste's sister, and at once seized the advantage; with Naida in his power he could dictate terms to Alceste, which he had not dared to do before. Naida's warning message had rushed Malabar into preparations for the "showdown," and he had put through his call to Washington for official action. They knew him there merely as Naida's brother, working with her on the Cairo case.

V

"It only remains to add," Malabar concluded, "that with the death of Von Strom and the recovery of the missing antiques and the jewels, which represented the wealth of the 'Order of the Golden Scarab,' Naida's work has found successful conclusion, and the criminal organization in the East is now on the way to a complete break-up. We discovered, Kent, that Von Strom was trying to engineer a coup by smuggling a fortune in precious stones into the United States, using Professor Caron as a catspaw. How he got the Frenchman into his power so completely—what took place between them at the so-called 'lost tomb' to which they journeyed—that probably will never be known. It was there the 'treasure-chest' of the organization was concealed, and it is my opinion that Von Strom was attempting to turn traitor to his companions in crime by walking off with the whole thing. Undoubtedly Professor Caron was acting under compulsion, and was killed because he threatened to reveal what he knew.

"As for Alceste's connection with this 'Golden Scarab' crowd, we discovered that while Alceste had helped them to rob certain rich men in Eastern countries, he had proved himself a 'thorn in the flesh' by insisting upon most of the proceeds from these forays being given away to the poor and needy. This Dick Turpin mania appears to have shocked the brigands and made Alceste so unpopular that apparently he had been 'black-balled' out of the secret council of the order if, in fact, he had ever been admitted.

"Yet Professor Caron was in great fear of Alceste, and the statement 'his evil lives after him' would seem to indicate Alceste as the founder of the sinister society of the scarab and directly responsible for its acts. I have given this some thought, and the only conclusion I can reach is that Von Strom told Professor Caron a great many fabulous tales about the ruthless Alceste, much as one tells a child about the terrible giant who lived at the top of the beanstalk; he would do this in order to build up a bogy with which to frighten the Frenchman as to the consequences of disobedience.

"Naida has been able to supply definite information regarding the golden scarab gem itself. Do you remember the startling robbery of St. Peter's treasury in the Vatican at Rome some time ago, when international crooks succeeded in penetrating to the sacred jewellery strong box? Such a sacrilege had never been known before. It reminds one of the ghouls of ancient Thebes Professor Caron was telling about that night you and I called upon him. The theft, you will remember, included the sacred ring belonging to St. Peter's statue in the basilica, a gold cross set with pearls and rubies, and given by the Colombian Republic to Pope Pius IX sixty years ago, and certain other rare gifts donated by monarchs and emperors. Among the items not mentioned in the newspapers at the time was the Great Ruby which many years ago found its way, from some secret, conscience-stricken source, into the sacred treasury. When the collection of stolen Vatican gems was recovered, shortly after the theft, only the Great Ruby was missing. But even that is now on its way to Rome—"

"The golden scarab!" murmured Addison Kent with interest.

"Yes. It was the very ruby at which you and I gazed in this room the night Professor Caron showed us the golden scarab. It had fallen into the hands of this secret society and evidently was mounted in its golden scarab setting to become the symbol of the Order. The lure of it undoubtedly turned Von Strom's head and emboldened him to risk everything in one mad effort to become a Crœsus.

"That is all, Kent—except that I owe you apology for the worry I have brought you and for my seeming abuse of your friendship. That friendship has come to mean a very great deal to me, and the half-hour we spent in this room last night was bitter punishment for the hurt I was causing you. The knowledge that our friendship meant something to you also—it was not easy to dissemble—to go through with the programme which appeared necessary. I ask your forgiveness, old chap."

Addison Kent was on his feet. There was nothing to forgive now—nothing but deep appreciation of the nightmare which this friend of his had been living.

In a long steady grip, more eloquent than any words, their hands met in their man's way, while Naida's eyes shone in sympathy.

30
The Luck of the Golden Scarab

I

It was about an hour later that the restlessness of Mr. Addison Kent finally took him out of the library into the hall. Mysteriously he poked his head around the portières and beckoned surreptitiously to Mr. Richard Malabar. And when Mr. Richard Malabar, obeying the warning finger raised to the novelist's lips, excused himself and left Miss Naida Malabar alone in the room, gazing pensively into the red heart of the fire in the grate—when he reached the hall—

Addison Kent deliberately stuck a fresh cigar into the journalist's mouth and lighted it for him—deliberately seized Malabar's overcoat and helped him into it, then jammed Malabar's hat upon Malabar's head.

"I say!—"

"You are going out for a breath of fresh air if I have to carry you!" whispered Kent fiercely. "For the love of Heaven, take a stroll about the grounds! Go and see a man about a—*mule!*"

With a slow grin of dawning understanding, Mr. Richard Malabar went.

II

The stars looked down upon that shadowy figure which paced to and fro in the twilight, hands behind back, head bent in thought. The stars twinkled.

Eleven keys and a little black book, small enough to go inside a cigarette case!—a legacy of Fate! What did the Future hold in store for him? What relics of the Past would those keys unlock? Through what Gates of Hazard would the way of duty lie? Along what shadowed Paths of Mystery must he retrace the footsteps of Alceste?

Alceste was dead—and buried! True enough, so far as deeds of crime were involved—so far as the police were concerned. True enough, perhaps, as Kent said, that Alceste had confined his activities to the single crime of theft—that the very name under which he had operated was taken from Molière's *Misanthrope*—Alceste, an enemy of social hypocrisies! True, perhaps, that Richard Malabar was no more responsible than one insane. Nevertheless, was he not called upon to make what restitution he could? Would there be any peace of mind—any rest for him in life—until he had followed backward, step by step, along this Thread of Ariadne which had been placed in his hand—until he had recovered from the underworld and restored as much as possible of the loot which Alceste had helped to steal?

No, Alceste must reappear in the haunts that had known him; but it would be in a new role—in the guise of a lone bloodhound, hunting down his quarry and snatching from their very jaws "the kill"! A dangerous business! But that way, and that way only, lay Redemption.

Back and forth, tirelessly back and forth, paced Richard Malabar, wrestling with his problem. And as he fought it out with himself and reached his decisions out there under the quiet stars, something of their peace descended upon him like a benediction.

Almost without volition his feet trended towards the portico, upon which fell the subdued squares of light from the library of the great house. On tiptoe he approached until he could look in upon the lovers—just a glance. For a moment his gaze lingered upon those two heads close together. Addison Kent's arm was about her shoulder, as if in fond protection, and Naida's head was resting upon that broad chest—what wonderful mates they were! The look on their faces!

Softly Richard Malabar withdrew. A quick moisture stung his eyes. To him she had always been the "little" Naida of the Storm; now she had come safely into her Port of Happiness!

And as Richard Malabar raised his eyes to the constant stars, a lonely figure in the shadowy night, his heart was filled with a greater contentment than he had ever known.

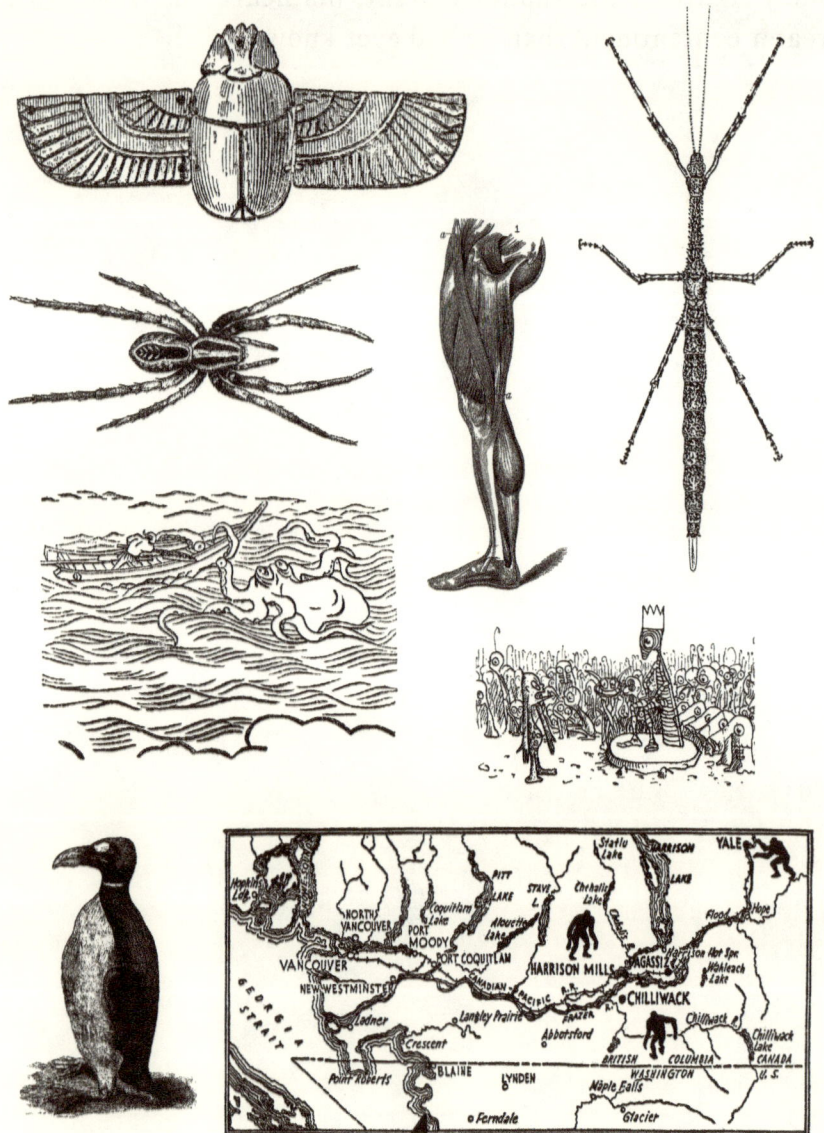

Sherlock Holmes
Volume 1
Arthur Conan Doyle

SHERLOCK HOLMES

Volume 1: ISBN 1-61646-006-7

Volume 2: ISBN 1-61646-007-5

Volume 3: ISBN 1-61646-008-3

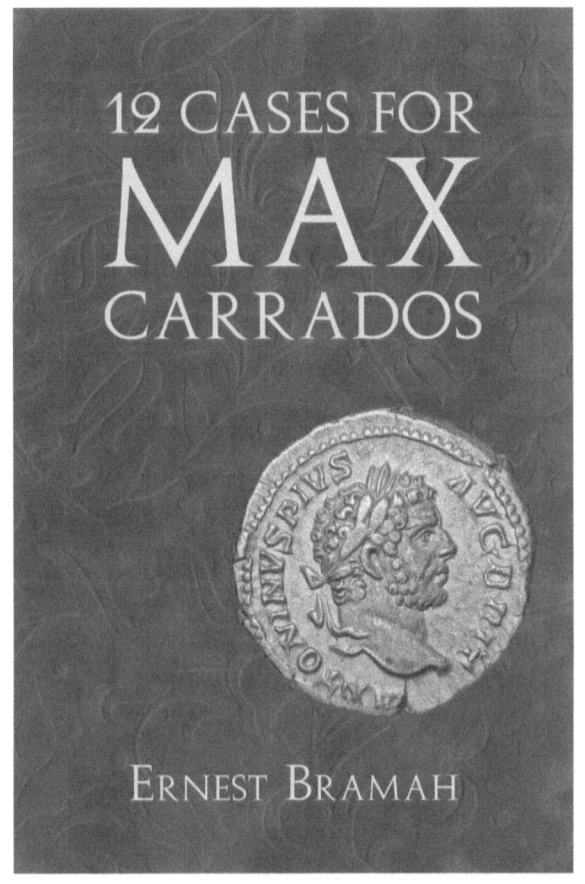

12 CASES FOR MAX CARRADOS

ISBN 1-61646-018-0

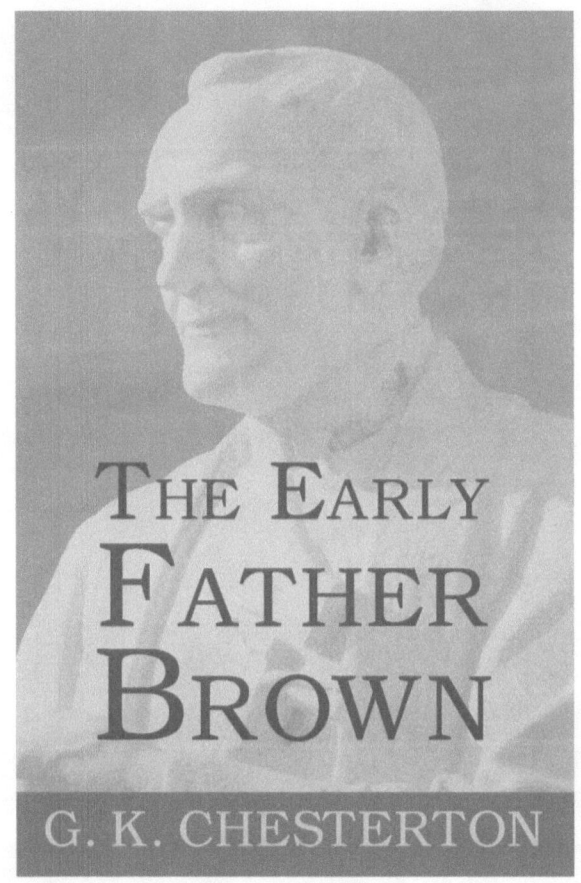

THE EARLY FATHER BROWN

ISBN 1-61646-012-1

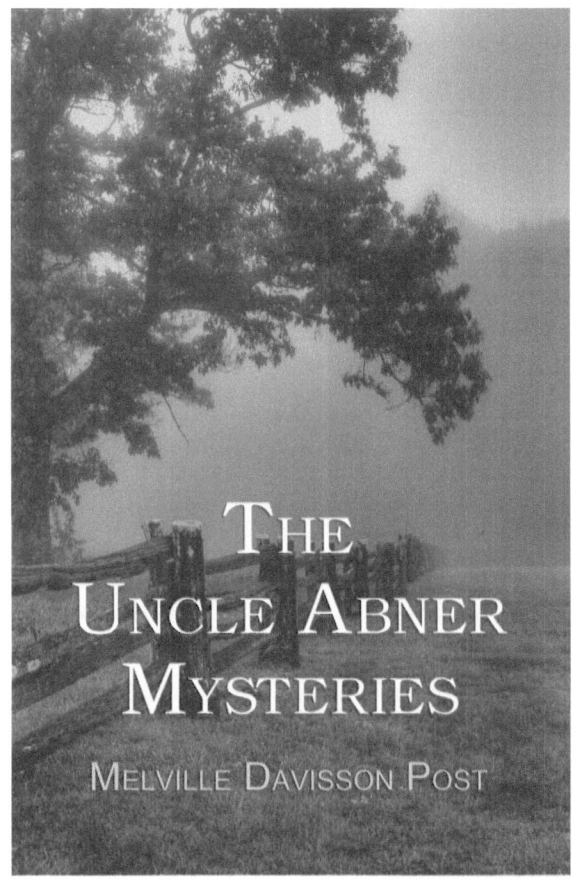

THE UNCLE ABNER MYSTERIES

ISBN 1-61646-016-4

www.ingramcontent.com/pod-product-compliance
Lightning Source LLC
Chambersburg PA
CBHW020918020726
47495CB00002B/235